THE FACE OF BOUDICA

THE FACE OF BOUDICA

Rebellion Against Rome

JOHN AUBIN

© John Aubin 2018

Published by John Aubin Books

A CIP catalogue record for this book is available from the British Library.

ISBN 978-0-9933425-5-4 (ePub)
ISBN 978-0-9933425-6-1 (mobi)
ISBN 978-0-9933425-7-8 (Paperback)

Book layout and design by Clare Brayshaw

Cover illustration: Christopher Rawlins (christopherrawlins.co.uk)

Cover design: Black Swan Book Promotion (blackswanbookpromotion.co.uk)

Prepared and printed by:

York Publishing Services Ltd
64 Hallfield Road
Layerthorpe
York
YO31 7ZQ

Tel: 01904 431213

Website: www.yps-publishing.co.uk

In memory of a good friend, John Ashurst,
with whom I first explored the great matter of Boudica.

CONTENTS

I

I heard the riders approaching from a long way off, their horses' hooves thundering on the gravelled embankment beside the canal. I stirred in my chair set on the brick floor, raising my head and cupping my ear, thinking at first it was the wind buffeting the red-painted columns of the portico or chasing amongst the tiles above. Shadows from my mulberry tree swept across the sunlit spaces of the garden before me. Yes, the wind was still high, but this was another sound. Suddenly troubled, I began to rise to my feet, my old bones creaking louder than my chair. My steward, Gavo, came up at a run.

"*Domine*, men are coming! Many men. Myru has just come into the kitchen. She says she saw them earlier at the bridge. They are in armour and carry standards. She hid from them as they frightened her."

My nerves fluttered with a fear impossible to deny, even for an old soldier. I knew straightaway who these men would be. I had understood from talk at the canal dock that my neighbour, Appius Claudius Numicius Secundus (to accord him his full names), had been selected to entertain them at his villa when they came to inspect the estates. But his was a big house, with much land spread across the higher ground above the marshes, and Numicius, being of the equestrian order, was an important man, the *praefectus gentis* – the chief administrator of these half-drowned lands wrest from the conquered *Iceni*. He reported directly to the Procurator, second only to the Legate, the governor of the province, himself.

I had heard some time back from Numicius that the Emperor, Publius Aelius Hadrianus, was visiting his province of Britannia and that he was interested in my tiny corner of the Roman world. Not for one moment, though, had I thought he would be calling upon me! It was understandable the Emperor and his entourage would venture to see his *praefectus gentis*, but why should he wish to make the extra journey of several tedious miles to my house, where everything was so wet and unhealthy and of little interest, other than for the canal dock, of course, that I had overseen for so long? But it was only one dock of several on the canal. Why then did he want to visit mine?

"Gavo! Get everyone together, the farm hands too and the women, and stand them at the gate. You have time. They will most likely stop at the jetty before coming in." I grabbed at the man's tunic with a claw-like hand, an action that pulled up the cloth so I glimpsed his large member dangling down. "Change your tunic for a clean one and – in the name of all the gods – wear something underneath so that long rope of yours does not hang out. And put on your sash of office!"

I just had time myself. Let it not be recorded that Gaius Modius Celer was caught napping when his Emperor paid a visit. It had been a very long time since I had even seen an emperor – and that had been two (or was it three?) emperors before this present one – and then only from afar standing in rank on a parade ground with five thousand other legionaries, and he a distant white figure on a podium skirted by crimson, with the green blob of the laurel about his head. But now, if the Emperor was coming here to my very home, I, and my *Lares*, at all costs must make him most welcome and give him proper obeisance – could I do that now with my creaking limbs? – or should I not simply greet him as one soldier to another, standing up straight?

This day might prove the grandest of my life – certainly the grandest since I left the Eagles, and that now was a very long time back, with a wound given me by those northern *barbari*: my left shoulder still ached from it when the air lanced cold. The Emperor would be surrounded by many armed men, as well as by his advisers and his household, but it was possible I might be required to speak with him. After all, this was my house by the dock he was coming to, albeit, in truth, I owned it courtesy of the Emperor himself. Surely, there was nowhere else he could be headed for but here, as there was nothing beyond the dock but endless swamps and marshes.

These thoughts filled my head in a rush as I hobbled to my dressing room, calling out for my body slave, Diseta, and clapping my hands. "Come! Come! Why are you not at my side, you tiresome girl?"

She helped me drag off my own worn, sun-bleached tunic, and in its place slide my best long, ivory-coloured tunic of Egyptian cotton over my shrunken body, with its bony ribs and the white crossed slashes of my wounds – almost a skeleton already, but not quite; my heart still beat strongly in its cage. Old as I was, of eighty years, fast approaching eighty-one, I held hope yet of seeing more summers than this present one which was bringing, most astonishingly, the Emperor Hadrian to my door. Why should he wish to visit me? was the thought still beating in my head as Diseta pulled a woollen cape over my head and about my shoulders, too heavy and too warm for this summer day although the wind was chill. I knew I should really wear a toga to greet an Emperor, but there was no time to hunt out the only one I owned, at the bottom of a deep chest somewhere riddled with moth holes. I must needs then meet my Emperor looking like a cross between an Egyptian sybarite and a peasant.

From the shuttered window, I could see, as ordered, my slaves, and my bailiff and the other free workers from the barn, gathered in lines by the outer gate, with Gavo busy pushing them into place. Then, above the low stone boundary wall with its cracking plaster, I had my first sight of the riders arriving – a swirl of light and colour throwing up clouds of dust behind, bronze helmets gleaming, standards thrust high, the greens and reds of banners whipped back in the wind. The sounds came to me as well – the jangling of bridles, the thud of hooves, the rasping rattle of armour, the shouts of the riders, the snorting of the horses: they brought back to me, taut in my stomach, long-repressed memories of battle, as fresh again now as the slick, silver shininess of cuirass, the tang of warm, rubbed leather, the harsh clashing of steel, so that the blood rose in my veins once more.

Leaving the house, leaning on my staff of oak, its round, polished head carved with the Bull of *Legio VIIII* – a present from my fellow commanders of *optio* rank when I had left the Legion – I made the short walk from the portico steps along the stone-paved path across the garden, with its great tree and low box-hedging, between the facing lines of my servants.

Gavo, now at my side, swung open the iron-studded gate. I passed through, in that absurd long tunic, holding my arms out wide so that the embroidered sleeves hung down loosely about my wrists, in the traditional gesture of greeting. As I faced my visitors, I had one quick, leaping thought that perhaps I had misunderstood, and it was a party of discontents and brigands which had come to my gate and not the power and authority of Rome. But there, amongst the mass of stamping horses' hooves, with their tossing heads and foaming muzzles (they must have been ridden hard, I thought), with the glinting of the soldiers' armour and their standards all about me, and the coloured pennants and the banners flapping, through the many unknown faces looking tautly down at me, I recognised, in the act of clumsily dismounting, the bulky body of my neighbour Numicius.

On the few social occasions when I had seen him, he had been dressed in expensive fabrics, a fabulous silk dining robe once at a banquet to celebrate his wedding, decorated with flame-spouting dragons from lands of the East, way beyond our Empire's reach – it must have cost him a fortune – and, as a citizen from Italia itself, with friends in high places, he would favour the formal toga too; yet now he wore a soldier's garb of a moulded, brown leather cuirass and breeches fringed with tassels at the knees, and high fretted boots of an ugly tan colour: if the occasion had not been so important, I would have laughed outwardly. Our roles were reversed. Now it was me, of far humbler origin, I who had been honoured to wear the uniform and armour of Rome for twenty-five years of active life, and since, usually just the plainest plebeian clothes, who stood before him in what I would usually curse as effeminate finery.

Numicius made an elaborate show of greeting me with a kiss, something I could not refuse here but which I had always sought to avoid, much preferring the soldierly greeting of clasped arms. "Celer," he said, calling me most familiarly in a way he had never previously done, "this is a day of honour – for myself and also for you."

I murmured some appropriate response, while at the same time becoming aware out of the corner of one eye of a soldier on a high, black horse moving forward. From his blue shield carried against the horse's shoulder, with its emblem of a crescent moon, the white crest of his helmet, the elaborate, moulded design of his silver breastplate, and his most arrogant bearing, I knew this was an officer of the Praetorian Guard, probably the commander himself – the *praefectus praetorio* – since he must surely be accompanying the Emperor.

I had never had a great deal of time for the Praetorians, considering most I had come across – few admittedly, but I had heard many stories – vicious rather than brave, perfumed like women and over-aware of their own importance. They were said to hold the fate of an emperor in their hands. So it was better to keep your view of the Praetorians to yourself, certainly when you were an elderly ex-*optio* with one of their commanders above you on a prancing horse, whose hooves might at any moment grind you into the dust like *barbari* sculpted on a cavalryman's tombstone.

Beyond the Praetorian *praefectus*, I could see a small group in military uniform who had dismounted approaching. One, at the centre, stood out at once in a red cloak and highly burnished armour. The *praefectus* wheeled his horse, and with a grand sweep of his arm, bowing his head intoned, "Your Emperor approaches!" In this way, with Numicius also sweeping a low bow at my side, I came face to face with the Emperor Hadrian, he, soldierly, in his gilded cuirass and cloak of crimson, and me like a common man in the marketplace, the two of us standing straight and exchanging arms, as one soldier to another, despite our great disparity in ranks – myself, a proud but lowly veteran of Rome, and he, the Lord of the World.

Really, I was in such shock at this sudden meeting that I did not know what to do or say, realising how far beyond convention my greeting must be, and sensing the shock of the others beside me looking up from their low scraping. So I stepped back and bent stiffly at the waist, saying in a voice that did not seem to come from me, "You do me the greatest honour, *maiestas*."

The first thing I noticed about his face were the deep-set blue eyes that – as our poets might write – shone like two twinkling suns against the light tan of his skin. He was moustached and bearded, with thick brown hair curled across his brow catching the sunlight. Most of his head was covered by a round leather cap such as charioteers wear, plain without crest or plume. A broad visage, neither plump nor sunken, with the unsullied flesh of a man in the prime of life, bore a good shaped nose and firm mouth. He stood about a hand's breadth taller than me, so his face looked down into mine.

He spoke in reply, and, as he did so, his tongue licked over his lips. I thought, he is probably dry from his ride. I must provide refreshment.

"Modius Celer. Our greetings to you. Our friend, Numicius Secundus, has spoken of you and of your many years in our service and of how you can remember the old times in this land long before any of us here were born."

He paused, looking intently into my face while I searched in my mind for something to say, and how best to say it.

"That I can do, most certainly, *maiestas*."

He reached across and placed his hand on my upper arm. "Old soldier. You need not call me that." He laughed. The sound was high-pitched, almost girlish. "Caesar will be sufficient."

"Yes, Caesar. I thank you." I gathered myself, spreading my arms wide again. "My house welcomes you. Everything I have – yet I fear it is not much – is yours to use as you will.

He laughed again, perhaps at the humbleness of my expression. "What we want from you, my friend, will be in your head, not amongst your possessions. We come fully-prepared, I assure you."

I was in more wonder at those words. Why should he want what was in my head, or was it my head itself that he wished? In the name of everything I worshipped, what *was* he doing here?

Hadrian turned, and addressed a torrent of words to those behind him. The coloured scene of horse and men had for a few moments been frozen, even the breeze seemingly stilled in the flapping banners; then, as the Emperor's voice spoke out, it broke into life once more, various parts surging back and forth, orders being shouted out, a line of slaves, all dressed in green linen, coming at a run from the rear.

I had given up my great staff to Gavo, and with the Emperor's left hand on my arm again – I noticed the heavy gold ring with a black intaglio on his middle finger – he steered me, rather than me him, back through my own gateway with its peeling red paint, between the deeply bowing ranks of my servants and up the steps onto my portico, where only a very short time before I had been peacefully snoozing the morning away. Behind us, I was aware of a scrimmage of bodies as my slaves, released by Gavo, became tangled with those wearing green, some of whom were bearing embroidered cushions and folded chairs, others with pots and dishes and flagons in their hands. In amongst them, I glimpsed Numicius, knocked by a burly green shoulder carelessly to one side, an accident, of course, but he looked cross as Gavo gathered him up and sent him on after us. The Praetorians – a file of them with their commander – were with us too, gazing about suspiciously with hard faces, hands on their sword hilts, as they were accustomed to do, making sure this place – my home – was safe for the Emperor. Beyond the outer gate I could see the confusion of horse and men still wheeling about.

"They will set up camp by the canal," said Hadrian in my ear, seeing the direction of my gaze. "Have no concern. Your land will be left clean. We bring our own fodder for the horses. The supply carts will arrive soon."

"Caesar." I bowed my head.

"We will sit here, I think. It is pleasant in the sunshine out of the wind."

At the Emperor's words, I saw a plump, green-clad steward snap his fingers, while Gavo, looking put out, pushed his own slaves forward, and in a trice the folded chairs with their ebony and ivory decorated backs were set out with cushions on the herringbone patterned brick of the portico, small tripod tables of metal placed between them. Stools were set at our feet, as the Emperor seated himself, with me to his right and Numicius to the left. I could see the worn old chair I had been using earlier made of willow sticks and padded horse hair being hastily bundled away by my own slaves.

"Caesar," I said, now that we were seated, feeling somewhat more emboldened at being the host. "Indoors, you could recline. I have a couch in a room I use in summer. It has painted walls and a good floor of red *tesserae*. There is a brazier there if you are chilled and a window of green glass that looks out on my orchard of apple trees."

The Emperor raised his hand, looking upon me with a smile. "We are most happy to sit here in the sun."

"Gavo," I called, turning in my seat. "Bring out our best wine."

"*Domine*," he said, looking unhappy and could not say any more. I understood. The green slaves and their steward had charge of everything. Even now, chased cups of silver were being placed before us and wine poured into them from a gleaming flagon around which a portly Bacchus tottered amongst his vines. A slave, I saw, drank first from the Emperor's cup, and then after a suitable pause – presumably to see if he died or not – Hadrian raised the vessel to his own lips.

"Friends," he said. "We are pleased to drink with you."

Numicius and I hastened to raise our cups too. The wine was from a yellow grape, of a full, sweet taste which I was not used to after the thin, sour stuff that normally came my way from Germania through the traders in Duroliponte.

"The wine is excellent," I found myself saying, wiping my mouth with the back of my hand as I replaced my cup on the table, realising then that it was probably not my place to comment on the wine before the Emperor did so. A slave immediately offered me a white, starched napkin, which I took feeling awkward at my bad manners. I had lived on my own for many years since the death of my wife and was little used to high company now.

The Emperor did not seem to be in any way annoyed, however, but on the contrary gestured by a flick of his fingers for my cup to be refilled, and raised his own cup to me, saying, "We drink to you, Modius Celer, and to your ancestors, and to the *Lares* of this house."

I tried to bend my head in acknowledgement while seated, but found this was a difficult movement to make in my heavy cape while holding the cup, so merely dipped my chin, mumbling something about my debt and gratitude, and the debt and gratitude of my forebears too, which Hadrian waved away with a sweep of his arm, looking a little impatient. Numicius, I could see, was sitting forward in his chair, his cup scarcely touched, which I knew was unlike him. I had seen him some years ago dance a drunken Bacchanalia with his household slaves: today's Numicius, I thought, seemed anxious. The time for the pleasantries was coming to an end; the reason for this extraordinary visit must be at hand.

I signalled to Gavo and he released me from the cape which had weighed on my shoulders, I who had once marched the length and breadth of Britannia with a mule's load on my back. I sipped at my wine, watching the Emperor, seeing his steward place a set of opened wax tablets in his hands, which he examined briefly, flicking from one to another, then thrust back, catching the steward unaware so they nearly fell to the ground.

"You have controlled the barges at this dock for many years," Hadrian said. It was a flat statement, not a query as such or a compliment or a complaint. I waited, feeling my heart beating faster, although I knew of nothing to be anxious about.

"Yes, Caesar. What you say is true."

"And you came here when you left the legions and took your grant of land."

I nodded, and then felt that speech was required of me, so I said again. "That is true too, Caesar."

"That was in the Principate of my divine ancestor, Caesar Domitianus Augustus, we believe."

"Yes, Caesar. The fifth year. The Emperor himself was Consul then together with Aurelius Fulvus."

Out of the corner of my eye I saw Numicius blow out his cheeks in a manner that suggested astonishment. I realised that to him the date of my discharge would be meaningless. He was less than half my age. The period I spoke of might as well have been of Romulus and Remus.

To the Emperor I added, "The date and the names are on my *diploma*, Caesar. I read them through occasionally to remind myself. As one grows older the past dissolves into mist – but memory will return when it is sharpened by fact, like a lost man who finds a guiding light in darkness."

"Ah, you speak of memory," Hadrian said. "It is of memory that we wish most to consult you. But first we would tell you what we are planning here."

My poor heart, already disturbed from its usually steady rhythm, vaulted a further beat or two at those last words, so that I had to gulp back my breath, like a gladiator who for a moment has lost the movement of his opponent's sword, fearing what must come.

When I recovered myself, I saw the Emperor looking at me with concern. "I'm sorry, Caesar," I said. "A little indigestion. It catches me in the chest at times."

I could see from the half-smile on his lips that he understood. "Our apologies," he said in a soft voice. "We have come upon you suddenly, and not unnaturally you are anxious why. You need not worry: we do not plan to take anything from you – your position here, your house or your land. The reports we have of the barge dock, and the way you have managed it over the many years, are most satisfactory. Speak, Numicius, to confirm what we say."

Numicius, slumping a little in his chair, started upright. He began to gabble in his squeaky, high-pitched voice, "Of course, Caesar. Modius Celer has been a most diligent servant of Rome. In all my time here as *praefectus gentis* I have never known the flow of barges to be other than on schedule, save only when the canal is frozen in winter or when there have been bad floods or when the towing path is being re-surfaced, as it was last year...."

"Quite," Hadrian said, raising his hand. He looked at me. "Modius Celer, you have performed wonders in this wilderness. But times and circumstances change, and now we must put in improvements and develop what we have here."

I wondered what was to follow, but felt my body stilling at the Emperor's last words as it had always done when danger was upon me after that first flutter of nerves – the frenzied barbarian charge, the lock of shield and sword, the missiles sweeping the sky like hail: I had learnt to meet these terrors with iced water in my veins, cool and clear at first to keep me safe; then, in battle, my blood rushing and boiling when there was no time for fear at all, only discipline and duty and endurance to the end. No, I could not be frightened by anything now, only by the anticipation of the unknown, which might still trouble me until it was revealed. I believed the Emperor in what he said. There could be nothing for me to worry about.

There is a great difference, however, in how we react between the optimism of resilient youth and the lonely dread of age. I did not want my life upset now, not in my enfeebled years; I wished to see out the last of them in the manner I had long grown used to, in the place I knew and understood, with the people about me who served me, and I they, until there was no more that I could do of anything in this world.

I had worked hard after my discharge from *Legio VIIII Hispana*. I had accepted a land grant at the edge of the great Eastern marshes – the *Icenorum magnae paludes*, as the area was known, a name which included that of the *Iceni* people who had dwelt there, although most of them were removed after the war – *bellum Icenorum* – that took place in the governorship of Gaius Suetonius Paullinus. Some had been kept as slaves to labour for us in chain gangs, digging out drainage channels and straightening and deepening a river course so it could be used as a canal.

I had built my own house, at times with my own hands and as the sole architect, which had meant a number of bad mistakes at first. The worst of these had required the total abandonment of my original site and a new start on a corner of my plot where a firm bank of gravel lay close beneath the surface of the wet, black soil. Now I could construct my walls in timber on stone foundations so they rose vertically true and did not slump sideways after a week or two like a drunken foot-slogger on the march. I had had the shiny stone that is famous in these parts brought from the higher land where Numicius was later to erect his fine villa. My dwelling, on the contrary, was a plain one to begin with – I have added to it greatly over the years – at first being of only three rooms connected by a portico at the front, with a floor of wooden boards and a roof supported by squat oak columns set into stone foundations. This roof was so low that, even though I was only of moderate height, I had to remember to bow my head beneath it. All the wood was brought up in barges from the north as it is a treeless country here except for twisted thorn and drooping willow, and my lone mulberry, whose seed I dropped into the earth with my own fingers. The sawn wood cost me a small fortune, although I obtained a good deal from an old comrade who had set himself up as a timber merchant in the *colonia* of Lindum.

Why had I taken my discharge in this wet and dismal part of the province when there were so many other places that would have been far more agreeable? – towns, for instance, with wine shops and baths and exotic native women, full of army veterans like myself; Lindum was one such, where the VIIIIth had had its depot for many years before moving to Eboracum to take part in the campaigns against the peoples of the north in which I had served. The answer was that I needed extra income over and above my discharge grants, being at that time quite severely in debt. One or two trading ventures I had dabbled in on the side as an *optio* had fallen as flat as the toppled statue of a disgraced senator. It was a lesson to me, learnt too late, that I should have stuck to the business I knew best, which was fighting the enemies of Rome. The wily world of the merchant quite defeated me in a way the *Brigantes* and the *Caledonii* had never done.

I had met with one of the staff of the provincial Legate, who was at that time the great Army commander, Gnaeus Julius Agricola, under whom I had marched with *Legio VIIII* during three long years. This staff member had journeyed from Londinium to interview soldiers in the military areas who were awaiting discharge. He had told me of several posts that would become available to veterans with unblemished service – and that, despite one or two small, wine-fuelled transgressions over the years, *did* include me – posts that came with good pay and sometimes more land than the general grant. One that had attracted me at first was as an inspector of roads in the lands of the *Cantii*, but I dismissed it when I learnt of the amount of travel that would be involved, staying week after week in a government-run *mansio,* and taking to the road each day with a slave survey gang, examining stone surfaces and cambers and culverts, tree clearances, side ditches, bridges and fords. Although the house in Londinium that came with the job was on a generous enough plot, I could see little chance of settling down and taking a young wife, which, of all things, I did most want to do while Priapus still lifted his head.

So, I suppose, having told of that, it may seem strange that the post I did take up was to be in a desolate countryside of swamps and lakes where my nearest neighbour was a good five miles away, on higher land which at that time you could approach only by boat. As regards having a gallery of lovely ladies waiting for me to view and take my pick, the nearest women who could speak some Latin and who at least pretended to Roman ways, were at Duroliponte, only then a small place on a scrub-covered hill, scarcely a town at all, smaller in fact than a settlement outside a soldier's camp. And many of those native women were short and squat and coarsened by hard work, with black hair on their skin in places where you did not wish to find it, whose idea of love-making was to hoist up their skirts and settle themselves astride you – sometimes taking it in turns – for the price of a drink in some dirty room above a bar. Which makes it even more remarkable that I was, in fact, to find my beautiful, delicate wife at Duroliponte – but of her I shall speak presently.

It was the freedom from direct supervision, I suppose, that appealed to me most, as well as the responsibility to manage and make my own decisions; and also, I have to admit, the broad extent of the land that would be granted to me, as mine to live on and develop as I would wish, although, in reality, it remained in the ownership of Rome under the Procurator. But then that was true of almost all the land in a conquered province, including the square slabs of ground set like chequer boards – just enough for a shack of a house and a piece of garden – given to the average legionary veteran around one of the planned *coloniae*, such as Lindum or Camulodunum. If I moved to the *magnae paludes,* I would be master of almost two hundred *jugera*. It had sounded good when I was told of this but the reality proved rather different, for much of the land was unusable, other than for fishing and catching birds and harvesting reeds for roofing thatch, being marsh and lagoon and small winding creeks to be penetrated only by flat-bottomed boats, lying under a vast bowl of a sky.

A canal, though, was being cut through this waste, partly for drainage and reclamation but also for navigation. To the north it would link up with other canals already dug, and take produce and supplies to and from the Army that had its camps over the far horizon. My post was to be the manager of this waterway when it was completed, and director of its barge dock, where the goods of hides and tanned leather, and barrels of beer and *amphorae* of wine, and sacks of corn and barley, and carcasses of sheep and bullocks, were to be delivered out of barges into two wooden warehouses, raised on wooden stilts; then to be re-loaded down a line of ramps made of black oak into yet more barges waiting to take the goods to the Army. In time, barges were to come here from both north and south: there could be quite a jam of them, with much hollering and cursing from the barge masters, and it was my job to see the dock was kept clear and working smoothly so there was little hold up in the steady flow of goods in both directions.

Yet, when I first took up the post, and came into the great marsh at the end of the newly-built road from Duroliponte, all I found was a flat clearing of trampled earth within a great, moving, rustling plain of sharp, pointed reeds that stretched away under the sun like a vast enemy host thrusting its green-tipped spears aloft. And upon this churned ground lay various heaps of stone and tile and wood, and a camp of low-slatted boxes like those that hogs are kept in, which were for the slaves who were digging the canal, in which they slept out of the sun and rain. A team of overseers had their leather tents nearby, and there was a small detachment of armed men as well, of which exact unit I never learnt, but they were from some trusted people of the *Britanni*. The men digging the canal, though, were *Iceni*, enslaved after their revolt twenty years earlier which had caused so much destruction to the province and killed so many of our own people. Most of these slaves were the children of those rebels, men and women born into slavery to become a most useful, self-breeding work force for Rome. It was not the first I had seen of the *Iceni*, as I shall be telling – in the main, a fine people, of an independent spirit, who chose most unwisely to fling themselves upon our swords and destroy themselves.

In those first weeks and months at this clearing, which was to become my home and my workplace too, I shared one of the tents on dry land next to the lengthening canal: it already stretched out as a stark line into the distance, beginning to drain the surrounding marsh. The tent was an ex-army one of the sort that a legion will use to house a section of eight men on campaign. It must have seen many years of service, for it had been much patched, and in places the goat skin was worn so thin that it let in the light and occasionally a heavy downpour of rain too. It also stank to high heaven under the hot sun that seemed to blaze constantly that first summer. "The goats are getting their revenge", I used to quip to the works supervisor from Aquileia, an ex-army man too, with whom I shared the tent. At least we had plenty of room; he for a small trestle table on which he would set out his plans, weighed down with lead balls taken at some time from a legion's artillery store, and me for my worldly possessions contained in two leather-wrapped packs brought up after me on mule back.

And so I had settled into my new life, which slowly grew and took shape, with much hardship and many set backs. My house was completed, and later – by saving my quite generous pay and through frugal living – I extended it with small projecting wings. A hypocaust for my winter room was dug out and the floor, which stood on stacks made of rounded tiles like a caterpillar's many legs, re-laid. When, a little later, my wife – my most lovely, fragile Senuna with her white skin and red-gold hair – came to live with me, I had a small bath house built at a distance from the house, with her own rooms beside it, so she could be warm the whole year round, for she felt the cold at all seasons, such was the delicacy of her flesh. And when she died giving birth to my son, I buried the two in a round mound that I raised in the local custom on the highest point of my land away from the dock. This was already busy with the barges that were dragged here from over the southern horizon, then slid away north into that great distance where Senuna and my unnamed son would now be at peace amongst the rich fields of Elysium. Only I could not see them, nor ever would again. And the rains began that day they died, and the culverts burst their banks and flooded the dried-out land of the marsh once more, as if the world itself wept and would never stop.

With these thoughts in my mind, the globe of my head with its sparse white hair tilted backwards, my eyes unseeing, I returned suddenly to that present moment which for a space I had been parted from, and saw I was spilling wine from my silver cup onto my sleeve and Gavo was looking on at me most anxiously. I pulled myself up straight in my chair, swept the spilt wine drops away with my fingertips, and said to those clear, sharp eyes that were watching me curiously, "Please forgive me, Caesar. I am old now and the wine goes straight to my head."

"It is no matter," Hadrian replied. "With your years, you are entitled – how shall we put it? – to drift a little in the wind. In particular when you have unexpected guests who most outrageously have disturbed your peace."

"Oh no," I began to protest, seeing Numicius's worried, unsmiling face through the lingering fog of my day-dreaming.

Hadrian raised his hand. "We repeat, have no concern. We have said, we are pleased with you, and this is your house and shall be your house for as long as you wish."

"I could not leave here, Caesar," I cried loudly, breaking in upon the Emperor while he was still speaking, a bad offence at the very best of times, even by those who were his closest aides and friends. My nerves must be very much on edge despite my previous assurance to myself that I had no grounds for worry.

"We do not ask you to leave…"

"I could not leave, *domine*, for my wife and child lie here and are at rest, and I have made a vow to stay with them always for as long as I draw breath – and forever afterwards."

There was some annoyance now in Hadrian's voice. "*Listen*, old soldier, to what *I* have to tell you. And when I have spoken, there are some things I will wish you to tell me of in return."

I think it was the Emperor's sudden departure from the third person formality of the imperial court to the direct and much more levelling first person – used by all ranks at all times in the legions, from legate to foot-slogger – which brought me out of my anxiety back to my senses, gathering my dignity about me again like a cloak, veteran that I was who had been bleating at his Emperor and commander-in-chief like some girl bewailing the loss of her virtue. The wine was now mercifully clearing from my brain. It had been many years since I had been able to drink during the day; the effect was usually to send me straight to sleep. This time it had not given me courage either but fed my fears like a poison. Never again, I swore beneath my breath.

I could see Numicius's face, still severely unsmiling, swimming before me once more. "My apologies for my weakness," I said to him with a flourish of my arm. I knew I had humiliated myself before him, but it did not matter. I did not care about Numicius or what he thought of me. I cared greatly about the Emperor, though.

I turned to Hadrian, "I am myself again, Caesar. I will listen now."

It was, in fact, quite straight-forward. I was indeed to be superseded. There was to be a new supervisor of the dock under Numicius. But he would not be given my house, nor live in it. I would stay on here; it would still be my land. It was hoped I would enjoy my much earned and honoured retirement in comfort. This should have come years ago, the Emperor said. Not every job is parted by death. If I am honest, I would agree with him. I had not really been up to the work for several years past. Much of it I had given recently to Gavo to organise and superintend: he may have been a slave of *barbari* blood but he was far cleverer than most men, free or in bondage.

The official coming up from Londinium, who would take my place, would have his own quarters in a great new building that was to be built on the far side of the canal on the higher land where Numicius's villa stood. I wondered what Numicius thought of that. He held his face inscrutable as the Emperor outlined the plans. It seemed that this building would rise as a tower four or five storeys high – on a model already known in the Empire, Hadrian declared – and the administration of the imperial lands would be conducted from it. Its high walls would certainly block the view from Numicius's garden portico, and, what was perhaps worse for him, there would be a small town built about it as well, with all the noise and smells, and all the quarrelling shouts, of the people a town would bring – the blacksmiths and iron founders, glue boilers, potters, tile-makers, carpenters, masons, hawkers and traders, prostitutes and soldiers, for there would be a small army detachment based there too.

Hadrian rose and paced the brick floor of my portico as he warmed to the task of describing to me the developments which he had decreed should be made. More canals were to be built, and roads laid down to run beside them, and the newly drained land which they created would be divided into exact squares for an army of freedmen, with a slave labour force, to farm efficiently, taking maximum advantage of the black, sticky soil that could produce three crops a year. The corn, and the other crops, that would be grown and gathered were to be sent to the north to feed the armies there. For here was the nub of the Emperor's plan.

He had become so eloquent by now that the words were tumbling from his mouth before he could form them properly, and he had to go back occasionally to speak them again. He stood beneath my porch on two solidly-booted feet, the sunlight gleaming on his armour and from the bronze bands about his wrists, his crimson cloak flowing out at each thrust of his right arm to emphasise a point. All the time, out of the corners of my eyes, I could see the hard faces of the Praetorians watching and listening, their eyes ever moving across the scene, looking for dangers that might suddenly come out of nowhere, even bolts thrown by Iupiter's own hands.

The Emperor told me a great wall was to be built across the width of the northern country, separating the province Rome ruled from those further lands which still lay unconquered beyond. This wall would be fortified with many camps, forts and turrets, and be protected by ditches to its north and south, and there would be roads serving the new frontier, approaching it from the south and running beside it from west to east. It would be as if the wall itself spoke out, 'Here is the empire of Rome. This is where our civilisation begins which all men should aspire to, and could be part of if they come in peace; but, if not, Rome will keep them out and may strike at them as she seems fit, and destroy them wherever they dwell.' This mighty wall, Hadrian declaimed – the greatest construction Rome has ever seen – will be known as the *vallum Aelium*, from his family name.

I could understand how vital, and how concentrated and reliable, the supply lines for this new military area would have to be. Not only grain, but large numbers of other goods would have to be transported through a smoothly efficient system by road and by canal – tanned hides, raw metals, timber, wool, plant fibres, skins, clays, ores, and rough-hewed stone – to be worked in the legions' own workshops, turning out armour, weapons and missiles, clothing, leather horse harness and tentage, roof beams, ropes and cord, tiles, bricks, and shaped blocks for the wall and its many forts. It was going to be a colossal operation. To be truthful, I felt a sense of relief that I did not now have a part in it, and that I would simply be able to watch it, as it were, flowing past me on my own canal, through my own barge dock, which I had tended these long years.

The administrators were going to pour into the town that would be built nearby and take up their office space in the great tower that was planned – the clerks and time-keepers, surveyors, record keepers, book keepers, accountants, census takers, tax inspectors, tax collectors: there would be no end to the posts created. What had once been a quiet backwater (literally that term), occupied only by the far-flung, white-plastered walls of Numicius's sprawling estate, was going to be turned into a busy market place. No wonder the Emperor had a name as well for his new town – Forum Aelium.

Now, if I were a young man again, starting out on a new career, or even if I had just taken my Army discharge, then I might have relished the challenge. These were going to be exciting and demanding times. But Hadrian was right. I had done my duty. I had earned my rest. Let others take up the challenge of life. All I wished now was to see the sun rise and mark its course across the sky. And to watch my ponies being brought from the stable and led out into my long pasture that bordered the canal.

I felt sure the Emperor would like to see my horses being ridden. For this was the land of the horse where the goddess Epona still held sway. She was a goddess whom the *Iceni* worshipped. I had adopted her too. When I had first come to Britannia to join the VIIIIth, my troop of rough riders had placed the badge of Epona on their harness. The goddess had afforded us many favours.

There is a small shrine I have made to her at the end of the long pasture where the ponies turn at the gallop. It is just a carved stone really of Epona standing between two horses and feeding them from a basket. I came across it in a mason's yard on a visit some ten years back to Durobrivae across the great marsh to the west. The mason told me it had been subscribed for by two patrons who were now dead, drowned in an accident on a boat. Epona had not come to their aid then, I thought wryly, as I haggled with the mason and purchased the stone at a cut price. It cost me more than I paid him to have it transported to my house.

Occasionally I have my ponies brought up to the shrine so that they will stand before it with their front legs bent and their muzzles touching the ground, as Myru – my slave who looks after them and trains them – has taught them to do. Then I will say my own prayer to Epona at the stone, and place sweetmeats that Diseta has cooked before it. Although I believe in the power of prayer – for Epona saved my life more than once in those days when the province was in turmoil – I am cynic enough to know the foods I set out are as gratefully received by the beasts and birds of the field. Perhaps, though, they are all Epona's helpers.

Myru must ride for the Emperor, I have decided. I will see to it.

II

We had walked into the garden. Under the yellow sunlight, the day had grown hot. A gravelled space was shaded by the mulberry tree. Here there were two stone benches either side of a small pond, the waters of which were murky with green weed. A fountain would have kept the water clear, but to engineer this, with an ugly pressure tank raised on stilts and lead piping from my well head, would have cost me a third of a year's income. I had better uses for my money.

Senuna had liked to sit in the garden and watch the small golden fish I had bought for her which somehow managed to survive in the pond. She had fed them with bread crumbs and tiny scraps of meat from the kitchen. One, she named Horatius, had grown very big. I think he had eaten most of the others. Then Horatius had been plucked from the water by a heron, which must have been plotting its meal for some time. Later I was to think this had been an omen, for within a month Senuna was dead too, my son twisted in her womb like the fish in the heron's beak – beyond the skills of the aged *Iceni* woman who had brought so many slave births into the world.

I had intended to have the pond filled in, but had changed my mind. Instead, I liked to think of the shade of Senuna hovering there in the uncertain dawn light, or in the evening when the sinking sun cast its shadows across the garden wall. Sometimes, drawing the shutters aside, I thought I saw her form hastening on the path, her head down, her hair tied with ribbons into a coil at the back, as she had been used to wearing it, but when I blinked my eye there was nothing there but the wind stirring the dust.

Now, most remarkably, here was I at the pond, seated on the lichen-stained stone of my bench, with the Emperor of Rome at my side, and across the pond, the equestrian, Numicius, seated also, watching us with a quizzical look. Spaced around the garden still were the Praetorians, their faces expressionless but their eyes always in motion. On the portico where we had just been sitting, the scrum of slaves were busy clearing away dishes, bowls, chairs, cushions, and tables. Gavo, I saw, was looking across at me uncertainly. I raised a hand to him and he came across at a run.

"*Domine*?" he said, then had the presence of mind to bow low in the presence of the Emperor, an obeisance I had never required.

"Gavo. Pick up three cushions from the steward in green and have them brought to us. My rear is not as well covered as it used to be."

I nodded at the Emperor and he responded with a smile "A man will one day make a bedfellow of stone but not while he yet breathes. Is that not so, Celer?" He accepted a cushion from an almost prostrate slave, as did Numicius. I placed mine thankfully under my thin haunches.

I was uncertain whether Hadrian had quoted from some writer I was not familiar with. I had never been a great reader. I riposted, "But some of us lie closer to the stone than others", at which he smiled again.

I liked the directness with which Hadrian now addressed me and the fact he used my personal name alone, as Numicius did also. The fact they did not call me by my family name. Modius, showed a friendly informality, which was comforting to me. I could hardly expect either of them to call me Gaius, which was for childhood only or lovers' endearment. The last person to call me Gaius – Senuna had had her own private name for me, which is still too full in my memory to set down – must have been my mother, her hands held out to me despairingly that day when I left her to join the Army. I was only seventeen and she had needed my help, my father having been killed when I was about to come of age, his head smashed open by a bucket of bricks falling from one of the Ostian tenements then under construction. No one admitted responsibility and my mother had no money to fight a court case.

My parents had had a small shop in Ostia, selling fresh vegetables grown in the many market gardens that border the Tiber estuary. With my father gone, my mother seemed to surrender to grief and despair. For a while I did help her – of course, I did – but we were now ripped off by our suppliers, and there was not enough money coming in to pay the rent for the shop or for the rooms we occupied above it. My heart was not in vegetable selling, anyhow, or in trading at all in the grimy, litter-strewn market place to which we resorted after we had lost the shop, with its jostling crowds, thieves and pickpockets, and the dogs that laid their shit beneath our hand cart or the beggars that sheltered there drinking and fornicating.

With my friends Aulus Rufinius and Gnaeus Naso, I made a visit to Rome – the first time I had ever seen that city, although I knew from my father that he had taken me there once when I was very young to see the Emperor Claudius's triumph for his British victory. It is strange how that visit, of which I retain no memory at all, should have presaged a lifelong association with the province of Britannia.

I had told my mother I would try to make contacts in Rome to supply the fruit and vegetable markets there, but our trip soon turned into one of whoring and drinking, and we saw little except the wine shops with their sickly-scented back rooms and the tarts who performed for us there side by side in threes. We became too boisterous at one place close to the river and were chased out by a local gang wielding knives, who called us country louts and other terms far worse. In our drunken state, we were lucky to escape, or perhaps Mercurius had leant us his wings. Ever since I have been a special devotee of the god, and I keep a bronze statuette of him with my *Lares*.

Rather more sober, on our way out of the city through the Porta Trigemina, fending off the grasping hands of the beggars who congregate there, we came across a large leather tent set up by a detachment of legionaries who were drilling outside it on a patch of waste ground, and had attracted quite a crowd. They were in full steel-plated strip armour and were demonstrating battle tactics – the advance with shields close together and swords drawn; the retirement, rank by rank in sequence while under attack; then, shields locked overhead in a *testudo,* used as a protection against enemy missiles. Each drill movement that was shown brought a round of applause from the spectators. Small boys ran up to the soldiers pleading to see their weapons more closely, or tried to dodge past their shields as if they were an enemy attacking, only to be cuffed away to roars of laughter from the watchers.

Outside the tent, with its entry flap rolled up, two standards were planted into the ground, each long wooden pole adorned with gleaming bronze discs and a crescent moon, and topped by a silvered hand, palm-outwards. Beside them was a fluttering square banner, its crimson cloth adorned by yellow frilled edges and, upon it, also in yellow, the device of the seagoat Capricorn with the legend LEG XXI RAPAX.

While the demonstrations were still under way, a centurion in a muscled bronze breastplate, with silvered additions, edged in black, of victory wreaths and the savage head of a snarling lion, his legs encased in moulded greaves and with a high crimson crest atop his helmet, stepped out of the tent and picked his way through the crowd to where the three of us stood at the back – the only youths watching, I suddenly realised, amongst the many older men and women and the noisy street boys.

I can't remember exactly what this vision in gleaming golden-bronze and silver said to us – I had never spoken with such a grandly-armoured soldier before, only discharged ones in civilian dress propping each other up in bars, and then usually to get a clip round the ear – but it was something like, "Are you fine young men thinking of a life with the Eagles? If so *Legio Vigesima Prima Rapax* – 'we are the greedy ones, greedy in battle, most greedy for glory' – is recruiting now for service in Germania."

His actual words, I'm sure, were far less formal than that, but the bit about being greedy I do remember exactly, for it was the catchphrase of the Legion, much-chanted on parade – as I was soon to learn. In any event, the soldier seemed to place a spell on me, and Aulus and Gnaeus also, and before we really knew what we were doing, we had followed him back to the tent, which we entered by an opening at the rear. A man in a plain tunic sat there at a table and handed each of us a strip of papyrus, which we read hazily, not really being able to make out the script in faded ink. The words, 'I declare truthfully' – '*in veritate dico*' – I do recall reading in several places, as these were written bolder than the others.

Age?" the man at the table asked.

"Fifteen," Gnaeus said. "Sixteen" was Aulus's answer. "Eighteen", I replied, although in truth I was less than half way through my seventeen year.

"You two, come back when you are nearer to eighteen" – he pointed at me – "*You* – you will need a letter from your father which confirms your citizenship, your district, your family, your name, your age, and recommends you to the Legion. *What is your name*?"

"Gaius Modius Celer, sir," I shouted out, standing up straight with my feet close together as I imagined soldiers should do.

"And why do you wish to join the Legion?"

Until that moment, I did not know I did. I was caught up in a sudden vision of manly adventure and weapons and fighting, uniforms, banners and golden crowns, and the adoration of the crowd, in particular of lithesome girls; and no more turnips and cabbages and turning the chamber pot out of the window at night, with my mother screaming at me from the smoking brazier in that high, rat-ridden room beneath the eaves where the two of us lived now. I did not tell the man at the table I no longer had a father. Any scribe in the market place could write the necessary letter for me. I would become a soldier of Rome. Why had I not thought before of following such a life?

"I wish to serve the Emperor, sir." The Emperor at this time was Nero.

He looked up at me, with a look that seemed half quizzical, half amused. "Being a legionary is a hard life and a dangerous one too."

"I am ready for it, sir." I think the wine was still buzzing in my ears.

He sighed. "Read the document. Bring your father's letter. Where do you live?"

"Ostia, sir. In the old town."

"We are here until the *Kalends* of September. If you come, be prepared to go away. Wear nailed shoes. Bring one small pack of your belongings, no more. Once you have taken the oath, there will be no going back unless we find you unfit."

"I understand, sir."

"Do you?" He looked up at me. I thought he looked tired and unwell. I noticed now there was a deep scar crossing his brow, picked out in a shaft of sunlight through the tent opening. "Yes, I think you probably do."

All the way back on that long tramp to Ostia, the other two ragged me about what I had agreed to do. They were still calling me a 'boot-wearer' when we came in sight of my mother hauling her hand-cart single-handedly back from the market place, seeing two of the street urchins at that very moment pinching apples from it. I rushed at them, knocking them howling against a wall, and embraced my mother, taking over the cart from her. Her face brightened at the sight of me, and her happiness was so restored that I nearly turned aside from my new resolution. It was a couple of days before I could tell her what I had decided to do, and the horror of her pleading stays with me still.

I was never to see her again, and I have no idea what happened to her, although I did in the early months of my service write to her, but her replies soon ceased. I tried to make enquiry of her through comrades going on leave to Rome: no return message ever came. However much I justify to myself what I did, and however much I excuse myself by reference to the remote and dangerous places to which I travelled and the fighting I took part in, nothing will ever remove the stain I feel to my soul at the way I abandoned my mother.

Mother, how I trust you are happy now in Elysium. I make most humble obeisance to you who gave me life and suckled me and brought me to manhood, and I pray to Juno for your forgiveness.

I joined *Legio XXI* in Germania Superior, in the conquered lands of the *Helvetii* people, reporting to the fort at Vindonissa, on a flat plain between two rivers and surrounded by mountains. The journey from Rome had been long and arduous. I accomplished it in company with some thirty other recruits and a train of mules, marching all the way and eating and sleeping at way stations (normally in stables or attics, where our raw recruit behaviour might not be noticed by other official travellers on the highway), sometimes huddled together at night in our cloaks, for the high air we came into was cold. A centurion returning from furlough was nominally in charge of us, one Marcus Lafrenius Paratus: most of the time he seemed not to notice us at all, only when the mules were badly loaded or we dragged behind, and then he lashed out at us from horseback with his vine-stick. I was hit painfully on the arm and on the back of my neck on more than one occasion, and (for only this one time in my service) I began to regret my decision to join up. But I had taken the oath, back in that tent outside the walls of Rome, standing on a rostrum before a bronze head of Caesar, with my right hand raised, and there was no way out now for twenty-five years except through ignominy or death: the ignominy would have been akin to a living death, anyhow, so it did not present an alternative.

We passed by winding passes through enormous mountains, the sort of landscapes I had never imagined could exist, having travelled little in my life up to this time, but then others of our small company had never seen the sea either, so we all had much to learn of the wonders of the outer world.

The garrison fort we reached at last had recently been rebuilt in stone and the barracks were roomy and warm: snow began to fall early that first cold winter almost as soon as we arrived, the first snow I had ever seen. Our group was split up between four cohorts of new recruits and partly-trained men: the Legion had been recruiting widely that year, so I was mixed with others from all over Italia, and even Hispania and Gallia. The one thing we had in common was that we were all citizens of Rome.

Our training began with route marches into the mountains to harden us and get us fit. We would be left on the wrong sides of rivers and would have to cross back by whatever means we could. Those who could not swim – and it was by now mid-winter with the waters half-frozen – had to put together makeshift boats from forest timber, or by ripping down the hut door of some native if he was not at home; or, if he was, after beating him and his neighbours up. This may sound atrocious, and perhaps it was, but, if we had not got back to the fort, we would have been left to starve or freeze to death in the open. Legionary recruits, in particular those like me without as yet any particular skill, had little value compared with those fully-trained and with experience of war.

When at last we were kitted out with armour, we had to learn to run and move in it, swinging a pickaxe, climbing trees, shitting, lighting the cookhouse fire, digging ditches – yard after yard of the latter all to a regulation size and depth according to a wooden template which our section commander would run along the earthwork, also checking the exact slope and height of the rampart we raised with the earth dug out. Then we were introduced to the weapons we would use as legionaries – the sword, the spear, the javelin – at first using wooden replicas, then building up to the weight and balance of the real thing. Whole days were spent on the employment of the shield, its use in attack and defence and as an overhead cover with the *testudo*.

By the spring of the next year, we were fitter and stronger and leaner, and knew how to put on armour and how to keep it clean, and handle our weapons, and we had learnt a hundred and one drill movements – endless drilling on the parade ground which lay beyond the bath house on the far side the fort wall, in section and century formations, then as a full cohort, then with all our four training cohorts moving in unison together.

Spring moved on to summer, and we were beginning to learn field and battle tactics as part of the complete Legion, or at least that part of it which was present in camp since many detachments were away on outpost duties, guarding signal stations, for instance, and patrolling the frontiers. And we still had not come up against, or even been within distant sight of, a real fighting enemy, although any number of captured ones worked as slaves about the fort or in the civilian camp outside.

It was to this camp we went when deemed to be smart enough to represent the Legion and be allowed beyond the fort walls – to the bars and brothels, the bootmakers, clothiers, knife-sellers, jewellers, curio sellers, all ready to take the money of fresh legionaries flush with their first pay. More recruits arrived; and those of us, having reached a state of full training, moved up in the pecking order of the cohorts. As summer spread its cloak of deep green over the flatlands by the river, beneath the mountains with their peaks of eternal snows, I had at last been admitted to the leading cohort of the four training cohorts: this cohort would have been Cohort VII of the entire Legion if it had marched out on campaign.

But at that point, in what had been so far the steady progress of my legionary career, everything was suddenly to change. News of a terrible uprising against Rome, far away in Britannia, came to us early one wind-swept morning of rain (I remember the time exactly as I had been on my first all-night guard duty at the main gate and saw the three exhausted dispatch riders on their blown-out horses gallop up in the grey dawn light). The news ran around the fort like Vulcan's flashing fire. Part of *Legio XXI* was to replace soldiers lost in Britannia. Some rumours said a complete legion had been wiped out, and that the province might yet fall to the *barbari*. Then orders were posted and shouted around our barracks. Four cohorts were to leave immediately for Britannia. The cohorts that were chosen were the training ones, mostly with legionaries that were, at the best, only half-prepared for war, nearly two thousand men in all. Perhaps our commanders thought we would best learn about fighting by actually doing it. And I was amongst the number. My involvement with Britannia was to begin – that province at the northern fringe of the Empire, balanced on the very edge of the world.

I had just reached my eighteenth year.

III

"You know, of course," Hadrian said to me from his position beside me on the stone bench, "that we could have sent any aide to tell you of our plans for Forum Aelium. The reason we have come in person is because we wish to consult you on a matter that interests us greatly and about which the dunderheads about us seem to know very little. We have been intrigued since coming into this country to learn what happened here those years back; we mean the great business of the *Iceni* and their rebellion against Rome. We have been told you are one of the few men alive who remembers those days"

Ah, I breathed to myself, so that is the answer to the mystery of why he wishes to speak with me. Otherwise I would have been much less noticed, much more expendable. I noticed, with a shade of anxiety, he was speaking to me formally once more, using the courtly third person

"Everything I can recall, everything I know, I shall be honoured to tell you, Caesar. But about some things my memory may not be as good as it once was."

"Of course." He slapped his hands down onto his thighs, resting them on the gilded leather strips that hung down from his broad metal belt. "But you were with the legions then, were you not? That is what Numicius has told us." He raised his eyes to his *praefectus gentis* seated opposite him, who nodded. "You must have seen many things which will be of interest to us. It is not enough for us just to visit and inspect a province. We must understand its history and its people too."

It was my turn to nod. "I saw very much, Caesar, as a soldier. And those memories live still and do not fade, although…" I paused, calculating…. "more than sixty years have passed. Concerning the background to the revolt, and why it took place, I am not so clear now. I don't believe it was ever exactly determined. The *Iceni* had been friends to Rome, yet they rebelled against us, I believe, twice. Their rulers must have wished to retain their people's independence while still gaining favours from Rome. They also, I believe, had great debts they could not pay back and thought they could avoid paying our taxes forever."

"Rome behaved badly," said Hadrian, surprising me by the baldness of the statement. I would not have dared to say this, although I believed it too. "Our Procurator here at that time – one Catus Decianus – was a fool. After the death of the *Iceni* king – as an ally of Rome, he had held the status of a Roman citizen – the Procurator entered his territory with a mounted troop, overthrowing the king's legal will – which, in fact, had left half of his kingdom to us – saying that Rome would now take all the *Iceni* lands, and demanding that money owed by their royal house to Roman creditors be paid at once. When the king's widow – his queen – appeared and denied these demands, she was seized and flogged by a soldier before her own door and in front of her own people. Her two daughters, scarcely out of girlhood, were taken as well, and the story is that they were raped by some of Decianus's men – but others have told me that is not true: they were merely held back when spitting and clawing like wild cats trying to protect their mother. Yes, it was a most shameful affair for Rome."

I could see from the Emperor's face and his clenched hands, he felt this shame deeply, and personally. Long ago, I had heard about the lashes given to Queen Boudica of the *Iceni*, each of which had been a spark that lit the flames of their rebellion. And I had heard too of the rapes of her daughters – the royal princesses – a story told in the barracks with much crude jesting. After her defeat, Boudica is thought to have killed herself rather than be captured and carried off to Rome like a caged animal, eventually to be executed. What happened to the princesses, no one had seemed to know. Perhaps they were killed in battle. Perhaps they were taken somewhere, unidentified, to become slaves. A battlefield is a confusing place of many horrors.

Hadrian continued, "We are not *barbari*. Our aim is to bring a superior civilisation to these peoples. If Decianus had only been much wiser, there would have been no rebellion, no fighting, no killing. The grievances of the *Iceni* could have been addressed in a way that Rome would have found acceptable. Rome has always given with the one hand and taken back with the other. Here we got it wrong, and many people died as a result. We cannot treat people as slaves and take their land when they are yet free and believe themselves to be our friends. On the other hand, we cannot tolerate armed rebellion either, and must crush it ruthlessly and at once."

There was a silence. I did not know how to answer. Politics – local let alone imperial – had never been of much interest to me. I believed in good and fair government, but I knew you could not rule a proud *barbari* people without being firm, even brutal at times. I had been a soldier first, an *optio*, a junior officer of the Legion. I had never aspired to higher command, to achieve the rank of centurion, for instance. I had seen many brave and competent centurions – they were the backbone of a good legion – but many bad ones as well, in particular when they were detached from the Army and employed as administrators. I had never sought the responsibility of greater power. Perhaps I had felt that advancement would have corrupted me. In truth, I cannot now thread back the years to know what exactly was in my mind. The job I had done as an ex-*optio* for so many years managing my dock and my section of the canal, I thought I had performed justly. Yet I had had my troubles at times and had needed to be tough. Serving Rome was tough. Toughness had built us an empire. Toughness, dealt out fairly, was how I believed people should be ruled. Strength was respected, weakness never.

"Tell us about your service here," said Hadrian abruptly. "You were with *Legio VIIII*, I understand?"

"Yes, Caesar. The Old Bull, as it was called; probably still is although the Legion has gone from Britannia."

"It is the Bull of Hispania still. It is based in Germania at this present time."

"That is good, Caesar. I hear nothing of the Army now. All my comrades are long dead."

"Which is why we wish to speak with you. You must be the last Roman soldier -the last, that is, from those days of my divine forebears when we first ruled in this island."

Numicius broke in, surprising me. I had almost forgotten his presence. He looked studious as if he was quoting from a text. "The Emperor Claudius, yes, he was deified – he was divine – but not Nero who was condemned by the Senate," I thought the intervention was daring, for it might not do to tell of one emperor's sins to another or indeed suggest that Hadrian was in error. In fact, he did at first look irritated, then gave a wry smile.

"Your learning distinguishes you, Numicius. What you say is certainly true. The Senate had declared Nero a public enemy and would have put him to death if he had not committed suicide. Such things could not happen now."

I did not know if he meant an emperor today would not – or could not – behave like Nero, or whether an emperor now would be unlikely ever to lose power in the way Nero had, and have his fate decided by the Senate. I thought it would be wise to keep silent. Those who had overthrown a Caesar had usually met a nasty end themselves, often at the hands of his successor. It was a tricky subject – dangerous even – to discuss with a man, already semi-divine, who held the ultimate power.

As the silence went on, feeling awkward and thinking Hadrian might have been misinformed about me, I said, "I only arrived in Britannia after the rebellion had been crushed in battle, although we had been ordered there before the victory."

My unease had been justified for he answered straightaway, "We did not know that, Celer. We had understood you had fought under Petilius Cerialis when *Legio VIIII* attempted to relieve Camulodunum."

"Caesar, I had been a recruit with *XXI Rapax* in Germania. They sent many of us out to make up the numbers of the Bull after it had been badly cut up. Then I took part in the follow-up operations to put down those rebels who still wished to fight after the Legate had defeated their main army."

I saw Hadrian swing a face showing displeasure towards Numicius, who spread his hands over his lap like a child, as if to say it was not me, *domine*, who broke your pretty vase.

"Not to matter," Hadrian said. "We are sure you will still be able to answer many of our questions."

"Of course, Caesar. What is it exactly you wish to know?"

"We want to learn more about that war. What exactly happened, and why? Above all, we want to go to the battle sites to see how they are marked and commemorated. Many Roman lives were lost in those battles, but no one on our staff seems to have any idea of how and where they were fought, or for that matter" – raising his voice – "*do they know much about the campaign at all*". We are at present a distance from anywhere and anyone who might help. We have only one thing to assist us – and that by the merest chance as it was published not long before we left Rome: a History. We ordered a copy to be brought with us, as the author – one of our better historians – writes of this province."

He raised an arm and made a swirl in the air with his fingers, a clear signal for something probably pre-arranged. Immediately, out of nowhere, came not a slave but a stooping white-haired individual, clad – incongruously, it seemed to me in this place – in a formal toga, and bearing a thick papyrus roll, which he held reverently by its black ebony ends. Where had this man come from, I wondered, having not noted him before? He must have been standing somewhere in the background prepared for the Emperor's signal. Everything was a bit dream-like – the clear sunlight, the softly-moving shadows cast by the mulberry tree, and now this tableau that was being staged in my garden, like a scene at the theatre with the porticoed front of my house acting as the stage. It had been a long time since my last visit to a theatre, I reflected, and that had not been to see a cultural Greek play but a dirty romp in Eboracum with half-naked players – scarce worth recalling.

"Lib. XIV. Cpt. XXIX," said Hadrian to the man in the toga, and he, standing over us on the bench, turned the papyrus, holding the body of the roll in his right hand and unrolling and re-winding into his left in a manner he was clearly long practised with. Eventually he presented the two ends, separated by a sagging length of papyrus, to the Emperor, and stood back.

"This is Eunothydius, our archivist – one of our staff," the Emperor said casually, looking intently at the papyrus passages before him. The information was clearly for explanation only; neither I or Numicius, or Eunothydius himself, made any acknowledgment of the introduction.

"Cornelius Tacitus is a most competent historian, but he can be so imprecise on detail. It is the detail we require and our historian is a thousand, two thousand, even three thousand miles away – however far it is that Rome is measured from here – probably wallowing at this moment in the waters at Baiae."

"That is another weakness of his, you know," the Emperor added, looking up at me. "Tacitus is an old man now; he may even be dead for all we know. He was always something of a hypochondriac, liking to soak his ills away in mineral waters. He told us once he had been to Britannia and recommended the famous springs at Aquae Sulis to the west, which we are due to visit at some time in our travels. Now, much more to the point, this papyrus contains the latest books of his 'Annals'. Book XIV deals with affairs in Britannia and in particular the *Iceni* disaster: he gives that great matter – the *clades Icenorum* – ten of his chapters, if I recall rightly, yet...."

He read on a while, then stamped his fist down on the scroll that drooped over the stone arm of the bench, so that Eunothydius stepped forward looking concerned, probably fearing the precious papyrus would be torn. Hadrian waved him away with a brush of his hand as if the reverent figure in his formal attire was an unwanted fly buzzing at his head.

".....Ah, you see, here it is, such imprecision on military matters. You would never think Tacitus himself had commanded in the field. Why, in our Dacian campaign under the leadership of my forebear, the Emperor Traianus, we recorded all our battles and carved them in marble, setting up monuments of victory – *tropaea*, as we call them – to celebrate the triumph of Rome and to honour our dead. Here, in Britannia, it seems now we do not even know where our battles took place, in a war that saved this most valuable province for Rome. It was a critical victory in our history, or else these islands would have vanished out of the Empire into darkness forever. And we know he – the historian Tacitus, we mean – had access to the Senate's archives, as well as a first-hand account from his father-in-law, the famed Gnaeus Julius Agricola, who had served in the war."

Hadrian thumped the papyrus against the stone once more, and some of the scroll unrolled in a loose coil against his arm. "So why, in the name of Mars, even in ten long chapters, is he unable to provide us with more detail of what he has learnt? Does he expect his readers – from senator to slave boy – to have to do the job themselves? What is the point of a historian if he does not set down the facts as they should be recorded? It can't all be done in stone. Stone is soon overthrown, its carving worn away by the weather. Writing, although fragile, can be copied and copied, and so will last forever."

"You see…here is a good example …Take this passage about the rebel attack on Camulodunum: 'The victorious *Britanni* met Petilius Cerialis, Legate of the VIIIIth Legion, as he was marching to the rescue, and routed and killed all his legionaries. Cerialis himself escaped with his cavalry to the camp'…"

"Why doesn't Tacitus say *where* Cerialis's column was attacked? Is that not an important matter about which he should be much more precise? Cerialis was as rash then as he was impetuous later. He was a good legate, though, and a good consul afterwards. Two thousand men, perhaps more, were killed under his command… somewhere. How did that happen? We need to know where, why and how. If we study these things, we can hope to prevent them occurring again."

I was nodding as he spoke. It was these losses that I was sent out with the four cohorts from *Legio XXI* to replace. The number of legionaries who had been killed in that battle, and in the other fighting of the war, was close to three thousand, but only two thousand were ever replaced. I had never seen a memorial to those men, although we had honoured them on parade afterwards in the VIIIIth, and I assume the other legions of Britannia (the XIIIIth, the XXth, and even the IInd, which didn't cover itself in glory in the war) did the same.

"And look here also," continued Hadrian, stabbing at the text with his finger nail. "A better, even more important example of omission. Our historian, when describing the great battle which ended the orgy of destruction of the *Britanni* and brought the province to heel, states merely that Suetonius Paullinus, the Legate and commander-in-chief – we will read it to you – 'selected a position approached by a narrow defile and shut in at the rear by woods, so that he knew there could be no enemy except at his front, where an open plain stretched away giving no cover for surprise'. But *where was that*? Where was this battle site where our legionaries and auxiliary troops fought to save the province? Surely a town or a fort could have been named with the number of miles from it to the battlefield, or it could have been said to lie beside such-and-such a road or in the valley of whichever river flowed nearby. But *no*! We could be in the very middle of Britannia, or at its coast, or in the hills somewhere – he *doesn't say*! And what is worse, no one about us now knows. We might as well be asking about the campaigns of Hannibal – yet that is not a good example, for we have visited many of those battlefields to study the art of war and they are *all* commemorated."

Irritatedly, he pushed aside the now crumpled pile of papyrus, which Eunothydius, while seeking to retain the folds of his toga as best he could, swept forward to collect and carry away.

"Great Caesar," I said, bending forward in my seat, "it is ever like that. The deeds of men are like the leaves that fall in autumn: they are covered by fresh leaves the next year and the earlier ones are forgotten."

"But they shouldn't be, Celer! That is why we have historians – to set down the actions of our fathers, and, when those have been of high prestige and valour, to commemorate them in writing as well as in stone. After all, he – Cornelius Tacitus – succeeded much better with his earlier History of this province, if I remember rightly in his Book X of this same work, published some years back. Is that not correct, Eunothydius?"

"Yes, my Lord. And Book IX too, Caesar."

"He chronicled the invasion of Britannia by the divine Tiberius Claudius Caesar," Hadrian continued, speaking quietly now so that I strained to hear, "and he set out the campaign in detail, recording landing places that have now become towns, and the battles that were fought, and the alliances we had then, which peoples welcomed our entry into the province and which resisted, as well as Claudius's own dramatic journey with elephants to Camoludunum where he took the surrender of the *Britanni*. When he wrote of the later campaigning in the province, however, he seems to have grown lazy and often gave just a brief summary, so we do not know the course of events or even the commanders who were fighting and their legions."

"Can you imagine such a state of affairs from our Dacian War, which was chronicled exactly as it happened and then commemorated in marble? Much work was needed in the archives and libraries of Rome to recover knowledge about Britannia before we made this journey here, so necessary because the works and settlements we propose now depend much on Rome's earlier actions and arrangements. However, for reasons we cannot undestand, the great revolt of the consulships of Caesennius Paetus and Petronius Turpilianus – you see we have these inconsequential names in my mind from our friend Tacitius but not the military details we require – was *ignored*." He looked angrily about him. "We blame our advisers: many are Greeks with little interest in our western provinces, being obsessed with the heritage of their own territories."

I had heard – I think it was at one of Numicius's banquets, the last I had attended – amongst all the rumours out of the Roman capital spread by my social superiors, which I usually ignored, that the Emperor himself was a 'Greek-lover', but I bit my tongue hard to avoid making any such comment.

Instead, I said, "Caesar. I can tell you much from what I witnessed myself, and from what I was told later by others who were there. I think I could find again the place where *Legio VIIII* was ambushed and fought long and hard – the fighting was over a mile of country – for I went there with a detachment of the Legion after the war was over to clear up the site and collect the remains of our dead: those, that is, that had not been taken away by the *Iceni* and hung up in their groves. And I can tell you much about their cruelties too and of the many atrocities they inflicted on our people."

Seeing I had Hadrian's fixed attention, I continued, "But regarding the final battle fought by the Legate, Suetonius Paullinus, against the red queen of the *Iceni*, Boudica as she was known, or Bodig in the local tongue" – (here, I pronounced the name with the guttural sound of the 'g'at the back of the mouth which the *Iceni* usually affect, as also in their own name, the 'c' being spoken as a hard, guttural 'k' and the first 'i' normally sounded and written as an 'e') – "I do not know the place, although long ago I had an account of it by some who fought there. I believe the site lies somewhere to the south of Duroliponte close to the borders of the *Iceni* kingdom, not a great distance, in fact, from the place of Cerialis's ambush."

My mouth was very dry. I would have liked to drink some water but did not wish to break the flow of my own narrative. "I recall the Legate had trouble bringing the rebels to battle, as many of their war bands, laden with plunder, had gone back to their homes and they did not seek a major engagement with our army. So, to bring matters to a head, the Legate advanced against Icenia itself – 'Icenia' was the name by which we knew their territory then: it is little used now – and took up a position, carefully chosen, within their borders, close to some of their most sacred places. This was a challenge that their fighting men and their Queen could not ignore. The numbers the rebels could put into the field were so huge compared with Paullinus's army, the small size of which they could see now for the first time, that they thought they could extinguish the Romans like fire burning in a field, by surrounding it with many men and stamping it out."

"The *Iceni*, I was told, brought their women and children out in wagons to view the battle, travelling the chalk trackway that leads from their kingdom into the settled lands of Britannia. It was at the gates of Icenia that the battle was fought. For many of the fighting host and their watching families, this was only a day or two's travel from their homes, about as far as they could have gone, anyhow, in that wet season with their heavy carts. Few of these watchers – even the children – were spared after the defeat of their army, such was the rage of our soldiers and of the Legate at what the *Britanni* had done."

I paused. The Emperor had risen to his feet and was striding up and down on the gravelled path that fringed the pond. He raised his hand, and I saw the green-liveried slaves immediately stiffen, then run forward with their steward to the fore, my Gavo also close behind.

"*Domine...Domine*," they panted in unison.

"More wine here," Hadrian called out, raising his voice. He seemed agitated now, like a lion on the prowl circling the pond, uncertain of his rest or his prey. "And bring us some food. Anything. Meat and fresh bread will do. And move your fat arse!" This to his own steward, who for some reason seemed to incense him, standing before him with his arms across his flopping belly.

I nodded at Gavo whose eyes were on me alone. "Help him," I said cruelly, apeing the Emperor's irritabilty. "What are you waiting for? Saturnalia?"

It was a poor joke, most unfair on my loyal Gavo, but it made both Hadrian and Numicius laugh. Saturnalia, of course, is the festival when slaves exchange places with their masters – or pretend to do so.

When the wine was delivered in the ornate silver cups, with glass bowls of water placed beside each of us, and glossy red plates piled high with meat and bread (from where the last came I did not know; not from my kitchen, I felt sure) and Hadrian had settled himself again beside me, he turned to me and, fixing his bright sapphire-blue eyes on mine, said, "Now Celer, you have wine and food and you have comfort for your old bones, and you have an audience of your Emperor. Pray continue your account, and tell us everything you know of this red queen, Bodig, as you have named her" – he made a good effort at the correct pronounciation – "she who is known to us as Boudica – or so Tacitus writes – and of how you first came to Britannia, and of what you did and saw, and of everything you learnt, during that fateful time."

"Yes, Caesar." I did not need the wine, for my mouth was still sour with what I had drunk before. Instead I cupped a hand into the water bowl beside me and splashed my lips and my gums. I felt the cool water trickling to the back of my throat. I placed a piece of bread on my tongue and worked my jaw upon it for a moment or two, as if it was some moving part affixed to me that I was testing.

Then, swallowing, I began.

IV

"If I may, Caesar, I will start with my own service in that war..."

The four training cohorts of *Legio XXI* were summoned to move immediately to Britannia, but, in fact, it took us two days to get under way. A column of almost two thousand legionaries, with escorting cavalry from an auxiliary squadron that had been brigaded with us, marched out through the small wooden houses and sheds of the settlement of Vindonissa on a paved road slippery with a light covering of early snow: the month was yet September. Behind us trundled wagons carrying our heavy equipment, and a line of mules, roped together, treading nose to tail with panniers lashed to their sides. The cohorts marched in files of four, with our coarse campaign cloaks tied tight about us against the weather, wearing leather breeches and studded boots stuffed with wool. We carried our immediate necessities on long marching poles, and wore helmets, full strip armour and side-arms, with our covered shields slung on our backs. Our javelins were borne in light hand carts towed by slaves, rumbling along behind each century. Against the snow, we were like a long dark snake coiling its way beneath the white-topped mountains.

Although the cohorts sent to Britannia were formed of the training cadres, which had not been on campaign before, nonetheless numbers of experienced legionaries, fully-trained and many with fighting experience, had been transferred from the more senior cohorts, and mercifully we were able to leave behind the most recent of the recruit intakes. Many of our senior commanders as well were veterans of five or more years, so we marched with a battle-ready core at our midst.

All this seemed to have been a late decision by our commanders, and the transferred men had come grumbling onto the assembly parade to be formed up into their new units. However, they quickly accepted the situation despite our differing seniority (after all, we served under the same Eagle, and to go to war away from static frontier duty was what every legionary hoped for), and became more helpful and friendly. They shouted out much advice as the geometrical squares and rectangles and single files on the parade ground, with standards held high and *tubae* blaring, wheeled and turned, gradually forming into the column of march. At the front and rear were the cavalry, and amongst them too on horseback was our tribune commanding, wearing a shining breastplate and with a great black and white plume on his helmet, while our first-centurion, usually on foot, for once rode beside him.

After a march of some five or six miles from Vindonissa fort following the River Arula, we came to the main docks serving the settlements on the plain, built at the point where the river joined with another. Here, century by century, cohort by cohort, we embarked on the great, flat-bottomed barges that were used for legionary transport. The mules were put on board, kicking and screaming on the wet gang planks, and the heavy baggage too was unloaded from the wagons and transferred to the barges. Heaps of javelins were handed down to us by the slaves and stacked along the gunwales. Our cavalry squadron stayed with us for the present, keeping pace with the towing parties that were beginning to heave the barges into movement. Long ropes, slapping against the surface of the water, were stretched from the bank to the barges, which were now sliding one after another down a series of connecting channels to reach the main river.

After some miles the mountains began to close in on either side of the pass and the track bordering the river became steeper and rockier. We could see the lash being applied at times to the slaves doing the hauling, and occasionally teams of horses would be brought up and hitched to the towing ropes to help them. Later that afternoon, we joined with another greater river, which the man beside me, who was one of the experienced old-stagers, told me was the Rhenus. We threw off our towing ropes here and fixed oars into place at the centre of each barge; with these and the increasing pull of the river we eventually gained a good momentum forward, after wallowing and turning like fat ducks at first until we became more skilled with the oars. We could see our cavalry still accompanying us on the shore.

We travelled for two days like this, rowing in relays and sleeping on the barges overnight, with our shields and helmets beside us, anchored away from the shore – a most uncomfortable night with little sleep possible, cold and cramped and unable to lie down. We were fed from a galley at the rear of the barge, and we had to urinate into clay pots that were passed amongst us and emptied over the side. Anything else was impossible – although I did see several men in the barge behind with their arses stuck out over the gunwale – and there was a general and literal relief when we were allowed ashore towards the end of the second day. This was at a riverside settlement of thatched shacks beside a long quayside built of massive oak baulks. Barge by barge we were towed in, and the men disembarked, rushing for the latrine sheds, adjusting their armour plates, loosening their helmet cords, and stamping their cold feet. Local people brought foodstuffs and drink down to the riverside for us to buy, as well as enamelled trinkets and bronze and clay pots, but we had too much to carry already so little was bought. Even in this unlikely place, prostitutes plied their trade against the shed walls. And then it was back onto the barges, making sure we regained the same positions as before, having marked them with our shields. Our escorting cavalry left us here: we were considered to be safe now from any unexpected attack out of the mountains.

We put into mid-stream and for the first time, stowing oars, we hoisted our sails, the wind being behind us, and our fleet of twenty barges, now bunched together and having at times to fend each other off with long poles, made good progress. The mountains gave way to a flatter landscape, although there were still high hills in the distance, covered with thick forests. Occasionally, where the hills came closer to the river, we could see groups of huntsmen gathered on their lower slopes, some on foot with nets, others mounted and bearing spears, with packs of dogs which they were unleashing into the undergrowth. Women washing pots and clothes, and sometimes bathing at the riverside, we cheered and whistled at, and occasionally they waved boldly back. The weather was milder now and the sun shining. Smaller boats, seeing our flotilla approaching, sculled hurriedly for the banks: nothing was to get in our way for our journey was by urgent imperial order.

We began to pass larger stone-built towns on either bank and then military outposts and a fort or two, which signalled to us from their high semaphore towers. We spent another uncomfortable night on board while we sailed on with lanterns lit at stern and bow, the sky now clouding as darkness grew on and it started to rain. Despite old tarred sails hurriedly erected over us, we were soaked on our benches. The sky cleared with the dawn, and the sun shone over broad pastures sweeping down to the river, with a towpath seen now on the far bank and vessels beside it being hauled slowly upstream.

We put into the jetty of a large stone-walled fort, which jutted out into the river, the barges taking it in turn to come up to the jetty and discharge us. *Tubae* and *bucina* sounded out from the walls, and flying pennants, colourful against the bright sky, were dipped and raised again. Columns of white smoke drifted upwards from the town that lay beyond the fort, separated from it by another channel. The rumour went around – there was always someone in the know or perhaps the centurions had been ordered to instruct us – that this fort was garrisoned by *Legio VIII Augusta*, which had a particularly ferocious reputation. By batches, we were allowed to use the fort's bath house; only the quickest of bathes and shaves carried out by the attendant slaves, and then we were out again and back to the barges, where we were reunited with our weapons and armour at the quayside. Another rumour now came flying amongst us that some men from one of the last barges to dock had been set upon by men from the VIIIth and several badly knocked about, and for a while there was an uproar to leave the barges again and avenge the situation, but in the end discipline was restored.

We set out once more, barge after barge, with our mules braying as loud as the trumpets that sounded forth, using oars to get us back into mid-stream, and as we drifted on the river we shook unfriendly fists at the faces that could be seen on the fort parapets. My comrade beside me – Sextus, his name – told me the *XXIst Rapax* and the *VIIIth Augusta* had once been brigaded together at this same fort and there had been bad blood between them ever since. It was my first experience of the animosity of one unit to another in the Army – legion to legion, cohort to cohort, squadron to squadron – a situation which prevailed widely at that time, and most likely still does.

We had one more night on the river after that. Some *amphorae* of wine had been seized from a barge moving upstream; judging by the angry voices that were raised and the clipped words of our centurion, no payment was made. The barge owner wore a flat, red woollen hat and had a crew of two, including – I recall – a woman with wild, unkempt hair, who screamed oaths after us. Their barge was hauled by a tired-looking horse with its head-lowered, which kept stumbling to its knees. I hoped they escaped the attentions of the rest of our fleet.

The *amphorae* were shared with our barge, and a number of others around us, and as a result, the night being milder now, we rested in greater comfort than before, with the unwatered wine hammering in our temples. The clay pots were passed repeatedly amongst us, although some men, I saw, staggering to their feet amidst the jumble of equipment on deck, managed to urinate over the side, streams of piss arching out along the length of the vessel and catching the moonlight. Sleep was not easy because of the carousing that followed the wine, so that we drifted on the shining waters like a noisy pleasure barge on Lake Nemi. As dawn came, a series of sharp orders, echoing from barge to barge, brought us into silence.

We were allowed ashore once more at an empty timber fort near Confluentes, where another broad river merged with the Rhenus. This fort seemed to be used as a transit base for troops on the move for much litter was spread about, and even some abandoned equipment – harness, worn-out saddles, and the like – which, judging as well by a myriad of hoof marks by the leaning camp gates, and piles of horse shit, showed that some mounted unit had been here last, and quite recently.

There were further scuffles here, when other cohorts waiting to come into the fort were pushing forward trying to hurry us up in our ablutions, and some punches were thrown and equipment piles kicked over and trampled. For the latter offence, two legionaries were put in chains and hurried away under guard. I think the residue of the wine was to blame. We all calmed down after that.

We were making very fast progress now. We were lucky that the strong wind behind us continued to blow consistently, sweeping our flotilla of barges along. The river traffic, as we passed towns on the banks, became much busier, but individual craft kept well out of our way, other than for one small fishing boat which was hit by our vanguard barge and rolled over. We could not see if its occupants escaped. Certainly we did not stop to rescue anyone.

The river narrowed to pass between steep gorges, but that increased the speed of the current so that it grew hazardous for our steering crew to negotiate the bends. Our barge was towards the front of the flotilla and I could not see much behind me, but the rumour began to be spread that one of our number had grounded and been wrecked: I think it was the vessel carrying the mules and the tribune's horse, having higher sides than the troop barges and being more unwieldy. I did not see these animals again – yet I am not certain of their loss as they could have been diverted for other purposes. The tribune when I saw him next in the distance was certainly riding a horse, although I could not say if it was the same one that had left Vindonissa with him.

We passed a great city on the right bank, which Sextus – who seemed to know most things – told me was the colonial capital of Germania Inferior. Some of our officers took a boat to the quay here – to organise supplies, we were told – although there were several cheers after them and shouts of 'Have one for me', and similar obscenities.

When it was growing dark, we entered a landscape that was much flatter than we had seen so far, and the river began to divide into channels, some of which led off into the misty darkness through swamps fringed with reeds. The fertile fields beyond the reeds, where cattle grazed, then began to give way to a barer landscape of sand dunes and shingle flats under a vast open sky. I could smell the sea now, and shouted out to my comrades that we would soon be in sight of it, but many looked at me blankly for this was something they had never seen before or even imagined. In fact, we had to wait a while yet before we reached the ocean, and I received some strange looks as if I was a man given to delusions. We were all famished for we had had nothing to eat since last going ashore, and then but a handful of bread and some preserved olives in oil, which had affected the stomachs of many men in a way I do not like to describe.

At last we put into the shore on the left bank of the main channel, with our other barges taking in their sails and wallowing beside us in the inky water. At least there was a full moon, so our barge crew had light enough to steer us in with oars and we grounded at one of a series of jetties which stuck out here into the river estuary, like the fingers of a giant god reaching into the waters – perhaps Neptune himself. Beyond the jetties, many flares were burning, and we thought we were at a town. When we grouped and marched inland, however, we saw it was a vast camp of tents laid out and ready for us. We were impressed. Our arrival was expected and had been prepared for. After the somewhat haphazard nature of our long river journey, this was a most pleasant surprise. The camp, we learnt later, had the name Albaniana, perhaps named after the white sand of the dunes or the white of the wave tops when torn by strong winds.

We were to stay two days in this camp, and during this time came to learn that we were not the only forces moving here to be shipped over to Britannia. Eight cohorts of Auxiliary infantry, several recruited from the local *Batavi* people but others from Raetia and Syria Palaestina, were gathered at a fort a few miles further downstream. Most of these units had also been brought out of Germania, but, unlike us, had been longer on the journey, having had to march most of the way. Other forces, we were told, including two auxiliary squadrons of cavalry (a thousand men with their horses), were yet to arrive. It was to be a substantial force that would eventually set sail for Britannia. But when would that be? Where were the ships that would take us? All we saw was our camp with its thick forest of brown tents spread over a flat plain, and beyond that, the masts and sails of trading vessels seemingly floating above the reed beds and sand dunes.

When would the sea-going transport fleet arrive, and when would we be off to war?

We ordinary foot-sloggers did not know it then but despatches from Britannia, signalled from far inland, and then by ships with semaphores at their mastheads, anchored at intervals across the northern sea, had reached our commanders on the Rhenus, having been passed from signal tower to signal tower along the coast of Gallia Belgica. Our presence in Britannia was not needed now quite so urgently. The imperial Legate, Gaius Suetonius Paullinus, defying the numeric odds, had reasserted Roman arms and won a great victory against the forces of the *Britanni* under Boudica: the province was saved, at least for the present.

Our role was now to be relegated to that of reinforcement and recovery. Above all, we were needed to make up the losses suffered, in particular by *Legio VIIII*, which it was confirmed had been badly mauled. Our transfer from the XXIst to the VIIIIth was thus likely to be long-term, and probably permanent. If we had been told these things then, our morale would have slumped greatly. We lusted for battle. We lusted for glory. If we were worried about anything, it was that the war would be over before we arrived. Of course, we had no idea then of the resistance that we were to meet from the rebels still in arms. Nor of the punishments that it would be necessary to inflict on the rebel territory. We were ignorant of the war: we were ignorant of the enemy. We were soon about to learn of both.

We were moved to another tented camp close to the sea; in fact, it was built at the edge of a broad inlet that served as a harbour. There was a long shingle bank protecting all but a narrow opening into this lagoon against which the breakers crashed high when it was stormy, as was increasingly the case now for it was nearly October – late for crossing the open sea. At one end of the shingle bar stood a tall *pharos*, built, it was said, under the mad Emperor Gaius Caligula who had mustered troops here twenty years or so earlier with a view to an invasion of Britannia. The *pharos*, and our camp site, were legacies of his ambition, curtailed, it was said, because of hostility to his rule back in Rome.

That our operation was still active, and was not in turn to be abandoned (we were growing anxious about the delay which had lasted now for ten days) seemed to be confirmed by the fact that the *pharos* tower broke into life one evening, with flame shooting from its top as the signal braziers were lit. Few of us slept much that night: we kept stealing from our tents to look at the fire glowing through the darkness, suspecting that something was about to happen. And, in the morning, as we scrambled blearily from our tents to the latrines and then to our duties, we saw that the lagoon, shrouded in mist and with clouds of seabirds screaming high overhead, was full of ghostly ships – twenty or thirty of them, I counted, with the blurred shapes of more coming in at that moment through the opening in the bar, feeling their way into the shallows with sounding leads cast out from the bows.

During this day, cohorts of the auxiliary infantry began arriving at the camp, and were quartered separately from us, both within and without our ramparts, but with no tents: they put up make-shift shelters and lit fires. They formed a large concourse of men, whose looks and equipment were alien to us, but their officers Roman. As darkness fell, their fires were spread wide like bright stars in the sky and their noise filled the air all night long, so once more we had little sleep.

We left for Britannia early the next morning, embarking in the first grey light of the dawn – a calm, clear day mercifully but with a good breeze blowing offshore so our fleet of transports (part of the fleet, the *classis Britannica*) soon cleared the coast once the vessels, one by one, had passed through the gaunt, grey shingle bar to the ocean. Many men were sick as soon as we hit the first of the sea swell. For some there was a place below, and for our senior commanders the deck cabin at the stern, but most of us had to sit in full armour crammed onto the middle deck, leaning against our shields and being sick into our helmets, messy as that was, rather than over the legs of the man beside us.

There was a great discipline amongst the fleet. Their crews undertook their duties, largely in silence, ignoring we soldiers entirely, apart from one or two muttered comments about 'dumb ironsides' and 'poor, booted buggers', the usual slang insults between sailors and soldiers that might in a dockside bar have led to a fight, but here scarcely heard above the groans of the sick.

There was great order to the fleet as well, clearly the result of much planning. We had sailed in three divisions, and the left-hand division soon shook out its sails and steered away to the west, bound, it was said, for a harbour on Britannia's southern coast – this information probably coming from the all-knowing Sextus, who was somewhere on our ship although no longer beside me (how he would have learnt this, however, I could not imagine). Then, towards midday, the centre and largest division, including most of the auxiliary infantry with their cavalry too (I had glimpses of the tossing heads of their horses, closely-tethered behind high boarding on the decks), also began dividing from us, this time, I learnt, heading for the estuary of the Tamesis and destined eventually for the port of Londinium, which – another persistent rumour told us – had been burnt to the ground in the war. These transports, I knew – for I had witnessed their loading – contained two of our cohorts from the XXIst, leaving the two other cohorts, including mine (about nine hundred legionaries), together with the rest of the auxiliary infantry (two or three cohorts at the most), to sail on further north.

Towards evening we came in sight of the coast, a low grey-green line on the horizon which even the worst of our groaners struggled to their feet to see, causing a short series of harsh commands for us to sit down: the sudden movement had made the ship heel alarmingly to one side, bringing clouds of spray high over the deck. We were seeing at last the fabled land of Britannia, resting on the lip of the world, where strange monsters and dark gods could be invoked by the inhabitants, washing the land with blood and bringing our soldiers to near defeat. Eventually, I could make out the coastline from my place on the deck, having a clear view forward between the rigging and the swelling bow sail, which was filled with a great painted eye, the emblem of this particular ship, all seeing, all watching as it moved upon the green waters lipped with foam. It was a flat land we were coming to: I could see no cliffs or rising hills behind the white strip where the waves were beating on the shore. In one or two places trails of smoke rose into the darkening sky.

The wind died away as I was watching and the sails emptied, flapping against the masts. Orders were shouted and the crew pulled urgently at ropes all about us, swinging the yardarms to catch the changing direction of the breeze. But their efforts were in vain and our ship, together with its eight companions, rolled impotently amongst the waves, while the steersmen strained on their oars to swing the bows towards the shore. Orders were signalled by semaphore, the wooden shutters rattling in their sockets as the messages were spelled out. With a great splash, our bow crew released a heavy anchor, the ship at first straining against it with the current and then swinging to it like a great captured bird. All about us I could see the other ships had done the same.

We were fed hot food. The galley in the stern had been issuing comforting gusts of white smoke for some time, so we knew a meal was on the way. It had been a meal, however, intended as a forerunner to our disembarking. Now we were told that we could not make harbour tonight, but must sit out at sea until the dawn when it was hoped there would be enough returning wind to give us steerage way to the land.

No sooner had blackness settled over our small fleet, lit only by the flare of lights kept burning at prow and stern, then the wind returned accompanied with great gusts of rain. The shelter provided by sails hurriedly dragged over us did little to keep out the wet. By the time the first dim greying of the eastern sky came to bring back some outline to our world, it only served to confirm the misery we were all feeling – eighty men, or so, on my ship alone, haggard, cold, wet, sick, and hungry. Fresh water was brought round by the slaves who accompanied the crew. The water sliding down my throat and splashed on my face and into my tired eyes had an immediate restorative effect, as it must have had on my comrades. We rose to our feet, adjusted the straps on our armour, checked our weapons and put on our helmets. On an order from our *optio*, we slid off the leather covers from our shields and stood up in our places as if on parade.

The *optio* looked as immaculate in every detail of his appearance as if he had had eight hours of sleep followed by a massage and shave in the garrison bath-house, and had just spent a leisurely half hour putting on armour, cloak, and crested helmet. His name was Quintus Volcatius Pastor, and, indeed, he was very much like a *pastor* to us in those early weeks of service in the century he commanded. When eventually I reached his rank – the rank I was to retain, with advancing levels of seniority, for the rest of my legionary career – I modelled myself on him, in particular as I remembered him that morning as we stood ready to go onto a hostile shore.

As the light strengthened and the sun rose in a yellow ball above the rippling horizon, highlighting long strips of tattered, black cloud that were the remnants of last night's storm, and glinting on the armoured soldiers standing on deck, the *optio* addressed us, "We will be raising sail just now and heading for shore." He held a finger to the air and licked it. "The wind is back, I feel it. And in the right quarter. The sailors will put us ashore by boat onto a level beach. You must be patient and wait your turn. Then.." – he raised his voice .. "*no useless bugger will fall in the sea and get wet!*"

"We're wet already, *optio*," one wag called out to jeers and laughter.

"Now, keep your wits about you at all times. You are coming into a hostile land, although there will be an advance guard of those rough *Hispana* boys of the VIIIIth to meet us. They have been cut about by the rebel *Britanni* and they will be looking for bloody revenge. That's for sure. They will take command of our cohorts. You – I – will cease to be XXIst and become effectively VIIIIth. At least for these operations. After that, I don't know what will happen any more than you do. But we *have a job to do now* – and we will do it in the best traditions of the XXIst, and of the VIIIIth too. We are legionaries of Rome first and foremost. We serve under the direct orders of the Emperor."

A cheer was raised. I could visibly see the men's strength returning, and they growing taller as the sun rose and they were given purpose again.

"For most of you this will be your first real action. Follow your orders and remember your training, and I know you will behave well – very well. You will become proper soldiers, proper legionaries, not pretend ones. To take part in war is the best way to learn about fighting: the prime rule for you, as you are certain to make mistakes at first, is summed up in the two words, *endure and survive*. Keep yourself, your armour and your weapons clean. If I find any dirt – and worse – rust on them, you will wish you stood bollock-naked before the enemy rather than me. So, before you lay down your pretty heads tonight, make sure you dry everything and oil it. From now on it's the real thing. Keep your discipline. That is the most important of all. And when the time comes, be ruthless. These peoples have inflicted death and torture, not only on our comrades but on thousands of innocent civilians also, whose only fault was to try and bring civilisation to these *barbari*."

There was something of a growl at those last words, and Pastor raised his arm in salute, followed by roars of approval. He certainly knew how to rouse us. We would follow him every inch of the way. We would kill and avenge. The blood surged in me.

"And if you think last night was *uncomfortable*. Then think again. Last night was like a blessed night with Venus compared with what you will have to endure in the field. You will become toughened both physically and mentally: a strong body and mind working together, they make the perfect soldier. You will have the strength and endurance of Hercules, for you will need to march, dig ditches and raise ramparts, carry stone blocks, build palisades, and then seek out and fight the enemy. And when the fighting does come, you will not fear death. For you will fear *me* far more!"

Laughter rippled around the ship at that. I could see the crew at their stations ready to unfurl the sails.

"Honour and virtue, men. Above all things. We are soldiers of Rome – legionaries, the first and the best. Always keep that at the front of your mind. Now let's get on our way."

There was more cheering as Pastor turned aft to the deck cabin, and we felt the ship begin to move purposefully in the sea once more as the great flaxen sails opened wide catching the wind. Two hours later we were stepping onto the soil of Britannia.

"Caesar, I think it might help if I give next a summary of the strategy of the Legate Gaius Suetonius Paullinus in his campaign to lay waste Icenia."

"We are obliged, Celer. There is much that is at present unclear to us."

A detachment of *Legio VIIII*, with auxiliaries, consisting of about five hundred men, had sailed south round the coast from their temporary camp east of Lindum. The Legion had lost nearly half its number during this war, and most of the formations that were left had retreated to the shelter of its main fort in Lindum itself. After the final defeat of the rebel Queen Boudica, orders had been issued by the Legate, Suetonius Paullinus, to harry the *Iceni* homeland, known to us as Icenia. In particular, it was essential to wipe out any remaining pockets of resistance, and to capture or kill the *Iceni* hierarchy who had launched the rebellion against Rome. A particular objective was to find Boudica, who had fled with other members of her household after the great battle that had ended the revolt. It was hoped to seize her alive. Her death would assuredly follow – but only after she had been brought before the Emperor in Rome.

Detached units of *Legio XIIII* and *Legio XX*, which had fought that final battle, together with auxiliary cohorts, both infantry and cavalry, were to advance into Icenia from the west, while at the same time striking south against the *Trinovantes*, co-participants in the uprising and chiefly responsible for the destruction of Camulodunum and the atrocities accompanying it. The detachment of *Legio VIIII* sent to the east coast was ordered to set up a camp and supply base at a point where an inner lake and river system opened up into the interior of the territory, and to await reinforcements coming from Germania. It would then advance into Icenia from the east. To the south, the land of the *Trinovantes* was being scoured. To the north lay the great northern sea. The *Iceni* and their allies were thus contained. Suetonius Paullinus's intention was to ensure that no further rebellion ever broke out in this area of the province. Lands held by the *Iceni* for many generations would be confiscated to Rome. Such was the price of resistance in arms. '*Vae victis*'.

"So that was how the kingdom of Icenia was first delivered to Rome, where many lands were to be taken as our own estate."

"Yes, Caesar. Their Queen may have been beaten in battle, but there was yet much resistance in Icenia itself."

The sixteen centuries of the XXIst which landed on the coast of Icenia retained much of their original cohesion and command structure, although now absorbed into the VIIIIth and under that Legion's overall command. The centurion in charge of the detachment sent from Lindum took command as first-centurion. The legionaries of the VIIIIth – we had little or no contact with their accompanying auxiliaries – were not particularly friendly. They seemed to resent our intrusion into what they considered their war. Volcatius Pastor, who was still our *optio*, had been right. After their earlier defeat, they thirsted for vengeance. They saw us at first not only as newcomers, but as novices and interferers, and we were given all the worst jobs as a result.

That attitude certainly prevailed at the beginning of these operations. In time we came to prove ourselves and then were more generally accepted – even welcomed. After all, we were making up the numbers of the VIIIIth: without us, the Legion, which couldn't have recruited locally, might well have had to be disbanded and its numbers drafted to the XIIIIth, the XXth, or even the IInd. I was learning that to fight the enemy there were often many other conflicts as well that drained energy from the main purpose. A good Legate should be able to resolve much of this. But Gaius Suetonius Paullinus, was a long distance away and we were only one detachment of many serving under his orders. I was never actually in the field under Paullinus's direct command.

The VIIIIth fought under the sign of the Bull. The Bull was on their shields and on the buckles of their belts, and stencilled in yellow onto the leather of their tents. Yellow, in fact, was the colour generally favoured by the Legion. It predominated on the decoration of their shields, on the scarves about their necks, and on the helmet crests of their officers. Their cloaks as well, if not a bright yellow were of an ochre hue, so, when cast aside on the earth, they were hard to see in a dim light. I say this because, during my first days with the Legion, I had the misfortune to trample on one, discarded temporarily by its owner, and was shouted at as a result, lucky perhaps not to lose my front teeth.

The small fort we came to lay beside an inlet of the sea that thrust a long arm inland. It had originally been built in the early years of the conquest before Icenia had been accorded the privileged position of a client kingdom. Troops and equipment were being taken north by sea, and this broad estuary and the dividing river system beyond, with its many islands, had made a safe place for a staging camp. Here, supplies and troops could be held temporarily before being taken on to the combat zones further north.

It could be easily defended because it was divided from the mainland by several river channels, which in those early days were unbridged. The *Iceni* did not have the skills for major bridge building, relying largely on fords in their movements about their territory. Now, however, engineers from the VIIIIth (part of the advance party) had completed a floating causeway bridge over one shallow river arm. This was designed so it could be dismantled in an emergency and its individual parts towed to shore.

The fort, which we soon learnt had the name of Epocuria ('the assembly place of the horses' – an activity we were to continue) had long been abandoned before the VIIIIth reoccupied it, which had taken place some three weeks before our own arrival. In that time, the sagging palisade fence around the outer rampart had been rebuilt and strengthened, and various prefabricated wooden buildings – a small granary, a kitchen, a dwelling for the commander, part of a headquarters building, a latrine, and one barrack block which was intended to hold a century of eighty men, but into which a further eighty could be crammed – had also been refurbished and reroofed (with thatch of reeds), as necessary. The rest of the camp accommodation was tented. When our heavy baggage arrived, we were able to unpack our own tents and erect them in blocks of ten in our allocated camp quarter.

The auxiliary troops who had arrived with us were encamped with the VIIIIth's auxiliaries in a separate camp, just a ditch and rampart on the top of a slight rise some thousand feet from our own camp. In a palisaded enclosure set up across one corner of this camp were held prisoners brought in by fighting patrols of the cavalry. Most of these prisoners – mainly youths and girls – were intended to be used as slaves, but they included as well a number of older men who might have a status that could be useful to Rome politically, if only by their later execution. They were kept in a separate shed, and for the moment fed well. The others lived in the open, having food chucked into them usually at the end of our working day. I was to learn, however, that some female prisoners were treated rather better, having a particular value to the soldiers.

We had been in camp only three days when the order went out that men from our centuries who had experience of riding horses should put their names forward to their *optio*. I had often ridden (but more often driven) my parents' horses with the carts of produce coming from the farms to the Ostia market place, but I wouldn't have said I was, in even the remotest way, an expert horseman, certainly not when it came to actually being on board the animals. However, many of my comrades had been raised on farms, and were volunteering (they were short, stocky lads in the main, immensely strong, many, like me, less than twenty years old). Since action seemed to be promised, desperate as I was then to get into the actual fighting rather than spend my days digging ditches or erecting the heavy goat skin tents with their stubborn folds, loops, and pegs, I gave Volcatius Pastor my name too.

"You've ridden before, Modius Celer?" Perhaps he knew my background for his face showed his doubt.

"Yes, *optio*".

"And you're experienced?"

"They wanted me for the cavalry," I said.

He smiled at that. "Don't fall off too many times. The only heads we want you to break are the enemy's."

That afternoon, as I was engaged in cleaning out a drainage ditch beside one of the gates, I saw the horses begin to arrive, small ponies with long manes and forelocks, roped together in fours and fives, driven in by our cavalry, a troop from Gallia. They were corralled in a large, circular, plank-built stockade which units of the auxiliary infantry had just finished building between their camp and ours. Against the curving wall of the stockade were a number of open-fronted lean-to sheds which served as stables. There were some sixty of the ponies in all, taken from *Iceni* settlements in the hinterland. They were clustering together, obviously frightened, raising their heads and whinnying, some squealing, a particular high-pitched and unsettling sound.

The next morning, my name (as I had hoped) had been removed from the duty roster. I, with five others from my century, were to report instead at the stockade for instruction. I remember, it was a chilly morning, with the sun rising from the sea in a ball of crimson, the long rays stretching out over the land so that they seemed like the crown of Apollo himself, the god climbing out of the dark water and mounting the sky, the earth below gradually awakening with his light. And so, I thought, this is how creation is made, day by day, season by season, year by year, Apollo driving his horses of fire across the firmament. I was more poetic in those days than I am now. Then I believed – or half-believed – the stories we were taught in school and in the temples. Now I am not so sure of my beliefs when perhaps it would bring me comfort if they were stronger. As a boy, I had wanted to ride one of those horses of fire. As a soldier, this day should bring me the chance.

Our riding master, with the rank of *decurio*, was from the VIIIIth's cavalry squadron. His name was Marcus Albanus Primus. He was a thin, hard-faced individual with a large hooked nose – just like Julius Caesar, I thought, remembering the great man's profile on coins still in circulation when I was a boy. Albanus stood in the centre of the stockade while we fifty or so would-be riders lined its curving sides. The horses seemed calmed by his presence, as if they knew he understood them. Occasionally they would step forward and nuzzle at his hands, then snort and back away.

"We are going to raise a troop of mounted legionaries," he said. "You will be what are called irregular cavalry – rough riders, if you like, which expresses your role well. You will be divided into two smaller units – *cunei* – that will be able to move fast over any sort of country. We want you to break into villages of the *Iceni* and catch them unprepared, flush out their leaders, find any who have fought against Rome and punish them accordingly – there will be many such hiding away – kill them, and burn down their homes. These are the Legate's orders. In particular he wants you to seek out their Queen – the red-haired Medusa who escaped us in battle and is still at large somewhere. She is not to be killed but brought back as a prisoner."

"You will move on horseback, but, if you get into a major scrap, you fight on foot, as you have been trained as legionaries. These operations must begin as soon as possible. Time is of the essence. You have only a few days to get used to riding your horses – in full armour, carrying your side arms and a shield, and a spear too, as hunters use when pursuing wild beasts. I call them horses here, but they are ponies really, bred to be sturdy as *we* are sturdy and tough. For this sort of work, they are better than horses. They won't let you down – *unless you fall off*." He laughed, and we laughed too.

"Keep that picture of chasing wild beasts in mind, for that is exactly what you will be doing. It is beasts we are after and Rome wishes to avenge what the beasts have done – our soldiers hung up on trees, then disembowelled, our women raped and mutilated, our children swung about by their legs like clubs, their brains dashed out. Keep all this before you. It is what you will be about – to wipe out from these lands the stain on Rome."

It was a stirring speech. I felt the hairs on the back of my neck rising in anticipation – Of what? Of danger and excitement and killing. Could I kill? Of course, I could. No legionary ever asks himself that. Doubt and questioning and pity are for philosophers with their books. Killing is ever the business of Rome. We have even perfected it as a sport.

The practical side of learning my new role, however, turned out to be somewhat harder than standing around listening to speeches. The farmers' lads, of course, soon accustomed themselves to the ponies, which, it seemed, had not been running wild but were already schooled by their former *Iceni* owners to the bit and the saddle. Our own saddles were at first just a simple cloth thrown over the animal's back. As rough-riders, we were indeed going to ride rough – much as the *Iceni* did themselves.

The *Iceni* were expert with horses, as I was to learn when I came to live amongst them, although at this time there was not much good we wished to accord these people. Yet, we knew that, for all their brutality, they had courage. It took great bravery – or was it foolhardiness? – to take on Rome, and at first to beat the very best of her soldiers. While we wanted to hate them, we had a measure of respect too. In such a way, we will cheer enemy *barbari* in the arena if they overthrow the Roman professionals sent in to kill them. Providing, of course, that they in turn are killed and the Romans avenged. In Britannia, we were those avengers – carrying Nemesis on our ponies' backs.

At first, however, I had to find my seat on one of these ponies – then learn to keep it there. This was not easy, to say the least, in particular as in our first training most of us had no horse harness at all, not even reins. We practised mounting stripped to our tunics, oblivious of the cold air, for the mornings were often still gripped by the nights' frosts. Our lads experienced with horses had no trouble at all, vaulting onto their backs and sitting there upright, controlling the animal with their knees, their feet almost scraping the ground, for the ponies were of a short-legged breed with strong, broad backs. When I tried a similar manoeuvre, I landed in a heap on the far side of my pony, so that it kicked out its hind legs in sudden fright a few inches from my skull, to the roar of much laughter about me. Albanus, to his credit, was patient with me, and the ponies, on the whole, were well broken-in and equally patient. If they had been rearing and bucking, I – and other equally ill-schooled trainees – would have stood no chance of surviving this bastard cavalry, as we were apt to call ourselves early on.

Soon, by copying the others, and with the blast of Albanus in my ears by way of encouragement, I mastered the mounting, although how I was to achieve this under the weight of armour had yet to be worked out. I was also able to control the pony at a walk and at a trot, watching the skilled ones amongst us and copying their technique, pressing the animal's sides with my knees to guide it, and, at first to my shame, sometimes hanging on to its mane for support. We circled the camp, a line – or rather several uncertain, wavering lines – of ponies, with Albanus running along beside us, red-faced with yelling. I was very conscious of a number of auxiliary cavalrymen on much taller black horses watching us by their camp gate. Judging by the movement of their bodies, they were shaking with laughter. We will show them! – I thought – We will show them!

And we did. By the end of a long third day of training we were all becoming reasonably proficient in the basics of horsemanship (or at least we thought we were). But my buttock and thighs were being rubbed sore: I understood now why cavalrymen wore breeches. And on the fourth day those breeches were available for us too, three flat barges with much-needed supplies having been towed into our harbour by an oar-driven galley the day before. Unaccustomed to such garments, I chose at first a stiff leather pair that cut across my crotch far too sharply, threatening to make me a disciple of Cybele. So I resorted instead to a thickly knitted, grey-white woollen pair, tied at the waist with a cord, the leg ends tight about my calves. This was much more comfortable although not so long lasting: I wore through more than one pair during my time in the *equites Albani* – as we were to be known officially, but, amongst ourselves as the 'white riders', white being the colour of Nemesis, the colour of vengeance.

The Praetorians wear white trimmings to their armour and their uniforms. So we did too, wishing to be considered an equal elite; such was our aggressive conceit then. When bridles and reins arrived for our horses (with the same consignment as the breeches), we painted them white, using whitewash that we found in a store of the camp. It was hardened to a paste, but we were able to dilute it with acidic wine and brush it into the leather. Many of our breeches were of whitish material, like mine, and we wore white about our necks too, torn in strips from some old cloth we also found in a store. By chance as well – for, we were told, they had been brought to us from the stores of an auxiliary cavalry squadron now disbanded – the oval shields we would carry on horseback had a blue and white design, with a golden bolt of Mercurius at their centres, although the paintwork was much faded and the wooden surfaces knocked about and splintered in places, showing they had actually been carried into battle – damage that we showed off proudly. A number of my comrades too, in my particular *cuneus* of twenty-five riders, must have had friends in the VIIIIth's cavalry for they came on parade on our fifth day of training with copper parade masks, also painted white, which, when strapped beneath their helmets, gave a ghost-like look that even terrified me at first sight. Albanus made them take them off, although I think he approved of their effect.

"Put those away for now. We have more serious things to achieve. Now you must ride in armour and with weapons."

The last part of our training – once we were able to balance on a pony and control it – was the most important. Unless we could fight from horseback, as well as being able to ride the animal quickly across country to a place of fighting, we might as well have stayed with our fellow legionaries on foot. With bridle and reins fitted, and for some of us lucky ones, including me

– the distribution was made at first by lot – a saddle with high fore and aft pommels, held in place by a broad girth strap, there was something now to get hold of when mounting under the weight and constriction of armour .

All of our horse equipment looked well rubbed and worn, perhaps discarded by some other unit when they had been re-equipped: my saddle, for instance, had a split on one side and the horse-hair stuffing was poking out. I wondered, in fact, if it had been brought on after us from that fort we had visited briefly outside Confluentes, where we had seen much horse harness lying about abandoned. If so, our commanders had known even then what role some of us might have to carry out in Britannia.

The very fit and agile farm boys were still able to vault onto horseback despite their armour, although I winced at some who had scorned the saddle as they thudded down against the animal's spine. I was surprised at how steady and strong the ponies were against this sudden weight, but other than for a shuffling of their sturdy legs and a trembling of their broad barrel-like sides, with a lowering and tossing of their heads, they bore their riders well: they did not kick out, or worse, sink to the ground. Well-bred and well-schooled were those *Iceni* ponies: I recall them with pride.

One of our armourers, a bearded veteran of the VIIIIth who was putting in extra service because his skills were not easily replaced, had been busy mending the harness and other fittings that had arrived by barge. On his own initiative, he fashioned a number of iron pendants, mostly crescent moons and priapic devices, but a number as well showing the outline of a horse with a female figure behind. He told us this figure was the goddess Epona, and those amongst us favoured to wear one of the pendants on their pony should daily say prayers to her for she would protect them. And so it proved for I was one of those so favoured.

We learnt fast how to fight on and beside our ponies. I did not seek to emulate the most athletic amongst us, but found I could mount easily enough in my cuirass of strip-plated armour, although I left off – as did most of the others – the iron-studded leather strips that protected the groin: on horseback, we found that these threatened to do the job they were meant to save us from! The long mane of my pony (and by now we all had been allotted our favoured animal for whose care we were responsible: mine was a skewbald of brown and white) made a good hand-hold to mount, and I found the shape and tight fit of the saddle held me firmly in place when manipulating shield and spear. We practised our fighting skills, working long hours from dawn to dusk over those last days of our training.

We learned to dismount quickly, and make the pony stand close to us while we practised with sword and shield, thrusting and parrying. Albanus would move amongst us with a sharpened sword, delivering real blows while we did this, so any slowness might have led to a sudden departure from *equites Albani*: this only happened, in fact, to one of us and that was due to an injury through falling rather than by an unblocked sword cut. Then we would mount again as fast as we could and practise running down targets with our spears. The targets Albanus set up were made of wooden panels ripped from old packing cases, which he would set swinging from a gallows-type post he had erected outside the camp rampart. The skill was to pierce the wood with the spear, judging the rate of approach of the pony and the thrust of the spear. At first most of us missed by a mile, but slowly we began to gain a better coordination of hand and eye, coupled with a better control of our pony; and by the end of the day, as the dusk seeped from the sea across the river marshes, many of us were piercing the dangling wood at the first thrust and carting it away in triumph on the end of our spears.

The next day – our final day of instruction, as it proved – Albanus made the proceedings much more realistic. Our training was to make us able to fight and kill a real, savage enemy, on or off our ponies. So, to do that, we had to be savage too. As our two *cunei* rode out from the stockade that morning, an auxiliary cavalryman cantered up, harness studs and pendants flashing and jingling under a pale yellow sun, saluted Albanus, who was on foot, and delivered to him a heavy sack, which he slung casually over one shoulder. At the training gibbet, he placed the sack on the ground and we were ordered to dismount and gather around him, while holding our ponies' heads, the combined breath of the animals and men rising about us on the cold air like mist.

I suspected what was to come, as did others, I am sure. One of us was ordered out to stand by Albanus.

"Empty out the sack!"

Now we could see how stained was the fabric of the sack, the brown hemp oozing a ruddy colour. Our chosen comrade picked it up reluctantly, and tipped out the contents. Ten human heads rolled onto the grass. Some had little whispy moustaches and pointed beards, other were clean-shaven. One or two had lost their eyes, the side of one skull was split open, with brains, like grey fish roe mottled red, dribbling out. All were of men, some looking to be only youths – boys even – others much older men.

"Get to know your enemy! Groups of five. Sort yourselves out! Each group, take one head. All of you handle it. Get to know it. It won't bite you!

Its owner is now in that other world where *barbari* finish up. The first man of each group to spit a head with his spear can select a slave woman for tonight. Tomorrow you ride out."

I have to be honest, I was squeamish. One or two of my comrades were actually sick. And we had thought we were inured to death, having from early boyhood seen prisoners executed in the arena, heads cut off and blood jetting in spouts, soaking the white sand red. But there is something about handling the dead – the mutilated dead, in particular – that turns the stomach. A head, which contains the very spirit of a man, when separated from the rest of the body seems particularly offensive, frightening even.

And so each of the groups that we formed ourselves into nominated a leader to collect a head from the ground at Albanus's feet. In my group, a lad I simply knew as Titus fetched the head, holding it up by its hair. It was one with a curling moustache and beard, brown and gold hairs that caught the light as the head swung in his hand before us. One eye was closed and bloodied, but the other was wide-open, unnaturally so, I thought, as if someone had pegged the eye-lid back. It shone blue and accusingly. The lips were drawn up and parted, revealing a lower row of yellow teeth. I shuddered.

I could see Albanus watching us closely. "Each of you – all of you – take turns to hold a head," he ordered.

When the head with our group was handed to me, I took it by the hair, feeling the wet strands against my fingers, seeing the face turning towards me, twisted by the hair, so that I felt like dropping it and kicking it away as something unclean. Perhaps seeing my revulsion, Albanus pointed at me. "You – Celer, isn't it? – you can start us off. Fix that head up on the frame."

The frame was the gibbet structure upon which the wooden targets had been hung. Below the horizontal arm was a curving hook, and on the spike of this I had to drive down the head's severed neck, feeling the jarring resistance of sinew and bone. Watery blood dribbled over my fingers. There was a cheer from my comrades when I had completed the task. I walked back to my group, my hands bunched up into fists to conceal how much they shook.

My group of five practised first while the others watched. Part of the practice was to improve our speed into action. We armoured ourselves, took up our weapons, and mounted – left hand grasping the pony's mane with shield hooked over upper arm, right hand holding spear, short sword on right hip, right leg thrown over the pony's back, crutch sliding into the narrow saddle (those of us with sense had padded out this part of our breeches), mounted and seated upright, shield and spear ready to be used. To prevent the sword getting caught up in this operation, some of us carried it with the scabbard bound to the girth strap – but personally I did not like to be separated from my weapon.

A week earlier, I could not have done any of this, even without wearing armour or carrying weapons. Now we were all able to mount in quick order. It was a trick of agility more than anything else, knowing where to hold, how to spring and transfer weight – that and the patient steadfastness of our ponies. Albanus thought there was still room for improvement, though. Some of us were made to dismount and mount again, this time with the pony moving. Titus fell with a clatter on the ground. A roar of laughter came from the watchers. Undaunted, he chased after his pony, and, minus shield but with spear extended, managed to mount. This time, there were cheers

"Ride him down," shouted Albanus, his arm flung out towards the head on its hook.

Perhaps it was beginner's luck, or perhaps it really was skill, but Titus's spear went right into the remaining eye, removing its death stare forever. The head tumbled to the ground, split open and dribbling red slime.

"Another head! Five more of you mount up!"

And so we practised by the hour, wheeling, turning, and lunging, singly, in pairs, in threes, charging the ghastly heads spiked on the frame. We practised until we and our mounts were exhausted, and all the heads killed over and over again. And even Albanus, for the moment, was satisfied.

After we had finished, still in a type of frenzy, we dismounted and set about the mutilated heads on the ground, kicking out at what was left of them and beating them with the butt ends of our spears, until they had all burst open like rotten fruit and the grass was spread with vile heaps of red. We then mounted again, and rode back and forth over this ground for Albanus said it was good training for the ponies too. They reared up at first, and backed away from the awful smell of blood and brains, but eventually most of us were able to force our mounts over the gory, trampled grass. By this time we were satiated with the blood and violence, sitting back in our saddles exhausted. Tomorrow, we of the rough, white riders, with many of the VIIIIth and its auxiliaries too, would be setting out inland – to rekindle the war.

I remember how the sun that evening set in the greatest red ball I have ever seen, sliding slowly down the sky and floating above the flat landscape like a huge war chariot washed with blood. So vivid was the sight that there was much chatter amongst the men about omens of slaughter to come; not of our slaughter, was the speculation, but that of the pestilential, remaining rebels against Rome – the *Iceni* and their monstrous queen.

We drank unwatered wine that evening, then, as promised, we were allowed into the enclosure where the women prisoners were kept. I cannot bring to mind – a mind befuddled at the time – too much of what we did, but I do remember a girl's unblinking eyes watching me patiently until I was finished, and then she turning aside from me and weeping. And for that I have felt sorrow ever since.

V

The Emperor Hadrian was shuffling in his seat, wriggling his bottom on the stone slab. He raised his hand, saying to me, 'Our excuses, Celer.' In a trice, his steward was before him bearing a large shiny red pot, decorated with a moulded frieze of nymphs and satyrs, the sort of vessel that most households would show off for best on a table top. But this one was for a more base purpose – a pissing pot – and, turning his back to us, half-shielded by my mulberry tree, the Lord of the World now made use of it.

"You do not have the same need?" he asked, turning back to us and smoothing down his tunic front. His steward held out a bowl of water for him to rinse his hands. "You must have bladders like horses."

Numicius did signal for a pot, but I felt dried out by talking, glad indeed of a break and to take a sip from the wine cup which had stood untouched at my side. When my guests were seated again – I had to remind myself that indeed was what they were – I asked, "Shall I continue, Caesar?"

He said, "May we" – then, pleasing me greatly, changed this again to – "May *I* ask you, for I have read nothing of this and yours is the first such account I have heard, what exactly was our army's strategy at that time, with the enemy defeated in a great battle and Roman troops now occupying their lands? You tell of a landing on the coast and an advance with a small force from the east, and another advance by the main army from the west commanded by the Legate himself. Is that correct?"

"Yes, Caesar. The *Iceni* were defeated, but not destroyed. There were pockets of resistance everywhere and a clean sweep of their territory had to be made, their leaders caught and punished."

"I see." Hadrian leant forward, an elbow on his thigh and his chin in his hand, in a pose that suggested he was still puzzled.

"It was surely late in the year by now. Did the army not go into winter quarters?"

"No, Caesar. Not at this time. There was no respite in the Legate's actions. And, I recall, it was a bad winter too with snow." I smiled. "We kept warm by burning out the enemy."

"Yes, quite." There was a lengthy pause. "But in the end Suetonius Paullinus was recalled to Rome. I understand from our historian, Tacitus, an unfavourable report was made on him."

"I believe so, Caesar. That was not in my knowledge then, of course, or since really, although I have heard rumours at various times. The Legate was a hard man. He had saved the province, yet he had come very close to losing it. Thousands of our soldiers – legionaries and auxiliaries – had been killed. The province was ravaged, tens of thousands of civilians had been murdered, including many citizens. Such a disaster must have given him a terrible shock. As a result, I don't think he knew the word mercy. None of us did at that time."

Again a long pause. Hadrian retained his thoughtful pose. "Why," he said at length, "Why were you needed as mounted legionaries when the cavalry – the auxiliary horse – could have been used to seek out and destroy any enemy still in arms?"

Now it was my time to think awhile. I had not reflected on these matters for many years. I did not wish to present the actions of my Legate then, or of my comrades, or indeed of myself, in anything but the best of lights. There were things that were done then of which I am not proud – but *they were necessary*. I believe that, and will defend it to the very last. Yet, memories can still flare up to trouble me.

War is cruel. The *Iceni*, and the other rebels, had sought their freedom from Rome. However atrocious their actions, their motives were understandable, even noble, given the way Rome had treated them: I have to admit that now, but certainly not at the time. Our response was as cruel as anything they did to us. And they *were* cruel – most cruel. Their leaders, egged on by their priests, the Druids, held a perverted belief that the greater their atrocities, the more they honoured their gods.

So, in our revenge, we destroyed a whole people, killing their leaders and scorching their land. They have never recovered. Today they are mostly slaves, and their land we rule directly, bar some areas we have handed back to them for their own administration – just a token to say we trust them once more, while we squeeze them even further, as the Emperor now sought to do. The *Iceni* were rich once, but now they are poor. Yet the war had to be fought out in the way it was. It was they who brought war to Rome, not the other way round.

I replied to Hadrian, "Even with the reinforcements from the XXIst, the detachment of the VIIIIth was only a small force of legionaries advancing into unknown and dangerous country. Two cohorts had to be left behind to garrison Epocuria and protect the harbour. The *Iceni* were sailors too. They had many boats – small boats for coastal fishing in the main, but some larger ones as well which traded across the ocean – and they could have launched a raid on Epocuria from the sea. The auxiliary cavalry had its work cut out on the march scouting ahead and protecting the column's flanks and rear. That is why our small force was raised, as troops for shock patrols, with our whitened faces and equipment – we soon learnt the use of the local white rock, which we made into a paste and painted on ourselves – coming out of nowhere to seize and destroy, and then returning to the column with our spoils. On one occasion, a small detachment was cut off and killed. We revenged them later. But I am getting ahead of my story now, Caesar. Shall I return to that morning where I left you just now, with us about to break camp and advance into Icenia?"

"Yes, Celer," he said gravely. I pray you, tell me more of what was done."

In the early dawn light, the column of *Legio VIIII* moved out through the wooden gates of Epocuria, and took the gravelled road that wound between low sand hills crested by spiky grass to the bridge that connected the island with the mainland. The tide had retreated, and the floating sections of the bridge, lashed together with rope, were grounded in the mud, tipped sideways in places so that we had to be careful of our footing. Overhead swarms of seabirds watched our progress, as if screaming out their farewells to us, then diving to feed from the still uncovered rubbish dumps we had left behind.

The legionaries marched in battle order, the covers removed from their shields, without helmet plumes and wearing breeches and wool-padded boots against the cold, carrying javelins over their right shoulders. All baggage was on mule-back at the rear, guarded by cavalry. The standards of the first-centurion and his staff at the head of the column were raised high against the sky, so that, further to the rear, we were able to make out the vanguard of cavalry and the lead cohort as they reached the opposite bank of the river and began ascending the slope beyond.

We advanced only a handful of miles that first day. The *Iceni* scattered before us. We found their small settlements, alongside the hard white trackway that we followed, to be deserted: a few animals, pigs and goats and hens, grazed amongst the low, thatched roundhouses, with a barking dog, tied-up, throttling itself on its leash until we released it from its guard duties for ever. All the animals, we slaughtered for our supplies. A little further inland, we found some sheep on a hillside, driven into an enclosure made of hurdles, in the hope that we would not find them – but we did and our butchers slaughtered them also, and we set fire too to the dwellings, and left nothing behind us but waste. Many fields were full of weeds standing high amongst grey flattened crops of grain, dead and dying. It looked as if the *Iceni* had sown their fields but been unable to harvest them for lack of labour: the men, and women too, had most likely gone off to war and had not returned. What people were left must have been starving by now, existing on hedgerow fruits, and nuts and grasses. In the mid-afternoon, while preparing to lay out our camp, we came across some groups of women and children and old men hiding in ditches. Their bodies were angular with hunger, like people made with sticks, and their eyes huge in their heads, but still there was hatred of us behind their fear and they did not beg of us. We left them alone in their ditches. At that early time, before we had seen for ourselves what these people had done, we only killed, or captured, the able-bodied men.

The next morning, we of the *equites Albani*, the entire two *cunei* of fifty riders, led by Albanus himself, were allowed loose on our first mission detached from the column. We rode north in our two separate units, crossing broken country of marsh and river, heading north to where the land was higher and we could gallop over broad heathlands and feed our ponies on good grass, for the weather had turned warmer again, bringing in rain storms from the west. We burst into villages hidden away in valleys, villages that must have been largely innocent of the war for the *Iceni* here did not expect us, or even fear us at first, until we set about them and cut them down and burnt everything that we could see. At one village, built on a level shelf of land beneath a dense woodland of oak, our fellow *cuneus*, having reached here first, had already been at work, for smoke rose in thin spirals against a grey sky and flame crackled amongst the huts and cabins. A dead woman lay face down on the earth with her clothes rucked up at the back so that her backside was exposed, and a mangy dog was sniffing at her anus. Titus dismounted and put a spear through the dog, and then into the woman's arse while others of us laughed, but I felt sick to my stomach.

This had been a special place, not the usual straggling farmstead with round huts and small fields divided up by mud-filled tracks, but with a thick thorn hedge about a square compound of beaten earth, containing rectangular cabins raised up on posts, larger than any others we had come across so far. We saw the tied mounts of our comrades near one of the cabins, and a soldier emerged, his armour hanging open about his chest, bearing in his hands items that flashed in the grey-white sunlight – a golden torc as the *barbari* chieftains wear about their necks, and a silver one too, and some golden armlets and enamelled brooches in reds and yellows and blues. These he stuffed into panniers on his pony's flanks as another soldier appeared from the cabin pulling by a rope a captured man – a youngish man with a bushy mass of auburn hair. Tied together by a cord and hanging about his neck, were his hands, his arms now being but blackened stumps, cauterised by fire. The man, being led away, screamed, once, twice, while our brother soldier laughed.

"He was a sorcerer," he called out to us. "He was a maker of magical things, using metals that belong to Rome. He won't be making any more now!" And he laughed again.

In those early operations, we returned to the column at night, caring for our ponies before we bedded down ourselves in the horse lines used by the auxiliary cavalry, who regarded us with some disdain. However, on our second foray to the north, we followed their practice and brought back some heads fastened to our bridle straps, and from then on our return was more welcoming. This was a barbaric practice I, for one, did not approve of and most certainly did not like carrying out, but it seemed necessary at that time since our *cunei* were so inexperienced and we were trying to make a name for ourselves: it seemed part of a necessary initiation. Later, we stopped it entirely – but not the killing and the burning. We were still the ravagers of Nemesis with our horse harness whitened and with face masks like the shrouded dead.

The column was working its way slowly towards the centre of Icenia, sending out other mounted patrols in addition to ours, in particular to the south. It met with some resistance – some diehard attacks from warriors doped on berry juice, stripped to the waist despite the cold, their chests and backs covered in purple tattoos like the tangled stems of sprouting vines. They rushed at us in frenzied groups from both flanks wielding huge swords, cut down in a trice by our legionaries who marched in full battle kit and were ready for them. Two or three times as well, when crossing open land, a few chariots would sweep out of neighbouring woods, trying to cut off our rearguard, but were met by the VIIIIth's own cavalry. In these sudden encounters, amidst the swirl of horse and armoured men, and the great clash of weapons, the chariots would be overturned like toys, and their ponies, with tendons cut, left kicking and screaming in the traces amidst a wreckage of frames and wheels and yokes, snapped and crushed like twigs.

Most of the continuing resistance was coming out of the south where the *Iceni* land swept away to meet that of the *Trinovantes*. These people, as equally stubborn as the *Iceni* and of a stockier, dark-haired build, had perhaps even more to lose, as they had been conquered and occupied once already, whereas the *Iceni* had remained nominally independent until now, until Suetonius Paullinus had at last broken them in battle. Some of the worst atrocities had been committed by the *Trinovantes* in and around Camulodunum, and – it was being said – that the majority of the force that cut to pieces Petilius Cerialis's column had been of that people. So we had a particular score to settle with them, which, we were to learn, became the prime objective of Paullinus's army in the west.

After a further two days of march and camp, we of *equites Albani* were let loose once more – this time without Albanus who had been injured in the leg by the stab of a dying *Iceni* warrior. The first-centurion wanted the right flank of his column scoured of the enemy as far as the sea, which we anticipated (thinking of the return journey too) as lying more than a day's ride away; so we packed onto our ponies the equipment we needed for night-time as well, being mainly some cooking grids, dried meat and bread, and tarred coverings for shelter. We rode as two separate *cunei,* the one I was part of heading directly north – following a point midway between the rising and the setting sun – and the other on our left, crossing the land towards where it tumbled into the great inner sea known as Metaris. This time we were to be much more scouts than avengers: our mission was to inform. We were to ride hard and seek out any groups of the enemy, but only to engage them if we had to, and this time without plundering and destroying. Unfortunately, things went wrong from the very beginning.

We rode straight into large numbers of *Iceni*, on foot and in bone-rattling carts, travelling with animals about them, women and children too, many bare-footed in the cold mud. They cursed us, fearless, as we passed them on a ridge, and we let fly an arrow or two at them – I probably have not mentioned that we had some archers amongst us – but we otherwise left them alone. They forced us off the tracks, however, for such numbers of hostile people could be dangerous if we came upon them in an ambush, so we kept as far as we could to the higher grassland of the swelling hill tops.

We came to a meeting of trackways where there was an *Iceni* fort on a high point, carved out of the white rock, with a timber palisade topping its ramparts and a gateway of double wooden doors with a sentry walk above. We saw men on the ramparts, and smoke rising from within, so we suspected it was garrisoned by armed men, and kept well away. Beyond it the land descended to a flat, marshy strip by the sea. We could see the curl of the waves beating on a broad beach, and out to sea, a ship with a red sail beating against the wind – a Roman war ship, it looked, so we climbed up high on our saddles and waved and cheered. Titus fell off, I remember. Titus was always falling off, and getting up unscathed.

We rode down to the sea, and, although it was dangerous, for the higher land was above us and we could have been rushed by a war band, we galloped along the beach refreshing the ponies in the surf, then finding fresh water for them in a stream that made a pool here amongst the low cliffs.

The day was drawing on, and we rode back to the high land and along its crest to the west, until we felt we were a good way from the fort, whose occupiers would be unlikely to find us if they tried to seek us out under cover of the night. We camped in a circle, without a fire that would have given our position away (so the grid irons we had brought were not needed), but we eat the dried meat and washed it down with watered wine from our flasks. We posted eight of our number as sentries, flung well forward and all around us, being changed in four set watches.

In the early dawn, in the fourth watch, when I was sleeping, there was an alarm, and a soldier from our other *cuneus* with a badly injured horse was brought in by one of our sentries. He told us his unit, while encamped, had been attacked by a large force of *Iceni* earlier that night, and only he and one or two others had been able to get away. He had come upon one of our sentries purely by chance while leading his pony in the blackness, having no idea where he was at all. He had been most fortunate to find us as we could have been in any direction over many miles of country. But such are war's chances.

We were up and mounted within a quarter hour or less, our sentries called in, our covering sheets left on the ground. We cut the throat of the injured pony, as it was too lame to come with us and we did not wish to leave it for the enemy. It was a brave and faithful pony, with a particular long white mane, which I had ridden and knew well, and it upset me greatly to see it killed. I said a prayer to Epona that it might be reborn in the fresh, green fields of Elysium.

We rode out, with our comrade soldier doubled up with Titus on his pony at the lead. The direction was only half-known, as the survivor's journey had been made mainly in darkness, but a distinctive hill with a wood on its flank was a guiding landmark. We wound our way at first across open country, then directly across a grid of small fields, jumping the low hedges in sequence and surprising some terrified slave-workers who were making ready, with spade and hoe, for their day's labour. At last we reached the far side of the hill, at an open place with the wood behind, where the soldier said he thought his *cuneus* had laid out their camp and been attacked. He was not certain, and, as we approached, at first I thought he was mistaken, for there was nothing in sight but the long, grey grass swept by the wind beneath a dull sky threatening rain.

As we came closer, I could see that within a muddied hollow in the grass there were bodies lying, their flesh white against the earth, for they had been stripped of their armour, and tunics and breeches, and that the grass was all bloodied where the flesh and bone had been hacked about and the heads cut off. Some bodies, lying on their backs, we could see had had their genitals removed.

The sight made us retch in our saddles, and the ponies were shying away, threatening to throw us in their fear. I noticed that a fire had been lit at the centre of the hollow for here the ground was scorched and there was charred wood scattered about – at least I thought it was all wood until I saw that a man's limb lay there too with the white bone protruding from the blackened flesh. This *cuneus*, unlike us, must have lit a fire and that must have been their undoing, bringing armed *Iceni* to them in the darkness. Although piles of shit left by the ponies lay at one side of the camp site, there was no sign of the animals themselves – so they must all have been taken.

We forced our mounts to follow a trail of blood up the slope to the wood, but, no amount of kicking their sides or pulling at their heads would force the ponies in amongst the trees, so half of us dismounted, leaving the others on guard with spears poised, while the rest of us went into the wood. I was at the front of our file with sword drawn, and my legs felt so heavy it was as if I wore slave chains about my body. Not far from the edge of the trees, we came into a clearing, at the centre of which was the massive trunk of an oak tree, but its top and side-branches had been removed and it had been turned upside down, so the mass of twisting roots were now at the top, hanging down. And in amongst those roots, fifteen feet or so above the ground, we found our comrades' heads, set up on small wooden shelves nailed to the upturned tree, each with an earthenware bowl before it containing lumps of flesh, as if the frozen lips and protruding tongues were about to suck on what had been cut from the dead. The *cuneus* had been doubly unfortunate; not only had they lit fire to give their position away, but they had chosen as their camp a place close to one of the sacred groves of these *barbari*, where the Druids made human sacrifice to the goddess Andred. I was to learn that this warrior goddess particularly likes to receive the flesh of soldiers freshly killed in battle.

We had to leave the heads where they were; they were too high for us, even standing on our horses' backs, to bring down and bury. How the *barbari* had managed to place them up there, perhaps at first light before we arrived, I could not imagine. With swords drawn and spears pointing we searched all around the wood, but could see no one. No other escapees from the *cuneus* came into us either, so, wherever they might have been hiding, we had to leave them to their fate.

All we could do for the bodies at the camp site was to cover them, for their, and our, own dignity, with evergreen branches torn down from the wood. I knew this would not keep off the scavenging boar or the wolf for long. How close I had come to lying there myself. This mission, away from our main column, had been a foolish one. For a handful of knowledge about the enemy, we had left behind close to half our strength. The victory had been handed to the *Iceni*.

All that day we rode back south across a farmed landscape with many villages, and temples too – at least we thought they were temples, being square, post-built structures with shingled roofs standing apart from the villages, usually on higher land. It was a difficult ride, for we were much more careful than earlier to keep a close watch about us and to stay well away from the settlements, although we would have liked to have taken our revenge by burning and killing, and – being very hungry – to have found food. We crossed field after field, as we had done in the dawn light, by jumping their hedges and fences, until at last we came to a broad white trackway, which headed the way we wanted to go and seemed to be a main route of the *Iceni*.

The trackway was clear of travellers save for one cart that we came upon, drawn by two bone-thin women. When we rode up, we saw the rear wheels of the cart had gone into a ditch and the women were struggling to free it. The huge, frightened eyes of half-starved children peered over the sides at us. The women broke off their frantic tugging to protect them – but we rode on. We were not after women then; neither the place nor the time was right. Instead, later, we killed an old man in rags, who, at our approach, tried to hide in undergrowth at the side of the track. We took it in turns to spear him, riding by, yelling and cheering. He was dead by the time it was my turn. Titus dismounted to cut off his head, but made a mess of the job, getting blood all over his cuirass.

I was sick of this type of killing. I wanted to see the enemy felled in battle, cut down by us like wheat before the scythe. I didn't like the killing that made me feel a murderer. That was for cowards or braggarts, or the casual slave killers in the arena, not Roman soldiers.

A little later, we met up with a patrol of our auxiliary cavalry (a troop of *Batavi*) sent out from the column to look for us. We reported via Albanus to the first-centurion. No one was impressed by what we had done or seemed unduly interested in what we had learnt; so our losses were an unneeded disaster. It was the last major detached operation of the *equites Albani*. From then on we were to serve mainly as scouts to the column, subordinate to the VIIIIth's regular cavalry and commanded by them.

The next day after we had rejoined the column, the weather turned very cold, with a wind from the east, and it began to snow. Fortunately, the fall was not great but the flakes settled on the frozen ground turning the landscape about us white – a whiteness broken by the blackness of naked trees seen against a grey sky, and of rampart and palisade lines, where the snow would not gather on the upcast earth so that the camp's defences stood out sharply against the white background.

We were fortunate as well in our preparations for a winter campaign. Supplies of woollen tunics and breeches, socks and gloves had been brought up to us from Epocuria, as well as heavy cloaks dyed a deep maroon red, a colour which the long-serving legionaries of the VIIIIth were to adopt as their own, abandoning for the time being the dull yellow they had worn before. A long train of mules, guarded by cavalry, had carried these supplies to us on the same day as the snow arrived, treading out a long line of reeking mud across the otherwise hard earth. The shit left by the animals smoked on the cold air like damped-down fires.

We were somewhere in the centre of Icenia: the camp in the snow was the third the VIIIIth had built on this campaign. In the role of scouts, our small force – now only one *cuneus* of twenty-eight riders – was ordered forward on patrol while the camp was being broken down behind us and the baggage loaded onto carts and mules, guarded by two squadrons of cavalry and the VIIIIth's own horse. Our morale was low after the disaster we had suffered, and by our downgrading from active harrying of the enemy to the passivity of being mere observers and messengers – at least that was our expectation of the task of scouts. We were soon to be proved very wrong. Action was to come to us once more as fast and dramatically as an eagle diving out of a clear sky onto its prey.

Whatever our thoughts about our new task, however, we were grateful that we did not have the heavy labour of the legionaries, with frozen hands and feet, in dismantling tents and folding them up, and taking down the palisade of hundreds of staves and stowing these away, all of which would have to be brought out again and re-erected in the mid-afternoon before the short winter light, already dulled by cloud, diminished further towards night. This was the invariable routine on campaign: normally each day brought a further march with another new camp to be built. Battle would come as a welcome break to these wearisome, but necessary, duties.

As our twenty-eight men rode out of camp, by turning in my saddle I could see the quartermasters, with many oaths, supervising the loading of their stores, and the centuries' cooks, veiled in smoke, kicking out their fires and cleaning out their pots and pans, before hanging them from the harnesses of their mules – five to each century. Legionaries, not already in their armour and working, were standing beside the half-collapsed tents, buckling on their strip armour cuirasses over the wool and leather they wore underneath – adjustments necessary now because of their thicker winter clothing – and fastening their belts with their swinging apron straps; next putting on their battle helmets, stripped of plumes, and tying them by leather cords under the chin. Some were examining their weapons – their swords and daggers – rubbing their blades dry with lambswool before re-sheathing them, then inspecting the javelins they carried, with their heavy, pointed steel heads welded onto thinner iron shafts. Lastly, the curving, rectangular shields were slipped from the leather covers that protected them and hoisted onto shoulders where they were held by carrying-straps against the legionaries' backs.

The order and the discipline of a legion, when seen like this on campaign, were most impressive: I recall thinking that as I concentrated on controlling my pony and avoiding the snow-lined branches ahead. No wonder Rome had conquered the world. The VIIIIth was an experienced Legion that I was now proud to be part of. Its defeat at the hands of the *Iceni* had been as unexpected as it was catastrophic – an evil throw of fortune's dice. Perhaps the legate, Petilius Cerialis, had been rash in urging on the force he commanded, ignoring the strict rules of march into enemy territory. But there had been a very good reason for this; nothing less than a Roman *colonia* under attack that could only be saved by moving fast – by a rapid march that abandoned the usual prescribed precautions, such as we were practising now in Icenia.

The *Britanni* had been cleverly led: we had to admit that. They had surprised the VIIIIth, while it was extended in column on the road out of Duroliponte heading for Camulodunum, by erupting suddenly in large numbers from flanking woods and cutting through them in several places before they had a chance to deploy. The result had been the massacre of two thousand legionaries – the men our cohorts of the XXIst had been brought here to replace. Petilius Cerialis, his bodyguard, and many of the cavalry had been able to fight their way out of the mêlée and gallop for safety back to their fort near Durobrivae, pursued by chariots for much of the way. It had been a disaster. No worse defeat has ever been suffered by a legion in Britannia.

The desire for revenge was now driving on the VIIIIth. To have revenge gnawing at your stomach like hunger gives you a great will to endure, to surmount every hardship so as to be able to strike back at your enemy. The surviving cohorts of the VIIIIth had not formed part of the main army commanded by Suetonius Paullinus when he later achieved his victory over Queen Boudica. So, although that battle was a great triumph for the XIIIIth and XXth Legions which, with auxiliary forces, had fought that day, there was no satisfaction for the VIIIIth. They remained determined, however, to have their vengeance, unleashing retribution whenever and wherever an opportunity arose. It was good, they considered, that the *Iceni* still remained defiant. Obstinacy and defiance must be punished properly. The VIIIIth hoped that task would fall to them.

That day of our first patrol as scouts was to prove a memorable one. Forward of the column by perhaps a mile, we were surprised to hear the sound of many horses' hooves approaching, and immediately broke to both sides of the track in a wide screening movement, fearful of the sudden appearance of a large number of enemy cavalry. Such an eventuality at that time was still considered a possibility. However, something about the regular heavy thudding of the hooves, as well as the accompanying high call of a trumpet that sent the birds flying upwards out of the treetops, told me that these troops were Roman. And so it proved – an advance troop of Suetonius Paullinus's own auxiliary cavalry, of the *Picentiana Gallorum*, if I recall rightly, big bearded men in chain mail bearing red oval shields, seated on tall horses which made our broad, shaggy ponies look like the stuffed toys on wheels that infants push along.

Albanus, himself, now recovered enough to ride, was our commander that day, and he conferred with the troop's *decurio*, an elegant-looking young man with bright blond hair, revealed when he removed his helmet with a flourish of greeting. The two forces of our army, advancing from opposite points, west and east, had met up at last in the centre of Icenia.

At the rear of the column of cavalry was one unsaddled horse, tied by a rope to the saddle pommel of the mounted man in front. Across the animal's bare back, flung face-down, was the bound body of a man, who, by his unkempt look and the chequered pattern of his coarse tunic and breeches, was an *Iceni* prisoner. The bonds of this man were now loosened, and he was slid off the horse like an untidy parcel, being then pulled to his feet and held at the neck by one enormous auxiliary, like a mastiff shaking a hare in its mouth.

The auxiliaries from Gallia could evidently make themselves understood in the language of the *Iceni*, for the upshot of what was reported now was that this prisoner had delivered up some fanciful tale or other in a desperate attempt to save his life. The man was questioned again now in front of us, the horses standing, their breath blowing out on the cold air like steam, heads tossing, bridles jingling. I saw the badge of Epona on their harness, as some of us wore it on our bridles, and – for such a new rider as myself – dared to feel a sense of kinship with these soldiers from Gallia, who had probably been born into the saddle. On Albanus's command our scouts took up positions around the central group on the track, maintaining a careful watch against any surprise attack coming at a rush over the cold, white fields.

Whatever the prisoner said continued to save his life, for with a sword at his throat and despite being punched and kicked and shouted at, he was trussed up once more and slung back onto the horse. Then the troop left us, continuing along the track to meet up with the vanguard of our main force that would by now be advancing from the camp. Our first-centurion would decide what to do with the prisoner and whether anything further of interest could be extracted from him.

Albanus rode into the middle of us and addressed us. We had been his rough riders, now we were his scouts. He had trained us and must have felt the loss of our special status keenly. I am sure he blamed himself that he had not been commanding us in person at the time our lost *cuneus* was ambushed. Now, however, he told us he had another task for us.

"That prisoner says there is a party of women with some armed men to be found at a quarry some two miles to the south." He flung out an arm. We saw a bare, snow-covered field rising to a low skyline. Pale sunlight was trying to break through the thin layers of grey cloud, causing the sky to glow as if a light was being shone in the direction we should go. I was wary of omens like that. Had they not before been presages of doom rather than triumph?

"Amongst the women," Albanus continued, "the prisoner thinks is the Queen of these people, the one who led their revolt and has caused this war. She has escaped us so far. This may be a chance to capture her. I told my brother *decurio* we are the unit for the task. We will move fast, as I have taught you, we will find these fugitives, we will break in amongst them and we will capture this Queen. Are you with me?"

"We are with you!" we shouted back, full of excitement. "*Ave Albane!*"

I remember thinking we were going beyond our present orders, but it seemed a chance we couldn't miss. "*Ave Albane!*" I shouted too. "Let us ride!"

Albanus led us at a gallop over open heathland, our ponies' hooves kicking up the thin covering of snow so that it hung momentarily in the air like a mist about us. We reached the crest of the slope and saw a whitened landscape stretching away, with a belt of dark woodland in the distance, apparently devoid of any habitation. In what direction was the place where those we sought were said to be hiding? Albanus seemed to know. Whether he was remembering a complex list of instructions, or whether he was operating by instinct, I had no idea, but he led is off to the right, moving slower now in case of any holes or ditches hidden by the snow, until we came to a hedge beside a small plot of tilled land, with an opening that led to a track running uphill between thick woodland.

We proceeded more carefully now in case of ambush from the wood, with four riders out in front on point patrol to pick up any indication of a hidden enemy. Once through the woods and out into the open once more, the hedges on either side fell away and we all relaxed a little: I could tell this by the way the men sat back in their saddles and looked more carelessly around them, even talking until Albanus and his second-in-command ordered silence. The air was freezing on my face and I would have found it very hard to move my lips even if I had wanted to. The sounds of the ponies and their armed riders came to my ears muffled by the side-pieces of my helmet: the effect was to make everything seem as if it was happening in slow motion, giving a sense of unreality.

Reality came back to us sharply, however, when at the junction of a side track leading towards a rounded hill we came across an *Iceni* sentry standing in a pit by a lone tree. We must have surprised him with our arrival muffled by the snow, and he must have been half-frozen at his post, so was not alert at all. Suddenly confronted by our riders coming like death out of the whiteness, he tried to sound a warning on a horn pegged to the tree. It fell from his numb hands, his mouth opening wide in terror as horses and men surged towards him and three spear heads sliced into his chest. We pinned him to the ground like a pig, his thrashing body making bloody outlines in the snow.

Another sudden rush and a second sentry was flushed out, running away in frantic zig-zags, and hit by two of our archers with bolts in the back, falling to his knees coughing out blood, then sent into eternity by a swinging sword that half-severed his head. I thought our expertise was excellent. Everything was done in silence, only the frantic breath and the grate and groan of straining steel and leather told of the murderous affray. We did not shout out. We were the silent, white killers Albanus had intended. We had learnt our lessons well.

Albanus was circling us now, holding his hand up to his lips indicating the continuing need for silence – silence, that was, as far as the movement of horse and man would allow. It was a place of white cliffs we were entering, where the rock had been quarried in a great bowl-shape out of the hillside. The approach was by a narrow way with thick bushes growing on the banks either side, so we could make no movement to the flanks – a dangerous situation we could not avoid. In file, our ponies picked their way over the rough, slippery ground; only our sturdy, sure-footed animals could have done this. The larger horses of the cavalry would have slid and plunged and could not have ascended this path, so Albanus's insistence in training us as rough riders was at last justified. Such was the steepness of the way winding between the trees that some of us dismounted and led their mounts, holding the bridle in one hand with sword drawn in the other. Albanus, also dismounted, was at the front, a short spear balanced in his hand and his shield pushed forward. I was towards the rear, with Titus, wearing one of the whitened masks, beside me.

Ahead, we could see a white wall of rock overhung with creepers, and heaps of rock also beside the path where it had been cut out and stacked up in blocks, forming a funnelled gateway into the quarry floor beyond. A sudden shrill cry sounded out – of women, or birds, or instruments, or all of these things, I never knew, but it was repeated and repeated, a hideous cacophony, unearthly, chilling our souls. Now I could see movement coming against us as Albanus rushed the gateway with our men – some on foot, some, like me, still mounted – close behind him.

We were faced with wild warriors, with long unkempt hair and painted faces, swinging long swords and wearing armour on their chests that was of the legions: we knew where that had come from – our own dead comrades. Weapons clashed, oaths were shouted, we heard Albanus yelling out to us to force on, as we at the back, dismounting too, struggled against the press with our swords drawn. Our archers, lighter-footed than those of us trained with the sword, found a purchase high up on the walls of rock, and fired their arrows at point-blank range into the enemy mass beyond: there were as many of them, at least, as there were of us.

Albanus was through the gateway now and fighting with a giant of a warrior, who wore a helmet with horns and had a bronze mask too, cut out for the eyes and the mouth. Some of our men had fallen clutching wounds but I was able to scramble over them and get into the fight – my shield blocking blow after blow, my sword stabbing into bone and flesh, blood singing in my ears, my lungs bursting. Titus was beside me, and another of our number too, forming a short wall of shield and steel, as we had been trained, the enemy falling away before us so we were able to advance over their bodies to come to Albanus's aid. One of our men, still on his pony, hurled a spear that caught Albanus's huge opponent in the face, passing through his pretty mask – a rash, battle-maddened cast perhaps for it nearly sliced Albanus's neck as well. But with a spear-tip in his brain, the giant fell backwards like a boulder, and we were able to pour over his body in a flailing, rushing group of horse and men, as no training had ever taught us. As we advanced into the quarry, there were still more maddened *Iceni* rushing at us from the flanks, it seemed coming out of the very hill itself.

Such were the ferocity of these attacks, that we lost more of our men, cut down before they could swing round their shields to face them, both those on foot and on horseback: one mounted man, always the joker of our *cuneus* – but not now – I saw receive a sword slice on his thigh which severed his leg, tumbling him off his pony with a crash of helmet and armour, his body spurting blood.

We had thought we were winning, but suddenly now our own position was perilous, because coming out of the far corner of the quarry from behind a screen of bushes charged a wedge of armed men on ponies like ours, in mailed armour and with skull-cap helmets, long spears pointing. There were perhaps eight of these riders in all, but at their centre, closely guarded, were two other ponies, bearing figures wrapped in grey cloaks. One pony, I was able to see, carried two riders – women, I thought – crouched forward, the rider behind clasping the other round the waist. Their aim was clearly not to fight us, but to get through us, and, such was the impetus of their charge, they succeeded. One of us, however, was able to swing a sword at an outside pony, and the rider tumbled from his saddle, his leg caught by a strap, his head smashing against the rock. The pony beside him was the one bearing the two cloaked women, and, as they passed, in one of those moments that seemed to still as if suddenly frozen in ice, I saw the face of the woman at the rear turn towards me. It was the quickest glimpse that

I had of two blue staring eyes and a mouth half-opened in fright, the rest of her face being hidden by her cloak which also covered her hair. In that fleeting second, though – then and for ever since – I believed I had looked into the face of Boudica, Queen of the *Iceni*.

A well-aimed arrow hit another of their side-riders, pierced through the neck, but the rest thundered down that perilous track we had mounted so carefully, and no more fell. The last I saw of them, by scrambling up beside an archer onto one of the white block walls, was the group at a fast gallop crossing the field beneath the hill, the melting snow spurting up behind them. And then they were out of sight.

We could not chase after them. We were exhausted. We had lost six men and several ponies, and we still had some more killing to do. We searched the quarry and found their camp in a tunnel into the hillside. There was nothing there other than some crude earth cups and wooden platters and some worm-ridden furs. A fire still smouldered, the air full of smoke. On a shelf in the white rock, I spotted a bone comb, which I picked up. Amongst its broken teeth were a few strands of hair – golden red hair like sparks of fire. I meant to keep that comb, but must have lost it later because I did not have it with me when I got back to camp.

We had to leave our dead, but later their bodies were collected. All the enemy left at the quarry, we killed. The injured were in such a bad way they would not have made the journey with us even if we could have carried them: we had enough trouble getting our own wounded back to the column. None of us had enough knowledge of the local language to try and question the prisoners before we killed them. So we cut their throats and sent them to their own horned gods. I am sure our first-centurion would have liked to have interrogated them. He had to make do with the informant whom the Gallic cavalry had delivered to him. This man's information had proved sound, but he had clearly tried to use it to lead us into a trap. The next day at our camp, when the farriers had finished with him and there was nothing else to learn – to his credit he told us nothing, not even his name – we had him crucified on a post beside the main gate, and left him there when we advanced once more two days later.

The auxiliaries, and our own cavalry, sent out many far-ranging patrols but we never caught up with the *Iceni* group who guarded their Queen. She escaped us then and she escaped us later, until the time came when there was no point in searching anymore. The story went around that she had killed herself. What happened to her body, no man knew – although many, including myself, have wondered.

There was little further *Iceni* resistance that *Legio VIIII* experienced. Our consolidation of the eastern part of Icenia was accomplished when a week later – about the time of Saturnalia – we made contact with a forward detachment of *Legio XIIII* at a place we named *Castrum Harenae*, after the sandy soil there. Now, better tents were delivered to us, and we received supplies of fresh meat – pig and fowl – which we were able to cook on ovens constructed by the experienced regulars of the VIIIIth. By batches as well, we marched to a nearby place of the *Iceni*, said to have been a residence of their royalty, but now levelled by us and a fort built there. This had timber stores and granaries for the supply of our army in the field, as well as a stone-built bath house, erected in a few short weeks by the XIIIIth's own engineers, which was much in demand by units returning from the campaign.

By the time winter gave way to spring, the *equites Albani* had been formerly disbanded, its ponies to my great sadness dispersed, and I had returned to the ranks of my former cohort in the VIIIIth. I found that my old *optio*, Volcatius Pastor, was still there in command of my century, and also, my former tent-mate, the all-knowing Sextus. Still a bubbling fountain of knowledge, Sextus told me that the Legate was being criticised for his campaign and that a top-level emissary was to be sent out from Rome to review the situation in Britannia. The newly appointed Procurator of the province – one Iulius Classicianus – was said to be critical of Suetonius Paullinus's strategies in finishing the war, and was seeking to have him recalled to Rome. The blame for the whole war, and the near loss of the province, was being heaped on him, which Sextus (who had once studied the law, and politics too) said was absurd and a scandal, as it had been Paullinus, above all, who had saved the province by his brilliant generalship.

The opinion of his soldiers was that the Legate should certainly be sent back to Rome, but only to receive the thanks of the Emperor and to dedicate the spoils of the war to Iupiter (it was rumoured there had been some considerable gathering up of *Iceni* gold and silver, which might help pay for the damage done to the province – three towns destroyed, eighteen other settlements, thirty-three villas and temples, innumerable farms – and the former prosperous Icenia devastated and burnt, its fields left untilled, its people starving).

Paullinus should lead the legions of Britannia to more victories, was the view of most. Some *Britanni* peoples had remained loyal during the revolt but others had wavered: the latter should be punished and their lands taken too. The legions which had done the fighting, including the VIIIIth, were becoming restive: they looked for reward. If their commander was dismissed, the situation could become dangerous. To whom, and in what way, this danger would come, Sextus did not say exactly. At that point he rolled over in our mess tent and pretended sleep. I was too innocent of these things at the time even to speculate. However, I was unaware of any discontent amongst my comrades. Like most of them, I only wished to serve and to avenge further what these *barbari* had done to our people.

It was in the spring that we moved again – four cohorts of the VIIIIth, marching without cavalry, other than for a token screen. All *Iceni* resistance by now had been stamped out, and we marched for two days along the great white trackway that led out of their lands towards the south, seeing nothing but desolation about us. The grass at the trackside was growing green and fresh in the spring sunlight, but beyond, where the plough should already be turning the soil, the fields were grey with last year's ungathered crops and the earth thick with weeds. Every small settlement that we came to had been burnt to the ground, the round huts they had contained now just circles of charred timbers. There was a great stillness everywhere. The cattle and the horses, the sheep, pigs, hens and geese that had once moved upon this land were all gone. Only the occasional dark shape of a dog, with protruding ribs, slunk amongst the wreckage. I remember thinking even the wild birds had abandoned their haunts: nothing flew above us or about us when we halted to eat our food, and there was no bird song, only a long silence shaken by the wind. Further off, trails of smoke drifted up into the sky. The burning still went on.

Occasionally, a dispatch rider, or a group of cavalry, or even a half century of foot soldiers, would pass us going the other way, and once a litter carried at a run by six slaves, with armed men about it, perhaps bearing some tax-collector or other official going to see if there was anything else to be raked from the waste.

We spent the night under canvas in a prepared camp by a burnt-out village and took to the road again in the early morning. In the third quarter of this second day, we came to a junction with another paved road, branching off to our left – it looked newly made on a high embankment with clean side ditches. It led into a broad valley which the war must have passed by, for the land here was green and unspoilt. However, it too was empty of life. On our left side, a river curled through water meadows so full of bright yellow flowers one of our men near me called out as we passed, "Is it butter they grow here?" He was a lad from the dry southern lands of Apulia and had never before seen flowers so prolific and of such rich colour.

There were some barges on the river, being rowed by great sweeps, and a smaller oared craft, with a high bow and stern, which from the device on its raised banner, viewed distantly, I thought was of an Army command. Then, as if to confirm this supposition, we came in sight of a fort standing by the river, which must have been recently constructed – or at least extended and strengthened – for the turf on its outer rampart looked newly laid, although the inner rampart was well grassed. The barracks as well appeared new, for their posts and frameworks were of freshly cut wood, but other buildings, including granaries with brick foundations, had probably been built during earlier campaigns. Such matters did not concern me then. What did concern me and my comrades, looking eagerly around, was that there was no bath house, unless it was further down the river where I could just make out a small settlement of huts. We had grown used to our bath house next to *Castrum Harenae* during those weeks of winter. All too quickly, we had become soft, something that can happen easily to any army once it is moved to the rear away from the fighting.

The fort, which was large with the capacity to hold some five thousand men, had an annexe as well for a tented camp and cavalry stables. A number of formations from the Legate's own immediate command were brigaded with our four cohorts of the VIIIIth. These included a single cohort from the XIIIIth and two cohorts from the much derided IInd, which had arrived too late for the final battle of the war. A large number of *Batavi* auxiliaries also occupied the annexe camp, except for their senior commanders, who were quartered in the headquarters building. The name of the fort, we were soon to learn, was *Castrum Ikenorum*, the name for once spelt out much as it should be pronounced.

The Legate, Suetonius Paullinus, had his headquarters at this camp, although when the VIIIIth arrived he was away commanding in person a detachment of the XIIIIth on a march into lands of the *Trinovantes* further south. Trouble from this people had continued longer than from the *Iceni*, although led by a small faction of their leaders only. However, all suffered in the repression, although the destruction that was meted out was less severe than in *Iceni* territory. The ruins of Camulodunum had been occupied by the rebels, both *Iceni* and *Trinovantes* – and they had prepared a defence about the half-ruined Temple of Claudius by building a rampart and ditch in the Roman style: if we had done the same before the revolt, it might well have saved the lives of thousands. This rampart, we were soon o learn, proved but a small obstacle to the rightful wrath of Paullinus's avenging force, and many rebels were put to death on the same spot where they had slaughtered our fellow countrymen and loyal *Britanni* six months earlier.

At *Castrum Ikenorum*, we new recruits to the VIIIIth came into contact for the first time with those who had fought under the Legate in the defence of the province. The cohort of the XIIIIth with whom we shared barracks, had been present at the final battle when one hundred thousand – or so it was estimated – of *Iceni* and *Trinovantes* were overcome by seven thousand legionaries, with several thousand auxiliaries, an army of some ten thousand soldiers in all. In those words of Publius Cornelius Tacitus – "which you have read out, Caesar" – 'It was a glorious day, the equal of any of Rome's great victories in the past'.

The XIIIIth at first kept very much aloof from us. Many of their men, from the centuries we mixed with, were much the same age as ourselves, in their early twenties at the most, having not served long themselves under the Eagles before the war broke out. Notwithstanding this, they felt they were deserving of a special respect on account of the great battle they had so recently fought. And that, indeed, was what we gave them. The more we heard of that battle, the more we learnt of what a desperate affair it had been, despite the careful preparations of the Legate.

After a few days, rubbing shoulders with these tough legionaries of the XIIIIth in the barracks, we of the VIIIIth grew to know them better and to get along with them. We did not say too much about what we ourselves had done in our small way, marching across a land already bled by their own victories. It also helped, when we received some pay – the first we had had since leaving Vindonissa – to buy them tankards of the British beer that were sold in the civilian camp outside. The taste of this beer was such that, being unused to it, we spat out at first as much as we took in, but, as there was nothing else to drink other than plain water – and that was tainted – we gradually got used to it. It had a full, what I can only call 'brown taste', as if we were drinking the diluted mud of the river bed, made more gritty perhaps by the rough feel of the wooden tankard edge against our lips. The effect, though, was almost instantaneous, and seemed to separate our legs from the rest of our bodies, so that I – for one – felt I was spinning along like a dust eddy caught up by the wind. Like this, it seemed wise to sit down to drink more, and this we did with our comrades from the XIIIIth, soon friends as if we had been so for life, with the stories beginning to flow.

VI

"Ah, so, Celer, you *did* meet with men who fought in that final battle of the war. You can recall what they told you? You could take us to the place where it was fought?"

The Emperor had risen to his feet and was pacing up and down before me. Numicius, I saw (I had almost forgotten his presence) had slumped sideways on his bench, his back against a column I had had placed there – only a small column, broken off at a height of five feet or so, but it had come from the same bankrupt mason in Durobrivae from whom I had purchased my carving of Epona. Seeing the Emperor on his feet, Numicius was struggling to raise his paunchy body. He must have nodded off, I thought. Am I such a good story-teller then that I send my listeners to sleep?

"Yes, Caesar," I said. "I can remember what I was told of the battlefield, and its many features, but whether I could find the place, I am not sure. It might demand some hunting around, although I am reasonably certain of the approximate area. Some of the local people may have memories. Caesar, I have not been to that part of the country for very many years, but I would be honoured to help you in your search."

The last words, I added hastily, remembering how Hadrian liked positive people about him, not those with dragging uncertainties, pleading pitifully, "I don't know, I don't know...". In any event, the idea of a journey with the Emperor – to be one with his entourage riding in panoply through the province, trumpets blaring, banners flying, with a privileged position at his side – leading him in a quest that my wealthy betters could only wonder at, quite appealed to me. If only I was not so old. Would my aching legs and hips allow me to do this? I needed to be able to ride again, not be carried in a chair as if I was already dead?

Hadrian was removing his leather cap and scratching his head. The fringe of his brown, curled hair, where it had been compressed by the cap, now stood up in a ridge on his forehead. His steward and an attendant slave I saw hovering uncertainly in the background, not sure whether to bring forward the combs and brushes and polished mirror they had ready. Hadrian sat down again and snapped his fingers at them, so they came at a run and began to attend to the errant hair.

"We will set off tomorrow morning," Hadrian said. "You will ride with us, and bring with you whatever personal slaves you will need. It may be several days. Can your household run without your presence?

"Of course, Caesar. I have my steward, Gavo, who will be in charge."

"Good, that is settled. I shall issue the orders later. Now, come, I wish to hear what you saw and learnt of the battlefields of that terrible war. Numicius!"

"Yes, my Caesar."

"Do not sleep in my presence. It is rude."

"Oh, Caesar. My apologies, of course. It is the bright light in my eyes that makes me tired."

"Just that, Numicius? Not the flagon of Falernum you put down your throat last night. Does our best wine not have some say in it?"

"Of course, Caesar. Or rather, of course not..." Numicius looked flummoxed and unhappy. As I could see Hadrian was only teasing, I laughed. And then Hadrian laughed too, then suddenly everyone was laughing. Even the lips of the grim-faced Praetorians began to twitch. Numicius decided his best, and safest, course was to join in too.

When we were all settled again, and the steward and the slave had withdrawn, and Hadrian was beside me once more with the sun in his newly-barbered hair, I said, feeling stronger and more confident now, "Shall I continue first, Caesar, with a summary of the main course of the war? That's if my telling of these events would be of use to you. I am sure, Caesar, you will know the sequence of the war up to its great final battle, and, of course, you have your historian's account to consult too. But, now that I have thought back on those times of over sixty years ago – from that late summer when the war first erupted into fire, through the dark-white winter of our own march across Icenia, to the first greening of a new year when the last quivers of resistance were being stilled – my memory has returned – amazingly so, indeed – more fertile than I have known it recently in the present dotage of my years. The events – the people, the scenes, the colours, the victories and the disasters – come to me as if they were happening only yesterday."

"Celer, we would value such an overview, would we not Numicius?" – I could see the latter nodding his head vigorously – "For we appreciate

81

that what you tell comes to us directly out of time itself, and even if you were not actually present at some of the major events of the war, you were close by and have spoken to others who were. So yours will not be a story, heaped upon someone else's tale, then added to and altered many times, for whatever effect, for whatever purpose, over the years. Speak on now, we bid you, indeed we command you. We are most eager to hear more."

Who would think that one day I would sit here in the sun, nodding over those long days out of my past, having felt the world had long forgotten me in my little corner of remoteness, which was somewhere next to nowhere And then suddenly here I was, with 'the eager ear' of the Emperor of Rome beside me, my every syllable now under scrutiny, my every pause, deliberated, the rising cadence of my words, or the lowering of my breath, affecting the Emperor's mood, his opinion, as if indeed I was a player in the theatre, the play to be called – what should be its title? – perhaps, 'Bodig of the *Iceni* Fights Rome': a 'Play of Disorder in Two Parts'. Part II, of course, would tell of Rome's eventual triumph, sub-titled, 'How we Won back Britannia'. What else but that last would my audience be expecting? Yet I knew how very close to total disaster the real events had been. But for the courage of Rome's soldiers, and the skill of their commander, Queen Bodig of the *Iceni* might have triumphed, driving us out of the island and winning herself the title *Boudica Regina Britanni*.

The substance of this next passage I learnt from soldiers of Legio XIIII while based at Castrum Ikenorum in the early spring of the second year of the war. I have set it out here, as presented to the Emperor, together with my own personal comments at that time.

The campaign *Legio XIIII* had fought, together with *Legio XX*, had taken them under the Legate Gaius Suetonius Paullinus, on a march way to the north, at first through a mountainous land, and then, reaching the coast, across a broad water in boats to attack the island of Mona, where the priestly class of Druids had their stronghold. They had witnessed horrors there which were but a preparation for what was to come. News of the outbreak of the rebellion led by Queen Boudica of the *Iceni*, together with her allies of the *Trinovantes* and some other smaller tribes, came to Suetonius Paullinus on Mona, delivered at first by signal and then by a despatch rider, who had ridden, it was said, three horses to death in his dash from the south.

Paullinus had to move fast. The despatches delivered to him told of both the fall of Camulodunum and the defeat of the VIIIIth in its rapid march to relieve the *colonia*. He set out south with little idea of how the revolt was developing. Did Boudica – her name was given to Paullinus now although he had perhaps never heard of it previously – have a unified army in the field with a precise objective to destroy the whole of the settled province to the south, or did the revolt just consist of small warrior bands, plundering, looting and killing? He feared the former because the destruction of Camulodunum and the defeat of the VIIIIth's relief force showed evidence of good planning and command.

Paullinus and his headquarters staff moved south at once with a heavy force of cavalry about them, of *Tungri* and *Thraci* in the main. *Legio XIIII* with four cohorts of *Legio XX*, ferried rapidly from Mona, began their long march a full day behind Paullinus and the cavalry, using long-abandoned marching camps as protection overnight when they came closer to potentially hostile territory. They marched fast, leaving their baggage train well to the rear, trusting in fate that the rebels would not spring a surprise and attack the rear of their column, cutting off their supplies.

When he reached Deva, Paullinus sent messages ahead (the signalling system with its chain of towers beside the military road was still working) to his isolated forts and towns in the south to say that, given the sudden critical instability of the province, he and his army were marching to their aid. From Venonis, at a crossing of the military highways, further signalled orders were sent to the south-west where *Legio II Augusta* was based at Isca Dumnoniorum, alerting that legion that it might have to move at short notice. Reports had reached Paullinus that the army of Boudica which had destroyed Camulodunum, and which had largely dispersed afterwards with its booty, was now reforming with the likely intent of advancing on Londinium.

Paullinus thought at first he would be able to defend Londinium. Much depended on whether the formerly powerful *Catuvellauni* people were going to join the revolt. If that happened, it would be very dangerous to march his two legions through their territory to the relief of Londinium. He sent messages for the XIIIIth and XXth, still on the march somewhere south of Deva, to halt at Venonis and await further orders. The Legate, meanwhile, with a strong cavalry force of auxiliaries pushed on through the disaffected *Catuvellauni* lands. Reaching Londinium, he realised how open the city was to an attack from the north-east, out of *Trinovantes* territory. The situation with the *Catuvellauni* was still too uncertain to risk the northern legions advancing further south. Yet, a holding defence of some sort might be organised at Londinium if a detachment of *II Augusta*, of a strength of three cohorts, which he knew to be in camp close to Venta Belgarum, could march rapidly to join him at Londinium. However, this force, under the command of the Legion's camp *praefectus*, one L. Poenius Postumus, did not obey the Legate's direct and immediate order; instead, Postumus, worried by rumours of a further uprising that might break out to his rear, sought confirmation from his own legate at the IInd's base at Isca Dumnoniorum, much further to the west. By the time the order to Postumus had been repeated, it was too late. He did eventually advance with his force of a thousand legionaries towards Londinium, but by then Paullinus, without the reinforcement he had requested and faced with an imminent attack, had abandoned the city to its fate, taking his column across the river Tamesis and burning the bridge behind him. Several hundred civilian refugees who had accompanied him were able eventually to find shelter in the friendly client kingdom of the *Regnenses* further south, which was ruled by one Togidubnus, a loyal ally of Rome for some forty years.

Paullinus's mounted column, having seen the refugees towards safety, re-crossed the Tamesis downstream from Londinium at a place called Pontes, and in a difficult cross-country ride was eventually able to rejoin the main Roman road to the north at Verulamium. This town, although in *Catuvellauni* territory, also feared attack by the rebels. Although some individuals from the *Catuvellauni* did join the revolt, most of the people – traditional enemies of the *Trinovantes* – remained loyal to Rome.

Paullinus, now fully aware of the extent and nature of the rebellion and anxious to reunite with his main army, had in turn to abandon Verulamium to whatever fate might befall it. After a further dangerous march, he reached Venonis with his cavalry where the XIIIIth, with detachments of the XXth, were by now in camp. Having separated himself from his main command, his cavalry dash south might be considered a perilous operation, had the *Iceni* only possessed an effective army in the field under a competent commander following a military strategy rather than just seeking plunder.

Paullinus had hoped to save the province by defending Londinium – the nominal capital of the province and its wealthiest town – but the imminence of an *Iceni* advance (of an undisciplined horde intent mainly on loot and destruction, yet numerically strong) and the absence of any reinforcement by the IInd until his main force could arrive from the north, had put paid to that plan. Not only Camulodunum, but next Londinium, and then Verulamium – at that time, the three major cities of the province – went up in flames.

The rebel force of *Iceni* and *Trinovantes* that had destroyed Camulodunum, and also cut up the VIIIIth as it tried to march to the rescue, had initially been a large one. It had consisted of the warrior hierarchies of both peoples, supplemented by their households – whose men owed service in war to their leaders and who, before the coming of the Romans, had been well trained and armed as both cavalry (including charioteers) and foot soldiers. Their sons fought too now, taking up arms for the first time, pulling out weapons and armour from their hiding places, and joined by land workers from the rural fastnesses, who brought the tools of their labour to the fray – their scythes and knives and long-handled spikes and forks.

The attacks by this first combined rebel army had been well-directed, their results devastating. After the fall of Camulodunum, however, most of that army had retired with their plunder and their stories to their homes, leaving only the households and immediate followers of their chieftains in the field, organised into war bands of chariots, foot, and horse. These, though, contained some of the most determined and most vicious of the rebels, inflamed by the priests of the Druids who moved amongst them, telling of how the Romans had so recently attacked and destroyed their sacred sanctuaries on the isle of Mona. The Druids were a powerful force behind the rebellion. They had the ear of the *Iceni* Queen as well.

The rebel army that descended on Londinium was thus a much smaller one than had destroyed Camulodunum, although led by Queen Boudica in person. The atrocities of rape and murder and mutilation that accompanied it, however, were even more extreme than earlier. Those who specialised in such things had formed themselves into their own particular bands, encouraged by the Druids, who said these practices were necessary to appease their affronted gods. Thus, Roman women and their virgin daughters were laid out on hurdles and impaled lengthways with poles, and others hung up with their breasts cut off and sewn to their mouths as if they were eating them.

"This sort of atrocity, Caesar, I can attest to from what I saw in Icenia myself – acts intended so to outrage natural decency as to appear to overturn the world, a symbolism perhaps intended as well by the oak tree we had found turned upside down. Most terrible, it was to learn, that many of the worst acts were carried out by women."

A number of *Iceni* war bands, one in particular with Boudica's chariot at its head, crossed the Tamesis by an old, long disused ford and burnt the settlements on the far bank. Some, trying to rouse the *Atrebates* – long loyal to Rome – to join the rebellion, advanced towards the distant town of Calleva Atrebatum, where they clashed with the detachment of the IInd under Poenius Postumus, who had the help of auxiliary troops of King Togidubnus of the *Regnenses* people. This king served as a linchpin in keeping the settled south of the province loyal to Rome, for which actions he was later much rewarded.

Abandoning her initial intent to spread further destruction here, so far from Icenia, Queen Boudica's war band now re-crossed the Tamesis at Pontes, in the wake of Paullinus's force, and, gathering other of the war bands to her, fell upon Verulamium. The resistance here by the *Catuvellauni* inhabitants was more successful than that at Camulodunum, partly on account of the smaller size of the rebel army, but also because the defenders were able to strengthen ancient earthworks and hold off the attackers at several points, resulting in only part of the town being destroyed, before the attackers, seemingly content with the damage they had done, made off with their booty.

It was clear by now that the rebels were no longer seeking a major engagement with our army, but were much more intent on satiating their lusts for rape, loot, and revenge, the latter mainly expressed against their own *Britanni* peoples who had thrown in their lot with Rome. Since the rebel forces consisted of several war bands of their warrior elite, each with its own commander convinced he or she –

"in addition to their Queen, Caesar, shocking as this may sound, we found other would-be Amazons in arms"

- knew best how to act, the Legate's main concern now was how to obtain an opportunity to defeat them in mass. Much of the worst destruction in the affected area – of towns and other settlements, of isolated villas and trading stations –had already been carried out. Although some other of the peoples bordering the lands of the *Iceni* and *Trinovantes* were sympathetic to the rebels, nonetheless there remained important *Britanni* leaders who were still supportive of Rome, in particular Togidubnus to the south and another queen, Cartimandua of the *Brigantes*, to the north. The one people who might have tipped the balance against Rome, if they had come out in support of Boudica, were the *Catuvellauni*. They had been wavering in their support, but, perversely, it was the rebel attack on their ancient strongholds at and around Verulamium that brought them firmly back onto Rome's side, in particular on account of the ancient enmity of the *Trinovantes* with the *Catuvellauni*. The *Iceni* selection of Verulamium as a target of their anger can be seen to have been a great mistake, a mistake perhaps made by Boudica herself who was known to be with her troops in the field.

Now united with the force he had brought out of Mona – *Legio XIIII*, at virtually full strength, and four cohorts of *Legio XX*, with their auxiliaries, and others also from the fort at Venonis – Gaius Suetonius Paullinus, Governor and Commander-in-Chief of the Roman Army in Britannia, had an army of some ten thousand men with which to do battle with Queen Boudica, to end the rebellion once and for all. Because the numbers that the *Iceni* and *Trinovantes* could put into the field against him would be substantially greater than that – by a factor of eight, or even more – Paullinus had to be most prudent of how, and where, he offered battle. It was clear that a battle would not now be forced upon him by the enemy, which seemed not to want a general engagement but was more intent on seeking out unprotected places that might still contain rich pickings. The rebels seemed to be making the most of their remaining opportunities to stir up chaos before the inevitable retribution caught up with them. Some of those on Paullinus's staff thought that a solid show of force would be enough to end the rebellion. But the Legate himself did not believe that. Even if the rebels did not wish to fight further, he knew he had to make them do so. It was imperative that the power of these people be crushed in battle once and for all. Otherwise, other rebellions might follow.

Paullinus had to make the *Iceni* and their allies fight his army. He had to prepare for a decisive battle into which the enemy would be lured in the belief that it would give them victory. And yet, at the same time, the Legate had to make every preparation to ensure that, although numerically inferior, it would be the Romans who triumphed. If he misjudged, the outcome would likely be, not just the loss of Britannia to the Empire, but the death of every Roman and every Roman ally in the province, from north to south, west to east. This battle was going to be as critical, and as decisive, as any fought in the long history of Roman warfare.

Paullinus waited with his combined army at Venonis for ten days while he sent out reconnaissance patrols towards the south and west to gain information on the direction being taken by the rebel war bands. The campaign season had now descended into early autumn, and, after a long dry summer, the rains had come, the baked earth now churned by soldiers, horses and pack mules into a sticky morass of mud. Reports came in that all the rebel forces were returning – by chariot, horse, and foot –

towards their homelands. Prisoners, cut off and captured in swift violent actions by our reconnoitring cavalry, yielded the information that, given the onset of bad weather, the rebel chieftains considered the Romans would wait until the spring of a new year before launching any major offensive action. Their intention was to keep their peoples in arms throughout the winter, while building whatever fortifications they could – heightening and strengthening the ramparts of their forts, building palisades around their settlements, making earthwork barriers across the routes that led into Icenia. Because the preparations for revolt had brought their people from the fields, crops had either not been sown or had withered unharvested, and food had now become a vital priority in order to survive the winter. Accompanying the returning war bands were captured carts containing grain, and other foodstuffs gathered from Roman granaries and stores. Many of the prisoners our cavalry took had been accompanying these carts, which were recaptured in short, savage actions.

Paullinus, however, had no intention of waiting until the spring to put down the rebellion. When he was sure there was now no major rebel force in the field that could threaten the province further, to the south or the west, and that the enemy was retreating on its home territory, he ordered an advance of his whole army towards Icenia. Skirting the vast flatlands of marsh and lagoon – the area of the *magnae paludes* – he marched by roads then largely unpaved towards the firmer, higher land that lay to the south – the land of white rock that runs in a broad band into Icenia from out of the west, and is followed by many interweaving trackways providing a sure route into Icenia at its principal gateway. Otherwise, the kingdom of the *Iceni* is shut off by marsh and forest, and by river and sea. Paullinus wished first to settle affairs with the *Iceni*. He would deal with the land of the *Trinovantes* later. If he could lure the *Iceni* into battle, he knew their allies from the *Trinovantes* would be present on the battlefield as well.

There is a broad river valley that runs from Duroliponte towards the south, crossing the land of white rock, and marking the western borders of Icenia.

> "This is the same valley as we of the VIIIIth – as I have already described to you, Caesar – entered when we were marching out of Icenia to the fort at Castrum Ikenorum."

A line of forts had already been set out along this valley, from a campaign fifteen years earlier – at Duroliponte itself, for instance, and at *Castrum*

Ikenorum – and Paullinus now ordered these brought back into commission, enlarged and strengthened, and his army divided up and stationed in them. A series of signal stations on the higher land to the west was also established, so the Legate was able to be in communication with other of the province's remaining forces to the north and south.

This land was well known and mapped. The XIIIIth had been part of that earlier campaign: there were even some still in its ranks who had fought then. So Paullinus already had a good idea of the place he was seeking to give battle. The matter had been much discussed amongst his commanders on the march from Venonis, together with the battle plan that would be necessary to beat the rebel forces. Now, at last, he was able to carry out his own reconnaissance, instead of relying upon the memories of his senior officers or the reports on scraps of papyrus and tablets brought out from the legionary archives.

The land of white rock looking towards the Icenia frontier was largely open, flat grass and heathland, with marshes, lagoons, and winding river courses on its left side and a long, rolling ridge to the right crowned by thick forest. Ahead were further low grassy hills, with spreads of dark woodland amongst them, and off to the left, far in the distance, there could just be made out another dark dot, with white smoke spiralling up, which marked the position of an outlying *Iceni* fort.

As the Roman army took up its positions along the valley, it could be sure its every movement was being watched from that distant fort. Paullinus was not concerned. He wanted his army to be seen. He now knew for sure where he would offer battle. He wished the rebel commanders – perhaps Boudica herself – to see his army moving into position. He wanted the enemy to come out of their homeland fastnesses once more – in their thousands, their tens of thousands – so he could defeat them in battle. Only in that way would there be a chance of ending the war quickly. There was risk in this plan as well. But there is always risk in war. A good commander – a great commander – knows how much risk to take in order to achieve the ultimate victory.

The ridge crested by the trees wriggles like a serpent, with many indentations and swells of grassland overlooking the flat plain below, which stretches away, open and uninterrupted by any hedge or fence, as far as the reed-lined edge of the marshes. At one place, not far from the river valley –

"perhaps a mile or two, I have been told"

– is a long, steep-sided cut into the hill, as if it had been carved out of the white rock by some monstrous Cyclops. Behind are the thick woods, in front the empty plain crossed by the great trackway into Icenia. This is where Paullinus drew up his army, in and around that defile in the hills.

Paullinus at first did not give up his camps in the valley. He brought some of his force to the battle site, then the next day interchanged these with others. At night, fires burnt along the dark line of the hills. The third day, Paullinus abandoned his camps, bar for a holding cavalry screen, and brought his whole force into battle position on the hills. On the fourth morning, he could see the lure had worked. Numbers of the enemy were reported to be moving towards the place of battle out of the heartlands of Icenia – charioteers, mounted warriors, vast levies on foot, even lines of trundling wagons carrying women, children, and the elderly, all coming to see the Romans defeated. From afar, it must have looked as if the Roman army had placed itself into a trap. Against the green hillsides, our soldiers must have looked like a scattering of ants which had become trapped in their own nest. The forces of the *Iceni* and the *Trinovantes* moving upon them, led by the chariots of their leaders, with the flame-haired Boudica at the front, would surely stamp them out – as surely as the power of light replaces night.

VII

Seeing their eyes on me, their faces intent with listening – the Emperor beside me and Numicius opposite, but also in the background, poised for a sudden call, the slaves with Gavo amongst them and the green-liveried steward, even the stern Praetorians with their flickering eyes (I was sure they had all heard some, if not all, of my account) – I broke off suddenly, coughing. At once, a blue crystal jug of water was placed beside me and a cup of wine, and another of the fine Egyptian napkins held out to me on a silver plate. I coughed again, took some of the water in my mouth, and spat it out into a glazed terracotta bowl that Gavo held ready for me.

"Are we tiring you?" asked Hadrian, rising to his feet and looking down at me seated on the bench so that he could see my features that had been hidden by my hand.

"No, Caesar. Thank you. I am fine. It was just some phlegm catching in my throat. I can tell you more, though you may be wearied of listening."

The Emperor did not answer directly. He looked deep in thought. "About the battle," he said, speaking low as if to himself, "I can understand well the Legate's strategy and his dispositions. We fought similarly in Dacia on one occasion – to lure the enemy into the open and to capture their king." He raised his voice. "Eunothydius! Where are you? – curse you." And when the shambling, toga-clad figure at last appeared, "Bring me the History again. Quickly!"

"At once, Caesar."

Hadrian turned to me, "Are you recovered, Celer? Are you able to continue and tell us about how the battle was fought?"

My throat was drying again and I felt a little sick in my stomach, but such things could not be admitted to an Emperor. "I can continue, Caesar, but what I can tell of the battle is but a patchwork of memories that the veterans of the XIIIIth relayed to us of the VIIIIth over their evening beer. I do not believe I have ever heard – certainly not read – a full account of the battle, how it was that our army of ten thousand were able to beat a rebel host that over two days grew to a number many times as great."

Hadrian did not answer. He was watching Eunothydius approaching at a stumbling run, his hands once more full of the papyrus roll, which he began to unwind. I saw his long, white fingers were shaking. "Which Book, *domine*?" he quavered.

"As before. Book XIV, of course. Come on. Come on. Eunothydius, you are so slow we have become history ourselves by the time you finish." Hadrian chuckled at his own humour.

"My apologies, *domine*," said the unfortunate Eunothydius. I wondered what he had done so to irritate the Emperor, who was now seated once more and tapping the edge of the bench's carved stone arm with the heavy ring on his middle finger.

Eunothydius, in his nervousness, made a mess of trying to locate the requisite passage, and the papyrus began to unwind through his fingers and loop down alarmingly to the ground. I rose to help him, and at last we were able to present the correct section of the roll to the impatient Emperor, who offered us no thanks. He immersed himself in the rows and columns of black ink writing, set within red and yellow borders painted like the interweaving designs used on mosaic floors.

"Ah, here we are," Hadrian said at last, stabbing at the papyrus with a finger tip "Cornelius Tacitus describes the field just as you have done, Celer. The narrow defile, the forest behind, the far-flung plain in front, open and clear, with no hiding place from which an ambush could be made. And he confirms the numbers of our soldiers and says the *Britanni* had never before gathered together in such a host, so what figure can we give to them? – perhaps a hundred thousand, or even more if we include the non-combatants present. Many of those, however, must have been ill-armed, perhaps only with the scythes and axes and clubs of their daily work. The number of trained soldiers amongst the rebels, those with proper battle weapons and armour, and horses and chariots, was probably very much less, perhaps closer to the size of our own army. After all the *Iceni* had not been in arms since their first revolt, twelve years or so earlier."

"Caesar, the rebels had taken much equipment from the bodies of our own dead," I broke in to say. "The fallen legionaries of the VIIIIth alone meant hundreds of swords, cuirasses, helmets, and missiles falling into their hands."

"That is certainly true," agreed Hadrian, his eyes still scanning the manuscript. "I wonder how long it took for Suetonius Paullinus to slaughter the rest of their army once their finest fighters were down. Once we had control of the battlefield, they must have been herded together like cattle. Killing so many tens of thousands is an exhausting business and it seems from Tacitus that we killed the lot: he does not mention prisoners."

That last comment started a memory in me. "We did take prisoners, Caesar. I recall one of the XIIIIth – he had been a standard bearer in the battle – telling me his cohort had been responsible for guarding hundreds of them, many wounded, pressed up against the edge of the marsh where the rebels had lined up their wagons. The most severely wounded were pushed into the water by their own people. Many drowned there."

Hadrian nodded. He was still intent on his reading and I did not know how much of what I had said he had listened to. At last he looked up, making a tutting sound with his mouth.

"A great battle, one of the greatest of our age, and our historian uses but one short chapter to describe it. And that includes all the usual invented nonsense that historians seem to think is necessary, setting down the speeches before battle the commanders make – as if anyone can remember those, or even have heard them. Tacitus here gives a longer speech to Boudica than he does to Paullinus. I wonder who was able to translate and copy down her wild rantings. It's a pity Tacitus didn't use the space to give us more clear facts about the battle. But we do at least have something, which confirms many of the details that you have given us, Celer. Now, Eunothydius, Chapter XXXVII. Read it out to us."

For one so clearly nervous, Eunothydius proved to have a fine speaking voice. He must have received a good schooling in the art of declamation, I thought. He was like an actor, who when put on a stage, is able to shed his previous nerves.

He read: "At first the Legion stood its ground using the defile for protection. When the enemy approached, however, they hurled their javelins to deadly effect and attacked in wedge formations, the auxiliary infantry accompanying the advance together with the cavalry, which, with thrusting spears, destroyed any effective resistance. The *Britanni* sought to flee but their escape was blocked by a curving line of wagons. Our soldiers did not spare anyone, even killing the women and adding the speared bodies of baggage animals to the heaps of dead."

"You see," the Emperor exclaimed, "a great battle, merely summarised in one short passage. We need more, much more. What deeds of valour were done that day? Which soldiers were awarded decorations? Was any commander awarded a *corona*? We would like to know now where all this happened. Perhaps the legions which took part still have records that will tell us more. We shall ask when we join with them again."

Numicius, who had followed all this conversation, watching each speaker with his puffy eyes, but had said very little, merely emitting various grunts and sighs as comments he deemed appropriate, now spoke at last. Hadrian seemed quite startled by his intervention.

"Caesar, why was the Legate not given a triumph – an ovation at least – for such an important victory, saving a province for Rome?"

Hadrian swung his gaze upon him and seemed to study him for a while as if trying to make up his mind what to do with him. I remember thinking Numicius must be wishing he hadn't spoken. He was an equestrian used to command amongst his own rank, but he had no military knowledge and seemed out of place in this conversation with the Emperor. Yet, he had asked a good question – one that we legionaries had wondered about at the time, but one also which ventured into that dangerous territory of an emperor's prerogative to act as he wished, not to be questioned, even by the Senate. This unwritten rule lived on with successive emperors, who might also need to make unpopular decisions and did not wish precedents, or previous misjudgements, to be raised against them.

Hadrian's answer came calmly enough, however, but tinged with sarcasm which I felt uncomfortable to hear, knowing how unhappy Numicius must feel to be made fun of before someone of humble origins like me.

"Ah, Numicius, it is good to see you no longer sleep. And your stomach now seems quieter than it sounded before. It is best – and healthiest – to let your wind out when you can, and there is seldom offence given out-of-doors. Now, regarding Gaius Suetonius Paullinus, here I do have information from our state archives. He was recalled in some small disgrace for what was considered at the time to be an unnecessary prolongation of the war, and so the Emperor then – Nero – was advised that any formal victory ovation or procession would not be appropriate. Some prisoners were brought to Rome as slaves, and some fought in the great amphitheatre in various re-enactments of the war, but they were not paraded in the streets. It might have been different, of course, if only we had caught their Queen. I am sure Nero would have had her brought before him, flogged again, and then executed. But who knows? Perhaps he would have kept her alive to be shown off when the opportunity arose."

"What happened to Suetonius Paullinus?" I asked, suddenly curious. I recalled trying to find that out years ago when the war was still very much in my mind, but could never find anyone – not even those of equestrian rank, including Numicius, who were in correspondence with Rome and with whom I had rubbed shoulders occasionally – who knew the answer. The question had long gone out of my mind, only to surface now with all the other memories that were being awakened.

Hadrian looked as surprised by my sudden question as he had been by Numicius's. Perhaps it was not my place to speak before I was spoken to? I did not know the customs expected of the Emperor's court. His brow puckered and I thought he was displeased, yet there was no indication of that in his answer.

"Oh, Nero did treat him generously. Nero was like that. Generous to some, most cruel to others. After all, Paullinus had saved a province, whatever judgements might be made on the cause of the war and whether it could have been brought to a quicker – and less expensive – conclusion. At one point, it is said, after the main revolt was crushed, Nero told Seneca – his chief counsellor then – that he wanted the province given up as it was consuming far more money than Rome was getting in return. Happily, he was persuaded otherwise. It is not good to give up what Rome has conquered by arms. Our own present purpose is to make sure that we are administering each province as efficiently as possible, and, where that is at the edge of the Empire, we make its frontiers permanent for all to see. Rome must rule only what is productive for her people. She does not wish to fling her boundaries ever further, for no material benefit other than to say we rule this, and we rule that, even if those territories are largely sand and waste. Such a policy just uses up soldiers, who are about the most expensive things an Emperor has to pay for."

Hadrian paused to let his words sink in. I thought, if that is true where has all the money gone? Certainly not to me, or any of my former comrades. Then he added, "Suetonius Paullinus received a large estate at Pisaurum – I think I am right about the place – and he became a senator and consul only a few years after his return from Britannia. In the Civil Wars, he commanded legions again, but was on the wrong side and was lucky – I think – to be given a pardon. He then retired to his estates and was seen little more. He died early on in the reign of Caesar Domitianus. I looked that up especially, knowing old soldiers – just like you, Celer – can live a long time."

I was emboldened to interrupt, partly as Hadrian was once again speaking to me personally. "Caesar. We knew well of your predecessor Domitianus's rule in the Bull. For, out of jealousy, he turned back our great Legate, Gnaeus Julius Agricola, from conquering the whole of Britannia, having shown it to be an island by sailing the fleet around it."

Hadrian was silent, and I was immediately fearful of having overstepped the mark – as a gladiator knows when he has made his swing, and missed and lost his balance, and the arena is hushed waiting for his opponent's counter that may send him cartwheeling down into the arms of Erebus.

"That is a tale which Cornelius Tacitus also presents," he answered after a while, fixing me with his eyes, but – I was relieved to see – with a smile too about his lips, so that I knew I was still in favour, and whatever line I had crossed, I was able to step back from. "Have you been reading Tacitus, Celer? – his life of his father-in-law perhaps, a great commander, indeed, but I don't agree with his biographer's conclusions as to why he was recalled to Rome."

I was confused. I had not realised the historian was related to the commander under whom I had marched into battle many times. Instead of contesting the point, I decided to play the ignoramus, a ploy which has served me well at different times in my life. "I have little opportunity for reading, Caesar. All we get in this distant corner of the Empire is the occasional bawdy tale out of Rome, copied and re-copied by scribes in Londinium and sent up to Duroliponte for those to read who can not get enough excitement out of their wives or slave girls."

Hadrian laughed, which I was pleased to see. "It may be that both you and Tacitus are right," he said, greatly condescending. "But you must understand an Emperor's judgement at the centre of the circle that is Rome: he must assess many factors that are hard to understand by those, as it were, on the perimeter, or, for that matter, who are historians, having perhaps a particular grievance to write down."

"Yes, Caesar. I understand." I hoped now we could move back to the more certain matter – for me – of the *Iceni* rebellion. I had broken off my account with the army of Paullinus poised to give battle. We had just heard what Tacitus wrote of that great battle. Could I remember now what those legionaries of the XIIIIth had told me of their firsthand experience of the fighting?

When we were all seated again and the piss pots had been brought and taken away, and more wine poured, I resumed. I began by repeating what I had said earlier; that I had never heard – certainly not read – a general account of the battle, and I did not know exactly how it had been fought or how long it had lasted, but I thought very much longer, and more furiously contested, than indicated in Tacitus's brief passage. All I could summon up was what I remembered of those soldiers' accounts that I had heard those many years ago.

These were just fragments from men who had probably themselves seen little of the battle as a whole – legionaries and cavalrymen, standard bearers and signallers: perhaps a distant, confused view of the enemy, then a sudden, close up flaring of violence, a period of calmness in reserve, an advance again into furious battle, the killing over and over again – and, at the end of it all, after the enemy was beaten, the wide, disordered scenes of destruction and death, and of human misery almost too terrible to tell. All that, and the land itself too – the churned earth and the mud and the stripped branches of the trees, and the smoke rising; and the emotions felt – the fear and the exhilaration, the sickness and the exhaustion; and the weather – the clear day changing to one of grey cloud and storm, the rain blown sideways like flighted arrows, washing the dark soil into reddened pools and streams.

All these memories had returned to me as vividly as the day they happened, as I sat in the bright sunlight of today telling my Emperor of a great battle fought at a time of darkness which had saved a province for Rome.

All the veterans of the battle I had spoken with had fought on foot amongst the ten cohorts of *Legio XIIII*, some at the very front of the first action, but some at the rear, who came to the fighting later. I have tried to arrange their memories into what I think was the chronology of the battle, so there is a beginning and an end to the day, and indeed of the days after, for the work of identifying and disposing of the dead and clearing the battlefield went on for a long time.

I start with the land. It was a broad, grassy plain that *Legio XIIII* marched across when it first approached the battlefield, lying grey under a darker sky spitting rain. The grass was long and feathery, brushing the legionaries as high as the metal fittings on their belts and their sword grips. Their columns beat their way through the grass, leaving long trampled lines behind as if many scythers had come into these open fields and had started their cutting. In a number of places, groups of ancient burial mounds rose out of the grass like the round-capped studs on battle shields, the mounds far older than the people who dwelt in this land now. Of those people, there was no sign. No habitation stood on this plain, other than for one small palisaded farm of round huts in the distance at the very edge of the marshes. The farm was empty: the people had already fled taking their animals with them.

As the Legion approached the defile, set like a dark mouth into a low line of hills, some cohorts wheeled to right and left, climbing the slopes on either side. The defile mouth was filled thickly with trees and bushes. The first job was to cut and uproot these, and erect barriers made from their trunks and branches on the rising land to each side. The legionaries carried tools for this work. It took much of the day. The defile was long, rising into the hill behind, and narrowing. At the very top stood the trees of the forest edge, mainly large oaks with much tangled undergrowth amongst them. Work parties were also clearing this growth and felling some of the trees. Smoke began to rise from various points within the forest.

The legionaries of the centuries and the cohorts, when not working, sat on the ground in their allotted places, in full armour with their weapons beside them. As more of the defile's length was cleared, the men could be seen arranged in geometric order like pieces on a great games board, row after row of them, tier after tier, filling the land between the steep slopes. They eat in their places: food was brought to them by the Legion's slaves. They relieved themselves in pits dug at regular intervals at the base of the slopes. As night fell, they covered themselves with their cloaks and slept in their places, other than those detailed for patrols and sentry duty. The weather was kind. The rain that had threatened on the first day held off, and the nights were relatively warm.

Some units were exchanged for others, arriving in long single files out of the forest behind or departing into it, but most stayed exactly as they were for three long days and nights. During that period they could see little of what was going on – even the view ahead was largely blocked by the men in front. Occasionally a rumour would be passed back that a tribune was inspecting or the Legate himself, and ahead one could see a ripple of movement as standards were raised, or hear the sound of cheering floating back on the wind. On the ridge tops above, horsemen might be seen passing by, silhouetted against the sky, and trumpets would blare out. Once, the horse of a cavalryman lost its footing on the slippery white slope where the grass was worn away, and came plunging down on top of the men below, both horse and rider turning over in mid-air. The horse had to be destroyed and the rider was taken off on a stretcher made of poles and leather strapping.

Early in the morning of the fourth day, even before a watery sun had made its appearance above the shoulder of the eastern hill, rumours began to be passed among the men, from in front, along the rows, then also from behind, that the enemy was now on the battlefield below in force. Circling chariots and horse had been spotted by our patrols, and a great mass of foot soldiers could be seen standing on the plain in front. The legionaries rose in rows, tended to their armour and their weapons, wiping steel as free as possible from the dew that had been heavy that night, slipped off covers from shields and javelins, went to the latrine holes, gratefully accepted bowls of hot gruel brought by slaves in relays running the defile's length and width, like attendants in the theatre showing the high-born to their seats. Centurions, *optiones*, standard bearers, and other officers – and a number of the wealthier rankers with connections – who had personal slaves were brought water and could even manage to shave, although beards on campaign were permitted by the Legion.

After that, it was one rumour after another. The legionaries were ordered to stand, then to sit down, then to pile all tools at the defile sides and take up battle positions with javelins to hand, then to stand down again. Occasional shouts and cheering could be heard coming from other parts of the Roman lines, but not yet from the enemy. There was a distant, rumbling sound on the air, becoming louder then falling away again, which may have come from the enemy's host assembling. Flocks of birds, in particular black crows and ravens circling high above, of which there had been many before, were now all gone.

The hollow rumbling sound had grown very much louder now. One legionary put his ear to the ground, and pronounced the sound to be from the hooves of many horses. The Roman cavalry was seen in strength on the left flank high above the defile, and amongst them a figure on a white horse in a moulded breastplate of gold and silver and with a red plume flowing out from his helmet. He was speaking with men gathered about him, both on horse and foot. Others could be seen listening, and they would occasionally raise their arms and cheer, but in the defile all that could be made out was a distant rippling sound like the rise and fall of the surf on a beach.

"It is the Legate!" one of the centurions in the defile called out. "*Gaius Suetonius Paullinus. Ave!*" And he set the centuries ranged about the defile floor cheering, so that the sound rose up to Paullinus who raised his arm in acknowledgement. He looked a small man with a grim, lined face, white against the darkening sky behind him that had begun to spot with rain. The rolls of cheering sounded like waves rolling up and down the long defile. Standards were raised, orders shouted, and the men knew the time had nearly come.

From my own experience of battle, the individual legionary sees little of what is happening other than the small area immediately about him. There can be exceptions to that when your unit is positioned in the front ranks of the army and you are able to see the enemy charging towards you wildly in long lines, or in fast-wheeling clumps of horse and chariot mixed up with infantry, like knots on a string that is being violently jerked up and down. My service had taken place in the northern wilds of Britannia, fighting the peoples of those lands. We marched under Petilius Cerialis, who recovered from his defeat by the *Iceni*, later to become Governor and Legate; and then under Julius Agricola, who led us to the very borders of the world. I have never fought against a disciplined enemy, one who will confront us in the Roman way, attacking by formation, in line and column and wedge, with cavalry protecting at flanks and rear, the sky full of javelins and arrows, and the bolts from the artillery *carroballistae* and other machines of war.

Legio XIIII were experienced soldiers. All the many formations of attack and defence had been practised over and over again, and then honed in battle. They could respond instantly to commands delivered by voice, standard, or semaphore. They were used to the savage charges of the *Britanni* and the weapons they used, the long sword and the battle axe, both wielded by a full, wide swing of the body, as if battles could be won by the strength of the arm alone. Their cavalry and their charioteers deployed long spears with huge winged points, and they had archers and slingers too, so they could fill the air with missiles as they delivered their charge. Their ethos above all was that of the individual warrior, well-armoured and helmeted, often a chief or one of his family, trained to be merciless in savage attack. The chariots would deliver these warriors to the main places of fighting, then stand ready to take them away to other hard-fought locations as the battle developed. All this free movement of individuals and small groups, although heroic and often overwhelming in attack, could be virtually useless in retreat where unit cohesion above all was required. Defence in the field – a lengthy battle of attrition where weight of numbers stood a good chance of grinding down an enemy and winning the day – was the one thing the *Britanni* never developed. Everything for them depended upon the success of the first, furious charge. If that failed, they were very vulnerable to counter-attack.

And so it was to prove that day, although such were the numbers involved, for a while it looked as if the rebels would overwhelm our soldiers simply through the immensity of their host. That is where the cleverness of Paullinus's carefully chosen main position in a narrow funnel-like defile can be appreciated. The defile concentrated the point of the *Iceni* attack:

their front was unable to deploy to envelop the legionaries occupying the defile owing to the steepness of the slopes, which were defended by auxiliary infantry and cavalry who could advance against them downhill. When the legions broke out of the defile, having halted and turned the *Iceni* attack, the greatness of the rebel numbers added further to their undoing. So many were pressed together, harassed on their flanks by our auxiliaries, that they died simply from suffocation without being able to use their weapons at all.

At the edge of the battlefield was marshland and here the rebels' baggage train had been drawn up, with spectators standing up high on the wagons to follow the course of the *Iceni* and *Trinovantes* charge, with its fantastic lines of running, shouting men, many naked to the waist, their swords brandished high, interspersed with horse and brightly-coloured chariots, all bunching together against the defile's mouth as they approached the Roman front lines up the slope. When this press of men was forced back by the Legion's counter-charge, it was pushed more and more against its own rear lines, and much of the killing took place amongst this trapped mass on the plain or beside the wagons at the water's edge. Other *Iceni* on the flanks were turned by our cavalry and herded against the forest where other of our auxiliaries awaited them amongst the trees, and few escaped.

One of the XIIIIth's veterans I spoke with I recall best of all. He was a legionary of five years' service, a hard man like his name meaning 'stone' which I also recall: it was Longinius Lapideus. He had been in the leading ranks of the first century of the first cohort in the defile. This is his account, as I recall it now. I give it as if he is beside me still –

"I was a second ranker, in the left century (no.iii it was, commanded by Aelius Longinus), at the mouth of the narrow way we defended. On the left, we butted onto a timber fence that we had built on top of an earth bank. Above it was the steep grass slope, with a small round wood on its summit. The Legate was there by the wood with his staff, standards all about them. I remember how their horses were bucking up high onto their rear legs, I think frightened by the smell and the noise of the enemy who were then advancing."

"We had seen them coming onto the field before us all morning, great masses of marching men flourishing their weapons, with horse amongst them, chariots wheeling about in and out of their formations, some of which, as they came onto the open plain before us, charged towards us at a gallop through the long grass, so that we made ready to receive them, before they turned away. The columns of the enemy seemed endless, and there were now carts amongst them too, heavy four-wheeled carts drawn by oxen. Where once the flat lands that we ourselves had crossed three days earlier had lain silent and empty, there was now a great host of men and horse and wheeled vehicles, so that the land was covered with a great, living mosaic of movement and colour; and also a growing cacophony of sound, for the roar of that host, which our horses had already picked up making them jump and snort, with the blare of their war horns, reached us now in the defile."

"I would like to be able to say I spotted their Queen, whom we had all heard about – that queen of blood who had disembowelled our soldiers and had our women in the cities raped and impaled – but I can't say I did, although there were a number of chariots at the front of their army, any one of which may have been hers. Some of their number we could see, even at a distance, wore bits and pieces of our armour and our helmets, and carried weapons and shields which they had taken from the bodies of the VIIIIth. It would be untrue to say we were not frightened – every true soldier is fearful of battle, whatever he might say afterwards – but the sight of what they had stolen from our dead gave us an anger that sustained us, in absence of food and strong drink, all that day."

"It was past midday when their first attack came in. We had thought they were going to delay the battle until the next day, when even more of their numbers might have arrived, but I think they were so confident that they could wipe out our small army on the ridge, that some of the more headstrong could not resist rushing at us, and then the great mass of them were all coming at us, sweeping up the long slope towards our front lines like water overflowing the broken banks of a river and flooding across the fields."

"We knew what to do. We had been trained for this and the orders had been repeated and repeated all that morning. We stood fast against the very first of the attackers, men fighting naked, or near-naked, their bodies smeared with blue, mad on mushroom and berry juice. Their blows thudded on our shields but we stood firm and met them on the point of the sword, so most of these *barbari* fell in front of us gurgling in their blood. Then arrows and stones began to rain down on us and we huddled forward against our shields as if against a hail storm, protecting ourselves with our helmets and our shoulder armour. Several of our century fell, and were dragged to the rear by the men designated for such work. In this compressed space, it was important to keep the battle front clear."

"We were waiting, not for individuals or another thin, charging line, but for the main force of their warriors to come up against us, and they were doing so now at a run, in rough lines and groups, pressing together in the mouth of the defile, with some horse and a chariot or two amongst them, all eager to get to grips with us, to drive us back into the forest, to surround us, and kill us. All this time, our arrows were flighting down on them, and the oval lead shot of our slingers too: the missiles were raining like black sleet out of a grey sky, down onto the middle of their mass as they struggled up the hill over the wet, trampled grass, and we could see them falling, getting up on their knees, then falling again, some lying still, others rolling over writhing on the ground."

"The cohort *tubae* sounded, echoing along the line and to our rear. Each legionary had two javelins with their weighted, black steel heads, sharp-pointed like a galley's ramming beak, the purpose much the same when cast with force, to split open and break up the enemy – as we did now. The front rank threw, then plucked their second javelin from the soil beside them, and threw that too, then in quick succession each rank behind, the forward ranks kneeling as the heavy weapons sliced the air from all sides, a great forest of wood and steel lancing at the enemy as if thrown by some mighty wind. I could see the points spitting the enemy, passing through their shields, going clean through armour, flesh and bone, splitting heads, as cast after cast followed, the cohort to our rear stepping forward now to deliver their javelins, throwing them high so they fell at a steeper angle onto the heads of the enemy."

"More *tubae*, shrilling loud, a series of peals, long practised. Despite the heavy soil and the sloping hill, we moved with the precision of parade ground drill into our attacking wedge-shaped formations, our forward ranks making a series of Vs like the teeth of a great saw."

"We advanced directly against the stalling, stumbling enemy mass, bearing down on them at a trot, our shields held forward, locked shoulder to shoulder, our swords like silvered points of fire between each man, stabbing into chests and necks and groins as the enemy reeled and tumbled before us. This is where one loses awareness of anything else going on but the immediate three or four feet before and beside you, your breath heaving in your chest, your arms rigid on shield and sword."

"The clash of sword striking shield, yells, screams and groans, helmets tumbling off, a sudden burst of blood somewhere close by, flecking my face; ahead at the wedge point, a legionary fell; I stepped over his body, the enemy rushing at me, bearded, hating faces, eyes wide, mouths open, shrieking; I thrust out my sword; it shuddered and grated, finding bone beneath flesh; I stabbed again; the bodies before me were falling back; our wedge was moving forward; trumpets; the centurion's yell, "Steady! Steady! Keep your position. Keep your position"; a missile glanced my helmet, making my ears ring; "Forward! Forward!"; war horns and trumpets braying and shrieking, all around the injured and the dying. The standards thrust up high. Follow the standards! Forcing our way through the press towards the standards, we made a quarter turn to face a swirling, dark, raging pool of the enemy; then our wedge point – that was me alongside our standard bearer – was into them; using the edge of the sword now, slashing from side to side, punching out with my shield. A blow on my shoulder made me lower my shield; I pulled back before a jabbing spear, which only glanced on my armour, but was able to gather myself, sweeping my sword across the neck of its owner so that his head toppled, his life blood bursting out like a fountain."

"To right and left, the cohorts were forcing themselves from the defile out onto the plain. I was not aware of this at the time, but on our flanks our cavalry were also charging against the enemy mass, and our auxiliary archers loosed arrows into them so close that the shafts were flighted like rods parallel with the ground."

"The whole mass of the enemy began to tumble back. Those behind were caught up in a scrimmage, wedged in, up to their ankles in mud, unable to raise their arms, weapons knocked to the ground. More javelins from our advancing cohorts were thrown into them. We were stabbing into their backs now as they tried to turn and run – but they couldn't. Yet the Legion was advancing, its golden Eagle held high. It advanced against the trapped enemy like a mighty reaping machine; instead of stalks of wheat, it sliced away men's legs, slowly inexorably cutting everything down to the ground before it, yet the crop was not corn but flesh."

"It began to rain hard, the wet sweeping against our battling bodies, running down our bloodied arms and faces. We trod in mud and gore, and still the enemy was undefeated, yet trapped before us, like animals penned for slaughter, part still trying to advance, part retreating. We kept up the killing until another cohort came through us to take up the saw-edged front. Then we formed into square and retreated a little to the rear. There, we leant on our shields and we rested, sucking at the rain on our skin."

"Now at last I could turn my head to see our cavalry battling with the enemy horse and chariots on the slopes above us. The chariots were rendered useless by the mud, their ponies slipping and shrieking in the traces and the carts overturning, our mounted soldiers upon them with spears extended, piercing men and animals: the warrior chieftains, some in fine cloaks and with plumed helmets, thrown out and trampled under hooves, and cut up by the swinging long swords of our horsemen."

"I had never fought on such a field before: I don't think any of us had. This was a battle of utmost savagery. I saw our men breaking rank – a thing under normal circumstances forbidden – to slice the throats of fallen enemies who wore pieces of our armour or carried our weapons. And the rebels did not easily give up either, but, although badly wounded, would still grab at legs and hooves and try to stab up at us from the ground, until sometimes it took two or three legionaries to quell them and release them from their rage forever."

"It would be tedious to try to describe all the long killing that took place that afternoon and into the evening when the light, already dark with the rain, began to fail. We lost many men from the XIIIIth, and a large number from the XXth, who had held their positions for a long time on our flanks at the forest edge, There, they too fought off many attacks by the enemy chariots and horse. Many of the *Britanni* chiefs with their household guards led those attacks, and they were the hardest to overcome and kill. The auxiliaries as well repelled attack after attack in vicious fights of horse and foot, then advanced to encircle the enemy host from our left, cutting off its escape in that direction."

"My cohort, when rested, was returned to the action. By now the mass of struggling men had been forced right back across the plain against the rebel wagon lines drawn up at the marsh edge. The press was such that most of the dead here were not killed by our arms but by the crush. Our soldiers were crazed with the killing. They climbed up onto mounds of the fallen, some of whom were still alive and struggling to drag themselves clear, and stabbed down with long swords and spears at those writhing below them. When this was ineffective, the Legate ordered his archers to rain arrows down on the piled, trapped mass of men, until the whole ground became covered with heaving mounds of the dead and the dying, stuck with arrows like the quills of a porcupine. Only then, for practical purposes, did he order the killing to stop."

"This order was not in time, however, for those spectators on the wagons – women and children and the aged who had thought to make a sport of our expected defeat as if we were at bay in the arena. They were cut down by auxiliaries, who, although under Roman discipline, still favoured the practices of the *barbari* – raping women and girls tied to posts, then impaling them in the same way as Roman women had been impaled, seizing children and swinging them like clubs, cutting off heads and attaching them to their horses' bridles: even the baggage animals, they killed, throats and tendons cut, and pierced with spears."

And so ended Longinius Lapideus's account. The aftermath to the battle, I piece together from what others have told me, both then and later –

Many of the rebels, who had escaped the wrath of the Roman Army, did their best to escape through a funnel of land that led towards the river valley. Some were cut off by the Roman cavalry and killed, others got away – for the present at least – by keeping to the margins of the marshland, even hiding in the reedbeds up to their noses in the water. Most were flushed out in the morning and put into the wooden cages which were set up eventually to hold the prisoners. Some did, however, get right away, and these included the Queen with her attendants, who had probably fled long before the final defeat of the army she had led. Whether the Queen's daughters, who had been at her side at the beginning of the battle, escaped with her, or whether they were amongst the dead, unrecognised, was not known. There is a story that they were made prisoner, but of that there is no proof; neither is there any account of what happened to them later.

When a halt was ordered by Paullinus to the killing, the squares and rectangles of the cohorts and centuries spread across the plain, some still on the ridge above, stood in their ordered ranks, with shields and weapons lowered, backs bent, limbs trembling with exhaustion. Then a cry went up and was passed from unit to unit in a rolling crescendo of sound, a great shout of acclamation for the victory – the legionaries beating their shields and raising their swords and calling out the names of Rome and Caesar – and that of Gaius Suetonius Paullinus too, in praise.

For the weary army, though, there was still much work. Prisoners were herded together like sheep – many with wounds, their spirit gone. Until stockades could be made to hold them, as many as possible were roped together and made to lie on the ground where they were guarded all night at the point of the spear.

Food was found amongst the wagons: cheese, coarse bread, and sour beer for the most, and meat cut from the dead mules and horses and roasted over great fires that were lit from the wreckage of the wagons. *Iceni* women – those which had been spared from the killing – did the cooking. The soldiers were fed in their units, many sleeping amongst the enemy dead.

The cloak or tunic and trousers of a former enemy made many a hasty covering and a pillow for the long night hours with the rain still pattering down. Towards dawn the drizzle ceased and the new day dawned clear with a yellow sun revealing the torn battlefield and the carnage.

It was a terrible scene which the bright sunlight showed once the cover of darkness had lifted. Every detail of the battlefield, and of the dead and injured upon it, was lit up mercilessly. Only the edge of the field next to the marshes was still veiled by the drifting smoke of last night's fires, which would sometimes burst out again into flame. On the plain, maimed horses, some on three legs, some trying to pull themselves along the ground by their forelegs, kicked and struggled amongst the piles of human bodies, some of these bodies still moving, an arm or a leg twisting amongst others that twitched and jerked Over all was a long drawn-out wail of suffering.

Groups of cavalry moved amongst the dead, individual horsemen stopping and jabbing down, then moving on again. Behind them came lines of auxiliaries on foot, working through the bodies, separating out the still living and sending most of these down to the infernal regions with a slash or a stab of a sword. Some others were dragged to the prison cages that were now being built by legionaries with timbers taken down from the field palisades at the defile's mouth.

The Roman dead, an astonishingly low number for the fierceness of the battle – some four hundred and fifty were counted – were carefully gathered together, their armour removed, their bodies washed over and anointed with oils, ready for burning the next day when the pyres had been built. This was to be carried out on the higher slopes close to the forest edge, so there would be no contamination with the thousands of *Iceni* and *Trinvantes* dead below. Many of these, when stripped of anything of value, were simply left on the ground in grotesque grey-white spreads of naked flesh, or piled into heaps a man's height and more. Some bodies were thrown into pits dug by prisoners, or into the waters of the marshes, as was much of the wreckage of the battlefield – the broken chariots and wagons, fragments of armour and weapons not worth melting down, blood-soaked and muddied clothing, splintered boxes, broken earthenware pots, and great iron cauldrons. The last showed how the *Iceni* had been planning to celebrate their victory. They were not wanted by the Romans, their metals considered contaminated, and were heaved with their attendant spoons, ladles, fire grids and irons into the swamps. Now it would be the beasts who would be feasting here from the dead as soon as the soldiers had left – the wolves and boars from the forest and the hooked-beaked birds of the air.

VIII

"Where were the ashes of the Roman dead of the battle interred?" asked the Emperor. He had grown increasingly agitated by my account, drumming his feet against a leg of the stone bench as if matching his own body to those events of sixty years past, marching with the legionaries, forming line, his torso stiffening, his chin rising, seeing in his inner eye the flights of the javelins scoring the air and thudding into the enemy's bodies. A slave brought him the wine flagon, but he was waved away.

The air seemed hotter than ever, although it was well towards evening now when it might be expected to cool. I felt the sweat running beneath the linen of my tunic. I could do with a cooling bathe. Should I suggest this to Hadrian? He must be stifling in his metalled cuirass sitting here in the unshaded sunlight. He had probably bathed in Numicius's bath house this morning. My own bath house was not fired up at present, but we could make use of the cold bath of the *frigidarium*, which I always kept scrupulously clean.

"I don't know, I fear, Caesar," I said, answering his question about the men of my own generation who had died so long ago. "Is it not the practice of a legion to carry the ashes of their dead back to their own headquarters shrines? That is what happened with the bones of the VIIIIth we recovered from the place of their defeat. They were borne in honour to the fort at Lindum"

"Yes, you are probably right," said the Emperor thoughtfully. "Although that was not what we did in Dacia. We buried them on the field, and many also within the victory *tropaeum* that we raised."

"It is most hot," he said, rising to his feet, and flapping his hands across his face, which movements brought several slaves towards him, and the Praetorians' hands to their sword hilts. He waved them all back and re-seated himself.

It was my opportunity to mention the *frigidarium* to which – rather to my surprise – he assented straightaway, and with enthusiasm. "A kind offer, Celer. It is just what we require."

Now I issued the orders, calling for Gavo, who rushed back to the house and I could see him gathering together the household slaves, and amongst them Diseta bearing a pile of my best linen towels along the front portico to the side passage. When Gavo came forward and bowed to me, I knew all was ready. I looked towards Numicius but saw he had called for more wine and was sitting heavily in his seat, showing little inclination to bathe. I did not ask him to do so, realising in a flurry of thought that the honour of having the Emperor in my bath house had been granted by Caesar himself, and not the other way around, so it was his place to request Numicius's presence too, if he wished it, and he showed no sign of doing so.

The Praetorian *praefectus* came up, looking worried, and addressed some words to the Emperor, who waved him away impatiently, saying, "Your men can stand outside," and then to Numicius, "Tell Quintus here about your beans and how well they grow", leaving both men looking at each other awkwardly and, I thought, crossly.

"We shall not bathe long," added Hadrian turning away with me and accompanying me across the garden to the side of the house. He called out to the anxious, watching faces on the portico, with the plump steward at their fore whose hands were held up as if in supplication. "We shall *not* need a body slave. Our host here will supply our needs."

My bath house was but small, yet it contained a full suite of rooms, from *frigidarium* to *tepidarium* to *caldarium*. As I have told, I had it constructed for my wife, Senuna, who, although a *Britanna*, took to Roman bathing more readily than was my custom – I must confess – in this northern province. After my marriage but before the bath house was built, I had been used to going to Durobrivae to use the public baths there at least once a month. But that was a considerable journey in the two-wheeled cart I had owned then, meant for heavy agricultural use but converted by me to be more comfortable for passengers.

Senuna did not ride, and showed no inclination to learn, being unusually fearful of horses, so in order to travel together – other than by boat which we used often to reach Duroliponte – we had to make use of our slow cart hauled by oxen. The other problem was that there were no separate facilities for women at the Durobrovae baths, and, as Senuna did not wish to bathe in male company, as some women did – and nor would I have permitted her to do so – we had to wait until the end of the day when she could be admitted alone, or in company with one or two other ladies. Consequently, this meant in summer a very late return home, or, in winter, an overnight stay at a flea-ridden inn in Durobrivae, which for dinner served half-cooked pork washed down, it seemed, with cabbage water.

Hence, our own bath house was my present to my Senuna, to allow her delicate constitution the benefit of the warmth it provided, not only in the bathing rooms but through transmission to the rooms I had built for her alongside the bath house, the main house being without heating other than by braziers. Her enjoyment of it was sadly but short; scarcely a year had passed from the very first firing of the furnace to the day she passed from me. I only have the furnace lit occasionally now, although I do make more use of the *frigidarium* in hot weather – as I was doing now, so unexpectedly, with my Emperor as a bathing companion, an unprecedented honour indeed for a commoner.

We came – the Emperor Hadrian and I – through a small archway flanked by columns (this had been a late addition by my architect for a modest extra cost, the columns, carved of solid stone, of obvious quality: I did not enquire too much as to their source) into a small paved court, with the domed bath house on our left. The door was held wide-open by Gavo, who bowed deeply as we entered. In the tiny entrance chamber Diseta awaited us with a pile of towels. I was pleased the two lockers, which I had had put in for Senuna and myself, were freshly-painted in red, matching the crimson dado around the room, the plaster of the walls being of a plain buttery white decorated in places with coloured birds.

Hadrian pointed at these and made some comment. "For my wife," I said. "She loved to watch the birds in the garden. She had her own birds in cages. She used to walk in the moonlight and the birds would sing to her then as if it was day. She charmed the birds, I am sure."

"When did your wife die, Celer?" he asked in gentle tones. He must have been told by Numicius of that for I had not mentioned it.

"It will be twenty-seven years back, Caesar, when this year ends."

There was a silence. He looked at me. He had been unhooking his cuirass – Diseta had scurried to his side to help him – and now he stopped.

"She died giving birth. My son died as well."

"We are sorry. *I* am sorry. And you have had no wife since?"

"No, Caesar. I have not sought one."

He clasped me by the shoulder. "Ah, Celer. We have both been soldiers. What it is to suffer those things which a sword cannot prevent."

"You have had similar grief, Caesar?"

"The death of both my parents when I was a boy. My mother first. I missed her terribly although I had been nursed by slaves."

You have a wife, Caesar?"

"Yes, of course." He had recommenced undressing. Diseta took the heavy cuirass, with all its attachments, and, staggering a little under its weight, managed to lift it to hang on a hook on the locker door. Hadrian stood before me in his white tunic, while Diseta fussed at his feet to undo the leather strappings of his boots. What trust had been placed in me and my household, I could not help thinking. No wonder the *praefectus* had been worried. How many small, sharp knives, I wondered, might be hidden away in bath houses to release the vital life blood of oppressors? Was I too about to alter the course of history? The mad thoughts flickered across my brain.

"My wife – the Empress – is in Britannia with me now. She is in Eboracum, or at least she should be unless….." Hadrian broke off. He is confiding in me, I realised wonderingly. He trusts me because I have been a soldier and there is honour amongst soldiers, a loyalty that will never be betrayed – soldier to fellow soldier, soldier to emperor: the oath was the same.

Yet Diseta was present. She was a slave and unimportant, but she had ears. Diseta was removing my sandals now and helping me pull that awful embroidered tunic over my head. She took it and the Emperor's tunic, which he had shed himself, and hung them up too. She gave us our towels, and opened the double doors to the plunge bath, uncaring and unnoticing of our nakedness as she was long trained to do. Against the Emperor's firm, heavy body, deeply tanned on the arms and legs, neck and face, the chest thick with golden hairs, my own body felt white and hunched and shrivelled. His member hung firm and long, mine felt curled up like a thin worm, which even Diseta's ministrations could seldom stir these days.

My *frigidarium* was octagonal in shape, with small glassed windows high up on two of the walls through which sea-green light filtered as if deep within sunlit waters. A circular bath, lined with pink cement, large enough to take three bodies – perhaps four – was set in the tessellated floor, with a tiled shelf around its upper edge on which a bather could sit dangling his feet into the water. The water flowed in from an upper lead pipe, gravity-fed from a cistern behind the house, kept filled by a natural spring that bubbled up from the black soil – a most fortuitous discovery when my well was being dug. Another pipe, slightly below, drained out the overflow, and thus the water kept circulating, preventing the stagnation seen in my garden pond. I had been wealthy enough to pay for all this then; much less so now.

The walls of the room, above a blue dado, were plastered white, but with decorations of plump fish with open mouths and wings, which I had especially commissioned from a jobbing artist in Duroliponte – a young man with a nervous tic who hailed from Lugdunum in Gallia. His fish looked like none I had ever seen in the Ostia fish markets years ago, but the paintings, I had to admit, were competently executed. Senuna had loved them. Even at this moment, with the Emperor sliding into the water beside me and gasping at its spring-fed coldness, I could see her slim, milk-white body standing in the bath, her head thrown back, her red hair spread out on the surface of the water as she pointed at one of the fish which had been given a butterfly's wings, bubbling with laughter like a child.

The Emperor stood, bobbing a little in the water like a cork, his head with its dark hair and beard seemingly detached from the rest of his body, so that I felt I could pick it up and place it on the shelf beside him like the portrait bust of an ancestor. I entered the pool opposite him, carefully feeling my way down, with one hand on the edge and the other held by Diseta, my back for the moment to the Emperor – a terrible breach of etiquette, I knew, but these were unusual circumstances. I welcomed the embrace of the cold water. I felt it instantly reviving, as it swirled around my scrawny legs and my hips and my chest, and then I was letting go of Diseta, with my feet touching the bottom and my chin only just above the surface. How easy it would be to drown here, I had thought many times, and had retained this fantasy of release from all the sorrows that had followed Senuna's death and the death of my child. Far too easy it was, indeed, which is why the fantasy had remained just that. I did not believe in ease, for I knew that purpose and fulfilment, and any happiness, came only out of struggle. It was what the gods demanded. Whatever was to happen to me, I must either accept or resist, and not complain. Simply to escape by turning away was weakness, and an affront to everything I believed in.

"I see your scars, Celer," Hadrian said. I had turned towards him. There were two bronze handles set in the side of the bath, and I grasped them behind me: my feet floated upward and touched Hadrian's legs.

"My apologies, Caesar."

He did not appear to notice. He was pointing at my left shoulder, which dropped lower than the right, where the skin was all raised and puckered, whiter than the skin around it, so that it looked as if you could pluck at the scar to pull it away and reveal the bone beneath.

"I received that from the *barbari* in the north. In the war fought by the Legate Agricola. The camp of the VIIIIth was attacked at night and I caught the slash of a long sword on the rampart. The surgeon was skilful. He pieced what was left of the bone together."

"Did you serve on after that?"

"Yes, Caesar, but my front-rank fighting days were over. I still had my sword arm but I could not hold a shield. I obtained my discharge a couple of years later – after Mons Graupius."

"Ah, Mons Graupius." Hadrian splashed his hands in the water, sending a trail of drops over the hem of Diseta's tunic, she waiting attentively at the pool edge. "I've read historian Tacitus on Mons Graupius. He was able to give that battle a name, so why not others?"

"Indeed, Caesar. It is a field I could find for you, although forty years ago."

"You must tell me of it later. We have other things to do first."

I let me whole body float upwards now, keeping it clear of Hadrian who was trying to walk in the water, making swimming strokes with his arms. I could see Diseta watching him, moving round the pool with him in case of some sudden need. He laughed out loud. "I have swum in the Bosphorus and the mighty Danuvius, even the Tiber amongst the dead dogs, and now your slave watches me as if I am about to sink."

"Caesar, she is used to caring for me. Some days, one ripple here might sweep me away."

"Oh, Celer, I do not complain. These are the things an Emperor likes to see. Quietness and normality. And loyalty too. The loyalty of the low-born to the high-born. Would that I had more of such about me." He paused, staring at my body, now lying flat to the water. "You have a criss-cross of scars there." He thrust out his thumb at my chest. How did you come by those? It looks like you've been flogged with a steel whip. You haven't been, have you?"

I gave a chuckle. "No, Caesar. I've seen it done, though. As punishment for sleeping on guard duty. The flogging's made on the back, stripping the flesh from the ribs and the spine. Then, if the miscreant can still stand, he's executed by *fustuarium* – beaten to death with cudgels by his comrades whose lives he endangered."

"Quite," said Hadrian, in a taut tone of voice. "We have ordered many such punishments."

With dismay, I realised my error in telling the commander-in-chief his own business, in particular in regard to the discipline of his legions. The Emperor's power was sacrosanct from outside comment, unless directly sought, a bit like – I thought fancifully – a gardener preserving his hothouse flowers sensitive to the slightest whiff of outside air. If Hadrian was piqued by me, though, I was soon forgiven, for after a pause, while I carefully studied Diseta's painted toe-nails beside my head, he said testily, "Well, Celer, how *did* you get those scars?"

"In battle, Caesar. The *Caledonii* fight with a long spear that has a curving knife set on it, a bit like a field worker's scythe. Until we learnt how to deal with that weapon, many of the VIIIIth had their armour ripped up by its blade before we could get to grips with the wielder. In my case, I was without armour. It was the same night attack when my shoulder was smashed. I was trapped on the rampart, my legs caught up in some tangle or other against the palisade. One of those knives caught me on the chest and worked its way over me like a razor, making a chequer board of me. Then came the smash on my shoulder, and I was right down. Our cavalry drove them off, or I wouldn't have survived. The medical orderlies said I looked liked one of those criminals thrown to the beasts, gnawed and slashed, reduced to a piece of meat. I was lucky, though, for nothing too vital was cut. Some of the wounds healed better than others."

"The *Daci* also had a weapon like that. They used it with two hands and it could cut off the arms and legs of our legionaries – some of the worst fighting we have ever seen. We punished them later, but it altered our tactics and our armour."

"I think, Caesar, if the *Britanni* had been better armed and had fought better, we would not have defeated them. A good example of that is during the great rebellion, of which you are presently making such enquiry. The *Iceni* and their allies had a great opportunity to drive us out of their lands altogether, but they threw it away. It was their burning thirst for revenge that drove them on at first, and they had the luck of the ambitious, but did not follow up with any concerted strategy. And when they fought, they fought like wild men. They were brave, but they had no idea of formations, of tactics, of how to hold position, of how to attack. They accepted battle on ground of our choosing, and they hemmed themselves in so they could not retreat. That last battle was slaughter. Their Queen, and others of their hierarchy, fled and left their army to die. It was hardly glorious. It was the end of their people. They have never recovered. They do not now have the power and prestige of the other peoples of the province who were more pragmatic and did not resist Rome."

"And yet, Celer, the *Britanni* have fought well against us in protection of their liberties – from the days of the divine Claudius to the present when they still seek to make our lives difficult."

"I think, Caesar, they lacked good commanders, and, despite their ferocity, perhaps did not show the extreme fanaticism of other peoples, as you, of course, will know best of all – for example the *Daci* or the *Galli* or the *Ludaei*."

"Ah, the *Ludaei*. They have killed many Roman citizens in recent years. Cowardly murders. We may need to fight them again." Hadrian gazed at the water as if seeking some answer to rise, like an oracle's vision, from out of its depths. I realised at that moment – if not before – the vast responsibilities of an Emperor of Rome. Rome ruled by power, armed power. Soldiers cost money. Without money, there were no legions. Without her legions, Rome would fall. In Britannia alone were three legions. No wonder Hadrian sought peace here now rather than further war.

He said, "Thank the gods, the *Britanni* did not have a Vercingetorix, or an Arminius, or even a Decebalus. Then we would have had a longer, more bitter fight than your Bodig ever gave us."

"She roused her people. She brought them to war. Yet, in the end, she created a chaos and she destroyed her own people." I said this – I had tried to believe it over the many years – but I wondered how true it was. I remembered that frightened face I had glimpsed in the quarry of white rock. Bodig must have had a great command, a great presence, a great spirit, to bring her people to such a battle which they had expected to win. Whether she had led in person, or left the fighting to her chieftains, she had brought Rome to one of the most desperate battles it had fought for many years. If I belittled Bodig's achievement, then I belittled the greatness of Rome's victory – and that was something I most certainly did not wish to do. Rome had fought very many greater wars, but her victory against the *Iceni* and their allies had been a triumph of careful preparation, excellent command, and the great courage and battle skills of her legions.

Hadrian ceased his churning of the water and eased himself from it, sliding his buttocks onto the shelf and indicating to Diseta that she should massage his shoulders. Diseta was an accomplished practitioner, and soon the Emperor was groaning and rocking his head under her expert touch. I hoped these sounds did not penetrate outside the *frigidarium* or the Praetorians would be rushing in with drawn swords, stabbing first and asking question afterwards as they were prone to do. But Diseta was now working her hands down the Emperor's spine; his head had fallen forward and he was quiet. When she had finished, he waved her away, rising to his feet in his full naked glory. I concentrated on pulling myself upright while Diseta came around the pool edge to assist me.

"Your slave has a way with her hands," said Hadrian, pulling a towel about him, hiding a slight paunch in his belly. "If I were dishonourable, I would take her into my household and back to Rome." I could see the sudden fear that crossed Diseta's face. He laughed. "But of course I won't. There are thousands there with fingers like hers, but not so many here, eh?" He gave me something of a wink, and for the first time in the presence of the Emperor I felt myself repelled. Of course, I probably misunderstood him and I hastened to say, "Everything of mine is yours, Caesar. Take the girl if you wish." I could not look at Diseta, knowing the betrayal I would see in her dark eyes.

"No. No. I but jest, Celer. Apart from anything else, it would upset my household. They fight like cats for the privilege of body service to the Emperor. Even what I enjoy now with you, Celer, will upset their hierarchy. I shall receive some sour looks from my steward, I am sure, but why should that concern me....?"

"Why, indeed, Caesar," I felt obliged to say.

I saw him look at me sharply, as if to make sure I was not intending any insincerity, then threw aside his towel and slid his body back into the bath, the water closing over his nakedness. By this action he seemed to regain his dignity, not only as an emperor but as a man. It might be fashionable to present emperors naked in statuary, wearing just a wreath and clutching the imperial baton, but I preferred mine to be covered!

Seeing the Emperor settled again comfortably opposite me in the water, I ventured, feeling my boldness stirring my blood, "One more good campaign Caesar, properly resourced and commanded by a man who knows what he is doing – dare I suggest you, Caesar? – and Rome could conquer the whole of the north of this island and bring it into allegiance."

Hadrian sighed, blowing a trail of breath across the water like the bearded god Aeolus filling the sails of Odysseus's fleet – a story from my schooldays that had lingered in my memory. "And for what purpose, Celer? All that blood and treasure spent to add a land of rocks and water to our Empire, a land in the north where the *barbari* can live in caves and emerge to stab at us whenever they wish; not a land where we can introduce our peace and spread the benefits of our civilisation; nor" – he chuckled here, his chest heaving and sending a series of small waves across the bath to ripple against my body – "do they have anything we can tax them for, or indeed take from them, except miles of coastline full of seabird dung, some salting pans, and a rock or two from which we could extract iron. There was said to be gold in their mountains but our surveyors have found little. So, none of that's going to fill Rome's treasury; just the opposite, it's going to suck out much that's already there."

He turned onto his back in the water, holding onto handles as I was doing, and splashing his legs up and down, so that if I had been the Trojan Fleet, I would by now have been sunk. "To build a frontier – a great wall, our *vallum Aelium* – will be a far better policy for Rome, for we will be able to control goods going into the barbarian land and those coming out of it, and tax them accordingly. The people beyond the wall will want the luxuries of Rome and they will pay us for them with whatever we require in exchange – their seabird dung for fertiliser, their animal skins for boots, their savage dogs for our hunters, their wild bears for the arena, and so on. So Rome gains revenue without any of the costs of conquest."

"But we *must* retain a powerful army in Britannia," he added shaking the surface of the water with his emphasis "The Army is everything to Rome – our legions, our auxiliaries, our soldiers gathered from every province of the Empire. Above all, we honour our soldiers – which is why we have been concerned to learn of the neglect of their victories here."

And, I thought, there will be no future glory, no need any more for the legions to carry their Eagles to the very edges of the world, conquering all places, all regions, like an Alexander. But I did not put my thoughts into words. The Emperor – a soldier himself – may have been thinking the same. Some things are best left unsaid.

"Let's dress now and talk of other matters," Hadrian said abruptly. I was again astonished. He was confiding in me like a comrade – even a friend. The responsibility sat heavily on me. I did not know what it would bring. Never in all my long years had I been a confidante to anyone more senior than a fellow *optio* or a disgraced centurion, or, on one occasion, a love-sick tribune, who in his drunkenness had forgotten his status and probably retained no memory of the private things he had gushed out to me.

We both moved to lift ourselves from the water. Diseta stepped forward to help me, as she always did, but Hadrian, already out and stark-naked, came around the bath and seized my arm, pulling me clear of the water, virtually dislocating my shoulder as he did so (fortunately it was my better shoulder). We wrapped ourselves in the towels and seated ourselves in the entrance chamber, on benches I had had placed beneath the lockers.

Thinking we would dress straightaway, Diseta moved to help the Emperor, reaching up to open the locker above him, but I motioned to her to stop. I could see Hadrian wished to sit and talk awhile, before burdening his body once more with the heavy cuirass. I whispered to her to leave us, and, with a backward glance and looking rather petulant, she obeyed, pushing open the outer door. A wave of heat entered and with it a babble of noise from outside, of calls and shouting and the orders of the Praetorians. The Guard *praefectus* poked his head through the door, looking around anxiously, perhaps fearing to see one, or both of us, lying stabbed on the floor, but all he received was a shout of, "Get out!" from Hadrian, and, flashing an angry glance at me, he obeyed. Through the still open door, I could see both Gavo and the green-liveried steward in the background, hovering anxiously, and I tried to reassure them (Gavo at least) by raising a hand, before being aware that Hadrian had said something to me and I hadn't answered.

"I am sorry, Caesar. I did not hear."

He sounded cross now. "Do not worry about the slaves, or anyone else, for that matter. We are masters here. We do what we like for as long as we like, and I give the commands."

"Of course, Caesar." I waved furiously for Gavo to shut the door.

Hadrian's face broke into a sudden smile. "You respond to my whims like balls of grass blowing before the wind. But I feel you would not do that for ever, Celer, whether I am your Emperor or not. Now what was I saying? I was saying something outrageous, that I would change places with you, if I could. Just to be a soldier and sit in the sun full of memories, and have women to bring me wine. That would be very good."

I thought he talks like a simpleton. But I answered, "I am sure, Caesar, you would soon get very bored."

"Perhaps. But it would be pleasant for a while. You see, Celer, I am a plain man and I like plain things, not all this fawning over me that I must bear for the sake of an Emperor's dignity. I believe in command and discipline, though, make no mistake. A soldier's discipline. But courtiers and servants and secretaries and stewards, and dressers and bathers and beard-trimmers and dieticians, chefs and cooks, and those who wipe your arse for you and stand by to help you piss, they all drive me mad at times. I cannot rest with them. They are like children watching their father, seeing every move, taking notice of his spittle, whether his eyes are bright or dull, what mood he is in, whether to walk on his left side or his right….. Celer, there is never any peace."

"But you have the privacy of your household, your wife, your family, Caesar. Have you not? They must give you peace and comfort. You can relax with them?"

"Hah!" He rose to his feet, nearly knocking his head on what I realised now was a badly-positioned locker and began stalking up and down, holding the towels to his shoulders and waist. I sat and watched his bare feet and legs passing me. I noticed what extraordinarily long toes he had; they splayed outwards as he walked. "You might well think that, Celer, but it is not true. He sat down beside me and placed his hand on my thin shoulders, making me shudder at his touch: he did not seem to notice.

"My wife, the grand and most beautiful Empress Vibia Sabina, is in Eboracum – or is she? Perhaps she has visited some outlying camp, taking her women with her. They all have lovers amongst the soldiers; pass from one camp to the next and find a new set to fornicate with."

"Surely not, Caesar." I was genuinely shocked. I should have been frightened to ask, but the words came to my mouth before I could stop them. "You don't mean the Empress too?"

He took his arm from my shoulders and brought the hand down onto his thighs with a smack of flesh. "Who knows? She leads them in their flirtations. It is a game for them. They have nothing else to do."

"No soldier of Rome would dare approach the Emperor's wife," I said stiffly, coining the words carefully so that they came like glue from out of my gullet. From what I had heard of previous emperors, I knew that was untrue. When I was but a boy and learning my lessons with my idle fellows under the portico of Ostia's forum, we had all heard the stories of old Claudius's wife, Messalina. Many a stained bed-sheet was occasioned by those tales. I had been beaten for trying to discuss them with my parents before I really understood what such things were.

"You were lucky in your love, I think, Celer. I have been unlucky. The fault may be mine. I speak to you now, you understand, as a comrade and not as your Emperor: you should not repeat anything I say."

"Of course not, Caesar. But are you sure you wish to talk of such things to me? I am low born and not of your world."

"You have been a soldier, Celer, and with a fine record. I find I can talk to you as I could not talk to others. I have senators with me on this trip – my personal advisers, or so they are said to be – who would listen to me and give me their confidence, and then laugh behind my back and tell everything I have said with much glee at their next banquet."

"You must have honourable men about you too who would not betray you and in whom you can confide."

"Find them for me, Celer. Go out there now and show them to me. They are all self-serving. There are few of them I would trust, even amongst the

Praetorians. They all wet their fingers to see which way the wind is blowing, and, should it change, then they change too. An emperor is never safe if he cannot bring success. They all want money and power, and if I don't provide these things, then they will seek them elsewhere."

I was astonished. I felt I was but an innocent living in total unawareness of the ways of the Roman world.

"You may wonder, Celer, why I express my discontent with our historians with such passion at times?" He looked at me and I thought it wise to nod, although, if I were honest, I had thought it just an eccentricity in him – the sort of prejudice the high and mighty tended to acquire for no particular reason.

"Have you heard of another Suetonius – Suetonius Tranquillus?"

My expressionless face, which masked an increasing concern at what I was going to hear, prompted Hadrian to continue.

"He is an historian too – an equestrian from a good family, but not the same one as our Legate of the *bellum Icenorum*; at least I never heard him make such a claim. He was also until quite recently my personal secretary, a position he had held as well under my predecessor, the divine Caesar Traianus. Many aspire to that position. Above all men, he can expect to have the confidence of the Emperor. Here was a man I should have been able to tell my heart to, as I do now with you, Celer."

"You do me great honour, Caesar." I had to say that, although all I wished, in truth, was his silence.

"No, but I make use of you, Celer. It helps me to speak of these things. Suetonius was in charge of the imperial archives at Rome. If anyone could have sought out the documents I required to learn about the wars of the *Britanni*, it was he. He had an advantage even over Tacitus: I don't believe they ever collaborated. Tacitus, I know, thought little of him as a historian and a man. Suetonius's histories were of what we might term, the sensational type. He would piece together all the rumours and stories, dramas and tragedies, sexual conquests, lusts, and unsolved murders that were being discussed in Rome, and build them into a series of publications with titles like, 'Lives of Famous Whores'; "Wantons of Rome; 'Assassinations on the Palatine' He did write some more serious works, but everyone wanted the juicy, not the dry, history. A few years back he produced his *magnum opus* – if that is the right term – for what was not a philosophical work or a serious history, but a racy bestseller, 'The Lives of the Caesars' – a scandalous account of twelve of our predecessors, from Julius Caesar to Domitianus. It was certainly entertaining to read but did very little for my prestige as the present Emperor. I was furious."

He paused, looking down at his feet, then continued, "I was even more furious when I found my wife, Sabina consorting with him quite openly, in a very familiar manner which made me suspect a far greater intimacy than was respectable – and I dared not think what else. Sabina and I have always slept apart, in our own suites of rooms on either side of the palace. Treading the long passage between the two, having risen early one morning, I came upon Tranquillus coming in the opposite direction, in just a plain tunic, looking unwashed and disarrayed. I asked him what he was doing and he gave me some story about being woken in his own rooms early by the sound of doves, and seeking to find a slave who could have them removed. Of course, I could not prove otherwise. When I demanded an audience with my wife, she was all jewelled and fragrant perfection, looking at me with a curling smile of contempt. I have never achieved much union with her, you see, Celer. She has not been to my taste – but she is still the Emperor's wife and accompanies me everywhere. I dismissed Tranquillus from the palace, and also his friend, Septicius Clarus – the then Praetorian *praefectus* – of whom reports, now made to me, said had also been giving excessive and improper attention to my wife."

He took up a towel to dry his feet. I sat in disbelieving silence – disbelieving not so much about the facts of what the Emperor was confiding in me but that he was doing so. Who was I, an old soldier, breathing out my last months in these dismal swamps – not anyone even of particular note – to receive such confidences? Perhaps to Hadrian I represented some lasting totem of respectability and trustworthiness, out of an imagined golden era – which, of course, had never existed. Perhaps it was my age that led him to trust in me, as if I were some ancient, learned god of the Greeks, dispensing justice from a marble chair, before whom he could prostrate himself and make confession of his fears. Or was it that I represented a father to him before whom he could lay out his dirtied soul – at least his hurt and muddled soul – to seek a parent's strength and understanding? Did Hadrian love his wife, I wondered? Or did he have other loves, he was ashamed to admit to himself, and was this the real thing he sought understanding for?

They were fantastic ideas, I knew – absurd even – but I could do no more than simply accept what was happening and, at all costs, not show that I thought there was anything unusual in the Emperor's confidences. His wife's behaviour, and the betrayal of those he had felt to be his close friends, had clearly affected him badly. It was not surprising he was unable to discuss such matters with the fawning, self-serving companions of his journeys or the grim-faced soldiers of his bodyguard. The Empress Sabina, could not be much help to him either, probably scornful and dismissive, although he *was* the Emperor. If he suspected her dalliance, why did he not simply send her away? For the behaviour of betrayal – such as he intimated – he could have her put to death. But then – a common problem in such circumstances, as Claudius with Messalina – he probably loved her deeply. What was most tragic was that he seemed to have no way of expressing that love.

How amazing is the little business of man, I thought, trying to be philosophical (as I did occasionally) of the things I had learnt – these immense changes that had come to me so suddenly out of nowhere; one moment, asleep in my chair, the next, host and intimate to the greatest man in the world. How could he, a man so powerful – powerful in the armies he commanded and the trumpets that would sound out for him wherever he went, but also powerful in the strength of his body and the soldierly virtues that he had shown on many a deadly battlefield – be reduced to such a weak and tortured state? Behind the strength and the toughness, there obviously dwelt a most sensitive soul. Hadrian was clearly a vulnerable man. I, Gaius Modius Celer, vowed I would do all I could to help him, as my Emperor and my comrade.

All this I had decided in the long silence that lasted while he wiped at his feet with his towel, carefully separating his toes and drying between them. Unsummoned, Diseta slipped back into the room bringing with her a fresh white tunic – where from, I had no idea – which she slid over Hadrian's head, he, the Emperor, standing there naked with his arms raised like a child, as she did so. What did Diseta think, I wondered? I had known Diseta for many years. I knew her body well and she mine. But I did not know her mind at all – just the occasional glance or the flicker of an eye, and a misting of its brightness, that told me she stayed with me, not just because as my slave she had to, but because she loved me too.

IX

When I was dried and re-clothed as well, I said to Hadrian, "Caesar, if it is of help to you, I will say that you have behaved well and have been let down by those from whom you might have expected far greater loyalty. I cannot, of course, speak of your wife – you would not wish me to – but of those of your household who have betrayed you, my advice, Caesar, would be to root them out without mercy."

He looked at me steadily. The blue eyes glittered in the light coming through the outer door which had been left ajar. The hum and buzz of the watchful crowd outside came to me like a swarm of bees. Let them wait. Let Numicius wait and wonder what the Emperor is saying to old Celer, or what tales of Numicius's laziness and extravagences I am giving to the Emperor. For once in my life I felt at the centre of everything, and people waited to see which way I moved before they moved themselves. It was just for an instant – a few poor seconds – I knew, but here I was and it could not be taken from me.

"I may well follow your advice, Celer" Hadrian said. He was formal again now. My moment or two in the sun was nearly passed. "We are grateful to you for giving it to us."

"And now," he added, rising and contemplating the cuirass that Diseta was holding out to him, "We will sit here yet awhile – before we return to that babbling crowd out there – and you will tell me of your wife, Celer. I would like to hear more of her, for I think you have been one of those luckier in love than I."

"Yes, as you wish, Caesar." But I did not really wish this, for the story was yet locked tight within me and I had rarely spoken of it with anyone. Diseta here knew most – for since she had been with me, some ten years or so now, I had cried with her regularly on the anniversaries, such was the pain that returned to me, seeming worse to bear, not easier, as the long years passed, and I had cursed the gods and disappeared into a dark mist for many days. At such times, she and Gavo and the rest of my household had watched me anxiously, keeping my house and my land and the dock properly managed, until I returned to them in the fresh spring light, and life began anew.

"We must help you to start your tale, Celer. How old was your wife? Was she younger than you? I think she must have been. And how long were you together? And, my old soldier, you are so remiss you have not even told me her name."

"My wife's name, Caesar, was Senuna. At least that was the Roman form of her name and the one by which I knew her: I can only assume she bore it from birth. She was clearly of a *Britanni* people, perhaps – or so I had thought – of the *Catuvellauni*, who had adopted Roman ways and used the Latin tongue. She would not speak of her upbringing at all, or tell me anything of her family, which may seem strange, but she was most resolute in that determination and would not yield, even in our most intimate moments. I have never been able to solve the mystery of where she came from, and I suppose I never will; for she has long gone from me, and it is of little account now. She was educated and could both speak and write good Latin, and her manners were in all things refined. I feel quite sure, therefore, she must have been of a well-born family that had welcomed Rome, for she knew our customs and traditions. The reason for her reticence about her background was surely because of the circumstances under which I found her. I can make guesses out of one thing she did tell me, yet I am reluctant to speak of this, Caesar, unless I am commanded to do so, for these things are without honour to Senuna, or myself."

"We are intrigued, Celer. I *do* command it."

I was surprised by that. I had hoped, out of his former familiarity with me, he would have allowed me to keep my silence. But now I felt the ground opening up and myself falling into a pit of my own digging, for I need not have mentioned Senuna at all, only I had not wished to give the impression to my Emperor that I was some sad, old soldier who had never known love other than that of the brothel, or who could not even find some matron to sit with him and knit him socks. Did I sense a sudden change in Hadrian, now more abrupt in his manner, perhaps a consequence of his own admissions to me which he might already be regretting?

"Of course, Caesar. I was only concerned that I should not offend you by anything I tell."

"Continue with your story, Celer. Do not keep looking for approval like one of the fawners outside."

I took in a deep breath. This was a change indeed, for I was now being criticised in my own home. It ever was with men of power that they could abandon the conventional formalities as they wished and set some up to let others down, or play one person's feelings off against another. Or perhaps I was just imagining what was not there. One might spend a lifetime learning to dance within an emperor's court, and I was an old man who knew next to nothing of such things.

"I shall not speak of anything you tell me beyond these walls," he said, a smile on his lips and holding out a hand as if to ask forgiveness.

He may be the Emperor, I thought, but he is a complicated man who shifts like sand at the sea's edge. Yet, I found I did trust him. He would not use anything I said against me at some future time or, in his cups, carouse with his entourage making fun of me. Diseta, who was standing by attentively, her face impassive, would hear what I said, but then she knew, or suspected, most things, anyhow, and would not talk. Good slaves have the virtue of invisibility. What they think is of no account, in any event. If they spread tales about a master, he can have them punished as he wishes, or even have them put to death.

I licked my dry lips and began again. "As you may have understood already, Caesar, my first meeting with Senuna was not in some fine villa or even in one of those rustic round houses of the *Britanni* that you still see everywhere, or in a potter's workshop, or a milking shed, or at a forum market stall, but in a bar in Duroliponte of bad repute; in other words, Caesar it was a brothel – what some in these parts call a *lupanar*."

I felt my heart beating fast as I said these words. I seemed to be condemning Senuna by them, betraying her, to repeat the fact that she had been a prostitute – a *lupa* – the woman whom I had grown to love so very much. I had told few people of this, certainly not while Senuna still lived, and only a couple of friends since her death, to ease the pain that would not leave me. I had long come to terms with the situation that I found her in, knowing that what she did she had been driven to by desperate poverty.

"As I have said, Caesar, she would never tell me how she fell on such desperate times, or who the father of her baby was – for she had a tiny girl, Caesar – or what family had perhaps cast her out. She must have been so stricken by what had happened to her, and filled with so much shame, that her mouth was sealed on these matters entirely. However much I tried, she would not open up to me, and, if I tried too much, she grew displeased, which I wished least of all."

Senuna was fine featured and delicate, with white skin and golden-red hair, and well-spoken too, quite unlike the other girls in the *lupanar*. They – the other *lupae* – called her the *domina*, using our word for a high-born lady. They were all *Britanni*, some very young, scarcely into puberty. They received gifts from the men who used them, so they had money left over from paying the mistress of the *lupanar* to buy themselves fine raiment, and they had polished mirrors and jewellery too, and a large room with painted walls to sit in while waiting for the next client. That upstairs room reeked of cheap perfume which penetrated to the bar below, so that as a man went up the wooden stair, the other patrons would yell out, "Don't bring down more of that pong on your prick".

It was a vile place. So what was I doing there? I was lonely, and on furlough from my work at the dock. I had scarcely seen a woman in two years, other than for those coarse female peddlers, built like filled sacks of grain and with skin like tanned leather, who came up the river to sell goods to me. They would raise their tunics for an *as* or two, but I never took up the offer. The sight of their thick legs covered with hair was enough to suppress anything but the most grotesque lust.

When I first visited the *lupanar*, it was in company with a fellow veteran of the Bull passing through the town on his way to Lindum: we had been drinking and reminiscing much of the day. I remember we staggered up that stair, full of the bravado of Bacchus, an empty bravado indeed, for sloshing tankards of beer in the gut so often inhibit performance, and such was it for me that night: I was not like golden Dionysius, brave and upright, but more like his other form – ageing, belching, unsteady Bacchus, trying to get his equipment to work, that our satirists often depict.

"I give you such detail, Caesar, in all honesty of shame at my behaviour when I first set my eyes on Senuna."

"You paint a living picture, Celer. We have all fallen from virtue, even the gods."

She sat in a corner of the upstairs room, with its high, sharp fragrance disguising other smells, its walls with cracked plaster and worn-away pictures, and a dirt-smeared ceiling that had a painted sun at its centre. At first I did not notice her because the other *lupae* girls (in truth, they were not all girls but a mixture of ages, some quite old) in fancy tunics and veils of differing colours were flashing bright smiles at us, one or two with missing teeth, their faces thick-painted, with crimsoned lips and shadowed eyes. My companion went off with a young girl whose thin, frilled tunic was low cut to show her breasts: I remember she had many rings on her fingers and bronze hoops about her ankles. Giggling, she led him to her room off the narrow passage outside: the girls all had rooms there; they were just small cubicles really with a padded shelf that served as a bed, and little else.

It was now I saw Senuna, half-hidden away in the flickering shadows cast by the cheap pottery lamps. Unlike the others, she wore a demure woollen *stola* of some subdued colour, with a mantle drawn up over her hair, and she sat up straight in a basket chair with her hands laid on her thighs. It was clear she was older than most of the others, although still far from my own age, approaching then forty-six years, if I count back rightly. Her face looked very pale in the leaping, grey light. She was not smiling nor was she frowning; if I had to describe her face at that first sighting, it was accepting. Ignoring the others, who were holding out their arms to me, one even clasping at my tunic hem, I went over to this woman in the corner. Her demure look appealed to me, neither brazen, nor shy really, just – that word again – 'accepting'. I raised her up with my hand under her chin, and she stood straightaway.

"Do you want me?" she asked. Her Latin was good.

"Yes, I want you," I said. And I added, because I was somewhat befuddled and thought it necessary to show respect to this lovely woman, even in a *lupanar*, "If you are willing."

She gave the briefest of smiles. "Come," she said, and took my hand.

"Some things, Caesar, are best veiled in silence. I will not say more of that first meeting other than that I paid twice what I was asked for by the procurer, who came knocking at the door when the time was up, a raddled hag with bony, scoop-like hands into which I dropped my sestertii."

By that extra payment, I gained another twenty minutes during which I was able to guess at something of the woman's inner desperation, despite her apparent calm. I asked her her name. She told me, Senuna, in a quiet voice with her eyes to the floor, as if she was ashamed to say the name in this place, at this time. She told me she had a little girl, scarce two years old: I think she offered me this information as if it alone was an explanation of what she did here and why she did it. I don't believe she had thought I could have any interest in her other than for the reason I had come, so when I asked her where she lived – was it here or some other place in the town? – for the first time she looked up at me and met my gaze. Her eyes were a deep blue; at least that was the colour they seemed in the uncertain light of the smoky terracotta lamp, the flame of which guttered at the end of the extended prick of a Priapus. She had uncovered her hair, and it fell down straight either side of her face, some strands stuck to her cheeks. As I was to learn, in daylight it had the colour of glowing gold, but, lit here by the flickering lamp, it flared like fire.

She did not answer me directly, but told me that around noon each day she went for water to the public well that stands in front of the circular temple of Nodens near the river ford. I am not sure why she told me that. Was it a suggestion that I should seek her out at the well? Or did she hope for me to return to the *lupanar*? I couldn't say, but I left with the image of her face in my mind, and the feel and the scent of her body on my skin, so that I couldn't sleep that night but writhed and turned in my narrow bed in the *mansio* outside the town.

My friend left for Lindum early the next morning, and I was due to return by the canal to my newly built house at the edge of the *magnae paludes*. I couldn't leave yet. I missed one fleet of barges that were being towed out from the wharf. Instead, I walked about the town and had a snack and a tumbler of well-watered wine at a street bar, waiting for the sun to approach its full height above the painted wooden gables and heavy orange tiles of the basilica's roof. Then I went to find the well Senuna had described. As she had said, it stood in a gravelled yard in front of a post-built temple with a curving white-plastered wall and conical shingled roof. There was a queue of women, and some boys, waiting to fill the vessels they bore – pots and pans, jars, jugs, and squat, flat-bottomed *amphorae*. Some women wore leather harnesses in which two tall jugs were slung, one against each hip. The well was topped by a four-posted cover building with open sides that held the windlass, which two muscular slaves, bushy-haired in short grubby tunics – *Iceni*, I thought, from their fair, sunburnt skin – were turning to the accompaniment of a street musician playing on a set of pipes.

There was no sign of Senuna. The high-pitched music continued to pierce the babble of the streets and the queue moved slowly up to the well, where water was sloshing onto the ground from the raised bucket and running away in the gutters. Then suddenly I saw her. She was dressed in a ragged grey tunic, her feet in wooden clogs, and her bright hair hidden by a threadbare shawl thrown over her head and fastened in place by a tarnished metal brooch. She was carrying a tall earthen jar, which she hugged against her waist with one arm. She joined the end of the queue, exchanged words with another woman whom she seemed to know, and then stood there, her gaze cast down. Her whole attitude expressed great weariness. If she had been hoping I might have come to the well, she did not look around her to find me.

I waited until her turn had come at the well head, and, as her vessel was filled from the bucket and I saw her struggling to raise it, I stepped forward. She had one hand under the base of the jar, and was trying to fit its globular side into the curve of her narrow waist.

"Let me help you," I said, taking hold of the jar and pulling it from her. Her white hands clung to it for a moment, and then released it, as, startled, she turned her head to look at me. I was aware the other women in the queue were watching me too. I was dressed in my finest tunic, with high boots of fretted leather, and wearing my striped cloak, with a brooch that denoted I was a citizen and veteran of the legions. A babble of comment rose on the air, some of it obscene. I pulled Senuna away. "I'll carry this back for you," I said.

"Oh, no, you mustn't." She was reaching for the jug again, but I had it firmly in my hands now, water slopping from its neck. Her voice was high and anxious. I noticed how white her face was in the sunlight and how dark the rings about her eyes.

"Where do you live?"

"I don't want you to see where I live." Her Latin was quick and fast, but with the accent of the *Britanni*. I took her to be freeborn and not a slave. How had she become a prostitute? She was unlike any that I had ever come across. Last night she had exuded a calm dignity, even in the very act itself, that was unlike anything I had ever experienced before from the pliers of her trade. I could understand she only did what she did out of a resigned desperation rather than any sense of calling – as some *lupae* indeed did term their ancient profession, asserting and promoting their qualities with a dedication worthy of better things, intent on making as much money as possible in the quickest time. But why she? She was attractive. She seemed intelligent and spoke well. How had she come to this situation?

"Why then did you tell me you came to this well?" I placed the jug on the ground and thrust my face at hers in the way I had done with errant recruits on the parade ground.

She did not answer the question but her eyes did not flinch from mine. I could see the tiredness in them. "We'll walk to the river," she said. "We can talk there. If you want me again, we can arrange it for later."

I was angered by that. "I came here today to see you as a person, as a woman, not to fornicate. I told you last night I thought you lovely. Your loveliness to me is in your eyes and in your hair and in your voice, not in…" – I could not say what first came into my mind and concluded rather lamely – "….not in any fresh conquests of Venus."

"You will not wish to be with me when you understand how I live, and you see the things I must do."

"I know already what you do. But you are not like the others. I feel sure you are not in that place out of choice." I put my hand to her face, which brought out a further chorus of derision from the women at the well. "Senuna, there is a quality about you I would like to understand. I *will* walk with you."

I picked up the heavy jar. She looked at me, her face now quiet, unprotesting. She seemed resigned to my accompanying her. "Let me take this water to where it is needed," I said. "Is it for your little girl, the one you told me about?"

"She is not well." Senuna's eyes were suddenly filled with tears which ran onto her cheeks. I brushed them away with my fingertips.

"Then let us go to her now."

She led me into an area of the town to the north of the forum where the streets were narrow and connected by passages little wider than a person's shoulders. The timber houses overhung these alleys, so it was like walking in tunnels from which the sun's direct rays were shut out. Above our heads, washing hung limply on lines stretched between window frames. Grubby, bare-footed children, chasing each other, ran against our legs, while dogs barked at gates, pulling against their chains. At a corner an old beggar sat in her rags and filth with skeletal arms out-reaching.

Where Senuna lived proved to be a damp shack with a thatched roof mouldy with growth, two storeys high. Its facing plaster was black with age, much fallen away to reveal the woven wooden lacing of the walls, with holes in the earth infill through to the inside. The door was propped open. A crude wood stair, scarcely better than a ladder, climbed up just inside the door. Senuna, who had been silent for the entire walk, moving ahead of me with never a backward glance to see if I still followed, climbed the stair nimbly. Bearing the water, I struggled after her.

I emerged through a trapdoor into a small area of uneven boards, with the sloping thatch either side, lit by one small window open to the air. Green fronds growing out of the thatch curled around the window frame. A mattress on the floor made of straw stuffed into sacking was the bed where Senuna presumably slept. A shelf holding clay pots slanted crookedly against the far wall, and next to it were hooks from which clothing hung. That was all, except for a stool under the window on which a young woman sat, holding to herself a doll-like child with dark hair, and eyes so large and staring they seemed out of proportion with her face.

Senuna spoke to the woman in a babble of language I did not understand. The woman rose and handed her the child. She lay quietly in Senuna's arms, in her tiny, stained dress embroidered at the hem, her little legs dangling down. So still, so quiet, she was. It was obvious there was something badly wrong. I set down the water jar and went over to them, placing my fingers on the little girl's forehead. It was burning hot.

"She is ill," I said. "Can you get a doctor? I will pay his fee."

Senuna spoke to the woman, who, from her small stick-like shape, was little more than an undeveloped child herself. She disappeared through the trapdoor like a fox into its burrow.

"Is she going for a doctor?" I asked.

"No, she has her own sick mother to look after. I have no money to pay her to stay."

"I said I would pay."

"I cannot let you."

"Why, when I wish to help?"

Again, that silence which I was becoming used to with Senuna. "There is no doctor," she said at last. "Only an old woman in a place nearby who knows of some herbs and potions, and would hang a frog about your neck while she gabbles nonsense rhymes and rings a bell. I do not want that."

"I will go to the forum and see if I can find a doctor."

"No." She was cuddling the little girl now and crooning to her. "She is getting better. I have been praying to Minerva."

"Minerva!" I said surprised. "Why that goddess? Are you a worshipper?"

"I have been instructed in her wisdom," Senuna said. It was the only fact about her origin that she ever gave me. "She will help us, I know."

I remember arguing further with Senuna, offering money from my purse but she would not take it. She had an obstinate pride which showed in her face and by the set of her body with the child in her arms.

"Can I not get you food at least?" I asked. "If not for you, then for the little girl."

But she would accept nothing. "I shall work tonight and we shall eat tomorrow," she said. "I am not destitute, as you think. Do not concern yourself."

"Very well," I said, my own pride affected now that my offers were spurned. "But you must promise me: whenever you do need help, then you will come to me. My name is Gaius Modius Celer. I was once a soldier. I have a house where you and your child would be safe. You could stay for as long as you wish. You will not become indebted to me. I will not make any demands on you and I will not seek to hold you when you want to leave. I would like to heal you and your child and make you happy again, as you must once have been."

I told her how she must take a barge from the river below the town and how she must travel to the first dock the barge would reach on the canal – which the barge master would know well, as he would my name too – and where she would find my house by the causeway close to the water's edge. She did not interrupt, so I felt certain she had listened and that she might remember if she had a change of mind. Why I did all this, I was not sure. She was a woman I had met in a brothel. I had enjoyed her body for the few minutes that I had paid for. That's what brothels were for. There were plenty of other women available when I should need one again. But Senuna was different. I had known that straightaway. I knew I wanted her to be with me, not just now but in the future too – yet it would have been hard to explain my reasoning even to myself.

I left her and went down the trapdoor, and didn't look back. I had a heavy blackness about me that what I wished for could never happen.

Out of the corner of my eye, as I had had spun my tale, I was aware of heads coming and going in the bright light outside seen through the half-open door, looking in briefly, then retiring in frustration to resume their long watch in the garden. Once of these, I think, was Numicius, who must have been very bored, and frustrated by this extraordinary turn of events – the Emperor, he was host to, spending his time, in privacy too, with a mere ex-soldier of plebeian stock.

"What happened then? Hadrian asked: he seemed entirely unconcerned by any effect his conversation with me might be having outside. "How and when did she come to you? What was her background that she said she had taught the wisdoms of the divine Minerva, only to take up the life of a *lupa*?"

"I have never learnt, Caesar. She would not say a word, although I often asked. I could not punish her for not speaking and telling me the truth, although a husband has such powers. The last thing I would have done was to hurt her in any way – in her mind or her soul, or, least of all, her body. I have my suspicions, although I have never tried to find out if there is truth in them. I lost her, you see, Caesar, in such a short time – not even two years – it seems just enough to remember her and grieve for her still, and not to try and probe now into her past."

"What are your suspicions?"

"She had been raised somewhere where she learnt good Latin, and she had clearly been taught to bear herself with dignity and with self-control, the traditional virtues of a Roman woman – at least the virtues that we like to think remain with Roman women. As she had referred to being inculcated in the discipline of Minerva, I suspect she was brought up within a temple sanctuary, one perhaps dedicated to the Triad of Iupiter and Juno and Minerva in one of our larger towns, or even at some country shrine where Minerva might be worshipped with local gods, possibly not very far from Duroliponte. I say that for I think she returned there after I left her on that day I have described to you, and it could not have been at any great distance. But, as I say, all this is but speculation on my part."

"What happened, Celer, to the child?"

"She died. I don't know when. Probably not long after I felt the fever heat in her head. Perhaps – if I am right – Senuna took her back to the shrine to be cured, or perhaps to the father, whoever or wherever he was, asking him for help. She never told me anything except the plain fact that her daughter had died. I could not bring myself to ask more. Now that she had come to me, I wanted the past to be left in the past, however great the tragedy she had suffered. The only way I would have spoken of it is if she had raised the subject herself – and she never did."

"Tell me how she came to you, Celer." I saw him turn to the door, gesturing with his hands impatiently, and a trio of heads, which included that of my Gavo, abruptly ducked out of sight. "We would ask you to be quick now for our presence is much awaited by others. The Emperor can do many things but he cannot hold up time."

"I will be brief, Caesar." I was feeling chilled, anyhow, in the bath house and wished to be out in the sun once more. My brain had yet to catch up with all the words that had been spoken. Had a lowly citizen like me ever had such a long and private interview with his Emperor? I knew that later I would find myself disbelieving, thinking it all but a dream of colours I had dwelt within and nothing more.

"It was a very busy time for me then, Caesar."

The dock was newly opened and there was much work to do to ensure the smooth flowing of the barges, and to see that the warehouses were being stocked and unloaded efficiently. My house had only been completed a few months and still the decorators were in place, plastering and painting, putting a gloss on the tiled floors with mutton fat. The place was full of workmen and my temper was bad. I had fools to deal with at the dock and fools I tripped over in my house. My house slaves then were raw and untrained, *Iceni* most of them, and my steward had yet to learn the routine of my working life, that the right clothes were put out for me, that I had plenty of apples which I loved, that wild birds and fish were brought in from the marsh for my meals, that my chamber pots were washed out each morning, that the blinds in the *triclinium* were opened when the sun was in the western sky, that…..

"My apologies, Caesar, I will be much briefer….."

Day by day, I looked for her when the barges coming up from Duroliponte slid against the wharf. The days and the weeks passed, and the weather grew stormy as the summer changed to autumn. Still she did not come. I began to despair that she ever would. I had to accept it was unlikely, just a fantasy I had concocted. She had been so unwilling to accept my help. Perhaps, in any event, things had changed for the better with her. I had to hope that was true – that her child was cured, that she had found an occupation more honourable than the *lupanar*. I hated to think of her returned there, sitting silently in her corner, being led away by any man attracted by her serenity in contrast with the showy assertiveness of the others of her trade.

I was so busy with my work, training my clerks in the system of enumeration of cargoes and goods that I had devised, that I have to confess that on some days I forgot about her entirely. She was but a memory, a ghost that might have come back to a life of flesh and blood, but who remained in the shade. We were short of writing tablets, of both the wax and wood sheet types, and also of papyrus and vellum which I required for my official reports. We were short too of rope and timbers and iron hooks and barrels and *amphorae* and of pitch and tar and…..

"My apologies again, Caesar, recounting those days brings back such detailed memories. I shall be as quick now as a kingfisher, as brief as a mayfly."

I remember it was a grey afternoon in early winter, with the sun already low above the reed beds, the waters of the dock glowing red and lit by sparks of silver from a strong wind whipping at its surface. I had left my office and was checking everything was stowed correctly against the possibility of a gale, when the last barge expected that day from the south, pulled by a single horse, nosed its way into the small harbour. I turned my back to it and, with two of my workers, began checking the strength of the various struts and ropes of the dockside crane as the wind began to buffet us more forcefully. So, when a slave said to me, "A lady is here asking for you, *domine*", I turned with no expectation at all, only a sense of irritation that I had a further delay before I could take the stone-paved path that led from the dock to my home.

She stood silently before me in a long grey cape, with a shawl across her shoulders of a checked reddish-brown pattern as the *Britanni* wear, fastened at her right shoulder by a brooch. Her head was uncovered, and her hair was pulled up and tied at the back by ribbons. Her face was white with exhaustion. She stumbled a little sideways as she stood before me, then caught herself and pulled herself up straight again, determined, almost defiant. By her side was a cloth bag such as pedlars use to carry their wares.

She said, "You told me I could come to you if I had need."

I was astonished. I said formally something like "You are most welcome". My knees were weak with shock.

"Excuse me Caesar, I shall be finished soon."

I called for my slaves and they carried her to the house where a room was prepared for her. She slept the long night through, although the gale thundered at the walls and upon the roof, and I feared the water would rise out of the canal and flood us. But it did not. And in the morning I left early to inspect the damage, which was thankfully little. When I returned to the house, she had risen and was eating a gruel of flour and eggs and milk that my cook had prepared. She smiled. I shall never forget that smile. It was the first real animation in her face that I had seen.

She lived with me a year and then I married her in accordance with custom. I was legally responsible for her and she was my heir. Three month later she was pregnant. And before nine further months had passed, she was dead."

I felt the tears returning to my eyes. Such softness in an old man who had been a soldier!

"I grew to love her more than I can ever say, Caesar. She was life itself to me."

I lived in her as I had never done with woman before. My life had been full of harshness: she brought me for the first time softness and beauty, not just glimpsed for a moment and then gone, but mine to hold and to keep. She and I made up the totality of everything, of all that we did and felt together; anything else was but a background, even my work at the dock, just a framework now for our conjoined lives. I had known this love would come to me, even from the very beginning when I first saw her sitting so patiently in the corner of that upstairs room. And perhaps she had felt something similar too, some chiming note of predestination. Was that why she had told me she came each day to the well – to give predestination a chance of coming true?

It did not matter what she had done and where she had been, nor what were the mysteries that surrounded her. I lived in the present and not the past. And when my present ended, I had no life left at all. I was stuck still, frozen in memory. There was no future. It took me many months to feel I was moving forward with time again.

"I have never really recovered, Caesar, from what happened to me then – that is, until now. I mean at this very moment. The telling of my memories to you, Caesar, I feel has released me from a spell. It is as if I have been trapped all these long years like an insect caught in amber. I am prepared to move on now – to a place I do not yet know. I may not have many years, or months, or days even, left for the journey, but I shall set out on it. And at the end, there will be my Senuna waiting for me."

I could see Hadrian looking at me, his head on one side, a remote look on his face as if he found what I said too personal, too intrusive, or perhaps he was simply troubled by it, or thought me half crazed. I had opened up my soul to him as I had never exposed that poor ragged, fluttering thing to anyone else before, not even Senuna. Of course, I *had* said far, far too much! But then Hadrian's face cleared and he smiled, and he took my arm in a soldier's grasp of friendship. "Come, old veteran. You have spoken well. Let us go out to the others now and enjoy our feasting."

"But…." I was horrified. Did he think I had left my servants such instructions?

He saw the sudden worried look on my face and laughed.

"Everything will be ready," he said. "As we ordered. Think, Celer, if the Emperor of Rome can raise legions, ride ahead of his captured enemies to the Capitoline, carve through granite mountains and bridge the troublesome seas, govern a myriad peoples under the *pax Romana*, he can organise a simple feast for his friends."

X

The Emperor's camp was spread out across my far meadow – the furthest part of my land away from the house. Ground on which my ponies normally grazed was now transformed into a small town, with rows of tents, some small, some much larger, in a variety of colours – greens, reds, and browns for the main, their sides and roofs made of canvas or goatskin, some a mixture of the two. On the ridge points, pennants fluttered and drooped: the air was very hot and there was little breeze. At the centre of the camp, beyond a rectangular space that had been left clear (the grass here had been cut short with scythes) stood a high, crimson-sided tent with the golden imperial eagle painted onto the apex of its roof, and various animals in blacks and greys – lions and leopards and elephants – shown running or lumbering about its sides. Before its projecting porch, supported by gilded poles, was a guard of Praetorians, formed up in a small square, four ranks deep.

All about the camp, men were moving, some in military uniform, others in plain tunics, one or two even in heavy togas trying not to trip on the lumpy grass. Amongst them were fleet-limbed slaves, dashing by with messages, or bearing flagons and trays, piled high with sweetmeats and fruit. At the top of the meadow where I had grown a small coppice of birch, I could see horses tethered in amongst the trees, grazing on the sweeter grass that grew there: someone amongst the Emperor's travelling household certainly knew how best to make use of my land!

I was in the Emperor's main tent, feeling quite lost and lonely now, my embroidered long tunic exchanged for a shorter, more manly one, which showed my white, purple-veined calves. Hadrian was holding court on a podium raised within the main compartment of the tent, where couches with twisted ivory arms and mosaic-inlaid headboards had been set up, brought miraculously from whatever wagon or mule's back they had travelled on. He was seated beside the couches on a commander's folding field chair, which I supposed, ignorant of court ritual as I was, served him as a temporary throne. He was dressed still in uniform, but his cuirass had been changed for an elaborate gilded one, with moulded heroic figures stalking across it and the goddess Victoria raising up a wreath. Across his right arm was draped a cloak of purple, which must have half-emptied Rome's treasury by itself. To produce this imperial colour, I had heard, took the labour of almost as many slaves as the little sea molluscs they must gather to crush out each tiny drop of dye.

Hadrian was surrounded by his senior commanders, his advisers, his accompanying senators, even by a small number of women, who had appeared to my surprise out of nowhere and were making use of the couches, in transluscent *stolae* of saffron and lilac and white, with glittering ornaments at wrists and throats. They were sitting up balanced on their left elbows, hovered over by a number of men, one of whom I saw was rotund Numicius, now dressed in a tunic far too short for him, with floral patterns across its front as if he were some young suitor presenting himself at a lady's door. He pirouetted about on the podium on chubby legs, exchanging a word here, a smile there, and bearing bowls of fruit to the ladies, all of whom declined him with waves of their languidly-dangling arms.

I stopped a passing slave bearing a silver wine jug and took a beaker of well-watered wine. The slave was a huge man with a jet black face and gleaming white teeth – a Nubian, I supposed, for I had heard of such men who now served the imperial court. He was dressed in green like the rest of the servants. I watched him make off, having been signalled to by the steward to attend to the ladies on the podium. His short tunic showed broad thighs, a strong back and well-muscled arms, which I thought were wasted here serving this self-absorbed aristocracy. He would make a good front-rank man in an auxiliary infantry cohort, or even a standard bearer. What life was it serving grapes to pampered ladies? And even if he was brought in from time to time to serve them in other ways, which I knew was a possibility – and judging from the giggles rising as he moved about their couches, even a certainty – what sort of existence was that for a man? Better by far to be ordered to offer up your body to an enemy of Rome than surrender it to a worthless, idle woman who might hold an equal power of life and death over you?

"And our thanks are to our good friend, Gaius Modius Celer," I heard Hadrian say, cutting through a sudden silence, and I saw that all eyes on the podium, and around it from the various corners of the tent, were turned towards me standing at the tent opening.

"Attend to us here, good friend," said Hadrian, indicating I should come up on the podium beside him. Feeling strangely self-conscious, I did so, and to my astonishment there was a ripple of applause – the pressing of hands, the flapping of togas, the waving of napkins.

"Sit beside us." The command was fulfilled by another folding stool being opened up and pushed into place beside Hadrian: the seat was of red-stained leather, such as I had seen legates use in the field. My promotion to sit in a legate's chair beside my Emperor was an honour indeed, which here in his formal presence seemed even greater than the confidences he had just shared with me in the bath house.

I was required to drink with Hadrian, crossing our chased silver beakers, and delivering the oath, 'For the preservation of Rome forever', as we had made in the legions.

Then Hadrian made a further announcement, "We are all the guests here of Modius Celer and we are grateful to him for his hospitality. He will now provide us with some entertainment. He will show us his famous breed of small horses – ponies, they are called – of the type he once rode in war against the enemies of Rome. They will be ridden for us by his slave from the *Iceni* people, who were – and still are – masters of these ponies too." He whispered to me. "Is all ready, Celer?"

"It is Caesar." Earlier I had requested the honour of providing such a display and Hadrian had been enthusiastic in his approval. I had given Myru instructions, and time to prepare, and she would be waiting for the signal. She must be nervous, I thought, although I would not normally have associated her with such a state, being of tough *Iceni* stock. I too, though, felt the blood begin to pound in my body. This had to be a success or else I – and Hadrian too by association – would look foolish.

"Modius Celer says," said Hadrian, rising to his feet with a smile, "that he would have liked to ride for you as well, as once he rode for *Legio VIIII*, but he begs your forgiveness, as cruel Saturnus with his scythe has cut away much of his former nimbleness."

There was further applause and laughter at that. Hadrian and I had risen and were moving through the throng to the open tent porch. The Praetorians outside snapped to attention. Behind us, squeezed and pushed the spoilt, the powerful, the obsequious, the commanding, the knowledgeable, the alluring, each with a scrambling attendance of slaves.

With what seemed an interminable slowness, the crowd, in all its variety and colour, began to form up in a straggling line before the open square of grass in front of the imperial tent. I was suddenly very much on edge. What

I was planning to show this privileged company – many familiar with the far greater, more sophisticated entertainments to be found in the chief cities of the Empire, or even in Rome itself, but now gathered in a small beaten compound in the outback of one of its remotest provinces – would it prove to be a dismal anti-climax and I be ridiculed as a result? Oh, why, had I put to Hadrian my idea of showing off the skills of *Iceni* horsemanship? Did any of these here even know of the *Iceni*, except as a name, or as a territory now under Rome's dominion, to be exploited and trampled upon? Did they know anything of the history of these people? – how they had been amongst the wealthiest of this land we now called Britannia, and how their charioteers and their horse soldiers had once struck fear into Roman ranks. And indeed – I had to admit this – how once, if properly led, their forces might have swept us right out of our new province, driving us back to the sea. Yet, I held a fierce pride in my ponies, and in the controlling strength of Epona, and I knew that the goddess would not let me down – neither Myru either, for the show would depend on her. I gave the signal now, raising both my arms above my head, my finger tips together, knowing my servants were placed to pass it on.

I could see Gavo, with some of my field hands, keeping the approaches to the grassy square free of those spectators who were wandering away from the main crowd of watchers, some still carrying flagons and cups. A number of carousing Praetorians were clearly off-duty and they had wandered close to the gravelled causeway by which my ponies would approach.

Then I heard them. Above the babble of conversation about my ears, I could sense, as much as hear, the rhythmic trotting of the many hooves on the metalled path. The noisy talking at once stilled, like a wave frozen on its way to the shore, and people, noting the Emperor's attentive attitude, swung round to gaze in the same direction as he.

Through the growing evening gloom came my ponies, swinging round, forelegs stepping high, as Myru had trained them, with high, tossing reed plumes, laced with yellow flowers, fastened between their pricked ears. Their glossy black harness was covered by jingling brass pendants and small ringing bells that flashed in the low rays of the sun. Atop the centre pony in the front line of two now extending across the grass sat Myru, her black hair unfastened and blown out behind her.

She rode high on the pony's neck, her head close to its head, like a centaur, or perhaps like the goddess Epona herself, the horse's body seeming to flow with her as if rider and animal were one. In each hand, Myru clasped a thin wand of willow cane, which she held out, right and left, over the backs of the riderless ponies beside her, controlling them as if by magic. Behind, came the second line, approaching at a slow trot, and beside them ran Pyddr – only a small boy, bare-footed and bare-chested, wearing black calf-length breeches, whom Myru had found and persuaded me to take on: he too had a masterful control of the ponies, she had told me, so much so she thought he had been raised amongst them.

The ponies broke to right and left and came round in a perfect half-circle, the two lines merging into one now with Myru riding the black and white dappled pony at the head. She dismounted in a back somersault, so fast and perfectly executed it brought a gasp from the watchers. Each pony now in the line came up to her in turn, bent its knees and bowed its head. She sent it on its way with a quick stroke of her hand against its neck. At the rear came small Pyddr, and he too bent his head to be met by a thrust of Myru's boot against his rump, sending him tumbling over. There was a roar of laughter. I began to relax and took a sip of wine from my cup. The show had begun well.

It had been a long time since I had seen Myru's skills displayed in this way. She had stripped from her shoulders the round-cut leather cape she had been wearing (a traditional item of *Iceni* dress), and stood now in just a short hempen tunic into which some things that sparkled – perhaps small pieces of glass – had been sewn, for they shone and flashed in the sinking rays of the sun. The tunic was cut low across one shoulder so that Myru's small right breast, with its dark nipple, was exposed – a custom of the *Iceni* women, long practised. Her bare shoulder was blue with tattooing, a pattern of interlacing animals' heads and bodies that ran down her upper arm as well as onto the slope of her breast. I had studied these tattoos once, when she had had first come to the stable and stripped for riding. They were on her back too and around her hips – and elsewhere, for all I knew. I had marvelled at the tattooist's skill with an ink made of crushed beetles' shells, pricked out with a sharp reed pen, so many hours of slow torture across such a fine, soft-grained skin.

"Why?" I had asked.

"It is the tradition of my people," she replied. "And the tradition still lives with us when much else has died."

Myru – as with Diseta and, to some extent, Gavo, I allowed to talk to me directly as they wished. They were personal servants as much as slaves, valued members of my household. I have found no man, or woman, can give of their best unless they feel free to express the truth of how they feel. Some – such as Numicius – might find this a weakness in my authority, but I don't think I need to prove anything to anyone. My long life tells its own story. I have always treated those I like well, and those I dislike with an equal disfavour, regardless of their status. In consequence, I have normally got what I wish out of all men – and women.

Myru now put on a dazzling display of her skills. With Pyddr's assistance on foot moving amongst the ponies, cajoling and whispering, his hands stroking their sides, they wheeled and turned in perfect formation while Myru, mounted once more, sprang from back to back, riding against the neck, facing towards the tail, standing on her hands, wriggling beneath the belly, balancing on one leg, then on two, one foot on each of two ponies trotting side by side, all without pause, in a fluid synchrony which no one (least of all me) could ever have taught her, but seemed to spring directly from an ability she had been born with.

I could see the fascination on the faces of those watching. Even the Praetorians, both those on duty and those with wine flasks in their hands, gave her their full attention, their eyes fixed on the small nimble figure with the slender, tanned limbs, and perhaps on her nakedness exposed when her body somersaulted, of which, I am sure, she had little consciousness and even less concern.

The climax of the show came when Pyddr took up a set of reed pipes and played a strange, wailing tune, which brought the ponies up onto their hind legs as if they were dancing, causing gusts of laughter from the watchers. I was amazed by both Pyddr's skill and by the practise Myru must have put in to accomplish this act, so unnatural for an animal to perform. I had never seen it before and had been totally unaware of the training that would have been necessary. I realised there was probably much going on about my house which I did not know about now. Still, if it produced the sort of result that was being shown here, who was I to complain?

Myru had brought the ponies back into their two lines, and each animal bent its forelegs, muzzles low to the ground, as if in homage to the Emperor, while Myru and Pyddr prostrated themselves beside them, flat on the ground. The applause was deafening – and I have to say – most gratifying. Hadrian summoned me to take a bow, which I made, turning in rheumaticky circles before the throng, my hands with palms pressed together in the approved manner for receiving applause, hastily recalled. Then, finding a silver salver with a mass of greenery upon it being pushed towards me by a member of the Emperor's entourage, who was making appropriate gestures about his head with his hands, I placed one of the laurel wreaths upon my own head while summoning Myru and Pyddr to come up to me, and hung one each about their ears. One wreath remained, and I did not need anyone's hint to hand it to Hadrian, so that for a moment all four of us pirouetted together in a group taking in an increasingly frantic applause. Then, with my hands pushing at their backsides, my two worthy slaves scampered away, the ponies following them at a fast, jingling trot – a sudden rush of movement that cleared the arena in moments. People began looking about them, smiling and nodding at each other, clapping their hands, not now in applause but for the slaves to bring them wine and food.

Darkness was falling over the scene: the flat, reed-bound landscape with its twisting streams and silent lagoons, the ruler-straight black waters of the canal and the shadowy tile-clad roofs of my dock, all were merging into an ever-deepening grey gloom under the vast decaying eye of the sky. The taint of the stagnant marshes hung upon the air, a smell I had once enjoyed but which my Senuna had likened to that of death. Little had we known then how soon her sense would harden into reality.

Torches, set into tall, iron holders placed around the camp, flared against the darkness. Inside the great tent of the Emperor, many lights were now burning – lamps of metal and clay placed on tables, and lanterns hanging from the ridgepoles, lit by slaves balanced on ladders. The smells of roasting meats wafted on the air from the cooking area on the far side of the camp, quite blotting out those scents of decay which had earlier disturbed me. Music, plucked out from a *cithara*, splashed like rain drops amongst the company, who were piling glossy red plates with foods delivered on trays by the slaves. The Emperor eat with a select group at the top end of the tent, where a huge table of a dark, heavy wood (it must have taken more than one cart to carry it) was heaped with joints of meat and whole cooked birds and fish. Slaves cut and carved. The green-liveried servants of the household circled with their heavy burdens held aloft.

I felt weariness growing upon me. I could eat no more. I could certainly drink no more. Perhaps Hadrian noted my head falling, my eyes glazing, for he said with kindness. "Go to your rest, Celer. Put beeswax in your ears for it will be a while before the noisy ones are finished here. Be ready by the sixth hour, for we will march then. Has your servant the instructions?"

For the moment, I had forgotten I was setting out tomorrow with the Emperor and his party to find the battle sites of *bellum Icenorum*. I could not admit that, however. All was indeed ready.

"He has, Caesar."

"And we will take your horse-girl slave too. What is her name?"

"Myru, *domine*."

143

"We fancy she will be useful. We may need a good speaker of the *Iceni* tongue."

"Of course, Caesar. I have already told her."

"You have? You think like a *legatus*, Celer. We shall ride together and tell stories of the past. Of great Rome and how we conquered the world."

"I shall be honoured, Caesar."

He clasped my shoulder. "But the great days are over, Celer. The glory days have passed."

He leant on his hands, propped over one of the tables of food. I could sense the Praetorians, watching, suspicious, on edge now. "Sometimes, Celer, I feel everything is at an end. We shall soon not even be a memory."

"Never, Caesar. Your name, and that of Rome, will resound through history forever."

"Perhaps. Perhaps. But will we be *understood*?"

He stood up straight. "We begin our search tomorrow, Celer. If we don't know and set down our past ourselves, how can we expect future generations, in a thousand years, two thousand even, to learn of us?"

I did not know how to answer. He dismissed me and I went to my bed. I requested Diseta to join me, just for the comfort of her warmth against my body.

I suddenly felt very old and full of fear.

XI

It was a pale, clear morning. The sky had been washed pink by the rising sun, the colours suffused by the wetness of the heavy dew. Sounds were clear on the air – the scrape of feet on a step, the bark of a dog in the slaves' yard, the rattle of a chain, the whinnying of one of my ponies.

I had risen before the sun, dressing by the light of two guttering lamps for which I was short of oil. I barked orders at a sleepy Gavo to make sure he purchased an *amphora* of the best, non-smoking oil from the first barge to come through that day. I thumped him in the back with my fist to make sure he understood. I was displeased. Gavo was not happy either: he was not going to accompany me today. I would be making use of a body servant of the Emperor.

Diseta dressed me in a tunic I had last worn at a reunion of veterans of the VIIIIth some ten years back. It bore the red bands of a legionary veteran and had the Bull insignia embroidered onto its right shoulder. Over it, I put on a brown, leather corselet, which dated from the last years of my service and which I had kept well polished ever since. It was a little loose on my shrunken chest, but Diseta had padded it with sheep's wool and it now fitted me snugly enough: it had an attached skirt of segmented leather flaps that covered the hem of my tunic and allowed my legs to move as easily as my old bones would allow. My boots were of single pieces of tooled leather, impressed and decorated in the native style, high on my thin calves: my days with cold, rough feet from open sandals were at an end. The boots were old: my slaves had kept them well-greased over the years and they were still as supple as they had ever been. They had been a present organised by Senuna, although, of course, I had had to pay the cost, which had been considerable, nearly *x denarii* as I recall.

The Emperor with his bodyguard came clattering on horseback up to my outer gate before I was fully ready. I was surprised at how small the party was – Hadrian himself, of course, his secretary and his archivist too, looking diminutive on their tall horses in brown tunics and capes, his chief steward with an attendance of perhaps twenty slaves, leading pack mules laden with baggage, the Praetorian *praefectus*, in full parade armour and helmet, and some forty Praetorians in armour on jet-black chargers. The Emperor's banner of a golden eagle on a crimson background was carried by a Praetorian standard bearer – and that was all.

As I came out to make my bow to Hadrian, I looked along the causeway to see if more were not approaching, but the long, cobbled track, lined with willow trees, was empty for as far as I could see. Many of the concourse from yesterday, I had learnt, were staying with Numicius at his villa, eating the equestrian out of his house and home – the penalty of his class at such times. Others would have slept at the camp on my field, which was due to be cleared away today. Some would be moving south to meet up with the Emperor later, but most would be taking the long road to the north to rejoin the Empress in Eboracum.

Our greetings were short. Hadrian was clearly eager to be on the way. He wore a much plainer dress than yesterday, other than for the gilded moulding of his cuirass, little different from mine. He had on the same round cap as yesterday, whereas I was bare-headed, despite Diseta's pleas for me to cover my thin, white hair with a hideous, tall woollen thing, with a flopped-over top, that she normally pressed on me. I have always felt that the fresh air keeps the brain cool while warmth makes it stew. Even when on active service in the VIIIIth, I would take off my helmet as soon as I could.

The Emperor's horse wheeled and pulled, tossing its head, equally anxious to be away from here. Gavo with some other servants brought out my small leather-bound campaign trunk, studded with my name and *optio* rank. The Emperor's slaves seized it from them and lashed it with straps to the back of the rear-most mule. A horse was led up to me. It stood patiently, a quiet animal I was relieved to see, and smaller than most of those the others rode. I was attended carefully while mounting, and more or less hoisted into the pomelled military saddle of familiar memory. I sat up straight and did not fall off: it had been some time since I had ridden, other than for very short journeys. I could have been carried, I knew: a litter could have been found for me and carried by slave bearers almost as fast as I could ride, but I did not wish that. I wished to be mounted beside my Emperor in this search into the past – into my past too. My honour and my manhood demanded I ride onto those old battlefields. To be carried would have been a disgrace. As a soldier, you are carried only when you are dead. And so I rode out this morning into the living air.

As we prepared to move off, I turned in the saddle and saw that at the rear, on the best of my ponies – I had named it Ajax – Myru had joined us. Her tightly-rolled bundle was lashed across the pony's neck. She wore a short, grey tunic with her round leather cape about her upper body, her legs bare to the top of her thighs: I hoped she carried some other clothing to protect her should the weather change. I saw her kick out angrily at a slave who had come too close to her, perhaps to help her by holding Ajax's head while she fiddled with a twisted rein. Myru I knew had the hot blood of the *Iceni*, uncrushed, unbowed, even with me at times. I had learnt to ignore her sudden outbursts. I knew it was just her temperament and she meant me no disrespect. But who really knows the secret workings of anyone's heart? I raised my hand to her and she waved a small hand back. To ride with the Emperor was an even greater honour for her – an unimaginable one, indeed, for a lowly slave outside of the imperial household. I would try to see she was safe from any lustful Praetorian at night.

As Hadrian, surrounded by Praetorians, led us forward, I saw faithful Gavo raise his hand to me in his misery and bow. I felt mean at my outburst to him earlier: he was as loyal as a dog and put up with much without complaint. Beside him, Diseta stood weeping with her cloak pulled up about her head. She was thinking – I knew – that I would not return. She had told me her fears in the night, when I had shared them too. For me, these had been dispelled with the morning light – but not for her. I saluted her with my hand held against my brow and tried to smile, but a lurch of my mount at that moment forced me to concentrate on my riding and I did not look back. Diseta, who could bring blood to my old flesh still and smooth my skin and give me comfort, as Senuna had – though yet a slave. I had vowed I would reward her in my will.

We travelled by the long, flat road to Duroliponte, the first time I had followed this way for two years or so, having preferred to make use of the barge service which was convenient and – for me – free of cost. Once the Emperor and his immediate retinue had felt the first rush of air on their faces, they slowed down and we went on at no more than a gentle jog, which pleased me as I tried to relax into the rhythm of my mount, feeling the jarring of my bones at the unaccustomed movements. Hadrian turned his horse back to me, with the stern, unbending *praefectus* beside him. His face was more animated than I had seen it so far this morning, his eyes running from the air, his skin flushed.

"How do you do, Celer?"

"I do well, Caesar. What a glorious time this is for me. To ride with my Emperor across the face of the world."

Those may have sounded the sort of words used by Greek panegyrists, whose eulogies are often posted up in the basilicas, or even cut into stone, but I *did* mean them. It was exhilarating to be away from all my cares and dull routines, from the same circle of the sky under which all I did now was to sit and contemplate death, and take part in such an adventure.

We reached the main highway and headed south. The landscape of marsh and creek, where the road in places was raised on high wooden causeways, gave way to one of flat, open fields, which the road crossed straight as an arrow's flight, the embankment now built up of stone, and its surface, a fine gravel that spurted out beneath the horses' hooves. We passed long lines of slaves working in the fields, and were held up at one point by parties cleaning out the side ditches and blocking our passage with their wagons. When we passed through, I was amused to see the overseers bowing low, almost to the ground, while their slaves chest-deep in the ditches looked on in bewilderment, they not knowing who or what our high party represented. That these slaves might well be *Iceni*, I was suddenly mindful of, and I turned to see that Myru followed and did not speak to them, being unaccountably relieved to see her small pony trotting on beside the mules, its rider neither looking to right or left. It was seldom since the war that I had felt such a sense of awareness – of guilt even – as to what we of Rome had done to her people.

An hour or so after midday, we came to the outskirts of Duroliponte, which were nothing grander than some wooden shacks by the roadside with mud-walled yards behind, from which white smoke billowed up, swirling amongst the buildings. We passed a small burial ground, set with weeping trees whose evergreen branches swept low to the ground, brushing against the painted grave posts hung with ribbons of coloured cloth and wicker idols of local gods filled with flowers. Here we halted while our rear guard of the baggage mules escorted by five Praetorians caught up with us, Myru at their head.

A party from the town council came out to meet us. Advance warning of the Emperor's arrival must have been sent ahead, for the mayor and his councillors were all represented, dressed in their best clothes, one even in a badly-draped woollen toga despite the rising heat of the day. This party led us into the grimy streets of the town, past the well where I had met Senuna that morning, past the *lupanar* where she had worked – or rather the site of it for a new building was being raised there, the labourers as we rode by for the moment stilled, gawping at our clattering column – and into the small forum of beaten earth surrounded by its timber buildings. Here we dismounted, the Praetorians forming a protective screen, while some of us, myself included, followed Hadrian and the council members into the basilica. This was a low, dark building, lit only by slit windows in its timber and earthen, white-plastered walls. It smelt of damp and decay and I could see green mould on the walls running up into the open rafters of the roof. I had a momentary panic that the whole structure would collapse suddenly, burying us all in a heap of mud bricks and splintered wood. The future of Rome depended on it not doing so.

Hadrian, however, seemed to show no such concern, perhaps only irritation. He clearly wished to get these formalities out of the way as soon as possible and to continue with his mission. The mayor delivered a lengthy oration speaking of 'this great day' and the 'blessed light brought to our small town that would last for ever.' Hadrian, as kindly as he could, cut him short, and in a few words praised the council for its welcome and for its good works, 'so evident all around'. I blinked in my seat as a shaft of sunlight, penetrating one of the narrow windows, moved inexorably with time to shine directly upon my face. I felt old and tired, my eyes rebelling against the light. I wished to screw them up and rest. Yet this great day had scarcely begun.

The Emperor and the mayor next shared some wine and meats and bread on the raised platform at the head of the basilica, reclining on uncomfortable-looking wooden benches. We humbler mortals took our sustenance standing, delivered on trays by lithe slave girls, whom I suspected had been specially recruited for the occasion, perhaps even from whatever *lupanar* here was now functioning. There was something about the confidence of their movements and their pert smiles that indicated this to me.

Then at last there was a sudden bustle, and we were moving again, with Hadrian striding to the basilica's door, wishing to get on with the purpose of the day. As we came out into the daylight of the forum, he saw me scurrying to be part of the group about him and had the kindness to stop and address me.

"We go now to the *mansio*, Celer, which we will make our base. Then we will ride out tomorrow on our first reconnaissance and you will accompany us with your horse-slave."

"Yes, Caesar. I shall be ready."

"These fools know nothing of the war and its battles. The past, it seems, dies quickly here. One, however, said he had heard long ago, from his father, that battles had taken place nearby – somewhere in the country to the west, between here and a place at the crossing of two main roads called Competum, where there was a small *castellum* built during the war. The local people apparently still tell such stories. We will need to speak with them. But, Celer, you have said you will know where the VIIIIth under Cerialis was ambushed."

"Caesar, I may need time, and some scouting about, to gain my bearings from *Castrum Ikenorum*. It is many years ago and the country may be much altered. I recall landmarks, though, which should still be present."

"You will have all the time you wish. It is to *Castrum Ikenorum* we are going now. Only the place is no longer a fort but a small town with a *mansio* close by on a road that joins others leading to Londinium. It is known today as Civitas Ikelorum."

I pondered that. The fort had been named after Queen Boudica's people, recently defeated. Now it was known as the town of the people who had once been the *Iceni*; only the spelling of their name had been altered. It was as if they no longer existed; even their name did not matter. But, looking across the forum at Myru, sitting so firmly astride Ajax, watching us from amongst the company of the soldiers, I knew they still did. They had been defeated and enslaved, new settlements on barren land had been created for them under the watch of Rome in the territory that had once been Icenia – but their spirit was still very much alive.

Our small column set out from Duroliponte heading south. We had a guide now, riding at the head amongst the Praetorians and close to Hadrian and myself. He was a hunched, dwarf-like figure from the town – one of the *Britanni*, it seemed, although his Latin was fluent. At first a rabble of youths, with one or two older men amongst them, followed us on foot out of the town, waving leafy branches torn from the trees and cheering, until a couple of Praetorians turning their horses back were able to convince them to go back.

After about a mile, the guide directed us onto a branching road which, by the freshness of its surface and the cleanliness of its side-ditches looked newly made. Most roads in this territory, I suspected, followed the route of earlier tracks, but had been straightened and metalled. This one led us across a fringe of low hills that overlooked the plain on which Duroliponte lay. Looking around at the grassy hills with their stands of woodland on the crests, the lower slopes covered by grid-patterns of small fields, I did not recognise at first any feature that I might have known sixty years earlier, although certainly the VIIIIth had occupied this area at the end of the war.

Somewhere Petilius Cerialis's column had passed through this country on its way to the relief of Camulodunum, only to be ambushed in line of march as they passed between woods. That I knew, for I had been to the site to clear it of the scattered remains of our soldiers that the *Iceni* had left there: I had heard as well the stories of the few survivors. But where had the ambush been? As far as I could remember, there had been no Roman-built way then. Trying to blink back the years, I could recall only a track that followed a ridge top and passed between dark trees.

Sixty years ago, and more, is a long time to remember, and I was young then and full of blood, never thinking to set such details in my mind so I could pluck them out one day to inform my Emperor. Possibly – no, very likely – the route Cerialis had taken was this very one we were following now. It was said that his guides from the *Corieltauvi* people, sympathetic to the *Iceni* cause, had been responsible for choosing the route and creating the opportunity for ambush.

Then, to my right across the long curving slope of the hillside we had just climbed, I saw a round knoll that looked as if it had been shaped by man, with a clump of trees at its centre, like one of those priests of Isis whom I saw once in Londinium who has shaved his head at the sides leaving but twisted tufts of hair on the crown. The appearance of that round hill-top stirred my memory. The *Iceni* had taken the legionaries of the VIIIIth they had captured back to their sacred groves which lay within an earth and timber fort. The fort, I knew, had stood on the same round hill I was looking at now.

The work party of the VIIIIth I had been with at the end of the war had broken into the place, killed a few *Iceni* who had not had the sense to leave – many, in fact, had been drunk – and found evidence of the earlier sacrifice of our men to that repellent goddess of theirs, Andred – much as I had witnessed during our march from the coast. Together with the bones we had found at the site of the ambush itself, many chewed and scattered by wild animals, we gathered up all those we could here, and buried others beyond recovery that stank with decay. Many men were physically sick. Several otherwise innocent *Britanni* were killed as a result by some of our rougher elements. One of our number – Helvetius, who had been awarded a *corona* for outstanding bravery in battle – boasted of cutting the throats of local prostitutes after he had used them. That, we thought, had been a waste.

151

I called Hadrian's attention to the knoll with its crown of trees, approaching him directly and riding beside him, pointing out the place I meant. I could sense the Praetorian *praefectus's* displeasure at this: he tried to block my approach with his own horse, but the Emperor waved him away.

"I think it was on this very road, Caesar, that Cerialis was ambushed. It was just a trackway then passing between thick trees. The *Iceni* burst out at the column from both sides. The VIIIIth was soon outnumbered, as *Iceni* reinforcements, some in chariots, were arriving all the time. The column was then enveloped. Our cavalry, including Cerialis, were only able to escape by a charge that broke through the enemy. The legionaries sold their lives dearly. It happened somewhere here, I feel sure. Those that were captured were taken to that hill, Caesar" – I pointed – "and sacrificed inside its fort. I was here sixty years ago. I didn't think I would recognise the place, but I do now."

Hadrian did not say anything at first. But he reined in his horse while our small column ground to a halt behind him. He looked around him, and I had not previously seen such grimness on his face.

"We shall come here tomorrow," he said out loud. "And make a good search. And go to that other place of abomination as well." He flung out his right arm, pointing towards the hill top I had indicated. "But for now we must press on." He moved away from me, then turned and rode his horse back beside mine. "It is good that you have remembered, old soldier," he said. "We thank you."

"Caesar," was all I could reply.

I could see the *praefectus* looking hard at me. Why was he so suspicious of me? Was it because he had never been thanked, as I had, by his Emperor, and thought I might be seeking his job? I laughed so much inwardly at that, I started to splutter. When I recovered, the column was moving again, and I was now at its rear. Myru came up beside me, her pony, Ajax, so low in height compared with my horse that her head was at the level of my chest.

"*Domine*, are you not well?" she said.

"I am very well, Myru. I thank you. In fact, I have not felt so well for a long time."

She began to trot away, and I called after her, speaking over the backs of two mules which were being led between us. "I shall see you have a safe billet tonight, Myru. Your help most likely will be needed tomorrow."

She bowed her head and made a gesture of acknowledgement if not of thanks. I thought, I worry myself needlessly. That girl can look after herself.

I wonder what she will be thinking tomorrow when we come to those once sacred places of the *Iceni*. Far more of her people were killed in the war than were Romans and their loyal allies. The historian Tacitus – if I remembered correctly the figures Hadrian had read out – wrote of seventy thousand of our civilians killed and three thousand of our soldiers. Yet the numbers of *Iceni* dead were perhaps three times as many – very much more, in fact, if those who later died of starvation were included. And we have been killing them ever since, by slavery and hard labour, by removing their best lands, by causing their birth rate to fall, by forcing them into crime and prostitution. Yet, despite all that, the *Iceni* still retain their pride. You see it in Myru, in her breeding, in her looks, in the way she holds herself. She is a good slave, a good servant to me. Yet I would not feel safe with her if another Bodig – another Boudica – arose to lead her people once again. And that is not impossible. The Empire is overstretched. Our legions cannot be everywhere. One day, I fear, Rome may be destroyed too, just as the *Iceni* were – but after my death, long after my death.

I should not need to worry about such things now, not with the very power of Rome riding beside me – the god Mars, in person.

We came to a crossroads, where a shrine stood on a nearby hill to some god the *Britanni* here had equated with our Mercurius, favoured by me – he, son of Iupiter, with winged helmet and feet. Those were surely needed here because the road we turned onto at the crossroads was deeply rutted and in need of repair. As Hadrian's horse stumbled in a pot hole, I saw his face darken and he delivered some remark to an aide, who made a quick note on a wax tablet hooked to his belt. I suspected that some official or other, from whichever administration was responsible, as yet in blissful ignorance of his Emperor's journeying, would shortly be receiving a reprimand that would shake him out of his comfortable office.

We came now to a wide, green valley that I did recall well. It was the one along which we had marched from out of Icenia those long years back, with a swift-flowing river at its centre where oared boats, with casks piled at bow and stern, battled mid-stream against the current, their blades dipping and rising. After several further miles we came in sight of a sprawling town laid out beside the river, at a point where the land sloping down from the low hills made a broad shelf. From a terrace above cut into the hillside, a red-roofed temple with a central tower, looked down on the town. Smoke from one of its courts was rising against the wooded hill slopes behind. This was Civitas Ikelorum, developed from the fort that had once stood here, of

153

which there was now no sign at all. It had been where our scattered force of the VIIIIth, and of the XIIIIth and XXth too, had seen out the end of *bellum Icenorum*. Here the veterans of the great final battle of the war had given me their accounts. From here now, Hadrian wished me to ride with him to find the site of that battle.

We did not enter the town, but paused outside it while a delegation of civic worthies – as at Duroliponte – came out to pay their homage to the Emperor. Then, with formalities satisfied, we moved by a broad, white track around the town and took a road following the river. After a short distance, we reached the *mansio* we sought, the first of several such on the road from here to Londinium. Passing through a gateway in its high outer wall, we entered a large cobbled courtyard, with buildings ranged around on all sides.

Now, once more, there began a great flurry of activity, with presentations being made while horses stamped their feet and whinnied, while the mules brayed and sent streams of faeces onto the cobbles, while trumpets blew and Praetorians clashed their steel hob nails on the stones, while the slaves of the *mansio* met those of the imperial household, and fought with them, cases and bundles being off-loaded, dogs barking, a cat, I noticed, slinking around the balustrade of the wooden arcading above, doves fluttering around the window sills, smoke rising from the vents of kitchens and bath house – all was pandemonium and chaos until at last order was restored.

A carriage bearing a lady and a man of status, its sides decorated with painted emblems, and with outriders at head and tail, had met our column coming in and been caught up in the general scrimmage, unable to move back or forward. It seemed these people, having arrived not knowing the Emperor was expected, had been turned away. I saw Hadrian himself, still on horseback, involved in sorting out the muddle. "They shall be our guests," I heard him bellow above the throng. "Give them our rooms, if there is no space. We shall be content to sleep in the stables."

It was a fine gesture, one that would certainly be recorded to appear in some future potted life of the Emperor. I saw Hadrian's secretary making a discrete note on his tablets; perhaps he had plans to emulate his predecessor, Suetonius Tranquillus. But, of course, in reality, space was found for all, and the couple – a retired lawyer and his wife from the former kingdom of the *Regnenses* – later had an honoured position at dinner alongside Hadrian's couch. If anyone had to shift themselves, it was probably the landlord and his family.

There was music and dancing that evening in an inner court, which had a fountain and a space of grass overlooked by flowering trees. Some girls in costumes as light as the evening breeze danced to pipes, flutes, and bells. The Emperor, reclining full-length in robes of gold and purple, I could see was well-pleased. Seeking his permission, I retired early to my room – a dark hole buried deep within the attic of an upstairs range.

I had been given two slaves to attend me. They were *Germani* – tall, blond, efficient, but not friendly. They had been taught only to speak when spoken to. Retrieving Myru from the stables, where she had been tending to a small cut on one of Ajax's forelegs, I made sure she had a bed in a room – an even smaller, darker box – next to mine. The noise of feasting and drinking, and the clashing of *tympanum* and *cymbalum* from outside in the main courtyard, where the soldiers were entertained, continued late into the night. Some time in the early hours when it was growing light, I left my bed to urinate and could not find a pot. Seeking out my *Germani* slaves, I stumbled upon one of them wrapped over Myru, as closely and tightly as a limpet on a rock. That this was with Myru's permission, I saw clearly from her calm, dark eyes watching me over his shoulder. Then the huge-limbed slave began to untangle his body from hers, and I looked away. I peed and went back to bed. I expect they continued. I did not feel the strength to make it my concern, as perhaps I should have done.

XII

The Emperor Hadrian seemed testy. We had assembled early in the courtyard of the *mansio*. I had eaten some fresh bread and drunk some water. My eyes were dry with tiredness. I think Hadrian had not slept well either. I had the feeling that silence would be reigning tonight, otherwise assorted Praetorians and others of our party would be collecting up their bundles and taking the long road out of Britannia – or, worse, perhaps to the fighting frontiers to entertain the *Germani* or the *Caledonii* with their carousing.

We were an even smaller party now, perhaps ten mounted Praetorians with their *praefectus*, some slaves riding mules, the Emperor's secretary, one or two others whose status I never knew, and myself, of course, with Myru as well on Ajax, whose foreleg she told me was much healed. Speaking to her in the stables, she gave out no impression of tiredness, or of soreness, or anything else that might be expected from having a huge *Germanus* on top of her for half the night. I hoped he had not impregnated her. Myru was a valuable slave and I had always felt a friend and companion to me as well – as far, that is, as could ever be between *dominus* and slave girl. She was certainly much more of a confidante to me than Diseta ever was.

We rode hard for the places we had seen yesterday, leaving the slaves to catch up. We had no guide today but remembered the route well. Myru was beside me riding Ajax at a gallop. We rounded the town of Ikelorum, where chained slaves were working in the fields beside overseers with whips in their hands. No plan had been spoken before we left. Pausing to let the horses rest, I came up to Hadrian and gave him greeting which I had not yet made to him this morning.

"Caesar, I think we should take the track that leads to the old hill fort we saw yesterday. That will help give me my bearings. There may be *Britanni* there who can answer our questions."

"Very well, Celer. Let us speak to your slave."

I motioned Myru on Ajax to the Emperor's other side. The Praetorians bunched around us, their horses blowing and stamping.

"You speak Latin?"

"Yes, Caesar." She answered as I had instructed her before leaving my house. Keep it simple, I had told her, if he speaks to you – as he will. He is not a god – not yet, anyhow. He likes people about him who are respectful but plain in manner. He is Caesar, you are Myru. Those are the names you should use and no other. "I have only one name," she had answered, and I had laughed with her.

"And you know the *Iceni* tongue?" Hadrian asked her now.

"Yes, Caesar. The *Iceni* are my people." I tensed a little at her last comment, which was unnecessary.

"Indeed." He looked down at her, so far below him, and to my surprise he smiled – the first such smile that morning, which had so far been all unsmiling irritation and impatience. "You may need to translate for us."

"Yes, Caesar. I am at your command." Her voice was strong and clear. I tensed again. A simple 'yes' would have been enough.

"Tell us about your people," ordered Hadrian, and I was amazed as the two of them rode ahead of us talking from mount to mount, he halting from time to time, clearly asking more questions and she voluble in her reply – I could hear the rise and fall of her words, if not what they said – waving her free hand from time to time to emphasise a point.

The *praefectus* of the Guard rode by me. "Even a slave can talk to an Emperor, it appears" he said, sounding annoyed. "Keep her beside you, Celer." I bowed my head but did not acknowledge him. Who was he to tell me what to do?

The track we were following brought us below the hill I had seen from a distance yesterday, crowned with its distinctive grove of trees. As soon as we rode up to it, I knew for sure it was the one I had visited with the VIIIIth those long years back. I remembered the earth rampart topped by its palisade alongside a timber gate, although the palisade had now slumped inwards and the double-doors of the gate were missing: the platform above the gateway had fallen as well and lay across the path covered by grass and nettles.

"We fought our way through here," I said, gaining Hadrian's ear as he sat on his horse contemplating the wreckage, while the Praetorians reconnoitred a way inside. "It was only a brief resistance. They fled to their huts and we skewered many of them there. Then we saw what they had done here amongst the trees and we came back and killed the rest of them."

"Yes, Celer. Very good work, I'm sure."

I was troubled by that reply. This was a different Hadrian from the one I had spoken with before. He seemed on edge, looking up through the trees, seeing the sunlight filtering through the leaves and watching a grey bird, high overhead, fluttering its wings and flitting from branch to branch.

"What type of bird is that?"

"I don't know, Caesar. I turned and called out. "Does anyone know the name of that bird?" Ridiculously, I pointed upwards.

It was Myru who said to me softly, "It is an owl. It is sacred to the *Iceni*. It is a good omen to see it here."

To Hadrian, though, I reported, "Caesar, I am told it is an owl. Perhaps the goddess Minerva has sent it to guide us," and I thought then of Senuna, who had told me she had been brought up to know Minerva. Had Senuna then sent the owl to us? It was a fanciful notion, but a pleasing one.

Myru was beside me again, and she spoke most earnestly as Ajax browsed the grasses by the path. "*Domine*, the owl is of our belief. It will always have been here. The *Iceni* used to dedicate the heads of their enemies to it. The bird takes on the intelligence of the head, which is why the owl is considered so wise – as the Romans think too."

It was a very long speech for her and one that annoyed me, lecturing me before my Emperor – although I thought he hadn't heard, having moved some way off. But the *praefectus* had. I thought of the heads of my comrades I had seen hung up in *Iceni* groves, and for the moment the anger came back.

"Taking lessons from your slave, Celer?" sneered the *praefectus*, and at that I was angrier than ever. I was a veteran of the legions, of a fighting generation long before the decayed times that man was born into. I deserved greater respect. I did not wish to argue about matters of which he in his fancy armour had no knowledge at all. What fighting had he ever seen, anyway, apart from spearing a few of the plebs of Rome when they rioted before the Emperor because the amphitheatre games had been cancelled? That sort of fighting I could have done with my household slaves armed with clubs.

In line, we put our mounts at a gap in the broken gateway and came through into an enclosure, partly of cleared, beaten earth and partly rank with vegetation. On the far side, throwing its shadow across us, was the tall grove of trees I had seen standing up at a distance: they must have been a re-growth as we had cut down so many sixty years ago.

Close to the circling rampart by the gateway were two small, round huts such as the *Britanni* live in. The huts looked poorly built; walls were sagging outward and in places were just a mesh of broken wattle plugged with mud. The thatch of the roofs was black with mould. Smoke filtered through holes in one roof, snatched away in grey flurries by the breeze. Beside the huts, I saw that a narrow opening in the rampart had been hacked away, with a bridge made of tree trunks crossing the outer ditch. An ass was tethered to a post by the door of the nearer of the huts. Some ragged children, who had been playing outside, were now frozen in line, watching with wide eyes the foremost Praetorian, bearing the imperial standard, as his black horse entered the clearing, the rest of our party, in a bunch of horse, close behind.

Hadrian, together with the standard bearer and the *praefectus*, came up to the huts at a canter, their horses'hooves slipping on a sheen of mud where the ass was tied, causing the terrified animal to let out a loud braying and pull at its rope. At this, the *praefectus's* horse reared up, so he almost fell. I chuckled inwardly at the sight, my face still taut with anger. The line of children instantly broke up. They fled inside the huts, except for one who disappeared through the opening in the rampart and across the bridge, taking a last frantic look behind him as if we had ridden out of Hades itself.

Emerging from the far hut, the one from which the smoke rose, came a man and a woman, the first clearly very old because he was bent almost double and leaning on a stick, and the second, most probably elderly too, but I could not properly tell as she was wrapped in a brown woollen cloak, with a hood pulled so tight about her face that only a small, white oval showed.

The woman did not look overawed by the panoply before her, although she must have realised it was a delegation of importance, for the armoured soldiers and the banner told her so. She would have had no idea, however, she was addressing the Emperor of Rome. She spoke something in a high foreign tongue, with some Latin words amongst it, so I was sure she could have made herself understood directly if she had been pressed. I, who know a little of the *Iceni* language, could not make sense of what she said (the Latin she threw in did not help either as it seemed out of context with the rest), other than for the one *Iceni* word 'horses' – '*capailg*' – which is the term Myru often used with me in my stables.

Hadrian turned in his saddle and beckoned for Myru. She trotted up on Ajax, her small figure leaning forward to hear the woman better, who was shriller now and more voluble. At last, Myru, raising her hand to cut off the woman's flow, turned back to us. I made sure she addressed Hadrian directly and not the whole of our waiting group. I could hear, however, "Caesar, the woman says this place is her home, as it was her father's home:

her father is the old man. She asks, why do we come with our horses like riders who wish to do them harm? She has paid her taxes and they are free people allowed to live here and to farm the land below the rampart at this point to a distance of five hundred paces. The boundary is marked with stones. The records can be found in the town basilica, she says."

"And who are the children?" Hadrian asked. Some heads had appeared again in the doorways to the huts, pushing round the leather screens that hung over the entrances.

Myru asked the woman who answered, flapping her hands at her side to bring the children out to her. They gathered around her, all but the one boy who had disappeared through the rampart.

"Caesar, they are the children of her daughter, who has had to go to Duroliponte to work."

Hadrian turned, seeking out his secretary, "Valerius, find some money for this woman: a single *denarius* will suffice. Tell her we wish to look around here but we shall not disturb her further." And then he turned back to Myru, "Ask her if she knows what happened here – or perhaps the old man – in the fighting years ago."

I saw the woman's face when that last question was put to her. It turned from one of passive acceptance, of curiosity even, to fear. Now why should that be? I wondered, although I of all people knew what had been done here in the past.

"She knows this was a place where bad things happened," reported Myru. I wondered how much Myru might not translate. Myru was a slave but an *Iceni* first: she would not wish to speak ill of her people.

"What does the old man have to say?" asked Hadrian. He turned towards me. "He looks even older than you, Celer. He may have been living at the time of the war."

Myru put a stream of the *Iceni* tongue to both of them, and the man, whose gaze because of his bent back had been on the ground, now straightened himself as well as he could and looked directly up at us. His eyes, I saw, despite his age, were the sharp blue that many *Iceni* possessed. He wore a beard, plaited into a point, and the hair on his head, still thick, was white. He spoke now for the first time, and the gist of what he said, as translated by Myru, was as follows -

"I was a boy at the time of the war, not yet in full manhood It is hard for me to remember exactly, but I can have been little more than thirteen years of age."

I thought, so he is younger than me, yet his body is more broken than mine.

"I lived in the centre of Icenia in a small place of a few huts, surrounded by a thorn fence. We worked the land. It was heavy work on poor sandy soil. We kept pigs in the woods and sold their meat at market. When the war came, many men from our settlement, and others nearby, went off to fight. Some returned with terrible wounds: most did not return. When we learnt the Queen herself was to fight a battle that would bring victory at last, I joined the people who were going to the place where it was to be fought. My brother and I walked for two days: my parents drove a cart pulled by two bullocks, my small sister with them – she was about five. They placed their cart with others by a pool and a stream. There they were killed when our army was defeated: they were killed by Roman soldiers, my sister too. I was later told she had been speared right through like a wild pig. The Romans threw the dead into the water and burnt everything else. I escaped, although the group I was with were hunted all night."

"I saw the Queen. She rode in a chariot, with her two daughters beside her, all three brandishing spears. The Queen wore a cloak dyed in a patchwork of colours. I can see her now – as plainly as you stand before me. She had a mass of hair about her face, bright red in colour, and she stood up strongly, although her body was quite small. The daughters were red-haired too: they were dressed like men for the battle in leather tunics and breeches. I can see them clearly. They stepped down from the Queen's chariot to run beside it, holding their spears by their sides, as if they were hunting deer in the forest."

"The Queen was terrible to look upon in her anger. She had the courage and the strength of many men. She led the warriors from her own household into battle. How she escaped the Romans I do not know, and where and how she died I do not know either. Some say she still lives – or waits again for the call – but that is foolish talk, for she will have been long under the earth. Where that place may be, I have not heard. Perhaps there is no one left now who remembers. I may be the last of the *Iceni* alive who fought in that war."

Hadrian, and the men around him, listened to this story: I could see they were impressed by it. Their eyes never left the old man as Myru translated. When she had finished, Hadrian took off a bronze band that he wore about his right wrist, and handed it to his secretary who was dismounted, and by him to the story-teller, saying, "Keep this, old man, in remembrance of what has been and for the help you have given us."

The man bent his head even lower to the ground than it had been before. I doubt if he knew what Hadrian had said, and Myru did not translate. He must have understood its significance, however, for he took the band and placed it in the folds of his tunic over his heart. I knew the *Iceni* did that for things they valued, in the same way as they would place them in the ground to lie within the heart of their god, Camos, who sleeps below the surface of the earth: the rise and fall of the land make the shape of his body, the streams and rivers his blood, the forests his hair.

"Do you know where the last great battle was fought?" Hadrian asked. "Was it near here?" Myru translated and remained in conversation for some time while we waited on our horses, with the children now playing amongst us and the woman squatting back on her heels.

I could sense Hadrian becoming impatient. "Myru," I broke in. "What does he say? We have much to do."

She turned Ajax to us and addressed the Emperor.

"Caesar, he says he knows the sites of two battles, the one that begun the war and the one that ended it: they both took place nearby. He will show us. I have told him he will be rewarded. Have I done right?"

Hadrian looked across at me and smiled. "Our search is over," he said, "almost as soon as it has started. We have found this elderly Janus who looks both ways – into the past and into the present. He has a memory as clear as yours, Celer, and he will find for us what we seek."

I was a little piqued by that. Had I not lead Hadrian here? But I replied diplomatically, "The gods have indeed come to our aid."

First, though, we rode into the grove that occupied the upper area of the enclosure, furthest from the gateway. Straightaway, I could see why the woman had looked scared when we had told her the reason for our visit. I remembered the hideous, shrivelled parts of our soldiers that had dangled amongst the trees, and the skulls lined up in small clearings like sea-washed boulders with which you might border a path.

It was clear the place was still used for rites of some sort or other, although the *Iceni* practices had been proscribed at the end of the war upon pain of death. There were no human bones or skulls, but there were the parts of animals laid beneath the trees, and a cow's head or two hanging in the crooks of branches. Wooden troughs, still holding stalks of wheat and once probably filled with milk, were placed out in one clearing that had been cleared of vegetation. Everywhere else, though, was very overgrown.

There was only one path in amongst the trees, running between fallen, moss-covered trunks and dense branches covered by ivy and brambles. Hadrian and I alone followed that path to the inner clearing. Within minutes, he looked as anxious as me to get out again. I felt I was suffocating. The air was dry and seemed to fill my throat, so that I choked and coughed. There was scarcely space to turn our horses. When we emerged, I could see the relief on the *praefectus's* face. Hadrian said nothing, and neither did I. Everything had already been said.

Why I wondered had this woman and her father come to live here? I put the question to them, through Myru. The woman was feeding the ass and twisting a rope harness about its head. Perhaps she was going to ride it into the town to tell of the things that had happened today. The man leant on his stick beside her. Once again, Myru, who now seemed strangely subdued, put my questions and gave back the answers.

"The man says he had nowhere to live. All the land of Icenia was torn apart and scorched with fire. There was no food anywhere apart from in these border lands. Here, you could just about live. He said he wanted to be near the place where his family had been killed. That's why he came back here and struggled for years to provide for himself. In time, he was able to take a woman and have children. He has grown old here and the old ways too have stayed with him."

"Who places the offerings amongst the trees?" I asked.

"He says he does not know. It is not he, or the woman. Some men come occasionally, and they still make sacrifice."

I did not know how true any of that was. I think the old man knew rather more than he said. Perhaps he still lived in those old, dark ways. I thought, if anyone looked like the picture of the Druids handed down to us by the poets, it was he.

163

XIII

The old man's name was Catrig – in Latin we might spell that Catricus: it means something like 'one born in love'. Well, like me, it was a long time ago since he had come into the world, in love or otherwise. He was too old to sit one of our horses, although he might have ridden the ass that the woman was preparing to ride. He was eager to be our guide, however, once we had told him of our plans, and the Emperor ordered one of the Praetorians to take the ass from the woman. She, however, let out such a wail, rolling on the ground, with the children, thinking this was a game, rolling with her too, that Roman mercy intervened. I think she may have thought both the ass and her father would be going forever, and nothing Myru could tell her would stop her hysterics. It was my idea to have him ride Ajax with Myru: the pony was strong enough for both; after all, the breed had carried we of *equites Albani* in full armour. I was sure the two would have much to share together, and translation would be more immediate.

"So let it be done," said Hadrian, dismissing the matter with a wave of an arm. Seeing the ass being returned, the woman stopped her wailing at once and rose to her feet, slapping out angrily at the children who had not thought the game over.

Myru had Catrig mounted before her on Ajax's neck: her own body kept his frail, bent form there, which a puff of wind or a stumble might otherwise have cast away. I knew she was used to riding like this; sometimes I had seen her giving my stable boys rides in this way: she had even ridden with one before and one behind her, although, when I had been watching, the one at the rear had tumbled off, fortunately onto soft earth, lying there winded but laughing.

We rode from the fort to the wooded ridge crossed by the road that we had been following yesterday. I had been sure then this was the site of Cerialis's defeat, the place I had come to with a half century of the VIIIIth at the end of the war, although the battle had been spread out along a mile or so of the wooded track that was now a metalled road. Myru, with Catrig's white head bent forward before her like a bearded centaur, led the way by narrow paths between the trees as we climbed the slope to the ridge. The *praefectus* looked worried again, and made his men deploy in a ring about us, their horses crashing amongst the undergrowth and the riders crouching low in their saddles beneath the branches. Soldiers do not like wooded country, as I knew from my long experience with the legions. Rome had had too many disasters – both large and small – by getting into situations such as the one we were in now. It would not be good to lose the Emperor to some madman's bowshot or to the swing of the axe of some deranged outlaw rushing out of cover.

I had thought Catrig's age and infirmity might have meant he was no longer the best and most astute of guides. But I was wrong, as from the start he showed himself certain of every track and every path we were following. This was a wonder to me, for I would have thought it was some time since he had last traversed these woods. Ajax, leading us on a path still thick with last autumn's leaves, but bordered with long, fresh green grass, was suddenly halted. I saw Catrig pointing into the trees to our left, which grew more thinly here in a hollow that was damp with moss and fern. Myru wheeled Ajax into the hollow, and Hadrian and I followed while the others hung back. Myru gave me Ajax's reins to hold and in one quick movement leapt from the pony, leaving Catrig perched there, both his scrawny arms about the pony's neck.

She looked up at Hadrian and me. Behind us was the Emperor's standard bearer, his pole raised now in this open space away from the twigs and branches that had clawed at his precious fabric. Horses' hooves crashed and squelched on leaves and dead bracken, beneath which the ground lay wet and muddy. Overhead, a song bird sang sweetly, and sailing high across a patch of blue sky I spied a flight of black ravens soaring and weaving in the rushing air.

"Catrig says," reported Myru, "that this is the particular area where he and others have gathered many bones and other debris from the battle, and placed them here so that they may one day be recovered and revered. They have done this over many years. The woods cover the ground now more thickly, and only a little is found these days. You must dig it out from beneath the trees, which he doesn't like to do. He feels that what is beneath the soil is safe and at peace, but the bones that have the daylight upon them still need to find their rest."

"Where are these bones?" asked Hadrian sharply. He was leaning forward in his saddle, his bearded face catching the rays of sunlight filtering through the tree tops. I had felt so familiar riding beside him that for a moment I was brought up with a sense of shock, realising, as if I had not known it before, that it was the Emperor of Rome who accompanied me. The confidences Hadrian had shared with me now seemed very remote. In this space in the woods, reality suddenly rushed at me. The imperial standard was catching a breath of the wind, stirring its folds, and the eagle it bore seemed to stretch its wings and its great hooked beak to open.

Catrig was helped to dismount by Myru. He stood, doubled up at first, his thin body like a bent stick hung with a coarse grey tunic, and with a black leather cape about his shoulders such as labourers wear. Then he straightened himself as well as he could: I could almost hear the links of his spine grinding as he did so and I could sense his pain. No, the man could not have come here for a very long time. Without help, such as we had given him, he could scarcely walk at all.

He was turning his head from right to left as an animal might do sensing the air, and then he seemed to find what he sought, for he took several, stumbling steps away from where we sat watching him on our horses towards the centre of the hollow. It was very wet here: I could see his rounded wooden shoes squelching in the thick grass, water splashing up about the toes. He stopped by the stump of a tree that, by the look of it, had been felled, or had fallen, a long time ago. The top of the stump was about four feet from the ground. Across it lay a mass of cut branches, which he began to pull away with difficulty, for some were thick and long.

I said to Myru by my side, "Help him," and she moved at once to Catrig's side, her lithe body with its long dark hair and tanned legs like some consort of horned Faunus bestriding the sun-dappled woods. I had never really appreciated before how lovely she was.

When the branches were removed, a plank of wood was revealed that may, I think, have been an old door. It was black and dripping with slime and mould. Catrig and Myru tipped it back, so it lay at an angle against the stump. And now Catrig, with his thin, pale arms, was reaching over the edge of the stump, his beard brushing against the top, and I realised that it was hollow and held something inside. In moments he had fetched out from the interior two bones, which he held up, one in each hand. They were large bones, unmistakably from a man's thighs.

I looked across at Hadrian and I could see his face had gone very white. Sensing the sudden tensing of his body, his horse began to prance, kicking out its back legs, and emitting a long-drawn out squeal like a human cry, a sound I had scarcely ever heard a horse make before: it made me shudder and the hairs stand up on my arms. I could see the other horses around were similarly affected, with their riders pulling at their bridles and cursing to get them back under control. Even, Myru's Ajax, trained from birth by her, tried to shy away, almost pulling me from my saddle as I hung on to the reins. A Praetorian fortunately was close enough to me to come to my aid.

"Enough!" cried out Hadrian in a furious voice. The *praefectus* was at his side in an instant. "Get the contents of that place emptied out! Cordon the area off. This shall be done now by our soldiers with dignity. We shall wait for the task to be completed…." – I whispered the necessary information in his ear – "….on the road nearby where we will camp and rest."

I must be fair to the *praefectus* of the Praetorians. I did not like him, and he may, or may not, have been skilful and brave in war as well as a golden boy on the parade ground, but he knew how to organise things – and quickly too. How he managed to obtain a large oak box, stained a deep brown, with a bronze lock at its front and bronze decorations at its corners, and have it brought to that miserable spot, while the Emperor waited on the highway nearby – only some three hundred paces away – I do not know. Perhaps he had the ears and eyes of the gods and could conjure things out of thin air, but the box on the back of a mule, with slaves attendant, arrived little more than an hour after we had set out our folding chairs on the road's stone surface. Our horses were tethered to trees at the edge of the woods, all except Ajax who stood like a very large, patient dog beside Myru on the road. We admittedly created an inconvenient block for travellers, but those that did approach us – on foot and in carriages – were probably happy enough, when they learnt of the Emperor's presence, to be halted and told they could go no further for the time being. I saw some in the direction of Duroliponte gathered behind a screen of Praetorians trying to make out the Emperor and his party two hundred or so paces distant. Amongst them were some cattle lowing miserably, their sound disturbing Hadrian, so he ordered them to be allowed to pass through, their drivers bobbing their heads in fear as they drove their animals on with sticks.

Seeing Hadrian's secretary, Valerius, scribbling at his tablets once more, I thought this will be another incident to be added to that potted biography of his. Some emperors, I think – like Domitianus who had both a raging temper and a fierce appetite – would have had the cows slaughtered and butchered there and then to provide us with something to eat. As it was we had very little with us, other than for some cold meat and rough local bread, and some coarse wine with little water to dilute it. Hadrian, though, his colour returned and now in better humour, seemed to be enjoying this impromptu meal in the open air. However, when the Praetorian searchers in the woods returned eventually with their burden – the wooden box now covered with a crimson cloth bearing the eagle of Rome and, beneath, the letters S.P.Q.R – then his mood changed once more. He became sombre and frowning, the crease lines of his forehead deep like the furrows of a field.

The box was borne by slaves, their green tunics, bare legs and sandals besmirched with mud from the hollow where the bones had been recovered. It was set down in the centre of the road and Hadrian went up to it, signalling to me and to Myru, who had been helping Catrig find a resting place against the grassy bank of the road, to attend him there. Also present was the *praefectus* and a guard of three Praetorians, now remounted on their black horses, as well as secretary, Valerius.

Hadrian commanded that the box be opened. Valerius, did this, first carefully folding the cloth covering and tucking it beneath one arm, then raising the lid with the other. I saw many bones of differing shapes and sizes, jumbled on the surface and jutting down into the depths of the box, some yellow, some white, some a darkish brown, of differing sizes and shapes – a hip joint perhaps, a broken rib, a chin still with teeth attached, leg bones, arm bones, some with cut marks on them, the dome of a skull. The box was deep. It was filled with the many bones of men who had fought and died for Rome. I did not wish to look any more. I saw a black beetle crawling on one long bone and I felt a wave of sickness in my stomach.

Hadrian, I thought, also looked unwell. There was perspiration on his brow. He ordered the box to be closed and sealed, which was done while we turned away to watch one of the *praefectus's* men unrolling a large bundle of green cloth – the colour of the slaves' livery, which it had clearly been intended for. Wrapped within its folds were pieces of broken armour – curved strips from breastplates, some still hinged together; more strips from shoulder protectors; an almost complete groin guard; the rim of a helmet; the domed top of another helmet cleaved by some mighty blow; many silvered buckles; a decorative plate from a belt; hooks, bolts, and locks; several javelin heads; a large spear head which must have been *Iceni*; and the broken blade of a sword – they all came tumbling out of the cloth, many tarnished green, or orange with rust. There were also two much-decayed leather boots, part of a leather panel cut from a tent, the hempen carrying strap of a pack, a broken cooking pot, the wooden hub of a wheel, and several other nameless, rotting objects of wood and leather and cloth.

"There is much more out there, Caesar," said the *praefectus*. "We could only take away the first of what we saw. The rest has been covered with earth."

"Not men's bones?" Hadrian asked sharply.

"No, Caesar. We have brought all those from within the tree stump. The other relics were in a heap nearby."

"We shall give everything honourable remembrance," Hadrian said in a low voice that I was only just able to hear. He looked around him, and, seeing Catrig and Myru, seated by the ditch, he strode over abruptly to them. Myru jumped to her feet, but Catrig was still struggling to raise himself.

"No matter, no matter," said Hadrian, indicating with his hand that Catrig's struggles should cease.

"Ask him," Hadrian commanded Myru. "for what purpose these remains were gathered here and not taken to the local authorities for rightful disposal?"

Myru put the question to Catrig, who I could see, as I came up to the group with the *praefectus* beside me, was shuffling and twisting on the grassy bank looking most uncomfortable. I thought he should rise, and I offered him my hand. He pulled himself up, bent as usual, and spoke fast to Myru in his native tongue.

"Some bones and debris were taken into Ikelorum, but the town council were not interested in them. They had them put in the rubbish pits outside the town." I saw Hadrian's face taughten and the muscles in his jaw ripple. Myru continued, "After that, Catrig thought it best to keep everything where it was found. Once he was active doing this, but now that he has grown old and infirm he can do it no more."

"What was his purpose?" barked Hadrian. He stood with his legs apart on the dusty road surface, his hands on his hips. I could swear the *praefectus* had his sword an inch from its scabbard, awaiting the order that would dispose of this decrepit *Britannus* who had insulted Rome.

Catrig's voice became high and appealing. He crossed his arms before his face in a way I knew with these people meant, 'Be merciful'.

"He says," Myru reported – she looked tense herself and I wondered if she was embellishing her translation to protect Catrig – "that he, and other *Iceni* in these parts, respect these remains – *in particular*" (she stressed these words, probably on her own initiative) "because some will be of their fighters as well as the Roman soldiers, *however wrong their cause*." (again, the last emphasis was her invention, I felt sure).

What she reported Catrig as saying, I knew was true. I had been here with the VIIIIth six months after the massacre and had seen legs and arms and trunks of *Iceni* dead still rotting amongst our own, although most of their fallen they had borne away. So there was good reason to think that some of the contents of the great box, now lashed onto the back of a mule – too heavy, I thought for the poor animal's tottering legs – were of *Iceni* dead as well as Roman.

I did not tell the Emperor this, however. He ordered the Praetorians to march on foot beside the over-burdened mule as we left that miserable place, their horses led at the rear by slaves. Catrig, reprieved perhaps by Myru's quick thinking, was back with her on Ajax, slumped forward on the pony's neck and in danger of rolling off. Myru, I thought, looked exhausted. I felt little sympathy for the bearded Catrig. I suspected he – and perhaps others – might have had a greater use for those bones than he would ever say. We would never know.

As we came out of the woods on the road to Civitas Ikelorum once more, Myru trotted Ajax up beside my horse. Catrig before her was now upright again – as upright, that was, as he would ever be. He was pointing wildly over the landscape that fell away to our right from the low ridge we were following. To my extreme right, I saw the clump of trees topping the knoll with its sacred grove that we had visited, and to its left a broad plain stretching away from the twisting ribbon of light that was the river flowing to Ikelorum. In the distance, to the left, was another line of hills, alternately grey with shadows from a clouded sky, then lightening brightly as the sun reappeared, so that the hill flanks shone a sudden brilliant green, their upper slopes lined with the much darker green of woods. I could see one place where the whole distant ridge of hills, despite the sun, disappeared into shadow. In front was open, flat heathland, broken in places by small squares of fields. Far, far away at the very edge of my vision, came silvered flashes of light which could only be from the sun striking on water.

I rode up to Hadrian. "Catrig says he can show the place where the great battle was fought. See, Caesar, he is pointing."

Hadrian turned his horse, and, shading his eyes with his hand, looked out into the distance following the direction of Catrig's wavering arm.

"That is good," the Emperor said. "We will ride there in the morning."

XIV

The White Way – the *Via Alba* that for centuries had been the main route into Icenia out of the west – ran across the plain where we rode, its main course principally straight but with many side tracks branching from it, winding a small distance away, then joining again, so that from a distance their routes looked like the twisting, white veins of a massive arm flung out across the green earth. Most roads constructed by the Romans since their first conquest of Britannia ran broadly south to north, or north-west, metalled routes to allow the soldiers and their supplies to reach the fighting fronts as quickly as possible. Icenia, a client kingdom to the east, surrounded by marshland and the sea, had been largely left alone by Rome at that time in the early years of conquest. It was still served by its own local routes, trampled out of the soft white rock by generation after generation of travellers – traders, pedlars, artisans, metal-workers, drovers with their animals, and occasionally a speeding war band of horse and chariot. The most important of those routes was the *Via Alba* that crossed this flat country, leaving the lands of the *Catuvellauni* at the border river and passing beneath a swelling sea of low, grey-green hills to enter the *Iceni* kingdom at a place where many gleaming, white quarry pits scarred the hillsides around, forming a type of gateway, given by Rome the name of *Portas Album*.

Hadrian was rested and in fine, energetic form this morning. The *mansio* had been as quiet last night as any place with scores of snoring, waking, quarreling, window-slamming, copulating, defecating human beings – and their animals doing many of the same things – could ever be. The Emperor may have slept well, but I had had a poor night, twisting on my hard low bed until the square window that opened to the roof eaves had changed from black to grey, and then to white, with fat pigeons perched somewhere nearby cooing to welcome the new day. I rose irritatedly and threw a small pottery lamp out through the window, hearing it clatter against the tiles. The cooing ceased.

The noise brought my *Germani* slaves into me, and so I was washed and shaved, longing for a hot bath to sweat the grime and the tiredness out of me but knowing the bath house was in a wing on the far side of the outer court and that Hadrian had probably appropriated it for himself. I felt sure the Emperor's slaves would not turn me away if I turned up with my coarse towel and jar of oil and old rusting strigil – indeed Hadrian himself would very likely make me most welcome and give me his best attendants to knead and scrape my parchment skin – but I could not face the effort and the performance. I ordered a first meal of bread and cheese and figs, washed down with a hot bowl of thin chicken broth. I could not drink wine or cold water so early in the day.

After that, I felt a little better, and, finding Myru on the stairs, descended with her to the stables. There we saw that Catrig, who had slept in the straw with Ajax, was up and about and exchanging quips in a jabbering *Britanni* dialect with the grooms, who were hard at work on their masters' horses. The chatter and the laughter were cut off suddenly as they saw me enter. Catrig seemed quite at home here, seated doubled-up on a sack of straw, his face low to a wooden bowl, the contents of which he was sucking up through his beard and his broken teeth.

In one swift movement, Myru mounted Ajax and brought him out into the yard, checking his legs for any sign of injury – but there was none. It wasn't long before our party began to assemble: it was of much the same size and composition as yesterday, perhaps a few more mules bearing the supplies we might need and ten or so extra Praetorians: the *praefectus* would probably rather have his men with him than idling away at the *mansio*, trying to climb onto the cleaning maids.

I did not know where Hadrian had had the great box placed that we had filled so reverently yesterday, but I imagined the Praetorians would be mounting a continuous guard over it: if anything was going to anger Hadrian now, I knew it would be someone not showing the decreed level of respect, perhaps out of ignorance or carelessness. He had said to me last night when I had had the great privilege of a couch next to him at our dinner, "Celer, we are going to give the fullest honour to those men whose bones we recovered: they have been neglected for far too long. They will be interred in a special place we shall have built, in a ceremony with every rite of remembrance. The legions of Britannia will attend."

"How will that be done, Caesar? In what place? And when?" I asked these questions with genuine interest, but perhaps the questions were too many strung together. Perhaps as well my voice had held a tone that made him think I was querying the need for such commemoration. For a moment, he looked quite annoyed.

"We do not know yet, Celer, but that is what we wish. And it will be done – whatever you, or anyone else, may think."

"Caesar, I apologise…I did not mean…." I was horrified, seeing other eyes on me, including those of the *praefectus*. I was troubled. How could the Emperor, after all we had said and shared together, doubt my total loyalty to him? But then, once again – as had happened before – after a few short seconds my dismay was replaced by relief. I had not yet learnt – but I was learning fast – that this was the way of things when you lived so close to power, when your rulers seemed to ape the gods in their capriciousness. That's why all these courtiers and hangers-on went around with acid in their stomachs. Much as I had enjoyed – was enjoying – being at the centre of the Emperor's current obsessions, I realised I was only the subject of one hour, and that the Emperor's attentions would move on and I would likely soon be forgotten. It would be a relief to me anyhow, I decided, when the time came for me to return to my quiet home with its mulberry tree and the dark waters flowing near, and Senuna's shade to meet me at my door.

Hadrian had made an expansive gesture of his hand. "Forgive me, Celer" – his reversion to the first person had been immediately comforting – "I do not doubt your loyalty in these matters, you who have been loyal to Rome all your life. Come" – he clapped his hands making his steward jump – "Bring more wine for my good friend, Gaius Modius Celer, veteran of the VIIIIth, who has looked upon the face of the mad queen herself. What was her name, Celer? – it escapes me at this moment."

I thought, he has drunk more than usual. "Boudica, Caesar – Bodig in the local tongue. And, I only think I *may* have seen her, I am not sure. Do you remember, Caesar, when I told the story? – it was just a glimpse of a face that I had."

"You *saw* her, Celer, of that I am sure." He raised his silver goblet so that it sparkled in the light of the many lamps. "And you know, I think you will see her again."

The last comment, of course, was nonsense. Wine can get into the head of all men, even an Emperor. I did not think any more of it. I was simply glad to find I was still in favour. Even the *praefectus's* face had relaxed: he had rolled onto his other side and was slyly stroking the thigh of someone else's wife.

We rode hard that next morning, leaving the baggage mules trailing far behind. Hadrian's energy was transmitted to his horse, and we all followed him at a gallop through grassy, open fields. My riding skills had returned. I no longer felt an old pained man who had to be lifted onto his horse's back, but in co-ordination with the animal now, as I had been when much younger. I seemed to flow with the horse's movement, the breeze streaming through my thin hair, my sweat drying cold upon me. Despite my tiredness and stinging wind-seared eyes, I felt fitter than I had been for a long time.

And so we came to *Portas Album*, having ridden partly on tracks, partly on a paved road, and partly across open ground. Catrig, once more astride Ajax with Myru, miraculously had shown us the way, with only the occasional halt and a sideways cast of his head as if to scent the right direction. How did he know this, I wondered, in a landscape that might well have changed in detail since he was last here? – a fast-spreading copse here, a new fence line there, a house recently built with its back to trees, fresh tracks and paths, a heath burnt black by fire last summer. Like many things that were beyond clear reason, Catrig's abilities, had he been still a young man, would have been surprising – as an old man, they were astonishing. I had read that Druids kept the world's knowledge in their heads with nothing written down. But, no, I could not really believe Catrig was one of that priestly caste. From what I had read, you were born into the Druids and you died as one of them. Catrig had told us of his origins – how as a boy he had come to this battlefield towards which we were now journeying, probably by exactly this same route. The experience for him must have been so engrained in his mind that he could yet recall every detail.

The plain stretched ahead of us – the plain that I knew now was the one the historian Tacitus had written about in his battle scene. We crossed the river by a high wooden bridge that the Romans had built, its central pier set on a small island between two fast-flowing streams. The barges coming up the river to Ikelorum were halted here to take on tow ropes so they could be hauled past the bridge by oxen. Ahead of us, flat heathland stretched away, an open place of long grasses, studded with gorse bushes and small clumps of stunted trees. Here and there could be seen the bowl-shapes of old burial mounds.

As we advanced further, the line of hills to our left took greater form, so I could see the swell of the land there, falling away in places into broad hollows, dark with shadows, the rolling folds looking as if they had been carved and smoothed by some giant master sculptor. Bands of dense vegetation were spread upon the upper slopes and deep into the gullies, although the hillsides themselves appeared mainly open grassland, untouched by plough or spade. Along the crest of these hills ran a dark line of trees, showing their flat summits were covered by thick woodland.

We halted to allow the mules to catch up, and I saw to the far right of my vision, forward of the tree line, another of those knolls characteristic of this country: it stood, crowned by trees, at a greater height than its connecting ridge – a most distinctive feature. Catrig, who had dismounted for a piss, was talking with Myru, and she, jabbing her heels into Ajax's ribs, rode forward, past the *praefectus's* protecting arm, to Hadrian's side. He had been surveying the landscape with a hand held up to his eyes against the bright sunlight, and had been about to speak to the *praefectus*. Instead he turned to her. "Well", I heard him say. "do you have news for us?" She answered, "*Domine*, this is the place. That is what the old man has just told me."

We all turned now to Catrig, who had just lowered his tunic, and who, seeing our eyes on him, made himself as straight as he could and begun stabbing with his fingers towards the knoll on the ridge. Amongst the words of the *Iceni* language he was shouting out in a high excited voice, I could make out some of our own – *pugna* and *bellum*, for instance – and most significantly *locus proelium* – place of battle.

So this was where it had happened! – that battle which had saved Britannia for Rome in a distant war. Although I had heard the accounts of soldiers who had fought here, I had never seen the site until now.

We left the *Via Alba* and rode through the dry heath scrub towards the ridge. Ever so often, Hadrian would halt and call Catrig (now remounted with Myru) to his side. I hastened to stay beside them, as did the *praefectus* and his Guard, with outriders at a distance, perhaps suddenly fearful of this wide, open place. And indeed I sensed too a tightening of my nerves, a feeling of unease – scarcely surprising, for here the ghosts of some eighty thousand who had fought and died still stood upon the plain.

Now we were closer, the hillsides before us had come into much greater focus. We stopped often as Catrig began further long discourses that Myru hastened to translate, she being interrupted frequently by Hadrian's questions, occasionally as well by my own – all this to the accompaniment of much waving about of Catrig's skinny arms. So it would be best if I summarise straightaway the essence of what Catrig told us -

The army of the *Iceni* with their *Trinovantes* allies were drawn up in huge numbers on the plain where we rode – on the very ground where our horses now planted their hooves, there had passed many brave bands of mounted warriors, with pennants flying from their spears, some wearing captured Roman armour. Chariots, pulled by frantic ponies, had rushed about them, swerving and turning, with warriors from the royal households standing up tall on their shaking carts to inspect the Roman positions on the ridge ahead, while their steersmen lashed at the ponies' backs. Further back, behind us as we rode towards the hills, had stood the great mass of the rebel infantry, throng after throng of them densely packed together, not in regular formations as the Romans used, but drawn up by household and territory in rough rectangles, squares, circles and ovals of heaving, shouting men, with horse amongst them too, merging with each other, holding aloft spears and lances, pitchforks, long-bladed scythes, all manner of implements brought from homestead and farm, now turned into weapons for battle – and above them, banners of red, white, green, and black cloth streaming out, the air filled with a cacophony of sound, of trumpet and horn, carnyx, and dead beating drums. Further to the rear, behind the last scattered rank of this infantry, lay the rebels' camp, formed of many tents of skins and cloths, some low to the ground, others, those of chieftains, standing tall, tied by ropes to carts and wagons, which, with the horses and oxen that had drawn them, made a wall here of wood and flesh – and behind that wall, the black sluggish waters of lagoon and marsh stretching away. Thick coils of smoke rose against the sky from many cooking fires and the forges of the smiths and armourers who had travelled with Queen Bodig's army.

Waiting on the hills, looking down upon these tens and tens of thousands of men – and women, and children too, who had come with the wagons to watch the battle that would set them free – stood the Roman Army.

At this point I can supplement Catrig's account by what I had learnt myself of the dispositions of the Roman Army -

The Roman army of Suetonius Paullinus lined the ridge top, their ranks spread out evenly against the dark trees behind – from the high knoll to the right (as we looked at the hills) where squadrons of cavalry were gathered on the smooth, grassy slopes, across a great hollow where the hills curved inwards, up to a long, sloping ridge on the left that projected outwards onto the plain. Orders sounded out from *tuba* and *cornu*. A wooden semaphore clattered out messages with blocks of wood that moved its signalling arms. Its message was relayed by another signal post further along the hills to the south. In open areas of the wooded land beyond the hill tops, the Romans

176

had laid out their camp. Here, a few reinforcements, mainly of cavalry, awaited their orders. Here were the meagre stores of food and fodder, of weapons and ammunition – ballista bolts, javelin heads, arrows, and sling stones – and their few carts and mules. Here also, the surgeon and his small team awaited the casualties of battle. Had the Roman lost the battle, this camp would soon have been overrun

Had the Romans been defeated, they would also have lost the province. Such a disaster would have been one of the worst that Rome had ever suffered, as bad as the three legions destroyed in the forests of Germania – the *clades Variana* – during the reign of the divine Augustus Caesar.

XV

When at last we of the Emperor Hadrian's party stood at the foot of the ridge, Catrig then guided us to various locations on the battlefield that he had known at the time, or had visited since. He had taken part in the battle as a boy, not even yet a young man. He had been given a coat of stiff leather to wear, far too big for him – it would turn the Romans' swords, he had been told, and their arrows would bounce from it – but he had been bare-legged, and bare-footed too. He had been at the rear of the *Iceni* infantry raised by the chieftain of his district, which itself had been towards the back of the general advance against the Roman lines. When the advance failed and was pushed back, he was so crushed against the others around him that he nearly suffocated. As he was small and nimble he was able to squeeze through gaps, and over the bodies of those that had fallen.

He saw little of the battle – remembered little of it – other than for the Romans in the hills waiting for the *Iceni* charge, and the crush of the dead and the dying afterwards, and then hiding amongst reeds, up to his waist in water, while the Roman cavalry searched for fugitives. He had got away only through the intervention of his gods, he said – although he did not state who those gods were. Later, when the war was over – as he had already told us – he returned to the area and visited the battlefields to try and understand what exactly had happened and how it was that the great army of Queen Bodig could have been defeated by so few Romans. So – extraordinary as this may seem – he had already considered much of what the Emperor was so eager to find out.

Despite his age and his decrepitude, he made a good guide. His few words of Latin did not amount to much, but we had Myru to translate the *Iceni* tongue he spoke in. I was surprised he had not learnt more of the Roman language in all these years. Sometimes – as I have already said – I did not think he was exactly what he had told us. But I was not going to question him too closely. If my Emperor was satisfied, with him, then who was I to think otherwise? We were both old men and would be going soon to whatever places our separate gods would make ready for us.

First, we mounted the right-hand knoll with its crest of trees. A number of goats were running wild here, stopping to stare at us as we thundered up the hill, then disappearing at a gallop, kicking up their feet behind them. There were some small fields on the far slopes, once cultivated but now lying overgrown. Catrig told us these fields had not been here at the time of the battle. Some *Catuvellauni* had subsequently tried to take this land, but they had been driven off. Who owned it now? I wondered. The question of ownership had not previously entered my mind. The heathland of the plain was untouched by the plough, but here on the hillsides the grass was suitable for grazing. I managed to get Hadrian's attention and asked him if he knew who had responsibility for this land. It was the Emperor's secretary, overhearing, who answered, "It is likely to be part of the *territorium* of Competum, which lies some five miles further along the *Via Alba*."

Hadrian considered this, then said to his secretary, "Valerius, make a note, will you, that we must discuss this matter not only with the council of Competum but with the centurion for the district – the *centurio regionarius*. It is he who must take charge of the commemoration – the *caerimonia commemorationis* – we have in mind. Where can he be found?"

"I shall find out, Caesar, and send for him to come to you."

Valerius I haven't described previously – the taker of notes, whom I imagined as a future biographer of the Emperor. He was a skinny young man whose cream-coloured tunic with its checked black borders, I suspected, was of the finest Egyptian cotton, and his riding breeches of the thinnest, softest leather obtainable, probably from Italia itself. I imagined he was from a high-born family, likely of the senatorial class, although I did not know his full name. He was now consulting one of the tablets dangling from his belt, and said in a squeaky voice: "The town of Competum has grown out of the vicus of a former fort there: it now has a prosperous market. The council, Caesar, has been seeking permission to build a *mansio* outside the town on the site of the fort."

"We shall grant it!" cried Hadrian, urging his horse into a sudden gallop which took him to the very top of the hill. Valerius and I followed rather more cautiously. "They shall help in another task too," Hadrian called out to us, dismounting and leading his horse into the shade cast by the trees growing here We dismounted also, as did Myru and Catrig coming up to the hill's summit at a more sedate trot.

Hadrian leant back against the steaming flank of his horse. "Under the *centurion regionarius's* direction, monuments will be erected to commemorate the battle." He clapped his hands together excitedly. "Rome shall provide the money, but the labour must be organised locally. Valerius, mark this matter for the Procurator's attention in Londinium. All will be arranged, all will be done. This will be a matter that we will follow from Rome with the very greatest of attention."

"But Caesar, will you not stay with us to see these things finished?" I asked, using all of my recently-learnt obsequiousness. "It will be hard for those given the task to fulfil it as you wish if you are not present to see that everything is completed correctly."

"Celer, you cannot imagine we could stay long enough for those tasks to be done. We have other provinces to visit, other regions to placate, other frontiers to inspect, many thousand details to attend to. The gods do not make our days long enough for all the works that must be achieved. But here in Britannia, we have no doubt everything will be set right."

He paused reflecting, cupping his bearded chin in one hand. "For it has to be so, in every detail, exactly as we have ordered, whether it is the great wall that must be built to the north and will bear our name, or the swamps that must be drained and the crops grown to feed our armies, or, here – a smaller matter perhaps, but one just as important – that proper honour be given to those soldiers who died here to save this province for Rome. If *not so...if not so...* then we... then we *will* return and kick every backside we find until these things are completed!"

He finished the sentence with what sounded an angry roar, freezing us in shock, but when he turned back to us we could see he was laughing.

"Do not fear, we have trust in you all," he said more softly. "We have to have. Yet, it is almost too much for one man to achieve."

He strode away and I saw him stop suddenly, looking down at the ground. He kicked at something there with a booted foot. It lay in a pile of loose earth by an animal burrow. We hastened to him, I and Valerius and old Catrig, whose eyes were closest to the ground and sharpest of all.

"What is it, Caesar?" I asked. But Catrig had fallen to his knees and was pulling out with his hands a short length of black metal that ended in a sharp wedged point. He brushed the earth from it with his fingers, and I helped him to rise to his feet, his back bent, holding out the object before him. Hadrian took it and held it up to his eyes.

"A bolt head from a *carroballista*," I said before the Emperor could speak.

"Quite so, Celer." Hadrian's eyes shone.

There was something about that one object which seemed to transfer the past to us and make it real. No amount of imagining by itself can bring back to us the sights and sounds of the past, but that one piece of metal, held flat on the palm, seemed to chase away the years and return to this place the horses and the armoured men, the flights of javelins and arrows, the desperation, the determination, the courage, the whole wheeling kaleidoscope of fearsome battle.

"Perhaps Paullinus had a *ballista* battery here," Hadrian said.

"Those mounds," I said, pointing to a ledge just below the scarp of the hill. "They could be where the *carroballistae* frames were dug in." I turned to Myru. "Ask Catrig if he knows."

"He says," she reported eventually, "that many of the *Iceni* ranks were struck down by missiles that hit them, not from above, but horizontally to the ground, like an iron rain swept by the wind. But he does not know where exactly that happened. The Legate, however, spent days fortifying his positions before the battle. The remains of his banks and trenches can still be seen."

"Let us move on," said Hadrian impatiently, remounting. More of the Praetorians were joining us now, their horse circling the knoll, the hooves thundering on the dry turf. The sound brought a tight feeling to my throat. It was one of the sounds of battle I recalled most vividly. I could almost see and hear again the fighting days of my youth, This place had been one vast killing ground.

We rode across the great, curving hollow which I had seen from afar filled by shadows. This had been at the centre of the Roman positions. The ground here had held the soldiers as tightly as if in a glove, cohort after cohort of legionaries and auxiliaries squatting here on the steep ground awaiting the battle, their flanks protected by the heights above them to right and left.

"When friend Tacitus wrote of our legions occupying a narrow place, was that here?" Hadrian asked out loud as he stood surveying the view over the hollow and then out over the flat plain in front, which had once been filled with the enemy. "I think it must have been. It would have meant the enemy mass would have been compressed here, crushed together while trying to get at us, which meant we could attack them from both flanks with our cavalry and artillery."

The *praefectus*, beside his Emperor once more, looked as if he was about to comment, but I forestalled him. What would he know of real battlefields?

181

"I think you are right, Caesar", I said. I pointed. "Look, over there, those are surely the remains of earthworks built to protect the right of the position."

We climbed a steep hill, our horses picking their way carefully on the ridged turf, but Ajax, with Myru and Catrig aboard, came up at a trot, such was the sure-footedness of my *Iceni* pony. No wonder, I reflected, that the *Iceni* mounted warriors and their charging chariots had been so deadly to us.

We inspected the long mound of an earthwork running a distance down the hill, with trenches dug beside it in a V shape, pointing outwards. Those trenches, I knew, would have been filled with pointed stakes.

"Paullinus did well," muttered Hadrian. "A classic defence, it seems, straight out of the manual. It was well for us that the Legate knew his business.

"He had many able officers with him," I put in, a little hesitant to interrupt the Emperor's reflections. "One was Julius Agricola, under whom I later served. He was a tribune on Paullinus's staff at this battle."

"Indeed, Celer You are correct. Our Army in Britannia – *exercitus Britannicus* – was experienced and hardened by many years of war. We were fortunate in that."

We rode on and came onto the gently sloping ridge that I had seen earlier projecting out into the plain. On its far side – a surprise to us for its position had not been clear from below – was a steep-sided valley, narrow towards its top but opening out onto the plain like a funnel.

I saw Myru was helping Catrig dismount, and he stood on the ridge top, bent like a hook, talking and gesticulating. "What does he say?" I asked as Hadrian rode up to hear.

"He says," Myru answered, signalling to Catrig to cease while she gave the translation, "that this was the place of the fiercest fighting of the battle. The *Iceni* charged against the Roman positions here. Catrig was in that charge, although he was at the very back of the *Iceni* army and never got further than the mouth of this valley."

Hadrian looked at me and I said, "So we were wrong, Caesar, about the previous position. That was not the defile that Tacitus referred to – his narrow place – but here."

"What happened," said Hadrian. "It is clear to me now..." – I could see him sitting up tall in his saddle as a commander familiar with battlefields – "...is that the *Britanni* had seen Paullinus's right flank was weak, far weaker than the left. If they could have taken the ridge we are on now, then they could have attacked our forces from the flank, and without having to advance uphill. That's why the fighting in this valley was so critical. Tacitus, gathering details for his History, would undoubtedly have been told of it – perhaps even by his relative, Agricola – and, in that infuriating, abbreviated way of his when writing about battles, he placed that one action above everything else that happened. Fierce fighting must have been going on at the same time the length of the ridge, from this valley to the high point where the *carroballistae* were placed – quite a broad front to have held all day. And against an enemy some ten times our strength."

"Yet," – he lowered his voice – "at least Tacitus did emphasise the most important feature of the field, and the fighting that took place there. He got that right, so we can forgive him other things."

From my own experience – distant, as it was – I knew Hadrian was right. Paullinus's position had been chosen with the greatest of care. Such was the shape of the ground that, wherever the rebel army attacked the Roman lines, its sheer size meant that it was pressed together, losing the advantage of its numbers and making it impossible for individual warriors to make proper use of their weapons. Now, if they had only stood off more, and attacked by discrete formations, piecemeal by piecemeal, then the result might have been very different. But the way of the *Britanni* was not to fight like that. They favoured the wild mass attack, to overcome all before them by the sheer weight of the charge. Paullinus had known that, of course, and prepared the ground for such an eventuality, even building field fortifications to supplement the lie of the ground itself.

"The battle that took place in this valley," I said, indicating with a wave of my hand the steep slopes falling away before us, "must be the one described to me at *Castrum Ikenorum* by veterans of the XIIIIth. And now I can understand what they were telling me. The hillsides, they spoke of, where our formations were packed close together, rank after rank in depth, protected by the slopes on either side, were clearly those we see now. There is no other point on the battlefield that matches their accounts – and Tacitus's description – so exactly."

"And now we have this survivor's tale too confirming it," Hadrian said, gesturing towards Catrig who was seated on the turf with Myru standing by him.

The Emperor seemed suddenly relaxed, buoyant even, as if cares that had been troubling him for a long time had been lifted. This matter of the rebel Queen Bodig and our war with her that we had so very nearly lost, had clearly been of greater concern to him than I had imagined. Important as these events had been, however, the Emperor's need to recreate them in such detail after such a long time was remarkable, to say the least. Why did he have such an obsession with what had passed? It was not now going to alter the present, or, for that matter, the future. If I were a philosopher, I might surmise that he wished to be distracted from other more serious problems that could not be tucked away safely in the past, but which were very much – perhaps dangerously so – part of the present. Yet, it would not be for me to make any such judgement on my Emperor.

"Tell your countryman," said Hadrian to Myru, "that he has done well and we shall reward him. Tell him so, that he might remember other things as well." – and he laughed at his own sarcasm. But I was sure that Catrig had invented nothing in his telling. It was clear he was living out his memories in the same way as I had done. I felt a sudden bond with him – we two veterans of the same war who might once have tried to kill each other.

"On this spot we shall raise an *altarium Victoriae*," said the Emperor. "Let that be recorded: the goddess Victoria shall be worshipped here in the years to come." And I saw Valerius, fumble for his tablets once again and raise his stylus to make the appropriate note.

"Caesar, by what name shall I call this place?"

"Call it for now the plain of the great victory – *campo magnae Victoriae*. And give instructions for this land to be surveyed and a map drawn, and for these events to be set down as a permanent record on vellum, so that no one will ever be in doubt about them again."

We picked our way down the steep slope into the valley. With the Praetorians in their armour riding ahead of us, I felt a chill in the shadowed depths thinking of what the XIIIIth Legion had faced here, and of their advance in wedges against the screaming, howling host before them. The missiles scored the air once more – the arrows, the javelins, the rattling slingstones, the blare of the trumpets, the thrusting banners, the thud of shields, the ringing of steel on steel, the screams of men and horses.

We came out onto the plain, and rejoined our mules which, with the slaves, had remained below the hills. Then Hadrian put his horse into a gallop across the heath, following paths through the scrub made by wild animals, the *praefectus* struggling to keep up with him. Looking around me, I saw our party was now scattered widely At the rear of our number came brave Ajax, bearing Myru and Catrig, kept at a sensible walk by Myru, who had no desire to risk a broken leg in a hidden hole or ditch.

I wondered what Myru thought of having to translate this tale of her people's defeat. I had no way of knowing. It was not the sort of thing you talked about to your slave.

XVI

We made a small camp at the edge of the plain where it merged into reeds and swamps, outliers of the watery wastes of the *magnae paludes* to the north that I knew so well. The mules were brought up and we pitched our tents on a piece of raised ground that was dry, and cooked on open fires, the slaves bustling about us while we reclined on rugs and cushions spread on the grass.

Catrig looked uneasy and found it difficult to be still. He kept on asking Myru to help him up, and he would stumble around for a while, going to the edge of a large pond that lay close by and staring out into its black waters. A little further off stood a cluster of ruined round huts inside a compound of beaten earth, high with weeds, the roof thatch of the huts pulled down. We had explored these before settling on our camp site. The Praetorians had scoured them thoroughly for any dangers, and had tethered their horses to the hut timbers. The slaves with the mules had also made the compound their own camp.

I saw that Catrig kept on wandering there from the pond, and coming back looking agitated, and, through Myru, I asked him why.

"He says when he first came back from Icenia after the war, this was where he lived and where he met the woman who became his wife. He did not know the settlement had been abandoned, and he wonders why. Some of his own kin lived there, and he has no knowledge of where they have gone. This whole place has a particular meaning for him, because it was where the great camp of the *Iceni* and *Trinovantes* had stood during the battle. It was around here – if not on this very spot – that his parents were killed with so many others. The Romans killed everything, including the animals. They dumped many bodies and much wreckage into that lake he keeps staring over. The rest they heaped up and set fire to. The fires burnt for many days. The Romans also had their cremation pyres beside the lakes. They made a camp here. You can see the remains of its earthworks if you search the bushes and the grass. The *Iceni* dead were left to the animals – the wolf and boar and wild cats – that roamed here. Ravens as well descended in great flocks, so the land was black with them. You can still find *Iceni* bones out on the heath amongst the gorse, he says, although many were cleared away when they straightened the road. Slaves used to find the bones and use them for charms."

Hadrian who had been talking with the *praefectus*, with Valerius taking notes, looked across at our conversation and asked me what was said. I told him.

"Let us seek for some bones," he said. "There may be other evidence of the battle too."

So we mounted again, I rather reluctantly for my body ached and my thin backside was sore from the saddle.

Catrig did not wish to come, so we left him under the shelter of a tent with Myru, food and wine beside them. Catrig was still speaking, his voice now directed at the ground in a low mumble.

"Tell us what he speaks of," Hadrian commanded Myru.

"Caesar, he says that the day of the battle was still and dry, but with a mist over the waters here in the early morning as the season was late in the year and the air at night was cold. The sky was grey, the battlefield ringed with smoke rising from many fires, so you could not tell what was smoke and what the sky, both here at the camp of the *Iceni* and also on the ridge and in the forest behind where the Romans made ready for battle. Later in the day, however, unnoticed by most – for the dead cannot see and the living were busy – the sky darkened from the west and the last killing took place here by the waters in driving rain whipped up by a high wind, the ground churned into liquid mud. That was the weather he endured all night, and during the next day when he made his escape."

Catrig spoke again, thrusting out his bony arms. Myru translated. "He says that, just as on the day of battle, it will rain this evening – a big storm will come out of the west."

I was surprised, and looked up at the sky. I saw Hadrian, and others, doing the same. The day was still sunny, the light perhaps a little suffused – which I thought might be down to my eyes – yet I did notice a certain stillness and heaviness in the air which might have accounted for Catrig's prophecy. Could Druids then foretell the weather?

We rode out once more onto the plain. We stopped at clump after clump of gorse and bushes while two slaves we had brought with us, with heavy sticks, poked about around their roots. At last, we had a success, for a part rib cage was dragged out, green with mould, its bone ends gnawed. It was packed away in a saddle bag. A little later, other bones were added to it, and then, triumphantly, a skull. We had found various pieces of rusting metal as well, some arrow heads and slingers' lead bullets, and a broken pot or two. Hadrian called a halt.

"Enough!" He held up his hand.

Just then there was a great crash, and the sky split open with a flash such as I have seldom known before; out of a clear sky the bolt of light seemed as if hurled into the ground by great Iupiter himself. Clouds were boiling like dark steam above the hills. Our horses whinnied, their flanks twitching.

"Back to camp!" yelled Hadrian as the Praetorians bunched around him to protect him, even from the anger of the gods. They galloped ahead: I was left at the back, still fighting to control my horse, trying to steer it between the clumps of vegetation that now seemed to rise like impenetrable hedges before me. At last I came out into the clear and followed in the others' hoof marks. It was then that the rain began to fall, opening upon me as if Iupiter had followed his lightning bolt by emptying the contents of his bath upon the earth.

At last, back at the camp, the slaves took our frightened horses, and we dived under the shelter of the tents. There was little space. All propriety forgotten, I found myself wedged alongside the Emperor with the *praefectus* of the Guard on the other side. We laughed. We went on roaring with laughter for some time, like schoolboys who had escaped from some naughty prank. I remember Hadrian spluttering out, "What would the Senate think if they could see me now?" and we all began laughing again. "Or the Empress?" added the *praefectus*, and we collapsed in hysteria, our limbs beating the ground as the tent boomed and shook in the wind about us.

I changed my mind about the *praefectus*. I thought he was quite human after all, and rather more daring than I.

Later, when the storm had passed and we were preparing to break camp and return to the *mansio*, I found that I was shaking with cold, having foolishly allowed my wet clothes to dry on me. At my age, that was like asking Charon to row out his boat to await my coming. Myru wrapped me in some of the rugs we had laid on the ground and put me up on Ajax with her. Poor Catrig was consigned to a baggage mule, where his bent body was propped between rolled tents and the panniers full of bones. Myru had been concerned when she had learnt we had gathered these.

"What will be done with them, *domine*?" she had asked while wiping my brow and forcing some warmed wine between my lips to try and get some heat back into my body. She seemed far more concerned about these particular bones than those we had carried away from the site of Cerialis's defeat. Then I understood: these were the remains of her own people.

I felt sufficiently ill to be unconcerned about the correctness of passing on her query to Hadrian. He had come up to us as Myru knelt before me, chafing my body with her small, hard hands. She had not seen him, but I had.

"What will you do with the bones we have just gathered, Caesar?" I asked through chattering teeth. The wine ran in red streams from the corners of my mouth.

I thought he looked uneasy. Even with my hazy head, I could see he had not thought of a purpose. He had just ordered them hunted out like a trophy or a curio. Seeing Myru's black eyes swing round on him, he probably had in that instant the good sense to realise that *Iceni* bones were as important to her people as those of our soldiers were to Rome.

"Every bone we have recovered will be interred most reverently," said Hadrian ponderously. "I shall have a monument built where that will be done. This war shall be commemorated properly, with honour to both sides. For out of former battle our joint peoples have forged this province of Rome – Britannia – that stands today."

I remember thinking: does he really believe his own words? Does he forget now those things that Rome did so very badly? – its rape and destruction of a proud kingdom, once its ally. And yet in that final battle of the war – fought on this place where my sick body was now being hauled away by my *Iceni* slave – all the skills and courage had been shown that had enabled Rome to conquer the world. The historian Tacitus, had expressed it best – 'it was a great victory as in olden times.' Once, in the fineness of my youth, I had been part of such a victorious army, marching over lands without horizons, leaving the whitening bones of our enemies in the waste we made.

Philosophising always seems more satisfying when you are old and not feeling very well!

XVII

I spent some time at the *mansio* recovering from the chill I had caught. It was a dangerous ailment for one of my age because it went straight to my chest and brought up much yellow and brown phlegm, which the new slaves I had been allotted by the management took away in bowls, holding the vessels out at arm's length as if the muck was contagious – which it may well have been.

Hadrian and his entourage were leaving – to travel south to inspect the lands of the *Regnenses* which had recently come under direct Roman rule, without the blood bath caused by the end of the *Iceni* ruling house. Then – he had told me – he would be returning north to be reacquainted with the Empress Sabina: 'reacquainted' was his own term.

Hadrian, I had come to understand, sought most of all a companion of the soul: I deduced that did not necessarily have to be a woman. He was surrounded by young and most able-bodied Army tribunes, sons of the nobility he had brought into his household, servants of the state – his archivist, his secretaries, his stewards, his messengers – and, of course, by many freeborn servants and even more numerous slaves, all of whom were at his absolute command. Yet I don't think it was necessarily physical gratification he looked for, but someone who could share with him his private thoughts, his ambitions, his philosophies. He veered between the brusque and the soldierly, the intimate and the artistic. His was a wandering soul indeed.

For a brief time I had been that person he could confide him. I think at first he had seen me as the rough, tough ex-soldier, with my brain locked in my sword hilt. It was only when we had both confessed our inner thoughts to each other, that day in my bath house, that he had come to see there was much in me that was in tune with his own feelings. Perhaps that future biographer, of whom I have spoken before, will be able to penetrate Hadrian's mind.

I am certain, though, that it is lonely being an Emperor, despite the thousands around you whose task it is to serve you.

The one consolation I had, as I sniffled and snuffled and hawked in my small room, trying to regain the strength to go down the steep stairs to the courtyard and mix in with the world again, was that my bill, and that of Myru and my attendant slaves, was all being paid out of the imperial purse.

Hadrian had been concerned about me. "Recover well, old soldier," he had said, from the door of my outer room, but not venturing further inside: the honour of his paying me a visit at all was reward enough, without exposing himself to my malady, which might, or might not be, catching. "We shall be returning for the *caerimonia commemorationis*."

I had struggled to my feet, leaning against the wooden shutter that divided my bed space from the rest of my sleeping room. Between me and the Emperor – from inner to outer room – stood Myru and my other slaves, the latter, older men in long rustic brown tunics, unlike the green-clad *Germani* assigned to me earlier. She did not seem to be missing the one she had taken to her body, her face now holding that expressionless mask she habitually employed in the presence of authority.

"What form will the *caerimonia commemorationis* take, Caesar?" I spluttered fending off a bout of coughing.

"Why?" He looked surprised. "Have we not told you? Of course, you will have missed our planning. The *centurio regionarius* – Decius Salvius Leptis – has taken charge. "

I clung to my wooden support hoping he was not going to tell me my presence was still needed here. As soon as I was well enough, I longed to start on the journey home. I had been promised the use of a fast carriage with outriders of the *cursus publicus*. It would allow me a grand passage through the streets of Duroliponte. Perhaps Numicius and some of his patrician friends would witness my triumphant return and wonder what had passed between the Emperor and me. Let them wonder.

"We will be holding a commemoration of the great battle whose site we have relocated – now to known for all time as *Campo Albo* after the field of the white plain where it was fought. A cohort of *Legio XX* accompanied by two troops of *Ala Primae Thracum* will march from Eboracum. Escorted by the Praetorian Guard, we shall accompany them to the field. The battlefield will be dedicated to Victory and an altar set up. We have other plans too, which the *centurio regionarius* will announce later.

All this was said with such formality that I felt my body swaying with the weight of it. I had much preferred the informal Hadrian of my bath house when he addressed me in the first person.

"Will you need my presence, Caesar?"

"Yes, indeed, Celer. You will have a place of honour at the dedication. We will demonstrate the order that Rome imposes out of chaos and the peace she brings."

"Yes, Caesar. I shall be honoured."

"In the meantime, Celer, we wish you a speedy recovery. We depart tomorrow. A message will be sent to you at your house about the future arrangements. Your neighbour, Numicius Secundus, will be attending as well. You will travel with his party."

"Of course, Caesar." I felt my spirits sink at the prospect. Yet it was an enormous compliment I was being paid. And the proposed ceremony did sound magnificent.

When Hadrian had disappeared, with a final flourish of his hand, I had sunk back on my bed, while Myru and the other slaves hung over me, looking concerned. She shushed them away with a toss of her dark head. I heard both the inner and outer doors closing and the sound of their feet on the stair. Outside in the courtyard, a carriage was departing with a flourish of trumpets. There came the clatter of many hooves on the cobbles. The sound penetrated my head like the flying shot of *Britanni* slingers rattling against a *testudo*. I placed my hands over my ears and groaned. I could hear the rustle of Myru's tunic by my bed and sense her smell.

"*Domine.*" She said the word so cajolingly that I thought for a moment she was going to offer herself to me, something I had never asked of her. "*Domine,*" she repeated. "I have some information that I think will be of interest to you."

What Myru told me I was at first concerned by, then excited, then quite overwhelmed. I cursed myself for being ill. For I would have to deal with this matter now before I returned home. When would I be able to get back to my own bed? I ached for my quiet room with the apple blossom that brushed the window shutters and the breeze that blew in that rank, but oh so familiar and so much missed, smell of the marshes.

I was worrying about how Gavo was coping. What might have gone wrong? Had the dock overflowed and the water flooded my house? How were my ponies without Myru to keep her eye on them? I had good slaves and servants, but it had been a very long time since I had left them to manage

191

on their own for more than a night or two. Still, Gavo was competent. But if Gavo fell in the dock or was struck by lightning, what then? Would a message ever reach me? Did anyone even know where I was? So, my first thought had been: was it some terrible problem learnt by Myru that she wished to tell me of?

But she astonished me by referring to my long departed wife, who had been dead many years before Myru had come to me as a slave bought at Duroliponte: she had cost me as much as *xxxv denarii* because of the sign about her neck that had advertised her skills with horses.

"*Domine*, I would speak of your wife's name that is well known in these parts – Senuna. *Domine*, I have learnt from kitchen maids here that Senuna is revered as a goddess at a place nearby. It is strange, because with my people the name is usually spoken as Senu, a goddess of the waters."

My initial reaction was anger. My wife's name was mine to use alone. I did not know it was spoken about still in my household. I replied tartly, "What business is this of yours, slave?"

I saw a flash of anger in her own eyes. I had always used her name, from the very first time she had been brought into my house. "It is none, *domine*. I should not have mentioned it. I request to leave you. There is work I must do."

I uncovered my head and snapped at her, "Stay!"

She froze on her way to the door, and turned back to me. I desired her then – in her short tunic with the tasselled hem cutting her brown thighs and the small jutting mounds of her breasts, the scent of her still about my bed. I knew however that my sudden desire could not be matched by any performance.

"What else have you heard?" I asked. After the first shock, my interest was quickening, for the mystery of Senuna's background was as yet a darkness to me. "Where is this goddess, Senuna, you speak of?"

"They say she is worshipped at a shrine near Competum. It is a half day's journey away."

I knew where Competum was. It was the small town a few miles further west of the great battlefield Hadrian had named *Campo Albo*. Had Senuna been called after a local goddess then? I remembered how I thought she might have been raised in a temple precinct. She had told me she had been instructed in the wisdom of Minerva. She had held herself like Minerva, dressed her hair like Minerva. Had Senuna then taken on the attributes of the Roman goddess? Where exactly, and how, had she been raised? Could I yet find out? I found excitement rising within me. Then, I thought, why had I not been told of this when I had made my own enquiries many years ago? I suspected the story could not be true; it must be just some half-crazed gossip Myru had misunderstood and passed on hoping to please me.

"What do you know about this shrine?" I asked her sharply.

"*Domine*, I am told it is a thriving place where you can stay and drink of the sacred waters, and say your prayers and deliver up your curses and your wishes to several deities who dwell there – but the greatest of them is Senuna, and people come from a great distance to make offerings to her."

"I must go and see it," I said. My doubts were evaporating like mist in sunlight. This must be truth, which had not been brought to me before – after all it was more than twenty years since I last made enquiry, and much can happen in that time. I felt as if Senuna was alive again at my shoulder and was telling me what I must do.

"Yes, *Domine*."

"You will accompany me. Will Ajax carry the two of us?"

"Yes, *Domine*. But would you not be more comfortable hiring a carriage or a litter?"

"I want to ride on my own horse. I want to go to this Senuna by my own power, not someone else's. I would walk if I could. Whoever this goddess is who is named Senuna, and whatever greeting I will make to her, I must travel to her as I was when I last left my wife."

Myru bent her head and did not reply. I could not put properly into words what I meant. Something had moved within the orbit encompassing me – that same orbit which surrounds all people, where our *genii* dwell. Mine, long asleep – or so it has seemed to me – was now dancing before my eyes, beckoning me on. I had no choice but to follow.

We left three days later. I felt much stronger and had begun to eat again – some roast meat last night, full of blood which I hoped had entered my own veins. I had passed clear water too and a good stool, and knew I could ride. It would not be a long journey. I was even tempted to try walking, with my feet in the dust, as a penitent should come to a shrine, but Myru stopped my nonsense by hauling me with her strong arms up onto the special padding she had strapped to Ajax's back. And in this way, ignoring some amused looks from other travellers, we had clattered out of the courtyard of the *mansio* through the gateway that opened onto the road.

It was not a long journey to Competum, and we reached there by midday. We passed once more over the *Campo Albo*, and I turned my head – from the reedy, tree-lined edge of the marshes on my right to the grey line of the distant hills on my left – seeing again the battle that had been fought there, the smoke rising, the scent of death filling the air. I had seen many such sights in my life, but never on the scale that had been acted out here.

Competum consisted mainly of roadside strips of rough timbered cabins, with, behind them, yards and paddocks filled with sheds and barns, and, by the street, a roofed well-head beside which two donkeys trod in circles, roped together. At the centre of the settlement, however, where the *Via Alba* crossed another main highway, stood a stone building of two storeys with a colonnaded front portico: it was probably where the council of this small place met. Beside it rose another tall building, this one covered with dirty white plaster striped horizontally with a broad band of red, and with a balcony projecting from its upper floor. A board attached to a pole showed it to be an inn. A number of men in coarse, rough-hemmed tunics, some wearing capes and hoods, were carousing outside, holding up their wooden pots to us as we arrived, and laughing at the strange sight we evidently made for them.

"What is your journey, old man? From where do you come and to where do you go?" was the politest form of their questioning that I can represent here. Their eyes above their pots were all on Myru's body as she jumped down from Ajax and lead the pony, with me still on its back, up a brick-paved ramp to the front of the inn.

The men, I think, were all freeborn *Britanni*, and spoke reasonably good Latin, but in a guttural, local dialect which made some of their comments hard to understand – perhaps that was just as well, although I was in no mood for a quarrel. Myru – the one slave in our company – with her long, dark hair unpinned to her shoulders, stood sullenly but watchful at Ajax's head, prepared, I was sure, to come to my defence in an instant, whatever the consequences for her.

I sat up as tall in my make-shift saddle as I could, and pulled aside the red cloak I wore so that the vertical red stripe over the shoulder of my tunic was clear, indicating that I was a veteran of the imperial legions and a Roman citizen. The jeering and the laughter stopped as abruptly as if I had placed a hand across the collective mouths. The drinking pots were lowered, the faces moulded themselves into sobriety, the eyes cast down. These were boisterous field labourers – no more – probably celebrating the end of harvest. I could not be angry with them even if I had so wished. Their disrespect was my own fault for riding into their town like a jack sat up on an ass: my apologies, dear Ajax, for liking you to a donkey in this instance, you of a breed that was once braver than Bucephalus in war.

I addressed them through Myru, who would not have the trouble I would have in understanding the replies. Indeed, it suited my superior status to have my slave do the talking while these men were now subservient with lowered heads, their fists pressed against their temples. I felt sorry for spoiling their celebration. I would toss them a few coins to let it continue after they had told me what I wished to know.

Myru, to my surprise, spoke in Latin. Perhaps their dialect was not one she knew. So, despite the accents, she did not have to translate the replies.

"My master wishes to know where the shrine of Senuna lies that, he hears, is somewhere near this place."

A man, wearing a yellow shoulder cape and with brown leggings, standing taller than his fellows, his unruly brown hair revealed by the quick removal of a tall, rimless cap, answered. "Tell your master there is a sacred place outside the town, in a valley amongst trees some three miles past the old fort on the road to Burentum. I do not know the gods which are worshipped there, but I have heard of this goddess of Senuna and it may be she."

I said to Myru, bending low from Ajax to speak in her ear, "Ask him which gods he *does* worship."

The man was bolder than the others, less cowed by me than his companions. Perhaps the beer he had been drinking still ran strongly in his veins. He laughed. "It depends on the season and the need. Today it is Braciaca, tomorrow it may be Ceres. For today we have finished cutting and tomorrow we must gather. So we should drink next to Taranis and to Iupiter – the two together – that they do not send us thunder and rain until the harvest is safe."

"Wise words," I said out loud, and nodded at Myru who took from the purse that she carried for me *iii sestertii*, handing them to me. I held the coins up and the man raised his cap, his head now lowered. The coins chinked into the cap as I tossed them down. "Say a prayer too for Senuna," I said. "Work hard and enjoy yourselves while you can for death can come quicker than an arrow."

I felt a catch in my throat as I spoke the words, and turned Ajax by the pressure of my knees so that none could see the sudden moisture in my eyes. It had been a long time since I felt so close to Senuna, my wife.

Myru mounted behind me, and we rode off, some small boys and other onlookers, who had watched this small scene, running and shouting behind us, perhaps hoping for further gifts – but there were none coming.

As the last thatched huts fell away behind us, I made out amongst the flat fields on our left the outline of the dismantled fort that had stood at Competum: it dated from the days of *bellum Icenorum* and had been built by Suetonius Paullinus to secure his line of march during his approach to the *Campo Albo*. It would have been garrisoned by auxiliaries and abandoned within a few years of the end of the war. As we came closer, I could see the ridge that had been left on the ground by the fort's levelled outer rampart, with a curved corner where the rampart turned to run parallel with the road. A patchwork of square fields stretched up to the old rampart, and in places across it too, so that their hedges made a rise and a dip over the filled in ditch and flattened bank. The wheat in the fields had been cut and was standing in stooks: I imagined this was where our friends at the inn had been working.

I caught sight of some tumbled stones behind a thick briar hedge bordering the road. A small burial ground had been laid out here, now neglected and overgrown. Myru forced Ajax through a gap in the hedge, the briars tearing at our clothes. Wooden grave markers had rotted and lay on the grass. Some stones still stood amongst others that had fallen. One bore an inscription to a cavalryman of the *Ala Nerviorum, 'in bello interfectus'*, another, poorly carved, said simply, *femina Britanna* – there was other writing below, but it was too decayed to make out the woman's name. Myru turned Ajax, and we rode out once more onto the road. I felt depressed by this evidence of passing mortality, once lovingly tended, now forgotten and covered with weeds.

A mile or so further on, we came across on old man sitting by a stone pillar at the side of the road. The pillar bore a dedication to the Emperor Vespasianus, in the eighth year of whose reign the road had been made – *'bono rei publicae nato'*. The man had a stout stick at his side and a long-haired, black dog at his feet, which scarcely looked up as we approached.

"I can go no further for my dog is unwell," the old man said in a quavering voice.

"Why do you not then release him from his misery?" I asked.

"I cannot. He has been a companion to me these fifteen years."

"Why, then you are tied to your dog forever." My comment, I knew, was not helpful.

"Do you know where a shrine is in these parts?" Myru cut in, speaking the old man's tongue. I knew she was impatient with sentimentality. Animals to her were as people, to be looked after properly but not cosseted as a child would a toy. However, I could sense (or thought I could sense) the old man's grief. The dog was probably the only thing in the world he could call a friend.

I nodded to Myru and she cast down some coins onto the grass beside him. The dog stirred, and the old man straightened his back against the stone. "Buy yourself and your dog some food when a pedlar passes," I said, already sensing I had been taken in.

"The shrine you seek you will find down a side road a mile further," said the old man. He had picked up the coins and was rising to his feet. Myru urged Ajax away.

"*Vale, domine,*" the old man said, his voice stronger than before.

Was he mocking me? I had a momentary desire to turn and seize my money back, but such an act was beneath my dignity. "*Vale,*" I said in turn, waving my arm. "Long life to you and your dog."

We found the turning off the main road. It was a narrow, unpaved track, laid out on a straight course, with signs of being much used, for its surface was rutted by wheels and pitted with hooves. It ran down a slope between fields into a shallow valley. To the right, a stream meandered beside the track, twisting and turning across a broad, green pasture where small, brown cattle grazed. Seen through trees ahead of us, the red tiles of a roof came into sudden view, and after a short distance we entered a cobbled court before a tall, square building with a central tower, which rose beyond an enclosing wall. On the far side of the court, white smoke could be seen filtering between the leafy branches of surrounding trees.

Upon the cobbles stood a fine, four-wheeled carriage built of varnished wood, with bronze fittings at its corners and doors and along the edges of its roof. Its draw bars rested on the ground, empty of the equally fine horses that had probably been harnessed between them. I thought I saw where they might have gone – Ajax had pricked up his ears and was increasing his pace towards a square, wood-shuttered building at the edge of the trees, painted black with red brick arches above the wide doors and windows. It looked as if it were a stables.

Halting Ajax here, we dismounted. Myru helped me down onto stone slabs laid around a basin of water into which the pipe of a fountain slowly trickled. I dipped my hand into the basin and sprinkled my face with the cool water. A groom in a livery of a short, brown tunic with yellow hemming came from the stables and, without a word, took Ajax's head and led him, not reluctantly, away. Myru went to follow, but I stilled her with my arm.

"Let's find out first what goes on here," I said. "I may need your help. I'm not sure of the cult here and the manner of its devotion."

My worries were eased by the arrival of a group of other visitants – I think the carriage was theirs. They appeared on a path from out of the woods, and paid me greeting with hands raised, palms outwards, in the traditional manner. They seemed to be of a wealthy family, being richly dressed in coloured linens and fine woollen cloaks, with shoes of soft, red leather – two men and two ladies, the enamelled brooches at their shoulders glistening with many colours, the women with hair piled and coiled and held in place with gold bands. I would have spoken with the foremost man of the group, but as I was stepping forward to do so, another man – a thin man of middle years, wearing a long tunic of similar colour and pattern to the groom who had taken Ajax – came up suddenly beside me. Diagonally across his chest was a yellow sash, and he carried a bronze rod in his right hand, which from its various decorations I took to be a sceptre. I assumed, therefore, he was a priest, although in truth I have little knowledge of the ritual of any of Rome's many cults and religions beyond those sacred ceremonies we had practised in the Legion – dedicating ourselves, our standards, and our Eagle to Great Iupiter, the Emperor, and Rome.

Myru, I was pleased to note, had fallen a few paces behind; although a companion to me, she knew, as a slave, this was her place in the company of her freeborn superiors.

"*Salve.* Are you here to worship the goddess Senuna?" The priest spoke this in my ear with a hissing sound that sent a spray of spittle onto my cheek. I instinctively wiped it with my hand.

"I am curious of this Senuna," I said, stepping back from him, "for Senuna was my wife's name, and it is uncommon, I think."

His face showed no expression. The eyes were dark, the skin an oily brown, the features angular, with a pointed chin covered by whispery black hair. The sceptre, I saw now, had a box-like perforated end, which I thought was for burning incense.

"The name is divinely given. Senuna was born of the old gods into new life, new wisdom. She carries knowledge from out of our past into our future; through her, wisdom flows like water, which is why we name many of our rivers and streams after her. Her wisdom may be equated with your Minerva, yet she rules supreme."

So, I thought, this priest can see I am a Roman. He does not wish to offend my worship, but he is a *Britannus* and he proclaims the beliefs of his own people first.

"The name Senuna – or at least a form of it – may be borne by her servers, yet that is rare," the man added.

His eyes shone. I thought, he looks in a trance. I was no follower of the ecstatic religions that I knew to be coming into fashion. I believed in the gods of my household, and in Epona, to whom I kept a shrine, and in the values of Rome's traditional gods, of which Iupiter remained, for all time, the Best and Greatest – *Iupiter Optimus Maximus*.

"Who are the goddesses' servers?" I asked.

"They are women who attend her. Come, I will show you. Your slave can wait for you here."

He took me by the arm, an act which I would normally pull away from – other than when occasioned by a close friend or former comrade – but here, because of my curiosity, I allowed. He led me to a door in the enclosure wall of the square building, which I already knew, from its shape and form, was a temple. We were about to pass now into the sacred area of its *temenos*.

Within the *temenos*, a broad strip of fine gravel – so fine it shone golden in the sun and was deep to the tread like shingle by the sea – stretched up to a columned portico at the front of the temple, which continued around its four sides. Before the steps to the portico stood an altar, where the group I had seen just now, had gathered and were making offerings. One of the women had placed a tall glass jar on the white, carved stone of the altar into which the other was pouring a libation, while the men watched with hands clasped and heads bowed.

"Come," said the priest, tightening his grasp on my arm and taking me up the steps into the portico, the floor of which was formed of small red bricks. Ahead of us were great double-leafed doors leading into the inner *cella* of the temple itself. I knew that only the priests of the god or goddess worshipped here, and their assistants, would normally be allowed to enter that most scared place.

Did this priest, therefore, officiate in the rituals necessary to please and appease a divine Senuna? I had known a woman named Senuna with whom for a brief while I had shared my life. I had loved her in ways that were merely mortal, so I found it hard to equate her with one of the same name worshipped as a goddess. There was a puzzle here that I needed an answer to. Senuna had told me she had been raised in the wisdom of Minerva, which this priest now informed me was conflated with the greater wisdom of Senuna, a goddess of the *Britanni*. So could it be that she, having taken the name of the goddess – and that was possible under certain circumstances, the priest had said – had been brought up here and instructed in the way I had once suspected? If so, how was it that she had ended up in a sordid *lupanar* at Duroliponte?

The priest led me along the portico and around the far corner, our feet shuffling over the brick floor. My hips and back were aching from all the recent riding I had done. I longed to be sitting in a comfortable chair or, better still, reclining, with food and drink at my fingertips. It had been a long time since I had eaten. The food we had brought was in Ajax's panniers, perhaps now being eaten by the grooms. I hoped Myru had had the sense to wait for me at the stables. I felt sure she would not leave Ajax for long unless she was confident of his care

Attached to the wooden columns of the portico, and to beams of the projecting roof, hung various votives made of cloth and coloured wood, or occasionally of bronze and pewter, some shaped as leaves and fronds, others like the salvers upon which wine cups are carried. The ink writing on one particularly large wooden frond I noticed read '*Deae Senunae Firmanus votum solvit libens merito.*' I wondered who this Firmanus was who had so willingly fulfilled his vow to the goddess Senuna. Had he known my Senuna? No, that could not be. The dedication looked recent. If Senuna had been here in the period before I met her in Duroliponte, it was already a lifetime ago. Firmanus had probably not even been born then.

We rounded another corner of the portico, so we were now at the rear of the building, and here I saw, looking from the portico, was a long single-storey building, built of stone with small brick-framed windows and a pitched tile roof. It looked a little like a barrack block at a fort, and was built against the outer wall of the *temenos.* We descended a set of wooden steps and walked towards this building across a cobbled surface.

We entered through a narrow door at one end, painted brown like the colour of the priest's tunic, and came into a large, stone-flagged room with elaborately decorated walls – scrolling patterns of reds and greens, with trellis work and a yellow bird – I particularly noted – standing on a leafy branch. The lower parts of the walls were painted a brick-coloured red. Within the room, some seated at tables writing with styli on wax tablets, one reading a papyrus, two lounging on a side bench, their backs to the wall, were a number of men (perhaps eight in all), all dressed like my priest in long brown tunics with yellow bands across their chests.

The men looked up, but no one spoke, and my priest said not a word either. Instead he went to a far door, and knocked briefly before opening it. I followed him inside. This room, like the former, was set with tables and chairs, and there were a number of couches against the walls. These walls were plainly plastered in white, but with the same broad red band at their base as in the outer room. Shelves lined two of the walls, and on a third was a row of hooks from which clothing hung – cloaks of the russet brown colour I was becoming familiar with at this shrine. There was only one person present, seated at one of the tables wearing a plain white tunic, her back straight, her hair tied in a coil at the back, ribbons dangling. She looked up at me as I entered.

I saw the face of my Senuna!

XVIII

I have to admit to feeling a great sense of shock – and disbelief too – at the face I saw. The features were very similar to those of my Senuna, who had been dead more than thirty years. I saw my wife again shining out of this face before me, reborn out of memory: there was the same oval of her face, the same heavily-lidded blue eyes, the same pursed small mouth, the same red gold hair. Was I seeing a ghost?

"This is Sena," the priest said. "As a server to the goddess, it is allowed that she be called by a form of the deified one's name."

I thought that was a little strange, but I did not comment upon it. The priest spoke of the 'deified one', not of the goddess herself, one of the pantheon of the divine, as if she had been a mortal once who had later become a goddess. I was used to this happening to Rome's emperors, but I had not known the practice was more widespread. You see, I had become quite cynical about religions when they strayed beyond my own tightly-held beliefs.

The woman named Sena, who looked so like my Senuna when I had first met her in Duroliponte, sat calmly with her arms outstretched over the table top. By 'calmly', I mean that she made no comment, and had no apparent reaction, to the introduction made by the priest. Her face – so beautiful – held no particular expression, of welcome or rejection, or indeed of any emotion at all. I judged her age to be in the late thirties, possibly early forties: there was greyness in her hair and lines about her eyes and mouth. She may have had a resemblance for me at first to Senuna but, if I am honest, as I looked longer, I could see the many differences brought about by age (my Senuna, I had thought – I never knew for sure – to have been but in her mid twenties when she died). There was something else about this Sena that was troubling, something almost uncanny, although I could not put my feeling into words as I stared at her. It may just have been on account of my nervous system still in shock at that first recognition.

The priest said, "Sena, who serves the goddess, may have occasion to go from this sanctuary into the world outside. Yet it is inconceivable she should ever bear the full name of the goddess. If your wife did indeed use that name – the name of Senuna – it is most unusual; indeed it is sacrilegious. For it is our belief that the name was born here with the goddess and has come from no other place, and will always be here, alone of all places on earth."

So, I thought, why then had my Senuna called herself that? Was it just a whim? Did she not know her birth name? Had she been brought up at this place and chosen when she left – perhaps even in defiance – to use the name of the goddess in whose rites she had been instructed? Senuna was such a beautiful name, even when taken from its context of divinity. There may have been no other name she wished to be called by. Was it the only one that allowed her her identity?

"How long has your shrine been here?" I asked the priest. I realised at once, seeing a small frown form on the priest's forehead, that these words were clumsy, likening a place of the gods to a butcher's shop. I tried again. "How long has the goddess Senuna dwelt here?"

"For all time, of course," the priest replied with a thin smile. "She came to us out of Chaos, and all would return to Chaos should her rule here be ended. In any event, we do not measure earthly days in the presence of the divine."

The talk of Chaos disturbed me. Did he mean a Chaos of the gods or of mortals – or were the two same? His answer, anyhow, I knew to be preposterous. The shrine had to be able to interact with the real world beyond its gates, where time hastened on and did not stop even for the gods.

"Yet, you must keep records here, as every organisation does, of matters passing, whether of the secular or the sacred. I saw your people working from documents just now."

"Indeed," he said, as if that one word was an answer to my comment.

I turned to Sena, "How long have you served here?" But there was no reply, no movement at all of the face, only a slow blinking of the eyes.

"You cannot address a server of the goddess on wordly matters," the priest said. "You can only speak through her to the divine one herself."

I thought he sounded irritated, as if he had expected me to know this. But all this was quite beyond any experience I had ever had. I did not recall ever hearing of such conventions of worship before, but then – as I have said – my knowledge of religious practice was very limited. I supposed every religion had its particular rites of worship. After all, it was I who had trained my ponies to bow their heads to Epona – which may have seemed strange to some. The more involved the ritual, perhaps the greater the mystery of the god, or more likely the greater the opportunity to hoodwink people – or so that, hard, cynical part of my mind was still alert enough to point out.

But why then had the priest brought me to meet this Sena? What was the reason for her startling physical resemblance to my Senuna? Was it just coincidence or….? Suddenly, a door seemed to open in my mind and I saw a vision of what might have been – an impossible vision – and I felt the floor twist and steepen and fall away from me so that I had to clutch at the wall.

"Are you unwell?" asked the priest, looking at me narrowly.

"Just a little dizzy for a moment," I said, wiping my brow with the back of my hand, feeling the sweat upon it. "I think it is nothing more than too much travelling and too little sustenance."

"I will take you to a place where you can eat and rest."

"Thank you. But first there are some more questions I have to ask you."

"Ask what you will. I do not promise, though, that I can answer. We will go back to the other room. Sena is resting now, but soon she will be called."

"Called by whom?"

The priest gave me a searching look, as if to check I was not deliberately misunderstanding, or even mocking, or in some other way disbelieving, but he did not answer. Such reticence – such suspicion – did not make it seem likely I would gain the knowledge I was seeking – that which I was growing fearful of finding out.

Yet, quite remarkably, I was to do so. Looking back, it all seems dream-like now. Indeed, everything about the shrine appeared but a waking dream. Perhaps this blurred atmosphere was a deliberate creation, perhaps the white smoke I had seen rising had spread a drug upon the air which swayed the senses. I shall never know. It was enough to learn and then to go. But that was to be the next day. My poor health was to cause me to stay one night at the shrine. I have wondered since if the shade of Senuna entered my body then causing me to remain. If I had left that same day, I am sure I would never have learnt what I did.

When we returned to the room where the priests – or clerks, or whatever else it was they were – were working at the tables, I began to feel ill again, my head seeming to turn in slow circles so that I staggered and had to clutch at a table, scattering a pile of wooden tablets onto the grey stone floor, together with a horn of black ink. The priest made me sit on one of the wall benches until my head stopped swimming. My heart was beating fast. I had never had a turn like this before. Someone must have sent for Myru, for her small figure suddenly appeared before me. Through all my ill feelings, I remained most aware of the eyes watching me from the tables.

A travelling chair was sent for. I had not been carried in one of these for years, not since some twenty years ago when I had had a leg bound up after a fall and had to be carried everywhere around the canal dock to do my work. As soon as I was seated in the chair with brown-tunicked bearers to fore and aft, I began to feel much better and sought to get out. It was Myru's arm that restrained me. "*Domine*, please rest," she hissed at me – the hissing, I am sure, was meant to express the urgency of her feelings.

The priest's face came into my view. "There is no cause for alarm," I said as steadily as I could. "I have not been well recently and perhaps came on this journey too soon."

"An offering to the goddess may help her intercede for you," was all he said. He seemed to have the compassion of one of those creatures who clear the arena sand of the dead and the dying so the show can continue.

I felt sufficiently weakened, though, to find the idea attractive. I had felt the spirit of Senuna supporting me many times over the years since I had lost her. It would do me no harm to seek her again more directly through a prayer and an offering to a goddess of her own name, whom perhaps once she had worshipped and confided in. I fumbled at my belt, then remembered Myru had my purse.

"*iiii denarii*." It was my turn to hiss at her.

"*Domine*, no…"

"*Domine*, yes," I said as sharply as I could, and I gained some satisfaction at seeing her count out the silver coins, which the priest immediately placed in the breast pocket of his tunic.

"*iiii denarii* will allow the goddess to look favourably on you," said the priest. "A further *v denarii* will allow us to do the same for you. We have accommodation here where you can stay and recover. There is a bath house too, and food can be brought to you, and, if you wish them, slaves can wait on you."

He sensed my uncertainty, seeing my furrowed brow. In a conversation recently – had it been with Numicius who knew far better than I the changing ways of the world? – I had heard of shrines that were like *mansiones* catering for the travelling adherents of their cults. Some, it was said, were more like pleasure rooms offering riotous entertainment in the name of the god. But surely not here. Senuna in her Roman form, Minerva, was a goddess of the home, of wisdom and sobriety and modesty. Had that not been how my wife had dressed and how she had behaved? Yet I had never been able to free my mind of the memory of her in the *lupanar*. Something – perhaps more than simple poverty – had driven her to that.

"Your slave can lodge free," the priest added, perhaps as an incentive. "She can sleep in the stables, if needs be. There will be a small extra charge, though, for the stabling of your horse."

I thought, these people seem more concerned with the world of commerce than one of sacred duty. I nodded my assent to the arrangements – all except the provision about Myru. I thought I might need her beside me in the night. I watched her as she counted out the *v denarii* extra, thinking my purse must now be just about empty. It was as well I would be returning home at imperial expense.

The chair I was seated upon was a capacious one, well-cushioned on seat and back. It stood on the ground on four square legs, from which it was raised, swaying at first, by the two bearers, one each between the smooth rounded poles projecting each end. With my quest for more information about Senuna abandoned for the moment, I was borne away through a side door in the enclosure wall and out onto the path that I had seen earlier which ran into the woods. Behind me came the priest, and one of his fellows – a much younger man in the same colour and style of tunic, clearly the uniform dress of the shrine – with Myru bringing up the rear. I could see how anxious she was when I twisted my body in the chair and raised my hand to her, and received no acknowledgement. I knew that when Myru was worried by something, and her advice thwarted, she descended into a mood akin to a sulk – which was particularly unhelpful to her master at such times. I suspected she thought I would have been better served by being with her on the back of Ajax and returning to the *mansio* we had left that morning. Perhaps I would have been, but she did not understand the reasons I had come here – as yet unfulfilled.

It might be thought Myru and I were closer at times than the usual relationship between a master and slave, and that I allowed her considerable licence, yet I had little idea of what she was thinking at any particular moment. That she was loyal to me, I had no doubt. But, as an *Iceni* woman, I often wondered how she reconciled her two states of being – the one, of evident pride in her ancestry, and the other, of her people's – and her own – subjugation to Rome. One day, I thought, I must try to talk to her about these matters. Yet, despite the power I held over her, I had no more ability to penetrate the mind of a slave than that of a citizen – perhaps less so.

Senuna had not been a slave but a freeborn *Britanna* to whom I had given Roman citizenship by our marriage. That had been long before Myru had even been born. Did she – did my other slaves – know of Senuna's background? I had no way of knowing. When Senuna was alive, my house slaves had seemed wary of her. I had never understood why, for she had seldom been impatient with them and never cruel. Did they then know more about her than I knew myself? I had wondered at times – but there was no way I could ask. All of those slaves had long since left me, and most were probably dead.

I rarely spoke to anyone about Senuna now, which is why the telling of my story to Hadrian had been such a release for me. Diseta, though, would have sensed my continuing pain on the nights she slept with me. So what, I wondered, did Myru know about my past? She worked for me as a slave, but she had become at times a close intimate, closer to my thoughts and feelings than Diseta or Gavo ever were, and closer even than most Romans' wives would be.

I had long determined to give her – and others of my slaves – their freedom upon my death, and there would be no further marriage for me even if spared the years for it – which I had thought unlikely.

XIX

The path through the trees, over which I was borne swaying at shoulder height, opened into a broad, sparkling clearing of meadow-fresh grass across which two streams bubbled and gurgled. At a central point where the streams joined, a small altar stood upon a circle of grey stone paving. It was from here that the smoke I had seen earlier blowing between the trees was rising in soft white billows, and the air was filled with a delicious scent of roasting meats. A party of gaily-robed worshippers (for I assumed that's what they were) had set trestle tables and folding chairs upon the paving and were feasting, occasionally rising to tend the metal cage of fire behind the altar while pouring libations upon the altar stone itself. The plates and bowls they were eating from, I noticed, were of the best, glossy red tableware made in Gallia, a few items of which I kept for best at home locked in a cupboard: I had not ordered them brought out, I thought wryly, even for the Emperor's visit. Here, even as I watched from my lurching perch, an over-excited boy, reaching across for more meat from the griddle, dropped a plate onto the stone, the broken pieces being swept away at once by an attendant slave. If such behaviour was part of this group's – this family's – worship of Senuna, equated with Minerva, goddess of wisdom, I thought I did not wish to know too much more, only how my Senuna could conceivably have once been part of it.

On the far side of the clearing rose a single-storied building, roofed with red tile, with a portico along its front like that of my own house. The wooden balustrade of the portico was lined with many green-leafed plants set in pots, some of which were in flower, of red and yellow blooms, with bronze cages of singing birds hanging amongst them. Behind, more smoke, grey this time, rose from the white domed roof of a bath house. The whole place was like a luxury villa such as Numicius owned, only here, to my mind, the luxury seemed at odds with the purpose of worship – but perhaps I was simply out of touch with the way the Roman world had developed during the fullness of my years. Numicius, I was sure, would immediately have felt at home. I felt uneasy, though, still troubled by the role my Senuna might have played here and that astonishing resemblance of hers to the Sena I had met. Would I find any answers to these mysteries?

I was carried into a room off the portico of character and sumptuousness, with an apsidal end that contained a floor of coloured mosaic such as I had only ever dreamed of owning. It bore the head of a goddess, not Minerva or Senuna surely, for the face was of great beauty, framed by long, dark hair into which small, white *tesserae* had been set depicting jewels, and, underneath, peacocks with feathered fans – an attribute, I knew, of Venus, goddess of love. For what purpose should Venus be represented here, I wondered?

The room contained a wood-framed bed, inset with ivory, with sheets of fine linen covered by a woollen blanket woven to a local *Britanni* design, with swirls and loops of colour divided by coiling, green tendrils of plants. There was an outer room with a bed too, where I installed Myru, dismissing the need for, and the extra cost of, any slaves from the shrine.

I lay on the bed and rested for a while. Myru, I think, went to check on Ajax, but returned soon because she had not wanted to leave me on my own. There was no doubt she was very suspicious of this place. She wished to be on hand for my call should I need her – which, as we shall see, very nearly happened during the night. For now, however, I feasted on a meal brought to me on trays by more slaves in brown tunics. It consisted of roasted sheep's meat (from that same altar fire I had seen, I wondered?) and fruits, with a tangy cheese and fresh white bread, accompanied by a red wine that must have been brought from some distance for it was too good to have come from any vine grown in Britannia.

The long summer day at last gave way to a grey dusk, and then black night descended like a cloak, the sky covered by cloud, with no stars or moon showing. Occasionally I would hear the sound of feet on the paving outside. Torches of pitch were lit on brackets on the portico columns. Their flickering light seeped between the edges of the door frame and through the green glass pane of the one small window. Myru had lit an expensive-looking, bronze oil lamp in the room, turning the wick low so that the light was just a steady glow away to my left as I lay on the bed covered by the blanket. I had not felt like using the bath house, from which noise seeped into the room from time to time – rowdiness from fellow worshippers, it seemed. Perhaps I would pay a visit to the baths in the morning, for I had not bathed properly for some days. I slept.

I woke suddenly. Someone was in the room with me. The light from the portico torches burnt brighter now, so the door must be open. I felt a gush of cool air on my cheek and I saw the outline of a woman's figure near me, smelling her perfume like a drug. Her face bent towards me, the face so like that of my Senuna – but of Sena, the temple server, the woman of silence I had met.

She spoke now, *"Domine,* do you wish to approach the goddess through me?"

What is this? I thought. I was going to call out to Myru, but didn't. These were matters only I could sort out in my head. My world was revolving – my past and my present intermingling, my wife returning to me in another form, but so close, so much remembered, so much desired. My old lusts, long burnt low, now flared bright.

"I think you do wish me, *domine.* You seek fulfilment through Senuna."

She was raising her tunic. I could make out the long, curving lines of her thighs, with the darkness where they met – darkness coming closer to me so that I could reach out and touch it. For a moment temptation trembled at my fingertips.

"Get away from me, whore – evil one," I said, the words delivered low, spittle on my lips. I did not recognise my own voice. I realised now what I should have realised before, and the shock hit me like a thunderclap. Prostitution. Temple prostitution. I had heard about it. I did not know it actually happened – perhaps in some far away Greek province, but not here in Britannia. So that had been my Senuna's business, which she had escaped from only into further prostitution, and then had come to me. This place of supposed wisdom was nothing but a *lupanar* for the easy entertainment of those who could afford it, purportedly to bring them closer to the goddess. What hypocrisy! What vileness! The gorge rose within me. I felt sickness in my throat. Sharp bile tore at my chest.

She had retreated from me, her tunic lowered. I heard her breath and the soft patter of her shoes. She said nothing more, and I saw her dark form pass through the door. Again, I was going to call out for Myru, but didn't. No one but I must know of this. All my remembrance of Senuna depended on it. All would be destroyed if others knew what I did now. I eased my shaking limbs from the bed and padded on bare feet to the door. I looked through. By the light of the guttering torches, I saw the woman's shadow far along the portico, pushing at another door. Briefly, she turned and looked at me, and it was as if Senuna was gazing at me out of my past, asking me for forgiveness. I stepped back into my room and closed the door firmly.

For the first time, I saw a chain dangling there and pulled it across the door, fastening it on a projecting hook. Not to have done this before had perhaps been regarded as a sign of my wishes. I did not know. I felt I would not understand anything certainly ever again. I could not sleep, but rose when Myru came in to check on me at first light, allowing her to escort me to the bath house as soon as the fires were lit. I felt I needed to be thoroughly cleansed, both inside and out.

I was angry. My anger made me far more decisive and determined than the cautious, curious, fearing state of mind I had of late been reduced to. I was used to being decisive. My life had once depended on it. Old age perhaps had rusted the edges of my inner steel.

When I had bathed and broken my morning fast, I dressed myself carefully with items pulled from my travelling pack and went straight to the office to which the priest had taken me yesterday. I did not wait for him – or any other person in a brown tunic – to come to me. Nor did I discuss with Myru what I was to do. Announcing my intention, I caught her with a crust of bread in her mouth, which she dropped to scamper along after me. Her shrill calls to me, I did not answer. Had she seen anything of what had happened in the night? I did not know, I did not care. I felt strong today. I cursed the weakness that had led me to be carried in a chair yesterday, swaying about like a fat, bloated patrician. I would find out what I needed to know and leave here on my own horse: Myru could ride behind me now, not the other way around, or she could walk in the dust. I was Gaius Modius Celer, *optio* and veteran of *Legio VIIII Hispana*, and I wanted results.

I followed the path through the trees, walking swiftly, found that the side door in the temple enclosure wall had been left unlocked, and went through. I came up to the building where the clerks had been working yesterday and where I had met the temple prostitute, Sena. It was not she, but those in the outer office I needed to consult. I barged open the door and stood there in my red-striped veteran's tunic with its stiff pleats at the hem, legs apart in military poise, unbent despite my eighty years, with my crimson cloak about my shoulders, held in place by the bronze bull badge of the VIIIIth. Out of the corner of my eye, I had seen a priest – no, two of those sceptre-carrying, brown-dressed creatures – hastening towards me around the temple portico, but I ignored their calls.

The clerks were at their tables, as before, and they seemed to press themselves back in their chairs at the sudden sight of me, as if a strong wind had entered through the door and swept its force against them. I barked at a man with a papyrus roll on his table. "Get out for me the earliest records you have of this place. I want to know when your goddess Senuna was first worshipped here."

A tugging at my arm told me the priests had arrived, one of them the same man as I had spoken with yesterday. I spun round on him. "You touch me at your peril. I have an imperial order." It was not quite true, but it was near enough. The grasping hand on my sleeve left me.

"Please be seated, or would you rather recline?" the priest asked. His voice still held that smoothness that had irritated me yesterday. .

"I will stand. The Emperor himself is nearby. I have his orders and I act for him. He is enquiring into the war that was fought in these parts sixty years ago. In particular, he wishes to know what happened at this shrine at that time, so close to the place of battle."

Again, this was not exactly true and I only had my suspicions, not facts. But what I said, or perhaps the way I said it, produced an immediate response. There was no longer hostility or suspicion from the priests, but only concern. Was the misrepresentation of a religion to deceive its worshippers an offence, I wondered? Was there such a fraud in Roman law? And was the prostitution here, disguised as worship, even legal?

My eyes lighted on the yellow bird painted amongst leafy fronds on the wall. I had a second's crazed desire to cut that bird out of the plaster and to take it outside to set it free. We poor breathing, sensate beings so often trap ourselves in situations from which escape is difficult, and truth even harder to find. With my anger from last night still boiling inside me, I would have liked to have taken a section of my soldiers and set the whole miserable place on fire. The degree of my rage surprised me. Perhaps it was due to the solidity of things I had valued for many years now seeming to dissolve before my eyes, to be replaced by others I found contemptible.

"Florianus, fetch out our foundation scroll," commanded the second of the two priests, an older man than the other. He had a round, ruddy face like a sea-captain, or so the fancy took me as I gazed upon him with narrowed eyes.

The clerk in question rose from his table and went to a cupboard against the wall. From a shelf he lifted off a long scroll, wrapped in a cloth sleeve. He took this to a large table top by the wall and drew off its cover, unrolling the single sheet of papyrus lengthways on the table top, and holding it open with heavy stones wrapped in hide. The papyrus was covered by rows of tiny writing in black ink, the spaces between the rows decorated with small painted scenes in reds and greens: I saw one representing a building with a pointed roof, another of a women's face with her hair drawn back into a coil, yet another of a baby borne in the arms of a man who carried a sword.

"Here is a record that tells of the coming to us of the goddess, Senuna," intoned the priest. He had a deep voice that would have commanded attention whatever he was saying. Despite my earlier forceful approach, I now stood beside him, quiescent, absorbed by what he spoke. The story he read seemed too incredible to believe, and at that time it was yet only half the story – as I was to learn. I will summarise it here in my own words, not in the steady, formal cadences of the priests (for the second man too had joined in, both accompanied by the chanting of the clerks).

'Before we – the Romans – came to this land, the old gods dwelt here, known to the *Britanni* as the Sen. They were gods of earth and fire and water, and they demanded sacrifices of flesh, sometimes human flesh. Worship was made to them in groves by the streams that rise and flow through this valley. When we first began to build our civilisation amongst these peoples, such worship ceased. The woods and groves and fields, with their places of sacrifice, were bought by a landowner – a *Britannus* who had been raised in our ways and taken a Roman name – that of Tiberius Claudius Verus. He built a villa close by and founded a small shrine to the goddess Minerva, of whose wisdoms and truths and enlightenments he had learnt while living in Rome itself. The Sen of the *Britanni* were now consigned to earth; Rome lived on through the divinity of Minerva.'

'Verus soon died. His son had no interest in Minerva: he was said to have reverted to the old ways, although that is unlikely, his principal interests at that time being wine and fornication. The shrine, however, with one impoverished priest named Cecidius, struggled on. Then the war came – the rising of the people out of Icenia. They surged over this land following the highway to the west. Verus's abandoned villa was destroyed, the shrine looted of its gilded statue of Minerva, but otherwise quite miraculously spared. Cecedius too saved himself by hiding away.'

'The Roman Army arrived. They set up a fort at nearby Competum. A great battle was fought somewhere to the east. Survivors of the *Iceni* fled amongst the woods and groves of the old sacrifice grounds of the Sen: the Romans hunted them down there, the earth soaking up much blood once more.'

'After a time of some ten moons (a most propitious period according to ancient lore), a soldier from the Competum fort, which was about to be torn down, came to the shrine and found Cecidius at prayer in the decaying *cella*, having nothing with which to make sacrifice. The soldier carried a baby in his arms, which he told Cecidius had been born to an *Iceni* woman made a slave at the fort. She had died giving birth, and he made offering of the baby to Minerva in the hope that such a gift of new life would prove acceptable to the goddess, and bring back prosperity to the shrine. The soldier, who did not give his name but had the rank of *decurio*, brought with him a nursing woman who fed the girl infant from her own breasts.'

'Cecidius regarded the gift as coming from the goddess herself, one that united Rome in wisdom with the *Iceni* people after the terrible war. He had the girl named Senuna – the new goddess of the Sen – and he saw her as a personification of Minerva. She became the living image of the goddess to replace the effigy that had been stolen. She was instructed in the knowledge of Minerva and made to dress and sit and stand and in every other way look like the goddess. People, on hearing of this miracle, began to flock to the shrine, which was built anew by the now wealthy son of Verus, who had made much money out of the war. He constructed a temple, with accommodation for the many devotees who travelled here from afar.'

'And so began a period of great prosperity for the shrine.'

That is the point at which the history of the shrine, according to the papyrus spread before us, appeared to end. I could not read the tiny writing for myself: it was hard even to make out the cursive script it was written in. The incantations of the priests, and the chantings of the clerks, ceased abruptly, as if what they recounted had been from memory and not necessarily from the papyrus itself. That was now rolled up and I had no further opportunity to look at it.

My mind was racing. I felt both exhilerated and worried at the same time. I had suspected yesterday something hidden from me that I might yet discover, but these revelations were overwhelming. I thought I knew now from where my Senuna had come, yet I was still far from sure. What further questions might I ask to gain a greater certainty? I had to accept much would probably remain in darkness, many of my conclusions being but supposition.

This, though, is what I deduced: the baby brought by the Roman soldier to the shrine was clearly the result of a liaison between a woman of the *Iceni* and the soldier. As the man held the high rank of *decurio*, it was likely the child was his: it was difficult to imagine him becoming so personally involved with some other soldier's *Britanni* bastard. Had the mother – captured and used as a slave – been raped? Such women would have been readily available to the Roman Army after the battle. As I had witnessed, whole compounds of prisoners were often kept close by the camps, to be used by the soldiers as they willed.

She had died giving birth, and the *decurio*, with orders to move elsewhere – probably a long way distant – had not wished to be burdened with an unwanted child. So the solution was the temple nearby, damaged and half-abandoned as it was. I knew unwanted babies, past the age when they might legally be destroyed, were often delivered to temples to be cared for. However, I had never heard before of such a baby taking on divine status. Yet, many strange things were possible at times when the working of the normal world was overturned. The time would have matched the likely date of Senuna's birth. She had been in her early twenties, I thought, when I had met her: such a period of years matched the time of my service with the VIIIIth after *bellum Icenorum*.

I remembered the gravestone I had so recently seen in that small overgrown cemetery outside Competum: the inscription had read *femina Britanna*. Was there a chance then that this was the grave of the mother who had died giving birth to my Senuna? Other graves, as I recalled, had been to cavalrymen of the *Ala Nerviorum*. Had Senuna's father, therefore, been the *decurio* of that unit, which must have fought in the battle? If so, a hunt amongst the unit's records might provide his name.

However, I did not even know if the *Ala Nerviorum* was still based in Britannia. After all, these events were sixty years ago, and all Army units, including the legions – as well I knew – regularly destroyed the huge quantity of written records that they accumulated. I myself had ordered many such bonfires of old correspondence, rota and sick lists, movement orders, leave requests, requisition forms. Perhaps in Rome itself, there might be some permanent record of the commanding officers of Army units across the empire, inscribed in stone or bronze. But I thought it unlikely.

The fact my Senuna bore that full name, and not some abbreviated version of it, made it even more certain that she was the baby who had been brought to the shrine to be dedicated to Minerva, but who had given new life to ancient *Britanni* beliefs as well – as the chronicle had stated. I thought it likely that this rebirth was seen through a fusion of Roman and *Britanni* beliefs. Senuna had been brought up in the likeness of a new goddess, Senuna Minerva. She – like Sena, her successor today – would have served the goddess. Had she, when she was of age, also served her through prostitution?

The train of adherents coming to the temple would have provided much-needed income for the shrine. Services would have flourished – accommodation and food, the bath house, the supply of trinkets and souvenirs, the selling of votive plaques and altar stones. Money would have flowed. Senuna, the demure, living personification of Senuna Minerva, through whom the conjoined goddess could be more directly approached, would have provided a further lucrative source of wealth, one that might have been considered as part of spiritual devotion rather than crude, animalistic prostitution. Senuna, raised in isolation, would have been largely unaware of the world beyond the temple, and of how her body was being exploited.

As I thought these things, I became filled once more with anger, looking at those priests in brown about me, and their blank, all-knowing, yet all-unrevealing faces. They worshipped wisdom, or so they said. Yet their religion was a tainted one, an abomination, a travesty of the true worship of Minerva – and, I suspected, of Senuna too, whom I believed to have been a goddess of light, of the moon and the moving waters.

So what had happened? Why had Senuna left the shrine and gone to Duroliponte to be a prostitute, taking her child with her? Who had been the father of that child, presumably conceived in temple prostitution? And what had taken place between the time when I saw her in Duroliponte and when she came to me at my home? I knew the little girl had died, but I did not know exactly when or where.

Looking at the priests, their gaze upon me as I stood before them in my veteran's uniform, my brow furrowed with thought, I thought these were questions I would probably never obtain an answer to. It was unlikely the present occupants of the shrine even held the answers now. The past had long since been rewritten here to suit the present. I wondered how old their papyrus was. It looked old. But a papyrus would be aged after only a few years, and I was trying to rediscover events that had taken place a lifetime ago – my lifetime; and just think how old and shrunken and wrinkled *I* had grown beneath my clothes!

I said, "I would wish to enter the *cella* and gaze upon the image of the goddess? If I may be granted this, I shall make a gift of money, now, and regularly in the future."

I turned to find Myru, seeing her framed in the outer door, worry written plain upon her face. "Come," I beckoned to her. "How much do I have left in my purse?"

"*Domine*. I do not know. I have not counted. *Domine*, I would counsel..."

216

I raised a finger. "Enough. Tip it out."

The purse was attached to a strap at Myru's waist. I had to help her to untangle the leather cords, her own fingers brushing limply against mine as I did so. Her advice, I knew, was wise, yet I did not want to listen. I tipped out the purse onto the table top. Several silver *denarii* mixed with a few larger bronze *sestertii* chinked and rolled across the wooden top. The first priest – the one I had dealt with yesterday – eagerly gathered them up, his lips moving as he counted. I estimated from the silver at least *vi denarii* there. Would it be enough to satisfy these priests for whom money seemed to be at the core of their worship? I felt a surge of resentment at having to deal with them like this. No wonder Myru, who could know little of my reasons, was looking at me as if I had taken leave of my senses.

One priest spoke to the other. It was in a language I did not understand: I don't think Myru did either. Perhaps they had their own form of communication, one that locked their secrets even closer to themselves. They seemed content. Even now one of the clerks had come over to gather up the coins and place them in a metal box.

"Follow me," said the senior priest, holding up his bronze sceptre so that it flashed like fire in the sunlight filtering into the room.

I walked outside with the priest, and, as we prepared to climb the steps to the temple portico, I saw Myru move to follow me, but her way was barred by the outstretched arm of the second priest.

"Let her come," I commanded. "She can wait for me outside the *cella*."

The arm was lifted and Myru was soon at my heels on the steps. She carried the emptied purse in her hand, looking down at it in sorrow as if it was she who had lost the contents. "You cannot follow me inside," I said. "Fetch out Ajax. We shall ride off when I have seen what I must see; and put the saddle in place for me until we are clear of their gates. You will have to walk at first, I fear."

"*Domine,*" she said in obedience.

I was led around the portico, brushing against a party of worshippers who were engaged in placing a votive against a column and who bowed their heads to us. Then we were at the great double-leafed doors of the temple, made of a dark wood and hinged with steel. They must have cost a huge sum by themselves, I thought. On each leaf was a bronze handle shaped as the head of an owl. However, the priest did not pull at one of these. I saw now that, cut into the right-hand leaf, was a further small door, which he banged upon with his sceptre. It was immediately opened inwards. Bending almost double, I followed the priest inside.

It was dark. An oil lamp flickered on a shelf. A curtain of gauze cut off the entrance way from the interior. The gauze shivered in the gust of air from the open door, which the priest was pushing to. A woman in a fine white tunic and stola stood before us. Her hair was swept back into a coil and she stood very straight, her hands laid against her thighs. She must be another server to the goddess, I thought, but she was not Sena and nor, being dark-haired, did she have any resemblance to my Senuna. It was strange, but I felt a sense of relief at that.

With the server leading, the priest and I passed through into the *cella*. The space was much smaller than I had expected. The walls must be very thick, I thought, probably to bear the weight of the tower above. The *cella* was lit by candles and lamps set on shelves. Their light picked out the image of the goddess – a life-sized figure seated in a chair: a real wooden chair that was like a throne. She was clothed in an elaborate tunic draped over her knees to her feet, her hands laid on a bronze helmet held in her lap. What the body was made of I could not tell, but the head was undoubtedly of metal, the face painted white with jewelled eyes that glistened in the lamp light, the hair – a wig – of a reddish colour tied into a knot at the back. The features were unmistakably of Senuna. I fell on my knees on the hard tiled floor and I cried out. What I said, I do not exactly know now, but after a time I was helped up and taken back outside.

When my memories begin again, I was on the back of Ajax, at the junction of the track from the shrine with the road from Competum. Myru was leading Ajax by a rope tied to his bridle. By the side of the road was the same old man with his dog we had met earlier. He called out, "You have seen the goddess – I can tell so from your face."

"Old man," I said, "I have nothing left to give you."

"It is no matter, *domine*," he said, "for now you know truth."

And I believe I did.

XX

I returned home courtesy of the *cursus publicus,* riding in a coach drawn by two black horses, bred for their power and speed. The coach was lined inside with a dun-coloured leather that was also carried to the outside of the doors where it was embossed with an imperial eagle in yellow and the letters *C.P.* I had insisted Myru travel inside with me together with two other slaves of the *C.P.*

Gavo – as the good steward he was – must have received advance notice of my arrival for he was outside the house with my servants and slaves neatly lined up, wearing their best, when the carriage at last thundered up the long, rough trackway from Duroliponte, following the canal, and swept to a halt before my gate. It was almost a full month since the Emperor and his entourage had come here, and now the signs of their presence in my pasture fields had been expunged by the growth of fresh grass as if they had never been.

I was wearing my veteran's uniform, newly cleaned and pressed in Duroliponte where we had spent a couple of nights at the *mansio* so that I could recover fully through some days of rest. With Myru for a companion and with a bodyguard of the two slaves of the imperial service – huge lads in green tunics carrying cudgels – I had wandered beyond the town, following the river downstream. I had seated myself amongst the long grasses on the bank, watching the rippling waters and seeing the moorhens diving and darting. The barges passed in regular procession, travelling in both directions. One, piled high with barrels, was being towed, and I had to jump up to avoid the ropes being hauled by slaves. I waved my hand at the steersman, whose face I knew, feeling sad now that I would no longer have any responsibility for these barges at my canal dock to the north.

I greeted Gavo and Diseta with an embrace, something I would not have done if I had been in company, but I felt them to be of my family – and who was I to stand on formality? I walked through my garden, which had been kept, I was pleased to note, very trimmed and tidy, and up the short flight of steps to my portico, where I had sat with the Emperor at a time that now seemed strangely remote. Much had happened since. Action, not remembrance, I knew, was now important to prevent time hanging over me and adding years to my age. Gavo had had the wooden eaves of the portico repainted in red, and had hung them with garlands made of reeds and marsh flowers for my return. The columns too that had been cracking with age had been replastered and painted. I thanked Gavo, while anticipating the bills that in time he would present to me.

I made worship at the shrine to my *Lares,* running my fingers over the small bronze figurines I kept there – first, my household gods, then, Mercurius, Venus, Minerva, and Epona, until I was satisfied that I had given thanks enough for my safe return. I asked Gavo to leave bowls of oil and fruit and flowers before them as offerings.

Having splashed water upon my face, and drunk a draft or two as well, for the weather was hot, I walked by myself to the mound at the top of the slight slope behind the house where I had buried Senuna and my still-born child. Kneeling here, I looked through the crown of long grass that shimmered yellow in the heat, into the depths of the blue, over-arching sky, understanding better now – yet still not knowing exactly – how, and from where, she had come to me, and what her pain and suffering had been at that time. It was a relief to me that we had found such happiness together for that short while before the final pain from which there could be no ending. I saw her face, with its calm contentment, her golden air with the ribbons at the back, and her eyes, bluer even than the skies above me. And the boy, had he lived: what would have been his life now? He would have been – I found the calculation hard to make and the imagined reality even harder to form – in his mid-thirties, perhaps a soldier in a high command, far away from me on a distant frontier, or a merchant or a trader with a growing fortune, building himself one of those fine houses that are going up everywhere in Britannia in the river valleys and by the sea.

I spent some time here before the grave mound. The wooden plaque I had set up beside it, in the *Britanni* manner, had moved sideways in the ground and the lettering was becoming obscured with mould, and needed scouring out and re-colouring. I would tell Gavo to have this done. On such a matter he would not have acted without my command, so I could blame no one but myself for this neglect.

I thought back on what I had learnt so recently at the shrine. I was still trying to resolve it in my mind, to develop my reasoning, my fears and my hopes, into a narrative that seemed to make sense. The resemblance of Sena to my Senuna, and then to the image of the goddess, had been too remarkable to be simply a coincidence.

My Senuna would have been raised at the shrine and would have been instructed in all the attributes of the Roman goddess Minerva, which would not only have been knowledge of the Roman tongue and of the history and philosophy and virtues of Rome, but would have included her very appearance – the way she was dressed, the way her hair was worn, the poise with which she stood and sat, her almost ethereal stillness at times. Such qualities were then syncretised with her own *Britanni* origins, which I knew now were those of the *Iceni* people too, against whom I had fought so long ago. She came to represent *Dea Senuna Minerva* – two goddesses, made one and the same. That explained the quality – the air – she had had about her which had inspired caution, and even awe, amongst my *Iceni* born slaves.

What had Senuna herself known about her origins? She would, of course, have had no memory of her parents. Had she been told the story set out in the papyrus? It was possible, I thought, although its writing down was likely to have been much later, when the shrine had needed to make a virtue of its foundation. As the commander of a Roman auxiliary squadron, her father would have been a citizen of Rome. That meant Senuna was freeborn and a citizen too. She should have been free all her life, yet her servitude – her prostitution – had robbed her of those freedoms, which she may never have known of until she came to me. My marriage to her, therefore, had not given her freedom, but simply confirmed it. She had always held equal citizenship with me.

Thinking of how Senuna had been treated at the temple over more than twenty years made me angry again. How many of the trinkets at that temple, I wondered – the sceptres, the jangling chains, the incense boxes, the ritual crowns, the very bronze head of the goddess herself – had been bought with the proceeds of her prostitution? There was little enough I could do, I knew, to challenge the power that had made it possible. Unless, of course, I had a word in the ear of Hadrian....now, there was a thought! The Emperor was seeking to rid the Empire of corruption and to return it to Rome's ancient values. What would he think of landowners and members of town councils who turned shrines into brothels for their own gain and aggrandisement – for that seemed to me to be what was going on – shrines too that were meant to represent the virtues of the Roman people? Apart from any other factor, was not Minerva considered to be a goddess of chastity?

I walked across the meadow to my small shrine to Epona. Someone had scrubbed clean the carved stone, so that it shone white under the sun. Some foodstuffs – I could not make out exactly what – lay before it, and flowers too. Perhaps Diseta had done this, or one of the stable slaves whom Myru controlled. I would find out later and thank them. It was pleasing to see such attention to the things that mattered most to me.

I leant against the stone. It was high enough to support my thigh: my hip fitted snugly into a curve in the carving. I ran my fingers over Epona's face and over the heads of the two horses she stood between. Sometimes I sense such powers coming through the stone that my finger tips tremble. Then, I feel that stone is filled with light – the light of everything that has ever happened, which might yet be seen again by those who have the gift. Certainly I love to touch stone – and wood too – for they bring me close to that other world that has passed. As I thought of Senuna – my Senuna, both divine and mortal – and stroked the stone of Epona, I cried out to both goddesses that they would allow me understanding. And my thoughts at once coalesced and I *knew* – although there was yet something missing that I felt was being held back, perhaps the most important thing of all.

I thought back on what I had learnt – on how Senuna had come to the shrine, how she had been raised, how she had lived, and the prostitution that had become part of her calling. The inevitable pregnancies over the years from this prostitution – of Senuna at first and then of others – would normally have been aborted or, when first born, suffocated – as the law allowed – the tiny bodies being disposed of in the ground. At the shrine of Senuna Minerva, the situation, as I perceived it, would have been – and presumably still was – somewhat different from other temples carrying out a similar practice. It was girls in the image of the first Senuna – my Senuna – the image that matched the goddess herself, that were most desired. The prostitution produced money for the shrine, but it was also carried out as a form of selective breeding to help ensure its future (such as I knew Numicius's bailiff used with his black, short-horned cattle), the boy babies put to death, the girls allowed to live, in particular if they had the favoured features and colouring. Most men using the prostitutes would be unaware that the greater devotion to the goddess they had shown had resulted in a pregnancy: if they did know, they were unlikely to be concerned, or just possibly they would, in fact, be pleased that the girl they had sired in the image of Senuna would in the future serve the goddess.

My Senuna, being raised at the shrine, would have had very little knowledge of the outside world. As she grew of age, perhaps at a time eight or so years before I was to meet her, she would have been instructed that to give herself sexually to a male devotee was not only a natural, loving thing to do, one of the wisdoms of life she was being instructed in, but a sacred duty too, as important – if not more so – as any other rite of worship she would have performed.

I cannot say – I hardly dare to contemplate – how many pregnancies she had had over those years: perhaps the first were of boys who were taken from her, but she must in time – perhaps not many years before I met her – have given birth to a girl who was to grow up in her likeness. She may well have been allowed to nurse this child, until such time as it was taken from her. These are secret matters, known only to the rulers of the shrine, impossible for an outsider to gain knowledge of – impossible, that is, unless an Emperor should make it his business to find out. Yet, I knew that, however much I assumed a friendship with Hadrian, he was much more likely to take action to stamp out some financial corruption than be concerned with the morality of an obscure temple ritual.

It is very likely, I think, that Senuna's next birth was of the little sick girl I saw her with in Duroliponte. The girl had dark hair, so perhaps she resembled the unknown father over Senuna's own blood – which must, however, have been a strong line for it had predominated through at least two generations. Of course, I had no knowledge of Senuna's own parentage, other than that the father had been a Roman *decurio*: he was likely to have had the dark complexion of many of his countrymen. So Senuna's fair skin and red hair had probably come from her mother, such colouring being frequently seen amongst the *Britanni* – the *Iceni*, in particular.

For Senuna to have left the shrine and broken her vows meant that something terrible must have happened to her. Possibly her baby was going to be put to death because she was not in the image of Senuna, but bore the parentage of the father. Possibly as well, the father was not one of the devotees: he may even have been a priest. The baby may have been due to be smothered, and a distressed Senuna, her natural maternal instincts prevailing, took her chance of escape, and, leaving her first child behind, carried her new baby from the shrine up that long track we had followed and out onto the open road. For her, it would be coming into a world she had scarcely seen before. Somehow she came to Duroliponte, her main concern being to protect her child. The only business she knew – other than for the rites of temple worship – and the only way to make any money to live was prostitution. She was able to maintain her special identity, however – her temple education, her poise, her dress, her very separateness, which were the qualities that had first attracted me to her.

She must have struggled like this for many months, then the child grew ill. That was the situation I had found. Senuna would not join me then, although my offer of help must have seemed to her like a beacon of light sent by Minerva herself. The child died. Perhaps Senuna then felt she owed herself to the temple – to Senuna Minerva – so she returned. If so, it was a mistake. They were unlikely to have wanted her back, probably turning her away at the gates. Senuna's own daughter, born earlier, whom she had had no choice but to leave behind, would by now have taken her place, to be instructed in turn as the new Senuna – very likely, the Sena whom I had met, who had offered herself to me in fulfilment of her duty, as her mother – my Senuna – had been used to doing. Once Senuna had broken her vows, not only was she told the goddess was angry with her, but there was no place for her at the shrine any longer. She had to leave her two daughters behind – one dead, one still living in temple servitude. She came to me, instead. There was no other place she could go that would offer her life.

And we could have lived for so many years together, if only…..I looked back towards the small round mound showing like an upturned bowl above the long, green stems of grass….If only…..

We thought Minerva had blessed us. But perhaps the goddess had indeed been offended and we were to be punished. I find that hard to believe. My Senuna was gentler than the birds that would sometimes peck from her hand. She walked in the moonlight and sang to the birds beneath my porch, and they sang back. She did not deserve to have the cord twisted inside her, choking her and my son to death.

Whosoever's hand guides and shapes the world – whether great Iupiter or his consorts, or one of those gods they worship in Aegyptus, or a god yet to be born – I hope they do not deal out cruelty just for the sake of it, as some mad emperors of ours have done in the past. I have been a soldier. I have always held a stern view of the world. I believe in right and wrong. I believe wrong-doers should be punished and they should be given back the pain they inflicted on others. The innocent and the good, though, should be protected. They should be able to enjoy peace, and the rewards of their work and the happiness of their own company. They should not suffer for the faults of others. I believe there is need for a god who will bring a rule such as this to the earth.

I felt the sun on my head and bowed myself before it. Perhaps, then, Apollo should be the god I worshipped above all. The whole matter was very confusing, in particular for an old man facing long night, not knowing what would happen within that blackness after Charon had deposited my carcass on the far shore. Would Senuna be there to greet me, smiling her secret smile, behind which lay so many things – things I have learnt of now but which she was always so reluctant to share? I so much hope so. It is within hope that we continue living. Without hope, there is indeed only darkness.

A jangle of harness and Myru rode Ajax up to me, with three other of my ponies beside her, their manes and tails all combed out and flowing in the sunlight. They stopped in front of me at the altar of Epona, and the four ponies knelt as Myru slid off Ajax's neck to stand beside me.

"*Domine*, it is good to be home."

"I fear it is not long before the Emperor will summon us once more."

"I shall be ready."

"Myru, you have been a good companion and a friend. I shall not forget it."

"*Domine*, I am happy to serve you."

"If you have any problems, you must bring them straight to me. Don't worry about what Gavo or Diseta or any of the others may think"

She nodded. For some reason, the sight of her small figure, with her black hair now bundled up and her tanned legs set squarely on the grass, brought a choking to my throat and moisture to my eyes. She was dark like Senuna's tiny child had been. Perhaps in this moment I saw her as my daughter – as my granddaughter – who had never been.

I was not the hard soldier anymore. I was growing exceedingly soppy in my old age!

XXI

The weather was changing. Autumn was blowing in from the west, shaking my mulberry tree and sending a branch, laden with purple fruit, crashing to the ground. I ordered the fruits saved and then had the whole tree picked even though some fruits were yet pink. This is work I shared with my slaves, helping position the ladders and call out instructions to those aloft. My servants boil the fruits into a pulp: the pulp goes to the ponies, who like it mixed with their mash, and the juice is kept as a medicine against sore throats, which are common in this region when the weather grows wet.

My successor at the dock had begun his duties. I met him and invited him to my house, together with Numicius's works foreman and, indeed, Numicius himself, who arrived in an open carrying chair, rather like the one I had been forced to use at the shrine. It was the first time I had seen my erstwhile chief since we had all been in the company of the Emperor. He seemed grosser than ever: feeding himself must have been his main occupation once the inspections of Hadrian were over.

"So, Celer," he said to me from his lofty perch, held there by four slaves, one of whom had skin as dark as the veil of Nox, "you concluded your business satisfactorily with our Emperor, I trust."

"Yes, indeed, Numicius," I said, with a flourish of a hand – the one not stained by mulberry juice. "We will be summoned to him again when he returns to this region. There is to be a grand *caerimonia commemorationis* at the former battlefield at which Caesar will be present."

"So, I understand, Celer. I have heard you have made your mark with him. I congratulate you."

This was so unexpected, I did not know what to say. I bowed my head respectfully. "Come inside and take some refreshment, I pray you."

The new man was young, and as slender as a wand. He was full of a repressed energy, which burst from him from time to time in the form of a twitching of his mouth and urgent movements of his hands. He was a citizen of *Britanni* descent, from a good family in the territory of the *Dobunni*, which had long allied itself to Rome. This man, I thought, is going to make a success of things. But he will not live with the canal and dock, as I have done. After a year or so he will move on to greater purposes. He will not stay on here in these swamps like me.

When the visit was over, I changed my tunic for a workaday one and returned to helping strip the mulberry fruits. Diseta chivvied me for being outside without at least a cape around my shoulders. The sun was shining but the air was cool. Another year was approaching its end. How many more, I wondered, did I have left to see? The air was stilled, the light bright: all I could make out were pools of sunlight and shadow on the path – just like life itself, I thought, with all its small joys and greater sorrows.

The imperial summons came sooner than I had expected: it was less than a month after the stripping of the mulberry. The rains had set in early this year, and the canal moved high in its banks. The barges were covered by great sheets covered in hogs' grease and towed by horses with leather coverings on their faces against the driving rain. The towpath was being resurfaced with broken stone on the orders of my successor, since parts were being trodden into mud. The slave workers stood in soaked groups, the sacks over their shoulders as wet as the rest of them. I felt some pity for them as I made my daily inspection of my property, with Gavo in attendance. I would have ordered them hot drink and food, but I had no control now. The new man appeared untroubled by the sufferings of slaves who came from the same *Britanni* stock as himself. He may not care for them as human beings, I thought, but he should care for them as tools of his trade; like his horses they needed food and shelter or they would become an expensive waste to him. Yet, he has to learn these things the hard way. I did not try to intervene.

A messenger on horseback from Numicius's household brought the news to me. The Emperor was returning from the north by the direct road to the *mansio* at Ikelorum, outside which a camp would be established. He was bringing with him a great assembly of his household, including the Empress and her own entourage of court ladies, and a thousand men of the Northern Army. The presence of Numicius and me, and several other landowners of the district, was 'requested' – 'ordered' would have been a better term. We were to attend by the *pridie Nonas Octobris*. A personal note to me was also included – a wax tablet in a leather pouch, with the Emperor's seal attached. I checked carefully the seal had not been broken. Numicius might have been curious as to its contents.

It began, '*Mi Secunde carissime*', which caused me a quick intake of breath. It is not often that a simple citizen, albeit a veteran soldier, is referred to as a man dear to his Emperor. Numicius had been right to congratulate me. The message went on to tell me his work in Britannia had been concluded and he was returning for that *caerimonia commemorationis* which I had helped make possible. He was intent on celebrating a much neglected Roman war, a war that had led to the present unification and security of the province. He assured me I would have a special place of honour at the ceremony, and he requested that I bring my *Iceni* horse woman and her performing ponies with me as well. The latter piqued me a little. The ponies were *mine*. I did not consider them as 'performing' animals, not in the way you might find prancing horses at a country arena where bears are also made to dance. Myru had trained them to show off the ancient skills of *Iceni* horsemanship.

That small annoyance aside, I was delighted and flattered by the Emperor's personal message. How the sealed tablet must have caused Numicius and his fellow equestrians to wonder at the contents. Now they would be on their best behaviour with me, wary of how much of what I heard and saw I might pass on.

And so it proved. I travelled with Numicius, with his slaves in attendance, in another carriage of the *cursus publicus* – this one even more luxurious, with padded seats and a screened off latrine, which I hoped Numicius would not have to use as the smell before the bowl was emptied would have been dreadful. Fortunately, we stopped frequently, so bodily needs could be attended to at those times. We were accompanied by wealthy neighbours of Numicius, some of whom I knew, others not, who rode their own horses with slaves beside them. Myru, with Pyddr also who had performed so well at my show before the Emperor, brought my six ponies, in a tightly reined company of blowing plumes and tails, each animal immaculately decked out with gleaming harness and shining bronze pendants. My slaves rode bare-backed at the rear of our little column, a part of my own household keeping me company, which I found a great comfort at the periodic halts, turning around and seeing them there. Myru's eyes would meet mine with a small nod of her head that told me all was well.

We caused quite a stir in Duroliponte, a town which had seen more excitements as a result of the recent proximity of the Emperor than in all of its fifty years since foundation. We didn't linger in the town, spending just long enough to refresh the horses and for one or two of our companions on horseback to grab a dish of food or a cup of the local beer, and then we were on the way south once more, followed by the usual train of running urchins.

228

The countryside we passed through was by now familiar to me. I settled back against the rich cushions, accepted a plate of chicken pieces swimming in a spicy red sauce, and eat them, chucking the bones out through the raised shutter of the window. Numicius, opposite me, was asleep, his hands resting over the swell of his belly. Our two slaves sat impassively: they would take it in turns to open the door and step out onto a ledge before climbing the side of the moving carriage to sit beside the drivers. Their return would be announced by a rattling of the window shutter before making a quick, wind-blown entry. I admired their athleticism. They were only young lads with tanned, carefree faces. Numicius must treat them well.

As I reclined luxuriously, glad that I was not riding amongst the cavalcade accompanying us, I reflected on the *caerimonia commemorationis* that was to come and the role that Hadrian clearly wished me to play. Even if Numicius had been awake, the rattle of the wheels on the stone surface of the highway and the clatter of the many hooves outside, coupled with the lurch and sway of the carriage, would have made conversation difficult. I was best left with my inner thoughts.

The Emperor was going to assemble a great concourse on the battle site. Numicius had apparently been in touch with the Office of the Governor in Londinium and had provided me with some further details. The one thousand men of the Army would consist of a full cohort of *Legio XX*, accompanied by mixed units of auxiliary cavalry and infantry: they were already on the march from the north to the old battlefield.

Attending the *caerimonia commemorationis* would be a large number of dignitaries – from the governing councils of local towns and other settle-ments: Duroliponte, Ikelorum, Competum, and even distant Durobrivae would all be represented, and it was very likely – Numicius had declared – also the great towns of Verulamium, Camulodunum, and Londinium, which had been so badly damaged during the war. Accompanying the Emperor himself would be his staff and his household, which would include the Empress and her chosen companions, plus the Governor (whose name for the moment escaped me) and the man tipped to be his successor (whose name I also could not remember), and, of course, the provincial Procurator, with senior members of all their staffs, and representatives as well from many of the *Britanni* cantons, including the *Regnenses*, a people which had stayed the most loyal of all to Rome during the rebellion. As far as I could understand from Numicius, the *Iceni* were not due to be officially represented, which I thought a mistake, although it was possible there was no one now of their people who could perform such a function.

229

And I was invited, of course – the only surviving veteran of the war who could be found – the very last Roman soldier from that time. Myru, with my *Iceni* bred ponies, would stand on the battlefield in place of the great enemy host that had once ranged there, with their red-haired Queen in her chariot at their head. I wondered if anyone had thought to invite Catrig – that rogue of the Druids, as I still insisted on thinking of him.

The carriage lurched unexpectedly violently, and the jolt woke Numicius, who farted, blinked his eyes and smiled rather wanly at me.

"Where have we reached, Celer?"

Two miles or so on from our last stop," I said.

"How long before we reach wherever we are reaching?"

"Not far. The *mansio* is only a few miles more beyond Ikelorum."

"Will we stop there?"

"I doubt it, Numicius. We may make a brief halt while the people crowd around with things to sell."

"I must shit now then. Acacius, give me a hand."

The slave with us in the carriage helped Numicius to his feet and led him behind the thin wooden panelling that stood across the far side of the carriage where the other door would have been. I held my breath, pushed wide open the window shutters at my head, and tried to think of the Emperor, at the head of his column of one thousand men, even now riding south to meet us. When Numicius emerged, he was grinning like a small boy who thinks he has done something rather clever. I was just pleased there was no smell. I had not inspected the latrine, but I suspected there was a hole in the carriage floor, and whatever Numicius had got rid of would have gone straight out under the hooves of the riders following. At least he was more conversational now.

"Quite an event this will be, eh, Celer?"

I nodded, being unsure of what to say.

Numicius added, "I have been told an *altarium Victoriae* is being erected on the battlefield on the Emperor's orders. Apparently, there are doubts whether it will be completed on time."

I had not heard of that, although Hadrian had spoken to me about how the council of Competum would be responsible for building the monuments that he had planned under the overall supervision of the *centurio regionarius*, whose name I did recall – one Salvius Leptis. Presumably this man was sweating at the moment. If the work was not finished for the forthcoming commemoration with the Emperor present, then he was unlikely to be advancing his career much further. The Governor might be losing sleep as well. This matter, which had appeared of only minor significance at first – out of a mere whim of the Emperor, or so it had seemed – had grown into an affair of provincial importance; no, in fact, far larger than that, now one of concern to the entire Roman state, including the legions.

I thought, the VIIIIth will hear of it across the water at their camp in the country of the *Batavi*, and wonder why they have not been invited to send at least a delegation. As a veteran of the Bull, I felt this omission keenly, although I understood the reasons why. The VIIIIth had suffered a bad defeat in *bellum Icenorum* and had had no chance of sharing in the final victory, a fact which had jarred ever since and would not be helped by the Emperor's present commemorations of the war.

Legio XIIII were now serving even further away, at Carnuntum in Pannonia. They had formed the major force at *Campo Albo*, where they had won their title of *Martia Victrix*. I felt sure they would have wished to have at least a token presence with the Emperor on the re-located battlefield. I could hear the comment that would be made amongst all ranks when the story of what was presently being planned reached them. But perhaps the Emperor – or some on his staff – might have already had the good sense to send out explanatory and ameliorating letters. It is all very well commemorating old battles, but the Empire still has to be defended and essential duties attended to. Time would not have allowed either for distant delegations to have reached Britannia. In the case of the VIIIIth, however, just a couple of days' sailing away, that was not exactly true: I hoped, at the least, some veterans of later wars had been invited from the *colonia* at Lindum.

I said to Numicius, "And I understand the Emperor is planning a *mausoleum* to the unburied dead of the war. I wonder if that has been started yet."

"Is he? I had not heard of that. A *mausoleum* or a *tropaeum*, I wonder? There is a difference. I know his divine predecessor, Traianus, erected a great carved Column to celebrate his victories in Dacia. I have gazed in wonder upon it. I hope he is not planning something similar here: it would bankrupt us and bring all public works to a halt until it was completed."

"No, I have certainly not heard him speak of a Column. But I know he wanted a place where the dead of the war could be commemorated and where the bones that are still to be found on the battlefields might be placed, now that the legions and auxiliaries that fought there are scattered about the provinces."

Numicius snorted and wriggled his posterior on the seat as if to relieve an itch. "I suspect there are more *Britanni* bones to be found than ours."

"I don't think that matters in Caesar's eyes. Nor in mine now, if I am honest. All remains should be placed together to honour the unknown dead of both sides. After all, you cannot have a glorious victory without a valiant enemy."

"What, even one that's raped and murdered thousands of women and children."

"Time spreads dust over such things," I said. "It's best now just to remember the courage of men in fighting for, and defending, what they believed was right."

Numicius snorted again. "Sounds like age has softened the soldier in you, Celer."

I might have been offended by that, but I wasn't. I knew what Numicius said was true. I had killed the enemies of Rome without mercy, some in battle when I had had no other choice, others when I might have saved their lives had I felt inclined – but I hadn't. The desire for revenge had lain cold against me like the blade of a sword for a long time after *bellum Icenorum*, and I had carried that blade to the fighting I had seen under the Legate Julius Agricola in the north, where I had used it to shed much more blood, some of it unnecessary. I was proud of the fighting, but not of the excesses. There is no honour in cruelty, just for the sake of it. Who was Numicius, anyhow, who had never served as a soldier, to talk to me about such things? I didn't seek an argument with him, so I steered a different tack.

"You say you have been to Rome and seen the Column of Traianus?"

"Oh, yes, my dear Celer. I have travelled widely in the service of the empire."

"As have I, Numicius."

"Of course, I am not implying...."

"No matter. Tell me about the Column. I have heard it is a magnificent depiction of the Dacian wars, everything carved into stone and painted, with weapons and other adornments cast in bronze and attached."

"It is indeed magnificent." Numicius breathed out more contentedly, the irritations in his body evidently eased. Through the shutters of the window, I caught sight of two of our mounted companions passing at a gallop. Our slaves chose this moment to change over the outside duty, and the carriage door slammed shut behind one as the other re-entered, his tunic hem caught up high on his thighs. I saw Numicius's gaze momentarily distracted from the scenes being gathered to his inner eye.

He continued, "When I first approached it in its place of marble in the newly-completed Forum Traiani, I tried to follow the carvings upwards – they spiral around the Column, you see – but after a few feet it was hard to make them out. Others there were doing the same, walking around the Column, their necks craned upwards, knocking into each other."

Numicius laughed. It was a cackling sound he made, rather than a full-throated laugh, but it was all to the same effect. I could see the picture he described – all those distinguished visitors in their togas admitted to the forum bumping into each other, their necks stretched out like geese. I joined in Numicius's merriment.

He went on, "A friend then told me the best thing to do was to go into one of the two libraries that stand alongside the Column, and use a parapet on the upper floor to view the higher sculptures. A number of us did that, much to the annoyance of some elderly ex-senators who were studying *papyri* in the room as we filed by. There was even a guide there – a smart, young Greek – who seemed to know everything there was to know about the wars."

"There doesn't seem much point in creating something unless it can be seen," I ventured.

"Quite so. But the record is there for all time. To the eternal glory of Rome, of course." Numicius said the words, I thought, with a tone of cynicism. I was not sure why. Our wars against the *Daci* had been hard-fought. They deserved commemoration, even if the result was hard to view. At least people would have to cast their gaze up instead of peering down into gutters seeking sordid things. I realised that in old age I was turning into a cynic, a trend I would have to watch.

When we came at last to the *mansio* outside Ikelorum, it was to find the buildings stuffed full, it seemed, with every living being and every animal in the Roman world, not only within the *mansio* courtyards, but for a large area around, the countryside with its hedges and ditches having been flattened and covered with a gridded pattern of tents and wooden shelters, the latter little better than the huts my field slaves slept in.

A harassed official – a soldier, it seemed from his plain leather corselet, of indeterminate rank and unit, one of a number at the road side – halted our carriage and came up to the window, enquiring our names. Our accompanying party on horseback, I could make out behind him, were being similarly questioned. The officials held sheaves of *papyri* dangling from their left arms, covered in blocks of black ink that I realised were

233

names: these lists alone, I thought, with their copies, must have cost many gold pieces to produce. Papyrus – as I well knew – was not cheap, nor the labour of the scribes.

Numicius and I were assigned places, not in the *mansio*, but in one of the tented camps; not in the same tent, I was pleased to discover, but in quite separate places.

"You are beside the Emperor's own encampment," said the official to me, with what I took to be a note of respect. Reading further from his lists, he added, "Your slaves will attend you and your horses will be in the lines nearby….And," he added hastily, scrambling further to find a cross-referenced note amongst the *papyri*, "Decius Salvius Leptis is to see you this evening when you dine with others of the Emperor's particular party."

Decius Salvius Leptis, I knew, was in charge of all the arrangements. He would probably be informing me of the role I would have in the *caerimonia commemorationis*. I felt a moment of unease, but dismissed it at once as the simple yearning of an old man for his solitude and peace. What greater honour could be bestowed upon me than this?

"You, Septimus Numicius Secundus," said the official to my carriage companion, reading from his lists as if dealing with a commodity rather than a person of importance, will sleep and dine in Area X – Row XXVI. Your slaves will take you there." He barked at the two young slaves who were sitting upright with frightened eyes. "See to this for your master. Jump to it!"

And so, in this way, our group was divided amongst the various camps. Our carriage lumbered away to I know not where. Ejected unceremoniously from it, I had been relieved to find Myru beside me. Still riding Ajax, with Pyddr behind leading the other ponies, by some latent instinct that only one of the *Iceni* can have she led me without hesitation through a forest of tent poles and canvas, stumbling over the lumpy ground, with many others about us too, also stumbling, some tripping on guy ropes and falling against tents, all dignity lost – until, miraculously, we came into a clearing of fresh, smooth grass. Here an imposing steward, in the green imperial livery I now recognised, showed me to a tall tent of canvas, also green, decorated with yellow eagles with outspread wings. It was guarded by a group of Praetorians standing back-to-back around the Emperor's personal standard. Inside, already set up, was the luxury of a sprung bed, side tables and three couches arranged in a triangle, all resting on a wooden floor that seemed to have been fixed together in square blocks. I, who knew of the work involved in setting up and taking down each day the pre-fabricated elements of a legionary camp, was amazed by the work and organisation needed to erect these present camps. Decius Salvius Leptis, and his many helpers, were to be congratulated. I could no more have done his job than I could have grown wings and flown to the moon.

And there was much more to come that would amaze me. For the present it was enough to settle into my tent, to take my turn in the *mansio* bath house, when my allotted time came – I was borne there in a carrying chair which Myru must have organised – and to dine in the select company of some opulent-looking equestrians and their lavishly-dressed wives, whose names and positions I cannot now recall, before settling in for the night.

The Emperor and his main party had yet to arrive. They were expected in the morning – the day of the *caerimonia commemorationis*. A languid partner at dinner had drawled to me that the Empress was to have her own camp away from the throng and away also from the Emperor – "probably already on her back under the camp *praefectus*" he added, in a comment that was clearly treasonable. Yet I made no complaint – no comment at all – but was content to nod idly, hiding behind the senility expected of old age, as if some mere comment about the weather had been made. The weather, indeed, remained fine and warm for the late season, with no sign of rain that might have turned the commemorations into a muddy shambles.

I soon returned to my tent, but only after checking on my ponies in the horse lines, where they occupied their own boarded cubicles. I fed them some fodder out of their manger while Myru poured water for them from a great iron tank into a trough. The water had been brought from the nearby river by teams of slaves staggering under the weight of buckets. Was there ever such organisation as this – even to fight a war, let alone commemorate one?

The ponies nuzzled at my hands as I fed them. I stroked their muzzles, calling them by their names. Only Ajax stood a little apart, confident of my eventual attention. Oh, my four-legged brothers, what loyalty you have shown me. Don't let me down tomorrow, for I suspect you will have a big part to play that Myru would already know of. I didn't ask her. My confidence in her was complete. I just sought my bed.

Later, I felt her beside me in the tent, and she lay down beside me on a palliasse. When I heard her quiet breathing, I knew she was asleep. It was a long time before I could share her sleep. My thoughts threaded the blackness. I thought of Senuna, and saw her pale face and quiet eyes under her red-gold hair, watching me as she had done when we had lain together. I knew that, after her death, I had been fortunate to find companionship again though my servants and my slaves, who gave me such respectful attention, way beyond their calling. If our stations had not been so very different, I would have called them my friends – Myru especially so.

It was half way through the night – or later for all I knew – that I woke suddenly, realising I had not met with Decius Salvius Leptis, as it had been said I would. I did not know what role I would be asked to perform this next day. I turned over on my narrow bed and Myru stirred beside me.

"*Domine*, do you not sleep?"

"Tomorrow will be an important day," I whispered into the darkness, putting out my fingers and feeling her bare shoulder.

"The day will come, *domine*, whether we wish it or not. Go back to sleep."

"Myru," I muttered, the slumber heavy upon me. "You have wisdom greater than a philosopher." I felt for her face and outlined the hollows of her eyes. "I thank you, now in this life and will thank you when I have passed to the next."

"Sleep, *domine*, is all I ask of you. Tomorrow your ponies shall dance for you, and for that I too must sleep."

XXII

I had scarcely risen, and was contemplating a bowl of tepid water that Pyddr had brought for me from somewhere or other – perhaps the horse lines, from which direction I had heard the call of trumpets and much shouting for some time – when the long-expected Decius Salvius Leptis made his appearance, shown into the inner tent by Myru, already dressed in the riding tunic she was accustomed to wear for displays, but with a woollen shawl about her shoulders against the morning chill.

Salvius was lean, with a narrow face and hawk-like nose, and his mouth twitched wide with good humour – which, considering the pressures he was under at present said much for his quality. He wore the tunic of a veteran, with broad red edgings to the chest and a badge of the winged horse Pegasus woven at the right shoulder. A military belt was about his waist, its bronze fittings catching the dawn light through the tent opening. The belt with its embossed emblems denoted his present status as *centurio regionarius*, a position much sought after by the most senior centurions of a legion.

We clasped arms, one soldier to another. I knew from the shoulder badge that Salvius had served with *Legio II Augusta* – another of the legions of Britannia that would not have an official presence at the *caerimonia commemorationis*. As I have already mentioned in this narrative, *Legio II Augusta* had not distinguished itself during *bellum Icenorum*. Indeed, its camp *praefectus*, who had disobeyed a direct instruction from Suetonius Paullinus to march the detachment he commanded immediately to an assembly point south of Londinium, had later committed suicide because of the disgrace he had brought to his Legion.

Seeing my eyes on the badge, Salvius said, "Yes, *Legio Secunda Augusta*. We fought the Silures for many years and conquered their country with its great mountains and narrow valleys, building many forts and making our base at Isca – where the Legion serves now. Yet, we are still remembered for the mistakes made in that wretched war against the rebels, which now the Emperor wishes to commemorate. It makes my own role particularly difficult."

But, notwithstanding his words, he laughed out loud, moving his right arm to my shoulder, which he patted rather as if I was his favourite horse. "I used to mix with veterans of that war, but they have all passed on now. You are the only one I have heard of who is left now: it is a privilege to meet you, for I understand you served under the great Agricola as well."

I said, "My service in the rebel war was with the reinforcements for the VIIIIth: our job was to lay waste the enemy's territory, a job without too much glory."

He stepped back from me, looking me up and down, which, because I was still in my sleeping tunic with my bare arms and legs sticking out like white sticks, must have made a sight unlikely to impress him.

"You do yourself little justice, Celer. I have heard of how you distinguished yourself then, and later too. And of how impressed the Emperor has been in his meetings with you. Which is why – other than for my pleasure at meeting such a distinguished veteran – I am here now."

I looked at him expectantly. My throat was dry. I was feeling very tired and my bowels were not good. I should not be here at all, I thought. I should be at home, lying in my bed, watching the sun climbing above the reed beds.

"You must allow me a drink, Salvius Leptis. Then I shall be better able to take in what you will tell me."

"Of course, Celer." He swung round to seek out Myru, but she was already coming to my side with an earthenware flagon. She poured out some watered wine: it must have been left over from last night for it tasted flat and sour, but it wetted my itching throat. I felt a little strength returning to my arms and legs. I sat back on my bed.

"Now tell me, Leptis – if I may call you by that name – what is expected of me today."

It sounded straightforward at one level, potential chaos at another. The Emperor and his immediate entourage, including his detachment of Praetorians, had spent the night at Competum. The Army, including the cohort of *Legio XX* , were camped somewhere nearby, and would march, with the Emperor at their head, to the battlefield. They would reach there by the twelfth hour. By then, all we spectators must be in our places. It was several miles to the field, as I well knew. Many had already started on the journey – indeed had been travelling in the darkness – some in their own carriages, some on horseback, some in carts hired from the countryside around. The road, even the side tracks, were soon likely to be blocked. Some of those invited to the ceremony, Leptis thought, might never reach the assembly place in time: he did not consider that to be his problem. His responsibility was the staging of the ceremonies themselves, and making sure that the Emperor and his immediate entourage, with their most privileged guests, were present and comfortable. This latter category of guests, which included me, would therefore travel across country on horseback. A cleared route had been especially prepared. It would be best – Leptis thought – if I rode with Myru and my ponies.

I nodded. I didn't want to be one with the other hordes, separated and penned into some cart like roistering plebs on their way to the games, a cart that might never reach the battlefield in the inevitable confusion that would reign. I wondered how my earlier travelling companion, the equestrian Numicius, would manage. Had he fallen in with others who would help him? I could already see the scrimmage that would form on the main road. No wonder it had been decided that the Emperor and his Army would approach from the opposite direction, or they would have had to draw swords to cut their way through the throng – not a circumstance that Hadrian would have desired.

I felt sorry for the dilemmas Leptis and his staff had faced. What the Emperor had requested was clearly incapable of being fulfilled in its entirety. Yet the core of it – the essential reason for the *caerimonia commemorationis* – must be accomplished. Once that was achieved, Salvius Leptis would be content. The rest would have to take its own course. For a man under such pressure, he seemed, as I looked upon him, remarkably relaxed.

He told me, "The Emperor will give a speech. At the end of it, he will call several to him. I will be one of these" – he chuckled – "if I still live; but the Praetorian *praefectus* too and various of the Army commanders, including the Legate of the XXth, who is leading his men. And the Governor and his Procurator, of course: they will already be seated alongside the Emperor. And then yourself, as the only surviving veteran who fought in the war. And your slave here – he turned almost apologetically to Myru – will give a display with your *Iceni* horses. We have rounded up some *Britanni* as well – some *Iceni* indeed – who saw the war as children, including one old man whom I believe has already met the Emperor."

I thought, so Catrig will be present. For some reason I could not explain, I hoped he would not be placed near me or given the attention of the crowd in any way.

Leptis continued, "After the appearance of the Army on the battlefield, a select group – including yourself with your horse slave" – he looked at Myru, whose head was bowed: her shawl had slipped to one side revealing a bare shoulder covered with tattoos – "will ride to the point where the *altarium Victoriae* is to be erected. A short ceremony will take place there, conducted by priests from the nearby temple of Minerva. Amongst her many attributes – as I'm sure you know – the goddess Minerva has a power of victory comparable with Victoria herself."

I was shocked by that. It was the last thing I had expected. So Minerva – Senuna Minerva – was now to be brought forth from her *cella* to celebrate a battle – a battle which very likely, had led, by one brutish means or other, to the death of the mother of my Senuna. And would Senuna's own daughter, Sena, also be there? What a tangle of emotions all this produced in me. I wondered how much those priests – likely to include the ones I had met – would be charging for their services. Would I have the chance to inform Hadrian about this? I thought, no for I knew now I could never raise the matter with him. It would spoil his celebrations of victory and unification, and he very much wished an event that would provide a glorious memory after he had left the province. A squabble before the *altarium Victoriae* might create a scandal that was likely to be remembered longer than the *caerimonia commemorationis* itself.

I saw Myru's eyes on mine. She would be sharing my thoughts, imploring me to say nothing. My whole future welfare – and hers too – might depend on it. The Emperor had shown himself most friendly and confiding with me, but I knew – like all men of power – his temper could be turned in an instant.

"After the group's attendance at the *altarium Victoriae*, and the Army's march off the battlefield, the ceremonies for most will be concluded," continued Leptis. "However, the same select group will have the opportunity of riding with the Emperor to inspect the works, some miles off, where a *tropaeum* is being built to honour the dead of the war. I understand, the ground has been cleared, but little else done to date. The Emperor is anxious to inspect the site. Tents have been set up there, and a meal will be provided. An overnight stay is likely to be necessary. There will be use of a nearby bath house, so you – as an old campaigner – should be reasonably comfortable. Make sure you bring with you today whatever you will require, because you will probably not return to this camp until the next day.

I thought, yes. I am an old campaigner, but the emphasis is on the *old*. It is as well these events have come now because I am sure I could not do them a year's hence – even supposing I am still this side of the Styx then.

Perhaps Leptis saw some concern on my face, for he said with a laugh, clearly his way of hiding anxiety, "Say a prayer for me, Celer, that it all works out. The Emperor will either be very pleased or he will be furious – whatever the reasons, whatever the excuses. At least Iupiter seems content for the moment, for if he sent storm and rain all these preparations will be a disaster worse than a lost battle."

I looked him in the face. I had had enough of all the joking, the sarcasm and half-belief, whatever the justification for them. I supported Hadrian entirely in the need to commemorate what the Roman Army had achieved here sixty-two years ago. The *caerimonia commemorationis* must proceed with dignity and respect, however difficult the circumstances.

"Storm and rain raged during the last hours of the battle," I said. "I was told by those who fought that they killed while thunder crashed about them and lightning seared the forests with fire. Yet, the Army endured and did the job Rome asked of them. You – I am sure – will do similarly today."

Salvius Leptis looked startled by my comment. He stepped back through the tent opening, and saluted me. Then he turned away without a word.

The ride to the battlefield over the open countryside was like taking part in a broad front of advancing cavalry, or perhaps – a rather better analogy – a disorganised, retreating one, for Myru, Pyddr and I on ponies, myself doubled up with Myru again, with my other ponies bunched about us, kept coming upon fallers, or those whose saddles had slipped, or one or two who had slid into a mud-filled ditch. The track we had to follow was marked out clearly through the fields and over open heathland, but some riders, seeking to avoid the bunching at the gaps made in hedges, put their mounts directly at these barriers, only to come crashing down. The ride became a type of frenzy, a hysteria even, in which male riders, and some women too, in various forms of dress – some in tunics, others breeches, a few in most unsuitable flowing *stolae* – rode as if they were in flight from a rampant enemy. Litters and travelling chairs were borne at a run by gasping slaves seeking a way amongst the press, others had been set down, their occupiers – women in jewels – looking out with angry eyes. If this was the situation away from the road, I wondered, what was it like on the highway itself? For all his confidence, Salvius Leptis was going to have some explanations to make when the Emperor got to hear about this aspect of his planning.

At last, however, and with my party still in good order, the flat heath I remembered well with the line of low hills that bordered it on the left came into sight. And now I realised the extent of the preparations. At a place on the heath, roughly central between marsh and hills and close to where the *Via Alba* crossed, tiers of wooden seats had been erected, rising to a height of perhaps twenty feet, held in place at the back by a forest of criss-crossing timbers. The seats were built in a curve, rather like the quadrant of an amphitheatre: the architect, probably from the Army, clearly a man of great skill.

Tents and booths were set up to the rear of the stands, with drink and food being served, and at one side were long horse lines, with many slaves in attendance. Myru went off to them with Pyddr. I knew she would look after the ponies before herself. She would want them watered, rested, and groomed before the performance they were due to give. Some people, I saw, clutching baskets and eating food from their hands, were already taking their places in the stands. More officials holding long strips of papyrus with lists of names were stationed at the entrances, and were issuing seat numbers. Here, at least, was order, I thought. I was relieved to see that Leptis's reputation might be salvaged by the excellence of these preparations.

I went to relieve myself. A long trench had been dug for that purpose, with raised wooden boarding above cut with holes, and just a waving canvas screen, incongruously decorated with the imperial eagle, between the section for men and that for women. Slaves stood around with cloths and sponges for anyone who had a particular need. Fortunately, all I required was to piss.

As I returned, after purchasing some meat and bread from a stall, I looked around, and could see the long lines of people still emerging from the cross-country route that we had followed, and those coming in carriages and carts, or on horseback, by the road, which was jammed with conveyances for as far as I could see, groups of riders being pressed out onto the surrounding heath. Further vehicle parks for those now arriving had been set up towards the edge of the marshes, on the place where the camp of the rebel host had once stood. From them, dark trails of people were stumbling over the rough ground towards the main assembly area. The sun was climbing in the sky. It was yet – I estimated – two hours, or a little more, before midday when the Emperor and his party, and the Army, were due to arrive.

I began to feel a stir of excitement. I had spent some remarkable days already in the Emperor's presence, and done things that I would never have dreamed of being given to do, in particular at the end of a life that – I had to admit – had grown dull and routine. But now, this day…this day would be like no other. This day would contain the type of spectacle only seen in Rome itself.

I was walking towards the stands, thinking it was time perhaps that I took up my seat – which I judged must be at the front of the stand amongst the more important people, since I would have to make an appearance beside the Emperor at some point – when someone bumped into me, apologised, and then cried out, "Why, Gaius Celer, you old rogue: how are you doing?"

I spun round. In a tunic the colour of ivory, matching my own, with the embroidered Bull badge of the VIIIIth at the shoulder, stood a man I had not seen for some twenty years. I had to strain back to remember when that had been; probably when I had last visited him in the veterans' compound at Lindum, visits that as the years grew on had become less and less frequent. I had trained him from his days as a raw recruit and overseen his quick rise to *optio* rank. When I had left the Legion, it had seemed certain he would become centurion, for he had the education and the experience and all the right contacts. But something had gone wrong: I had never learnt exactly what, but it was a matter involving that usual soldiers' story of drink and a girl – the daughter of the first-centurion's woman, in this case, or so I had heard.

The consequence was a retirement, neither dishonourable or honourable, but early and without land – only cash, which for many men, in particular ex-soldiers, flows away faster than water. This was the way of the Army now, or rather more accurately it was the way of the provincial government. There was not enough newly conquered land – at least land that was more than rocky hillside and scrub – to give out to discharged legionaries. In consequence – as a rough rule that I knew had long been (unofficially) applied – if your career had any major blot on it, the chance was taken to rule you out of a land grant. You had to be content instead with a barrack-like home in a squalid compound of beaten earth, with a cash sum that would not see you through more than a couple of years, even if you spent it wisely, but with a nice engraved bronze *diploma* to hang on your door post.

So, instead of his expected plot of land to farm – as I had received with a job too in the imperial service – Tertius Curtius Farus had but a wooden cabin, twenty-five feet by twelve, surrounded by a strip of land no wider than a single plough furrow, with identical cabins set on a grid to right and left, occupied by other veterans similarly dispossessed. There was more privacy, less regimentation, on a parade ground. It was not a place either where any sensible woman, other than a slave, would want to live.

I greeted Farus with a soldierly embrace, and stood back at arm's length from him looking him in the face. "You look well," I said. And he did too. His face was fuller and without the strain in it that I had noticed years back.

243

He was much older and greyer now, and not quite as upright as he had been, but his eyes were bright and his cheeks flushed – it seemed with health rather than wine.

"You too, Celer." I think he said that kindly for I knew the advance of years had stripped me of much flesh and I must have shocked him by my frailness. "I have thought of you often, fearing you might have gone on to the next fight" – this was an expression we had used in the VIIIIth for those who had passed on – "yet here you are as sprightly as ever. Do you never grow old?" He clapped me on the shoulder and pumped my arm again. "How did we lose contact…?"

"I have been too much on my own of late," I said. "I lose the appetite to do more than look at the stars. Yet you have not written to me either. What is your excuse?"

"Nothing to do with the sky. But a woman who is now my wife and a new house, with a small piece of land too, enough to grow some vegetables at least, yet I would like more that I could farm."

We were walking towards the stands, people jostling about us. "Her name is Virinia," he said. "You must make the trip to Lindum to meet her and see my place – and my boys as well, two of them now."

"You are a fortunate man, Tertius. Is she a Roman? How did you meet her?"

"The daughter of a pot-maker from Hispania – a citizen. I came upon her covered in clay. She's beautiful, Gaius, as swift and lively as a swallow, close on thirty years younger than me. How can I have been so lucky?"

"It's your accustomed charm, I am sure. And what you keep on and below your belt." Unlike me, his veteran's tunic was pulled in at the waist by a broad leather belt adorned with bronze fittings, amongst which shone out an upright phallus, such as we of *equites Albani* had carried on our bridle leathers.

He laughed, "I've worn that for much of my service with the Bull. It's kept me safe and brought me good things; well, most of the time, anyhow."

We came to the point where one of the officials was checking names on his papyrus lists. People were standing in an orderly queue, many carrying baskets of food, and with blankets and cushions under their arms. Most looked disarrayed, windswept and tired, not surprisingly, I thought, after their journey to get here. Already the stand was beginning to fill up, many people climbing the ladders that took them to the upper tiers. The front rows of seats, I noticed, were largely empty. Other guests, apparently not accorded set seats, were spreading themselves out in rows on the grass at each end of the stand.

"You received an invitation, Tertius?"

"Oh yes, through the VIIIIth's veterans' club. There was a draw and I was one of the lucky ones. You see it works." – he ran his fingers over the metal phallus on his belt – "There were seven of us with winning counters. I haven't seen any of the others yet. They were bringing their women, which I thought would be a mistake."

"Come and sit with me, Tertius. I'm a special guest of the Emperor. I'll tell you how that has come about."

"Oh, I couldn't do that. I haven't got a seat in the stand. I'll settle myself somewhere on the grass."

"By all our comradeship, you will not!"

"But, Celer, you're a survivor of that war – a living relic, if I may say such a thing, and I do so with honour to you. No wonder you have a special seat here. I'm just a foot-slogger who saw out my time. I couldn't sit near the Emperor. I'd feel out of place."

"You served Rome for twenty-five years, Tertius. You fought under the great Agricola. The Emperor, I know, will be most gracious if he meets you. He likes to see his veterans of old wars and talk with them. He will be in a mood to reward those who have served Rome well during what he considers were the great days of victory. This commemoration is all about honouring such victory. Seize the moment, Tertius – *carpe diem*, as the poet wrote. If you don't think of yourself, think of your boys, and Virinia too, and how they might profit. You have nothing to lose."

I put my hand on Farus's belt and pulled him behind me up to the official with the lists. I gave him my name. He took a long time searching, and then, when I suspected he was about to give up and tell me I had no seat, he checked the top of the uppermost strip in his hand and found my name there. He became at once immensely deferential. He handed me a metal counter stamped I-X. "You are in the front row, *emerite. Sedes X* beside the Emperor's party."

"This man is with me," I said, indicating Farus, my fingers still hooked about his belt.

"I must check his name on the lists, *emerite*. A moment, please"

"He will not be there. He is with me. He is a blood comrade of mine, a veteran of the legions. I will not have him sitting on the grass." I dared to add, "The Emperor would not wish it."

The official was flustered, trying to be obsequious but still doing his job at the same time. I felt some pity for him.

"I will take the blame if there is any objection. There will be room for two in my seat. I am old and my backside does not take up much space these days."

The official gave in and waved the two of us through a barrier where a slave, taking my token, showed me to my place. The seat was only a section of a long wooden bench with the number X carved on its back rail. I was right, there was plenty of space between IX and XI for the two of us. The wooden planks were hard. I should have had the sense, like others, to have brought a cushion, or at least the rolled blanket I used for a saddle on Ajax.

As Farus, silent now and still looking worried, settled himself beside me, I looked across the ground before me. Much work had evidently been carried out to clear the heath of its bushes and long grasses for a wide space around, and the mounds and dips in the ground had also been carefully levelled, the spread soil tamped down and covered with turf. A wide, wooden rostrum had been set up at the centre of this cleared area, and, with a thump of my heart, I realised that I might be expected to attend there at some point in these ceremonies. This was the land I had ridden with the Emperor in the search for relics of the battle. Beyond, the line of hills shone in the bright sunlight, their green yellow slopes dark with shadows where the hill sides curved inwards, backed by the black line of the trees on the crest. That is where the centre of our army had stood all those years ago.

More people began to enter our row and the rows immediately behind, many in fine clothes as if they had just dressed in comfort and not had to slog to the field as most of the press around, some greeting us but others pushing past with a mere grunt. Amongst them were ladies in coloured *stolae* with veils drawn over their heads, their wrists jangling with bright bracelets and their scent reaching my nostrils as if from a flower garden. Despite my years, my body stirred and I could sense Farus wriggling in his seat beside me.

Then came a flourish of *tubae*, and some people were entering the row from our right, standing grandly and turning to the crowd behind, acknowledging their calls and their applause. Farus nudged me. "That's the Governor, Quintus Pompeius Flaco, and his family. The story is that he's due to be replaced by another in the Emperor's favour, who's travelled with him from Germania. If the two come together here, we might see the clash of blades."

He giggled nervously. Farus had been a soldier I would trust with my life, but socially he now seemed more like a gossiping woman. I was impatient with such stories. I was wondering how Myru and Pyddr were and my ponies. Were they ready for whatever display they were to give? These matters – although my ultimate responsibility – seemed to have passed entirely from me now

A hawker pushed himself along the row behind us, and by twisting sideways I was able to purchase a straw-filled cushion that I regretted as soon as I placed it beneath me, for the stalks stuck cruelly into my buttocks. Farus had bought a bladder of wine and a meat pie, both of which he shared with me. I was unused to drinking from a bladder and the wine was bitter, so I spluttered, and sprayed much down my front – not only a waste but one which did not improve my already unkempt appearance.

Looking up, I could see the sun riding high in the sky. The hour of the Emperor's arrival must be close upon us. The stands were almost full and a sea of people to my left washed the grass with many colours. I turned to look behind me. In a row well to the rear I thought I made out the portly, white-clothed shape of Numicius, dressed now in a toga, one of the few I had seen this day. I raised my hand to him but there was no response.

On my immediate right, the seats were entirely empty. Towards the centre of the row were seats with tall backs festooned with red cloth, and with a canopy above, clearly intended for the Emperor and Empress and members of their immediate entourage. On Farus's left was a further veteran, judging from his tunic, but a much younger man, who had a woman beside him (perhaps his wife) – an attractive young girl with blonde hair, wearing rustling silk and bearing a sky-blue parasol, which she was asked to lower by people sitting behind. Farus was talking with them.

He turned to me. "Celer, this is Marcus Fulvius Rufinus, former *decurio* of the *Ala Petriana*. I shook hands with him across Farus, thinking what elevated company we had come into – ex-*optiones* now mingling with high commanders of equestrian rank as naturally as if we had been born amongst them. I thought, there should be more events of this sort to bring all ex-soldiers of the Army together, whatever our ranks, or whether our service had been with the legions or the auxiliaries.

I was still pondering this when a further blast of *tubae* sounded out, and there was a general stir about me, with people rising and gazing expectantly to their right. Suddenly, around the far end of the stand, emerging onto the grassy arena in front, came the high-stepping black horses of the Praetorians, with their *praefectus* (the man I had grown to know well) at their head and a standard bearer beside him carrying the imperial Eagle. He raised the Eagle high against the blue sky so that the golden bird seemed to take wing and fly.

The Guard were in ceremonial armour, their shining bronze cuirasses decorated with white enamels bordered with black, the flowing plumes on their helmets also black, their fretted boots against the flanks of their horses shining a glossy red gold (much work had gone into polishing those, I thought).

More blares of *tubae* and then the Emperor himself appeared on foot, holding the hand of a stately and richly robed lady at his side – the Empress Vibia Sabina, without a doubt. A great sound – an intake of breath like a surge of wind – greeted them. Everyone was standing, some with both arms held out before them. The sound was replaced by shouts of acclamation, from individuals at first, then a concerted roar in which I joined too, *"Ave Caesar! Ave Caesar!"*

The Emperor raised his right arm in acknowledgement. In his hand, he grasped the white and gold baton that symbolised Rome's imperial power. He was dressed much as when I last saw him, not in ceremonial armour but a plain, brown moulded corselet over a purple-bordered tunic, his waist and upper legs covered by metal-studded leather strips, alternately brown and white in colour. His boots were short and of a dark colour inset with patches of bright red. Fixed high on his left breast was a round, leather helmet without plume or other decoration, as a cavalry man will wear for training, and around his head was a green laurel wreath, decorated with gold which flashed in the sun as he walked. The Empress beside him was waving a fan nonchalantly at the air. Her hair was coiled high and set with a golden tiara, her robes making a flowing mix of purple and white, open at the front to show her full bosom. A court slave raised a parasol trimmed with crimson and silver above her head.

Behind the Emperor and Empress, also on foot, came other senior figures of their party, who were directed towards the empty seats beside me in the front row. An immense woman in red and yellow, like a barge under full sail on the Tamesis, shuffled herself along the wooden bench up to me. She turned to me, then seemed to sniff when she saw my apparent plain tunic, and turned her head back to engross herself with her companion on her far side: he looked an old man, perhaps nearly as old as me, with thin, white knees that jutted out from a blue cape nearly enveloping him. Who these two were, I never learnt: I would imagine some wealthy landowners who had perhaps bought their way to the Emperor's attention.

When all were in position, the *tubae* blared out again, this time louder and more insistent than before. Hadrian and his Empress, escorted by the now dismounted Praetorian *praefectus*, were led by officials, bowing deeply and walking backwards, to their crimson-decorated central seats. On Hadrian's left, the Governor sat, and on his right, the Empress, with, beside her, a lady who was presumably the Governor's wife – a tall, slim woman with much jewellery in her elaborately coiffured black hair. Fully armoured guards took up position beside this central group, their right hands – in Praetorian style – resting on their sword hilts.

The crowd slowly quietened. Those who were still standing settled back into their seats or onto the grass. The sun was now at the apex of the sky and was burning hot. I saw more parasols raised and shawls pulled across heads. Hawkers began to move amongst the crowd again, pouring drinks into wooden cups. Hadrian, and those about him, were engaged in animated conversation. They seemed for the moment oblivious of the expectation of the crowd. The Emperor laughed: I saw his teeth in his tanned face flashing white. The Empress leant forward, her breasts opening out like plump fruit, speaking to one of her attendant ladies on the grass below. The Governor's wife simpered, looked away, and raised a fan to her cheek. Somewhere some wind pipes were playing – a stylised melody shrilling higher in sound than the murmur of the throng.

Then, stepping out into the arena, came the previously hidden musicians, each man wearing the imperial green livery decorated with yellow embroidered eagles at the shoulders – very smart they looked too, marching in perfect step. The instruments they were carrying, I saw, were curved *cornua*, usually used for signalling commands on the battlefield, having a deeper, more penetrating note than even the *tubae*. They turned to face the Emperor and, on a signal, issued a grand fanfare, the sound rising and falling, then slowly dying away to a ripple of applause. I had never heard *cornua* blown together like this before. The sound entered deep within me, bringing a sense of expectation, with memories too of the many times I had heard the mournful call of the *cornu* on campaign. It brought the faces of the dead back to me from a score of half-forgotten skirmishes.

The imperial party stopped their conversations. All turned to the arena. I saw Hadrian raise his baton and then lower it. The *caerimonia commemorationis*, for which we we had come all this long, crowded and exhausting way, had begun.

XXIII

To my astonishment, three chariots swept onto the grass, each drawn by two ponies – short-legged, broad-backed animals like mine – crossing the level area of grass before us at speed, turning and criss-crossing so that I held my breath thinking they must collide, but they did not. I was astonished because I did not think such skills survived, or indeed the vehicles themselves, which were built in the manner of the *Britanni* tribes who had first confronted Rome. They had low-set carriages, with half-circles of wicker panelling at their sides, and a long yoke, the woodwork being brightly decorated with red and blue, and yellow and green paints. I had seen some such as these racing to attack our column – as I have already described – during our march through Icenia.

At the sight of them, all my memories rushed back, and I held my breath, my fists clenched, my body bent forward in my seat. Some people behind were cheering and yelling as the charioteers, dressed in *Britanni* style in short woollen coats and full-length breeches, cast aside the reins and ran up and down the yoke at full pelt, recovering control and then pulling each chariot into a tight turn before bringing it to a sliding stop, in line with the others, before the Emperor and Empress. The charioteers bowed low, and the ponies dipped their heads and bent their forelegs, in much the same way as Myru had taught mine.

Amongst my surprise, I had a fleeting thought. Was it possible that Myru had had a role in training these chariot ponies? I had suspected she was involved in activities I knew nothing of. But no, that was ridiculous: there were no chariots anywhere on my property, and there could be none nearby either amongst the swamps and open waters around. If there had been, I would surely have heard of it. Later, I was to learn –from Myru herself – that the chariots were the property of one Aulus Canius, who ran a training school at Camulodunum, where such displays took place regularly in the *circus* there. I had no idea of such things, a further example of how isolated from life I had grown.

I was not so astonished when next, striding out onto the sunlit grass from a tunnel cleverly constructed under the stand, came what appeared at first sight to be a pair of gladiators. I was not surprised because I had expected some ritual combat of this sort to be enacted during these ceremonies. It was always the Roman way to celebrate old blood spilt by shedding new blood (such cynicism, I knew, was unbecoming for a veteran of the legions). I concentrated on the fighters, hoping this bright, cheerful day would not be spoilt by any unnecessary killing. The tens of thousands of the fallen who had lain here sixty-two years ago did not need any further death heaped upon them to give them greater meaning.

Closer inspection of the contestants, however, once they had removed their cloaks, revealed them to be: the one, armoured as a Roman legionary, wearing strip armour, burnished as brightly as I ever saw on a parade ground, and a plumed helmet (as worn on parade but seldom in battle), with a sword that he drew now, surely of a greater length and width than the standard issue, and carrying the standard pattern of tall, curved shield – and the other, in the fighting kit of the *barbari* (intended, I am sure, as an *Iceni* warrior, but not as I ever saw one), with leather breeches and bare chest, tattooed with swirls and loops, head encased in a bright pot of a helmet, long hair and moustaches flowing, a round leather-covered shield painted with a boar (or what I think was meant to be a boar) and a great sword with a long, cruelly curving blade, wielded by one well-muscled arm.

The two set about each other in a performance that I realised straightaway was a mock, probably a carefully rehearsed contest, intended to show how Rome fought and defeated *barbari*. I was ashamed of this make-believe as it had little to do with *bellum Icenorum,* or indeed any war that Rome's armies had ever fought, but was just a piece of theatre intended for the cheering masses. Indeed, they were cheering now, urging the man playing the Roman soldier not just to defend with his shield against the weak blows thrown by the *barbarus*, but to strike back himself. Round and round they went on the grass, weapon to shield, weapon to shield, crash after crash, about as realistic as a stuffed flying horse with flopping wings that I had once seen hauled by ropes across the amphitheatre in Ostia.

I was wondering how the Roman victory was to come, when suddenly I saw that a swipe of the *barbarus's* hooked sword had split the legionary's shield and sent a splinter into his face, because there was blood flowing on his cheek. This must have incensed him because his own blows, thrusting with his sword, became much more energetic and realistic. The *barbarus* was parrying them with his small shield in a way that showed an increasing desperation, certainly not rehearsed. Sensing the change in tempo, the crowd roared even louder than before. Then a sudden swipe with the hook caught the legionary below his shield and cut into his calf, fortunately for him only a glancing blow, but slicing the flesh so that the blood spurted and he fell to his knees. An official – the *rudiarius* – carrying a birch wand rushed out and placed himself between the two men. The contestants then left the grassy arena, the *barbarus* with arms raised in triumph while the crowd cheered, the pretend legionary hobbling on one leg, supported by the *rudiarius*. It was not the result that had been required for this make-believe: Rome had been defeated by her enemy – not an auspicious opening for the Emperor's *caerimonia commemorationis*. I thought Hadrian would be angry, and tried to see him along the row of dignitaries now rising to their feet, but could make out little around the red and yellow bosoms of my neighbour, who was bent forward stuffing what looked like a meat pie into her mouth.

There was only a short break in the proceedings, for, after a short interval, I saw my ponies coming into the grassed arena at a gallop, with Myru in front at their centre on Ajax, and Pyddr mounted as well, bringing in the ponies at the rear. My throat felt tight as I watched; such pride I felt. What had begun for me as a mere interest, and then turned into something of an obsession, was now being performed – for the second time, indeed – before the Emperor and all his high-born companions, including his Empress.

It was Myru I had to thank now for everything. These days I simply paid the bills. She did the training, the caring, the grooming, the riding, the planning...the everything. Without her, there would be nothing to show but the ponies themselves, and who wants to look at a squat, solid, hairy animal with four big feathered feet, a broad head and a wet muzzle, often lowered to the ground? No, it was Myru's training and her riding skills that had made this show, and had helped make my name with it.

The performance this day followed the same lines as had been presented at my house. Myru wore the same short tunic with one breast exposed, as she had then, and she sprang and balanced and performed somersaults on the ponies' backs with a skill and audacity that I found breathtaking, although I had seen it many times before. The audience were gasping and cheering and clapping, engrossed in the fluid movements of the ponies and the acrobatics of their riders. Pyddr this time rode as well: his role had clearly developed from that of marshalling and superintending the ponies on foot and serving as a clown to Myru's act. His own skills seemed to have advanced remarkably since I had last witnessed them. He sprang from his pony to Myru's at full gallop, then stood on his hands on the pony's back while it raced across the grass.

The climax of the show came when the ponies were brought in line before the Emperor and Empress, with Myru on Ajax at the front, making obeisance to them with a full bow of bent forelegs and lowered heads. That brought the crowd to their feet, roaring out their appreciation. I saw Hadrian, with the Praetorian *praefectus* in attendance, step out onto the grass and acknowledge Myru and Pyddr with a gesture of his right arm, while they lay flat on their faces before him. An official in green livery then raised up my two slaves, and they were presented with victor's wreaths which were placed on their heads – an honour for them, from the hands of the Emperor himself, that had scarcely ever been heard of for a slave, not even in the *Circus Maximus* at Rome.

While my ponies were leaving the arena to further applause, I was able to make out Hadrian at last along the row to my right. His head was turned towards where I sat in the shadow of the red and yellow woman, who had now started upon a great slab of bread and cheese that her companion had handed to her. The same official who had raised up Myru and Pyddr was coming along the seats, anxiously scanning our faces. "Where is Gaius Modius Celer?" he called out loud, but before I could speak to him, his eyes had lighted on me and he stood in front of me.

"Modius Celer?" – I bowed my head – "The Emperor requests your presence on the rostrum." Over the official's shoulder I could see that Hadrian, with some others, had already left their seats to cross the grass to the rostrum. They mounted it, facing the crowd. *Tubae* and *cornua* sounded out.

"Of course. I shall be most honoured," I replied, seeing the gaze of the woman beside me now fixed on me, her mouth still chewing, her eyes goggling. Turning to Farus, I said, "Come with me, Tertius. If I am so favoured, I know you will be equally so."

"Oh, I couldn't," cried Farus, the hero of several skirmishes that I had personally witnessed, the winner of two silver *phalerae* and a bronze *armilla* for bravery, now reduced to a shrinking girl, trying to shake off my hand on his arm.

"You are coming with me!" I insisted.

His resistance seemed to collapse like an inflated pig's bladder punctured while being kicked about at the baths. We climbed over the low wooden rail in front of the seats, aware of all the eyes watching us, so that I stiffened myself as straight as my old bones would allow and tried to pace a military step. I didn't turn my head to look at Farus but I could sense him falling in beside me, marching in time. We probably looked just a couple of old-timers trying – and failing – to tread back the past, but I did not care. I never felt such pride as then, marching out before this audience of my betters to come face to face with my Emperor once more.

I saw Hadrian's eyes flick over me onto Farus, and then back again. I climbed onto the rostrum, with my old comrade close beside me. Others already there, including the Praetorian *praefectus* stepped aside as we both made our obeisance.

"Greetings, Gaius Modius Celer," spoke Hadrian formally, looking down at me from the high point where he stood

"Greetings, Caesar."

I heard Farus mumble the same words, taking his cue from me.

"Are you well, Celer?" This in a lower voice.

"Yes, Caesar. I thank you."

"You have a comrade with you, we think."

"Yes, forgive me, Caesar. He is an old friend of mine from the VIIIIth. May I present Tertius Curtius Farus who served as an *optio* under the Legate Gnaeus Julius Agricola."

"You are most welcome Curtius Farus. We would talk to you later of those great days."

"Thank you Caesar – I mean, *domine... maiestas*." I felt Farus's awkwardness and uncertainty. He would have found it far easier storming a breach in the enemy's rampart than meeting his Emperor.

Hadrian turned to his steward. "Sestius. Make the announcement."

A man in the imperial green livery beside the Emperor raised an ornate metal speaking trumpet to his lips and read from a wooden tablet held up in his left hand. "Good people," the amplified tones bellowed out across the air. "We welcome you to this commemoration of the courage of our armies some sixty years ago when the enemies of Rome were broken at this place. You will have marvelled" – he hesitated and I realised he was adjusting the written words in the light of the combat debacle that had just occurred – "at the chariot displays you have seen and the skill of the riders of ponies used by Rome's enemies – enemies no more, but now one with the loyal populations of our province of Britannia. We wish to introduce to you a man who fought in that war – a veteran of the VIIIIth Legion who once looked upon the face of the *Iceni* rebel queen herself – we present Gaius Modius Celer!"

As my name was announced, amplified by the speaking trumpet so that its cadences seemed to tremble long on the disturbed air, Hadrian reached out and pulled me beside him onto the highest point of the rostrum. A standard bearer raised the imperial eagle above us. I looked out at the rows of faces watching me, amongst whom I could see the purple and white of the Empress with her women about her. Even from here I sensed the power of her presence – a presence, if I had understood Hadrian correctly, he liked to distance himself from.

"Raise your arm to the crowd," the Emperor hissed at me from the corner of his mouth. I had been standing as if frozen while the audience before me cheered and waved. I flourished my right arm and the applause grew louder. I felt something being pushed at me. It was the speaking trumpet. "Say something," the Emperor's hiss came again. "It is customary when you have been announced."

The mouth of the trumpet was running with the steward's spittle. I knew it would be the wrong moment to wipe it on my sleeve. "I am most honoured," I said, trying to shout into the trumpet, but merely making a nasty harsh, echoing noise."

"Don't shout. Spit your words into the trumpet," came the advice from Sestius.

I tried again. It worked. I could hear my words sounding out now like weighted darts soaring towards the crowd. "I am most honoured. I am a very old man now, yet in your presence I feel but twenty years again." There were cheers at that. I was fast learning the art of oratory, something I had had little cause to practice before.

"I am lucky to have lived so long. You must not think well of me because I have survived, but rather remember all those who died on this field and who never had the chance to grow old."

The applause came again and I paused. Perhaps they were really remembering as I had asked. The next words came out before I could stop them: I did not know how appropriate they were in this place, at this time.

"And do not remember only the Romans who died here, or were killed elsewhere in that terrible war, but those of the *Britanni* peoples who were our allies and also gave their lives. And even our enemies, for they died for what they believed in."

My heart was thudding. I should not have spoken the last line. But the applause that came in waves to me was most gratifying, whatever the Emperor and his Governor and the Praetorians might be thinking. A brave and victorious war usually required an equally brave and determined enemy. It was surely a good thing to commemorate human courage.

I had been going to end at this point, and I could see Sestius reaching across for the speaking trumpet. But I put it back to my lips. "I am pleased you have enjoyed my ponies. They are ponies of the *Iceni* people, ridden by *Iceni*. Are they not beautiful?"

And that brought the biggest roar of all. I turned to Hadrian. My tunic was soaked in my sweat and my hands were shaking. I felt the trumpet snatched out of my hand. Hadrian looked at me with a smile. "Well spoken, Celer," he said. "I should take you back to Rome to write my speeches."

I knew then I was not disgraced, but, on the contrary, had triumphed. Even the reluctant Farus shook my arm and congratulated me. On the rostrum now there was some discussion taking place. A legionary tribune – a young man in a burnished cuirass – delivered a message to the Emperor, with Hadrian stooping to hear it against the continuing hubbub of the crowd. Then the *praefectus*, looking out towards the far side of the stand, at a nod from the Emperor, raised his arm and let it fall. I saw an iron-caged brazier high on a post set into a low mound – in fact, one of the ancient burial mounds that studded this grassland – burst into sudden flame as it was lit by a soldier bearing a long firing pole. Red flame shot from the fire cage and a column of white smoke began to ascend above it, spreading out as it was caught by the breeze. I could just hear the crackle of the burning wood.

The noise of the crowd fell away, aware that something was about to happen. The steward with the speaking trumpet stepped forward again to the edge of the rostrum, his head tilted back, the trumpet raised priapic-like against the bright sky. He must have learnt his lines well for he spoke without notes.

"Look to the hills, you people, and see the mighty army of the Romans draw up their battle lines as they did six times ten years ago and advance against the enemy on this plain where we gather today." He paused. The flame in the brazier leapt up higher than before, red sparks showering from it, the smoke turning from white, through grey, to drifting black. "See they come!"

All of us on the rostrum had turned towards the hills. Then, for the first time, I saw the army Hadrian had brought with him from the north. They must have marched directly to the far side of the plain and taken up their positions on the hill tops, out of sight amongst the trees – in the same way that Suetonius Paullinus's army once had done. They had been waiting for the fire beacon below to summon them.

The green hill sides, with their sinuous, curving slopes and their open high places, began to be filled with lines of armoured men, rank after rank of them stretched from left to right of my vision, with amongst them too, like turning parts in some great machine, the troops of cavalry wheeling in dark blocks on the spurs that projected into the plain. The infantry – the legionaries of the XXth (for such they were, descendants of those who had fought under Paullinus) – were now moving also, gathered together on the slopes in a formation of pointed wedges descending rapidly over the humps and ridges in the grass to the flatter land below. Out of the distance came the sounds of *cornua* and *tubae*, as I had not heard them since I left the legions – not prettily played in unison as earlier, but the real battle calls of an army in attack: the XXth were clearly intent on providing as much realism as possible.

Closer and closer came the formations of armed men, now in wedge, now in line, now in squares by centuries, now back in extended line, standards and banners raised, the Eagle at the centre, with the cavalry charging at a gallop on each flank, turning and throwing long spears which sliced the air like dark rain. Auxiliary infantry were present too: I could not see exactly where, but perhaps towards the rear behind the cavalry, for a great cloud of arrows suddenly filled the sky, aimed high so that they fell to the ground some hundred feet or so before the front ranks of the Legion. As if this was a signal, the XXth halted and threw flights of javelins – the front rank first, then kneeling, the same with the second rank, then the third, the fourth, the heavy javelins thudding into the ground, throwing up clods of earth, sounding like a roll of thunder. The foremost century of the XXth and some of the horse were now less than three hundred paces from our rostrum, the churned ground between stuck with a forest of arrows and spears and javelins.

Orders were shouted, standards dipped, and the Legion's cohort advanced again, officers on white horses now riding to the front, with the Eagle borne amongst them. Behind them, the centuries, each with its standards raised, marched around the missile-strewn ground in as perfect a formation as I would have hoped for on parade. As they came closer, I could see more clearly the soldiers' appearance: they looked as if they had been long on campaign – their shields were muddied and dented, the bosses tarnished, their armour dull with wear and exposure, their helmets bare of crest or plume, their faces scruffy with stubble, some wearing cloths around their necks. Yet their bearing was magnificent, their discipline perfect, their lines straight with shields held forward and swords drawn, the blades flickering between the shields like silver lightning.

This was the first cohort of the XXth brought here on the Emperor's orders out of present battle in order to re-enact another, and whatever each man's own thoughts, they had carried out what they had been asked to do with as perfect a precision as any routine drill. I could understand how Hadrian had wanted his soldiers to look here as if they were truly at war: this time he did not require the perfect, polished look of the parade ground. The men looked tired, their faces unsmiling, yet their heads up – in fact, just as if they had endured some long drawn out battle. I thought they have probably not slept, nor eaten properly. They have been marched here at speed and hidden away, probably spending the night in the open, just for this one staged appearance. It was all at the Emperor's command, carried out without question.

The crowds were cheering the Legion, which stood, swords now sheathed, before them in blocks of centuries, the golden Eagle raised high at the centre beside the white badge of the Boar on its crimson banner. The cavalry too came to a halt before the rostrum, their tall horses ridden by soldiers in chain mail and knee-length breeches, some couching spears from which pennants and coloured ribbons dangled, others holding up standards with devices I did not recognise: I thought they might be part of a squadron from Gallia. Also coming into view at a quick march were the archers, tall men wearing high, conical helmets, in scale armour with their bows in their left hands and their quivers on their backs. Their faces were dark, so I thought they must come from Rome's most easterly provinces.

At the front of the Army, now drawn up for inspection, strode a magnificent figure in full burnished armour – an ornate cuirass studded with the discs of *phalera* shining gold and silver, silvered greaves on the legs, a crimson cloak fastened at both shoulders, and a huge fan of a crimson crest in an arc from ear to ear atop the helmet. Despite the mounted tribune at his side, who outranked him, the first-centurion had command of the parade. The parties bearing the Eagle and the banners of the auxiliaries formed up alongside him. The *cornua* brayed, the *tubae* blared. The standards were dipped, the Eagle too, now ringed with a wreath by an attendant *optio* – how often had I had the honour of performing that service – was lowered almost to touch the ground. The Emperor, standing, with his ivory baton clasped in his outstretched right arm, acknowledged the salute, and the Eagle was raised once more, soaring higher than the banners and standards clustered about it. The legionaries began a rhythmic beating of their shields, the sound rising ever louder until, with two great shouts of "Caesar! Caesar", it was suddenly shut off. In the ensuing silence, the crowd began applauding, first by clapping and then with joined cries too of "Caesar! Caesar!"

The first-centurion unsheathed his sword and offered it to the Emperor, who made the customary gesture of refusal, whereupon the soldier touched the blade in turn to each of his shoulders and to his face, and returned it to its scabbard. He turned on his heel and marched back into the ranks. Gradually, file by file, the legionaries and auxiliaries began to march away to the renewed sound of the *tubae*, the centuries that had stood in rectangles now forming column as smoothly as melting ice flows into water.

The Praetorian *praefectus* was speaking to Hadrian, I think offering his congratulations. The rostrum was alive with conversation. The Governor, Pompeius Falco, was in full voice, laughing with several others who wore military-style uniforms. I saw Decius Salvius Leptis come suddenly into view. He had been summoned before the Emperor from whatever station he had been occupying during the ceremony. His look was as imperturbable as ever – that of the true ex-soldier whose temperament I wished I too could have retained, having grown increasingly susceptible to irritations, depressions and nervous excitements as my years had advanced. If a man had good reason to be pleased with himself, I thought it was Salvius Leptis. Against almost impossible odds, he and his staff had stage-managed an event that had been supremely successful. As he had said to me, there was no need to be concerned about those who might still be trapped on the road, or who had fallen from their horses and had broken limbs or their necks crossing the fields. For the majority, this day would be talked about for a very long time to come. And the Emperor was pleased too, which was the most important result of all. Promotion and reward would surely follow for Leptis. I watched him talking with Hadrian, and decided to push myself forward on the rostrum too.

"Come, Farus," I said. "This is our chance."

Sometimes it is hard to gain an audience with an emperor; indeed, most times it is impossible. Now, however, it was as easy as taking a few short paces towards him, dragging Farus by his sleeve with me. As Leptis stepped back, saluting Hadrian with his arm across his chest, so I stepped forward.

"Ah, Celer," said Hadrian as familiarly as if I was one of his own family. "Our congratulations on your oration; and to your horse-girl too. She performed most excellently?"

"Caesar. I was fortunate in acquiring her."

"Indeed, as you have told us before. We should buy her from you and take her back to Rome. She would perform wonders in our stables."

I stood and said compliantly "Caesar", knowing he was teasing me. I would not sell Myru even to an Emperor.

Understanding I had a purpose in approaching him, Hadrian asked, "How may we serve you, Celer?"

"Caesar, you have been gracious in receiving my friend here, Curtius Farus" – I felt Tertius's anguished struggle against my restraining hand – "He is a veteran, Caesar, of twenty-five years, and I never served with a finer man. Owing to a cruel throw of Fortuna's arm, he has had to struggle since his discharge and seeks help for his advancement. May I present him, Caesar, to one of your officials who may look into his case?"

I saw Hadrian frown. Had I got it wrong? This was perhaps not the place or time for such a supplication? However, he answered. "Celer, We would suggest you raise this again with us later. Perhaps your comrade would like to accompany us on our ride to the *altarium Victoriae* and then on to the site of the *tropaeum*. We shall be holding a great feast there later. You will both be most welcome."

He turned away to address Pompeius Falco, who had been hovering at his elbow, looking on disapprovingly.

"Thank you, *maiestas*," Farus said to his back, bowing low as I lugged him away. "Enough," I hissed at him. "He has done nothing for you yet. He will, though, Thank him when he does."

All around, the crowd was breaking up, the stands emptying, people flooding away across the heath to the rear. The Empress and her entourage, separated from Hadrian, had already left. I did not envy them the struggle they would now have in getting away from this place. Already the horses were being brought up that would take the Emperor and his chosen party on to the next, and more private, stage of the ceremonies. Turning my head, I was relieved to see the ever attentive Myru, with Pyddr, leading up Ajax and my other ponies.

"You will ride one, Tertius?" I said. You can ride, can't you? I don't recall ever seeing you mounted."

"Not on a horse perhaps," he answered with a grin, his good humour now returned after the ordeal I had just put him through. "But, yes, I have practised my riding in recent years. I often hunt the boar amongst the forest beyond Lindum's north gate."

"Hopefully, we can gain better things for you" I said, hoping that my words would prove true. It might be necessary to beard Hadrian again when he was alone. I had not liked the look of the autocratic Pompeius Falco just now.

"I can't thank you enough, Celer," he said.

"You can thank me later. We must ride now. Do you have any belongings with you?"

"No, I came as I am. I had planned to take a carriage back tonight, but I see now it would have been tomorrow, anyhow, before I could have got clear of here. It might have meant a night for me spent out in the open."

The choked progress of the crowds, those coming down from the stand pressed in amongst the many others rising from the grass, was indeed slow, scarcely moving, in fact. I could not be too concerned about them, not even for my neighbour, Numicius, who should be able to find his slaves to carry him clear. The smoke of fires was rising in the distance, nearer to the marsh side to which the Army had retreated. I had overheard a great feast was to be held there for the soldiers. I dreaded to think what would happen when the XXth were in drink and the auxiliaries tried to secure their share of the feast. The battle might be re-fought yet again, this time with real casualties.

I mounted Ajax with Myru, while Farus chose Circe, the most spirited of the mares. I asked Myru and Pyddr to keep an eye on them. I wasn't sure if Farus could ride well, or even at all. All ex-soldiers live in a world of bravado, which they think stops them growing old. For Farus too was an old man now. I had forgotten that fact, thinking that everyone younger than I still enjoyed the first vigour of youth.

At a signal from the Praetorians, and a call from Hadrian's steward, our party of some thirty horse set out across the battlefield towards the hills.

XXIV

We crossed the plain with Hadrian in the lead, two Praetorians riding beside him with pennants snapping on their spears. The sun was sinking towards the hills: I hoped there would be daylight enough left for all the things to be accomplished that Decius Salvius Leptis had spoken about. He was riding with us too, on a grey horse taller than any other in our group. His slave rode beside him on a pony like mine, but not so broad set and solid as those bred in Icenia. I think this slave, in fact, may have been freeborn, because she was a young woman, perhaps Salvius's mistress taken into his service. She was dressed in a long straw-coloured tunic hitched up to her waist so her white thighs shone bare against the pony's flanks. A leather bucket full of papyrus scrolls was hung around her back. Old as I was, I found the sight distracting. Such distraction, though, was unbecoming at this moment, riding with my Emperor across the tangled heath where so many had died. I looked away at Farus on Circe. He was riding beside us and seemed to be managing well.

We climbed the side of the long ridge that jutted out into the plain and came to its crest at the point where I had stood with the Emperor before during our inspection of the field and discussed the likely tactics of the battle. This is where the fighting had been fiercest – the point where the XIIIIth had met the centre of the *Iceni* charge. Before us, the steep-sided, narrow valley where they had stood fell away, covered in clumps of gorse and long, rank grass. Nothing man might plant grew here; only a few goats picked their way between the bushes, their bells tinkling at their necks. Overhead two large birds hovered on outspread wings, awaiting the moment to dive on their prey.

"See, Caesar," I said pointing at the birds. "There is an omen. The eagles are gathering for you."

Hadrian, startled, looked upwards and grunted. "Those are not eagles, Celer, but some lesser bird. But, our thanks to you, it is a good sign."

Our party of horse must have disturbed the birds' prey, for, after a few circles, growing ever wider, they flew off across the plain.

Hadrian's attention was now taken by the small, square structure that had been built on the highest point of the ridge. From a distance, I could see it was not finished, for the courses of cut stone, laid around the opening for a door, were higher than on the other sides and the building was as yet open to the sky. We cantered up to it. The ridge was so narrow at this point that we could ride no more than three abreast. All around were the signs of the building party – wooden planks and heaps of stone and stacked tile, and a cleared circle where mortar had been mixed, with wheel barrows and tools, half-concealed under a canvas sheet. Of the builders themselves, there was no sign.

Hadrian was talking with Salvius Leptis, leaning from his saddle to do so. He looked annoyed, his voice raised. Leptis in turn spoke sharply to his woman, who dismounted and produced one of the scrolls from her carrying bucket. She unrolled it and tried to hold it up for the Emperor to see. Leptis snatched it from her and leant towards Hadrian, stabbing at it with his finger, while their two horses chewed at the grass.

"There has been plenty of time," Hadrian was saying. "You could build a *pharos* quicker than this." I knew that wasn't true, having grown up with the great *pharos* of Claudius rising year by year above the Ostia harbour.

"I had expected the ceremony of dedication today, nonetheless," said Leptis, gazing around, hoping perhaps to see the missing priests of Minerva rise out of the grass. A white path led off into the woods that stood on the main part of the hill, but was empty of life.

"Priests will not create a sanctuary out of the invisible," said Hadrian tetchily. "This has been ill-done."

"Caesar, see the plans," Leptis said urgently, hoping to redeem himself. "The altar cannot be built until the inscription is finished. And that has had to be made in Londinium because no one here has the skill. That is where the delay has been. Once the inscribed stone arrives with the carved Victoria that is also ordered, they can be placed inside and the altar built about it. Then the walls will be finished and the roof put on – you see, as drawn in the plan." He pushed the papyrus closer to Hadrian, who studied it briefly, then looked away, clearly still annoyed.

"As long as they don't make a mess of the words. Have you checked them?"

"Of course, Caesar. I have a man in Londinium working with the mason."

"Let us see you have them down correctly."

Leptis clicked his fingers at the woman again, who produced another scroll which she handed up to him. Unrolling it, he pushed it across to Hadrian. "See, Caesar. The wording is set out here."

Hadrian read. "It seems well. But I would much prefer '*magna victoria*' to '*clades Icenorum*'. We commemorate a victory here not a disaster."

"It may be too late, Caesar." Leptis for all his imperturbability was growing rattled.

"Have it done!" Hadrian urged his horse away leaving Salvius Leptis with a bundle of papyrus in his hands, which he thrust down angrily to his waiting servant.

I chuckled. I had liked Salvius Leptis, but his smooth unflappability had begun to irritate me. Now that was gone. Had a man ever been so raised up at one moment, then cast down at the next? Leptis must be wishing now he had never been handed this labour of Hercules.

We rode down from the ridge and set a course towards the east, the sinking sun behind us throwing long red rays over the land – as if Apollo himself wished to show remembrance of the blood shed here. I thought, at least I do not have to hear those dreadful priests of Senuna Minerva reciting some prayer to Roman victory. Perhaps that will happen yet when Hadrian's inscription is at last in place, but I shall not be present to witness it, nor the Emperor either.

The country we came into was more enclosed, the hills smaller, their slopes covered in thick woods. We passed farms of plain, white-washed buildings with red tiled roofs, surrounded by circular thatched huts. Slaves worked in lines hoeing the fields. Dogs and boys ran out to meet us, and were cuffed away by the Praetorians. Our route had been prepared, I noted. We came across the occasional Praetorian advance post set up to see there was no danger to the Emperor: this was standard procedure, I imagined, whether in Britannia or elsewhere.

We splashed through a ford across a wide river running at this point in two channels. The water came up to the bellies of the larger horses and almost drowned Ajax and Circe and my other ponies that were being led by Pyddr. I turned to see if Farus was all right, but he grinned broadly (I think Circe was actually swimming at that moment) and waved a hand in the air, his body and head tilted back like one of those riders in Campania I had seen who break in horses. I doubt if he had felt such exhilaration since leaving the Bull.

On the far side of the river we came at last to a paved road, and, with one of the Praetorians now serving as a guide, we followed this into a deep valley with a stream gushing to one side. At the foot of the hill, the road crossed an area of grassland, where two other streams joined, widening into a broad clearing on the valley floor. The streams gurgled and splashed in deep, earthy channels fringed by ferns, their waters catching the late afternoon light; birds sang and fussed amongst leafy bushes higher up the slopes. It was a scene that might be imagined in Elysium.

But not quite so. For a cast of the eye showed on one side the grass stripped and laid bare, and deep pits dug, with mounds of earth and white rock turned up into heaps. From here, the brown strips of interweaving paths led across the green sward to a place where the earth and rock were being dumped to form a great mound.

We were at Hadrian's side. "This was a holy place of the *Britanni*," he said. "We have been told their Druids used to perform their ceremonies here: the place of the three streams, they called it – *in loco tria flumina*. It was another spot where the living dead of the VIIIIth were taken to be sacrificed in their groves. Those have all long been cut down. Paullinus, himself, gave the orders for that." Turning to me, "You would know of that best, Celer. We should still be able to find the stumps of the trees here."

We rode on, our companions pressed as close to the Emperor as they could. The valley seemed to have cast a spell upon us. I felt a sense of unease. Ajax seemed to feel it too, for his head was down and his sides trembled. We crossed one of the streams where boards to make a bridge had been laid, and came up to the great mound that was being built. Once close up to it, I could see that it was being formed of alternate layers of rammed chalk and earth, this then no haphazard work of simple dumping that would soon wash away, but a piece of careful engineering. The mound was intended to last.

"This will be the core of the *tropaeum*," Hadrian said. "It will have an outer layer of chalk so it will shine white as if faced with marble, and on its summit will stand a tree hung with the arms of victory. The ashes of our dead, recently recovered, will be buried in a chamber within. It shall be done."

"But when?" he asked, raising his voice and turning to find Salvius Leptis, who, after his earlier reprimand, was hanging back in the line of steaming horses. The animals needed water after their long gallop, and we were having to force them away from the streams. The best way to keep them calm from the atmosphere of this place would be to allow them to drink, but I, of course, had no command here. Myru, riding behind me, I knew would be of similar mind.

Leptis rode to Hadrian's side. "The work is only ceased for today, Caesar. The workers have been employed preparing the camp that awaits us, "Work will recommence here just as soon as we have gone."

Hadrian nodded, but did not otherwise acknowledge Leptis. He had a way to go yet to return to Hadrian's favour.

"I asked. "Whose land is this, Caesar?"

He looked surprised by the question. "Salvius Leptis, will you give Celer an answer?"

Leptis was fiddling with his documents again, and looked so flustered that I wished I had not asked. His woman was handing him one scroll, then another and another, while the horses moved restlessly about him and Hadrian's eyes never left him. At last Leptis seemed satisfied.

"Tiberius Claudius Verus," he announced – I thought I had heard that name before, then remembered the man who had first bought the land upon which the temple of Minerva Senuna now stood – "or at least the fourth of that name for it is a lengthy dynasty. He is of the *Catuvellauni*, a wealthy man, who owns a villa higher up the valley. He has been honoured to give this land for the present purpose. He is away in Gallia at present, Caesar, visiting his estates there, and had hoped to return in time to be present – but I think, Caesar, he is nowhere to be found so he must have been delayed: I have heard nothing further. I believe his steward will be at our rest camp tonight."

"We thank him. Make sure he is notified of the Emperor's thanks. And you may bring the steward to us later."

Hadrian dismounted and, with the help of one of his attendants, he climbed the side of the mound where a path had been left for the workmen to use. He stood on boards at the top, looking down at us from the height of three men, or a little more. His attendant held him by the arm, for the boards were slippery. I could see the *praefectus* ordering two of his men to climb the mound as well: it would not look good for them to lose their Emperor in a sudden slide of earth. Hadrian, however, seemed unaware of any anxiety he was causing.

"There is much to be done," he spoke down to us. "This mound is yet a third – if that – of the height it must reach. About this present level, a passage will be let in from the side to reach a chamber that will lie at the heart of the mound. There, the ashes of the dead will rest. See, they are already setting up the planks that will form the walls of the chamber."

He turned and nearly fell. I saw his attendant and a Praetorian grab at him, but he steadied himself. We could see nothing from below of what he was referring to. He appeared again at the edge of the mound. "Is what we say not true, Salvius Leptis? Come up here, would you, and bring your plans with you."

Muttering something to himself which it was well for him was not overheard, Leptis drew a scroll from his assistant's bucket, and hastened up the curving earth path, at one point slipping to his knees and pressing the scroll into the mud. His curse of "*Stercore!*" brought a ripple of laughter from the watchers. Once Leptis had joined Hadrian, they could be seen towards the centre of the mound in close conversation. Then they returned down the path, Salvius sliding once again but gathering himself, Hadrian behind supported by his attendant proceeding more carefully.

Hadrian remounted. His horse in turning came close to Ajax. He leant across to me, "Tell us what you think, old soldier? Will this not be a fine memorial to our Roman dead?"

"Yes, Caesar. Yet will the dead be just our dead or the *Iceni* too? It will be hard to separate the bones."

"Both will be burnt together. In that way, we honour both our peoples. Through fire comes cleansing and new growth. Rome will grow and Britannia will grow. We shall build a fine province – an even finer province – and we shall keep it safe. That is our work. To consolidate our Empire so that it can grow stronger yet."

"Noble sentiments, Caesar."

"Oh, don't give me that fawning nonsense, Celer. What do you truly think as a soldier?"

"If I had fallen in the war and my bones left unburied and bleached, lying amongst those of my enemy, I would be honoured by your actions, Caesar. As I said in my small oration just now, our courage is the greater when seen against the courage of our enemies. Without the latter, there would be less glory. So I think it right now, after so many years, that the remains of the dead are mixed together and burnt."

He looked at me, his blue eyes piercing mine. "Thank you, Celer. You speak well. You should have been more than a soldier."

"I was in charge of a canal, Caesar."

"So you were. We had not forgotten. And yet there is more in you, we know, than despatching barges full of honeyed wine from a dockside wharf. You could have achieved greater things."

"I still live, Caesar."

He laughed, and urged his horse away. I was left breathless at my own temerity.

The camp beyond the *tropaeum* must have been long in the planning. Amongst all the tents and awnings and prefabricated wooden huts and stables was even a stone-walled bath house, all that was left of a villa that had once stood here, long since burnt down. The baths took their waters from one of the streams that flowed past to join with the others near the *tropaeum*. Salvius Leptis had certainly distinguished himself in getting them into working order in time: no wonder, I thought, progress had been slow on the *tropaeum* itself. There were only so many skilled builders that could be conjured up to work at a place in the middle of nowhere, however direct the imperial summons.

Others were arriving who had not been among our party which had ridden here. – the Governor, Pompeius Falco, for instance, and other officials, some wearing togas, who had been on the rostrum at the *caerimonia commemorationis* or had sat with the Emperor in the stands – but without, it seemed, their wives. The company was almost entirely male. There was no sign of Numicius, I noted: he had probably not received an invitation to this final event.

Suddenly, coming over the brow of the hill from the road, appeared a trail of runners, slaves bearing trunks and rolls of cloth and carpet, bronze lamps and vases, and even a swinging wooden bird cage, all scampering along at a pace much faster than walking, many out of breath and clearly exhausted; and behind them, a high-sided litter shrouded by yellow curtains, swaying alarmingly, borne by four half-naked, dark-skinned slaves, with four more in close attendance – the Empress Vibia Sabina, no doubt, with an escort of gaily-bridled white horse bringing up the rear.

The column passed into the Emperor's area of the camp, and we watchers turned back to our bathing and dressing. An open air *triclinium* was set for Hadrian's appearance, but he did not come, so we of his party ate and drank without him. Farus and I ended up seated side by side upon the ground, leaning against the stumps of trees that might once have been growing in the groves of the Druids.

The grey evening light gave way to blackness, yet a blackness lit by a rising moon, and the whole black vault of the sky became a mass of a million, million stars that seemed to flow like mist. Flaring torches of pine wood and pitch were lit and positioned at various points around the camp. The timbers of the *triclinium* were studded with candles and lamps, so they looked to me like the brightly-lit stalls of the Ostia market when trading had continued after dark, and, where, in the deep pools of blackness in-between the tables, I had first found out how human beings pleasured themselves. Here too there may have been some pleasure conducted between slave and slave, or even master and slave: I could not see and I cared less. It was enough for me to be pleasantly drunk and to be leaning against Farus's shoulder while he told me for the third or fourth time how he had cleft the chieftain of the *Caledonii* from the top of his skull to his chin, so that his brain fell out like a grisly pudding from a cooking pot.

I felt very tired and I allowed Myru to lead me, with Farus's help, to my appointed tent. Farus slept beside me, and Myru too, so she could be on hand for us. Pyddr, I believe, was with the ponies in the stables, from where the restless snorting, shuffling, screaming, and kicking out of the many apprehensive animals could be heard most of the night. I slept at first, but woke very early and could not sleep again. I do not know how long Myru slept, but she was on hand to help me when I wanted to shit, and, then, as soon as the fires were re-lit at the bath house, she accompanied me there, so that I was one of the first in line. Farus was snoring when I left our tent and he was still snoring when I returned – a man clearly with a calm equanimity of mind.

I did not see Hadrian until later in the morning, when he emerged from his great tent, and, pushing past his ring of Praetorian Guards, came out into the general circle of the camp where he was immediately surrounded by bowing officials and guests. "Have you slept well, Caesar?" Do you wish to dine?" Do you wish to bathe?", but, to my astonishment, he pushed them all aside and came up to me, signalling he wished to be alone with me.

"Caesar?" I said, apprehensive, even fearful, that he had found some fault in me.

"Accompany me to the bath, Celer. I would wish to talk with you." He paused. "As I did those months back at your house."

He had used the first person: I was surprised and gratified – my second intimate talk with my Emperor in a bath house: was there no other place such confidences might be shared? There were many from Hadrian's personal staff who could advise him. So why choose an ordinary veteran – an old man now – who was longing to return to his home? Why set me above all the high-born about us, which was bound to make me the subject of much unwanted and unnecessary speculation, and could even bring me danger? If I had been a young man, I might have been worried by the jealousy and suspicions aroused in others. As an old man, I was not too concerned. It would have been impossible, anyhow, to refuse.

At the bath house, the line of would-be bathers, which by now included Farus, had to wait for us, or go down to the stream instead to wash. There was already quite a mass of naked men at the stream side slapping at their bodies or getting their slaves to rub them down with towels. I think that, even in my youth, I would have preferred to stay dirty for a week rather than take part in such an exhibition. Naked flesh can be fine to gaze upon when it is trim and muscular. But, when bellies have swollen and muscles sag with fat, and legs are shrunken thin like willow sticks, when the penis has grown long with overuse or is shrivelled up to a mere button, then the sight is not one to be viewed either before or after eating.

"Celer," said Hadrian with a groan, lowering himself into a hot tub, while I sat beside him on a shelf that ran around the plain, heated room. I had not undressed. I would rather now sweat in my tunic while I paid attention to my Emperor than join him in the water. "Celer, I would speak to you again because I need the opinion of a man I can trust. You know of the ways of men and of the emotions of men – those emotions that can consume and destroy, whether the man be slave or free, soldier, patrician, or emperor: we are all made of the same bone and flesh, although in differing earthly stations."

"Quite so, Caesar." This was a commonplace enough observation. So what was it he wished to ask me in particular?

"You witnessed the Empress arrive here last night?" he asked.

"Yes, Caesar, I did. Was her journey here at short-notice? Her attendants and bearers seemed ill-organised."

"She was most displeased. She said she had been ignored at the *caerimonia commemorationis*; that neither the crowd or I had given her much attention; that a common soldier – she meant you – received more attention than she, the Empress."

"She mentioned me, Caesar?" I was alarmed. Powerful men – powerful women too – can have long reaches, even about matters that are trivial and untrue.

"Only as a way of pointing out how she felt neglected. It was when you spoke to the crowd. She knows nothing about you and would not want to know. You just provided an extra cause for her ill temper."

"I see." This was scarcely flattering.

"I did not eat last night, I did not sleep because that woman would not leave me alone. She was either telling me how badly I treated her or she was trying to force me to give her attentions I did not wish, not once but many times, in many ways – ways that make me ill now to think of."

I felt my stomach contract. The Emperor had told me intimate things before, but this was reaching new heights – or depths. I did not wish to hear any more.

"How can I advise you, Caesar?"

"I do not know how to handle her. I cannot simply get rid of her. She comes from a powerful family who have friends in the Senate, in the Army, in the Courts, in the Palace itself. I fear what would happen if I did anything too drastic to control her. You see, it is not me she wants really….. Yet I am Emperor. But, as soon as my back is turned…." His voice tailed off, and he hung his head looking miserable, his legs floating up in the water.

"If I understand you correctly, Caesar, that is treason. She could die for it."

"I have no wish to harm her, Celer. She was most loving when I first met her; when I married her. She was my Ceres and I her Iupiter. And yet I cannot love her now in the way she wishes. I wish to love most of all with my soul, not my body."

I may have been in awe of the Emperor, but there comes a time when even a slave will have had enough of his master. I overflowed with horror at his vacillating self-pity, and I was annoyed too that he had dragged me into such an intimacy that I had never sought

"Weakness is never the solution to anything, Caesar. It pains me to say this. But you *have* to act. You must either investigate and expose the Empress's betrayal or you must separate yourself from her entirely – or perhaps do both. You cannot live in a situation where she is able to rule you and act as she likes. That is not what the people of Rome would wish of their Emperor." I don't quite know how I summoned up those words. I felt chilled, and I was shaking, despite the heat of the bath house.

He gazed up at me from out the water. He looked perplexed. There was no decision in that face – Hadrianus Augustus, Emperor of the World. How could a man who lays his enemies low in war be so dominated by his wife?

"Thank you, Celer," he said, pulling himself from the bath. His face was set now. "We shall make a decision." And with those words he reverted to being my Emperor, and I just his servant – his most aged and loyal servant.

The Empress left not long after this. Indeed, her abrupt departure may well have been on account of something said to her by Hadrian on his return to the imperial tent. The litter, again heavily curtained, appeared with its entourage of porters and bearers, and was seen on its way from the camp with a blare of *tubae*, its small escort of horse clattering behind. There was no wave of a hand to say goodbye, no sound of departure at all once the *tubae* had sounded out, other than for the creaking jolt of the litter and the harsh breath of the bearers. Many of the bystanders of the Emperor's close party exchanged looks, but few made any comment. The camp was in a chaos of being broken up, with tents being flattened and rolled, slaves running everywhere with burdens of cooking pots, rugs, lamps, and trunks, carts being dragged by hand to be loaded while the horses, waiting to be harnessed, blew out white mist from their nostrils and stamped their heavy feet.

I crossed the beaten, litter-strewn earth – there were numbers of wine beakers and broken flagons spread about as if a wind in the night had torn through the roofless *triclinium* and showered them there, but probably they had simply been abandoned as wine suddenly overcame the muscles and brains of those stumbling to find their tents – and came up to the stables to see how Myru and Pyddr were coping with Ajax and Ceres and my other ponies this morning. I found the two of them in a passage between the wooden walls of the stable and a farrier's furnace on the far side: they were both stark naked and emptying buckets of water over each other, giggling as they did so like children. I did not know if this was suitable, even for the simple act of washing, as Myru was a mature woman and Pyddr still yet a boy, but they both looked at me with total calmness as I appeared, and I decided to say nothing.

Farus and I were making our preparations to leave, facing the long, uncomfortable journey by pony, on which Farus would accompany us for part of the way – I had invited him to my house but he had said he must return home to his wife, who would otherwise be worrying about him until a message could be got to her – when a slave in the imperial green livery appeared. I saw him asking a question of others, and then I was pointed out to him

"The Emperor requires your presence, Gaius Modius Celer."

My heart sank. Was this to be more of his feeble introspection? I did not think it could be. That time had been and gone, and would be no more.

I stopped what I was doing immediately and turned to follow the slave. Farus made to come too, but I held out my arm. "The summons is for me alone, my friend. This time I cannot take you with me, but be sure I shall represent your wishes should the Emperor allow me that opportunity: he did say to speak to him later, and he is a man of his word."

I was stopped by one of the Praetorians as I approached the Emperor's tent. I had to stand, my knees wilting with my tiredness under the hot sun, which, defying the late season, was now shining fiercely over the valley, cocooned by its surrounding woods. Eventually a message was brought back that I could proceed, and I passed through waiting courtiers and other hangers-on to Hadrian's inner tent, aware of the looks at me that said, 'Not him again. Who is this man whom the Emperor favours so?'

As I passed through to Hadrian's chamber that was lined with green canvas walls decorated with eagles and the faces of gods and goddesses – the identity of the latter unclear owing to the bulging and swaying of the canvas as slaves fanned the heated air – I saw he was seated on a low dais and was dealing with someone standing before him, a bearded man in a long russet-coloured tunic and dull-brown cloak, fastened in the *Britanni* fashion with a large brooch of enamelled colours.

"Ah, Celer," said Hadrian, immediately on seeing me enter. "This is one Frentius, steward to Tiberius Claudius Verus who owns the land where our *tropaeum* is being built. I have asked him to express our thanks to his master for his generosity in ceding this land to Rome."

At the introduction, Frentius made a bow to me, his thumbs hooked in a broad metal-linked belt that was of the sort worn off-duty by senior legionaries. I wondered where he had obtained it. I did not like the look of the man. His face had what I can only describe as an oily look, and his black eyes darted about everywhere other than resting on my own.

"We would wish you to serve us yet, Celer, by being in touch with Claudius Verus and his steward here about the *tropaeum,* and reporting its progress to us after we have left Britannia."

"You see," he said – indicating I should come forward and speaking into my ear while at the same time dismissing the steward with a wave of his hand – "Salvius Leptis is to be promoted outside the province and, with a new Legate in place, which will also happen soon – yet his time will be taken up by the building of the *vallum Aelium* – there is no one else I can trust who truly understands my requirements, to tell me truthfully how the work here proceeds."

"Of course, Caesar, I shall be honoured to serve you." I said this with a sinking heart, for I wished most of all to return to my seclusion and peace, there to see out my remaining days. "But it will be hard for me to travel to inspect these works."

"We would not expect you to do so without calling upon our monies, our accommodation, and our transport. Celer, you will have all the privileges of an imperial servant who holds direct orders sealed by us."

He saw the continuing doubt in my face. "But, if strength should fail you, you may appoint a deputy. Your friend and comrade – Farus, if we recall his name correctly – for whom you sought our favour, we believe."

"His dwelling, Caesar, is even further away than me – in Lindum."

"Not if he will take up a villa in Competum that can be made available to him – to be the steward of *Campo Albo*, and to superintend our altar and our *tropaeum*."

My face shone at that. It would solve all Farus's problems, and mine too. I need only write to Farus to gain the reports the Emperor required. "A villa, Caesar?" I said, feeling suddenly quite weak.

"Yes, of course. There is plenty of land. Five rooms? Six rooms? A hypocaust for winter? Even a mosaic or two, if he wishes them. And a piece of land of five *jugera* or more with field slaves so he can have an income above his pension, which we may increase to what it might have been. We have asked that his case be looked into. If he was wronged, Rome shall make good what he has lost."

"That is magnificent, Caesar. He will be so pleased, so honoured, so grateful. He is a modest man, and does not wish to push himself forward for favour. Shall I send for him, so you can tell him these things."

"No, Celer. We have done enough. We have not time now, for we will be leaving very soon. Tell him he will receive official notification and be visited by our agent in Lindum. If anything should go wrong, you must inform us directly, Celer."

"How should I do that, Caesar?"

Hadrian leant further forward, so his face was very close to mine. His breath smelt of garlic. I knew I was in favour when he spoke personally once more. "In writing, of course, Celer. You will be able to use the imperial service from Duroliponte. Just make sure your letters carry the seal of the *decurio* there, and they will be added to the official correspondence going through the Procurator's office in Londinium, In that way, they can come straight to me, unopened. I shall be travelling away from Rome for a long time yet; I am destined for Hispania next, and then to Mauretania – but correspondence will reach me wherever I am."

"I do not know how to address an Emperor, Caesar. In what style of language should I write to you?"

"You do very well when you speak, Celer. Now all you have to do is set the same words into writing. There should be no difficulty."

"You will have to excuse my rough ways, Caesar. I am no learned patrician, or equestrian even, no courtier smoothed by your service. My education was mainly with the Army. I have never written much besides soldiers' rotas and casualty returns."

"You worry too much. You worry as an old man, not as one who was once a soldier. Keep your days with the legions before you and all will become clear to you. All we seek is plain language, not the poetry of an Ovidius or a Vergilius. You can surely do that. There is nothing difficult in it, providing you can spell out your letters. We wish you long life so that you may do this important work for us well."

I thought, does he not understand that my life has been long already? In truth, the life I wished for now – for however long I might have left – was not, in fact, to be still in the Emperor's service – however great that honour – but to lie on my back in my own fields and watch the clouds slide slowly across the sky, and to see my ponies coming up to me through the grass to nuzzle at my palms, and to have my people smiling at the beginning of each day, and at the end of it, and for there to be no more fear or hatred of anything, anywhere. You see how far I had come from the stern soldier with his oaths, his steamy breath and his blood-stained boots, always raising his fist to the sky, seeking the next fight. What I wished for now was peace – such peace as allows remembrance; remembrance of the good days I have lived, and, above all, of Senuna, with whom I shared only a very few, but they were the best of all.

Hadrian must have seen the dreamy look that had come into my eyes, for he stepped back, clasping my right arm, and said abruptly. "I think you are tired, Celer. I must let you rest before your journey home. We – I" (again, that confusion between the personal and the official) "give you our thanks for all you have done for us – for me. I am grateful to you and would like to express my gratitude in some material way, but I think that – unlike your friend Farus – there is nothing you wish for, or need, just the comfort of your home and the safety of your bed."

He laughed, and I was startled, for he had shown how much he was able to follow my own thoughts and understand me, far more than his words might otherwise show. He is a sensitive man, I thought, who is called to rule the world when all he really seeks is his own inner peace.

He said, "I have confided much in you, Celer – much that perhaps I should not have spoken. I ask you to respect my trust and to keep what I have told you to yourself."

"Of course, Caesar. You have my word on my soldier's oath. I shall not speak of anything you have told me. Your trust is an honour to me and my house."

I meant that then, of course. Yet, as I have now written much of this story down – you see I did learn to write in that plain style Hadrian had chided me about – then I shall have to ensure that certain passages are destroyed at my death. I shall give Gavo the necessary instructions.

I made my farewells to Hadrian, and we clasped arms in the same soldiers' way as we had done when we had first met, incredibly, it seemed now, just a few months back. I returned to Farus, who, assisted by Myru, was busy attaching his few possessions to Ceres's harness. Taking him to one side, I told him what Hadrian had said to me. I doubt I have ever seen such a reaction of joy in anyone before, certainly not one disciplined by the legions who should be able to treat both triumph and disaster with equal equanimity. I recall once a legionary awarded the *corona muralis* greet the honour with as little emotion as learning he had just had his bread ration increased.

When he had finished leaping up and own, making Ceres start and fling up her hooves, and clasping me about the neck and – dare I record this? – kissing me (a sight which brought some merriment from those observing our little scene) Farus took me by the arm and promised me a devotion that would have put the loyalty of Mucius Scaevola to shame.

"You must be the first guest in my new house," he said – and I made a promise to him that I would be.

A little later I saw the Emperor's party depart amidst the high, shrill sound of the *tubae* that set the rooks flying out of the trees above the valley of the three streams. Hadrian was riding north again to rejoin his Army – and his Empress. Soon, I knew he would be leaving our island of Britannia, and I should not see him again. I saw him turn once in his saddle and raise his arm to us watching. I felt my eyes fill with tears – old, soft wretch that I was – because I knew that salute was for me and for all the soldiers who had served Rome, and were serving her still.

His gold burnished figure seen against the green woods that lined the high road, with his banners and standards raised about him, and the lines of black horse clattering along in his wake, seemed to represent everything I had ever fought for, which I shall be proud to take to my grave.

XXV

I sit at a bronze-topped table placed for me by Gavo in my inner room, the one where I sleep in winter for it has a heated floor and walls. The heat comes down flues from the same furnace that fires my baths. I am covered thick in woollen tunics, a little like the way the people of Aegyptus bind up their dead for eternity. The season has been very cold, with ice so thick on the canal that it has had to be broken each morning by a ramming barge rowed by slaves. Their breath rises about them like steam. The grating roar of the barge's iron beak against the ice reminds me of a starved lion in its cage before its release into the arena.

Such thoughts distract me from my writing. It is not easy to take up the iron pen and dip it in the ink well and form spiky letters on the smooth, grainy surface of the wood. But I must do so because of my promise to the Emperor. I have decided to write my letters on thin sheets of wood. It is the custom now in Britannia, for papyrus is expensive and tablets of wax are larger and heavier and might easily be altered or wiped clean. I wish my letters to Hadrian to reach him as I write them, and not as some busybody scribe might take it upon himself to 'improve'. You see, I do not believe too much in the protection of the imperial seal, for I have seen a forger slice one of these and reheat the wax in a quicker time than it takes for a hound to seize a hare.

I have other writing to do as well. I have begun this account of my extraordinary time in the presence of the Emperor Hadrian, and how we talked of *bellum Icenorum,* and of the battles that were fought then; and of how I joined the legions and came to Britannia and first found my wife Senuna, only to lose her and have to seek out her shade a second time; and of the Emperor's commemorations of the field of great victory, in which my ponies were ridden too; and – most extraordinary of all – of what the Emperor told me of his own life, of his worries and despairs – which I shall set down as well, although to keep my most sacred vow, those writings will be kept apart and marked for burning as soon as I sense the bony arms of Pluto reaching out for me.

I write my narrative on old *papyri* from the office at the dock – long lists of goods and of the barges that carried them and of taxes owed and paid, and of the names of my servants and slaves over the many years. All these *papyri* are already much used, new columns having been added beside the old ones until the space is filled, and due now for burning, or so my successor has ordered. I brought them with my own hands from where they had been dumped. There is space yet on their backs, if re-rolled, on which to write – and so I fill my time these short, dark winter days. When I do not write, I sleep.

But first my letters –

Epistula I
G. Modius Celer Hadriano Imperatori salutem dicit.

Caesar, I pray you keep well. Here, the winter has been hard. The canals are iced and the supply barges for the Army are delayed. I keep warm indoors. My slave with my ponies – you will recall her – tells me the ground is frozen like iron and slippery, so Ajax and Ceres and the others are only exercised once a day and that with care: they are growing as fat as idle slaves, she says.

I have received a letter from T. Curtius Farus who says he has moved to a rented house at Competum while his own villa is being built: he has begun his job as overseer of *Campo Albo*. He has been appointed by special edict as a member of the Competum council. I have not been able to visit him yet because of the bad weather, but I hope to do so as soon as the Spring comes.

I am sure you will receive copies of his reports, Caesar, which I understand are sent to the Office of the Procurator in Londinium. I have learnt the inscription for the *altarium Victoriae* has now been carved but has not yet been put in place or the shrine finished because of this same bad weather that has had the province in its grip for the past two months. The statue of *Victoria* is also ready, and is currently being stored in Duroliponte, wrapped against the frost.

I will write again when the weather improves and I am able to undertake a tour of inspection.
Vale

Publius Aelius Hadrianus Augustus Imperator G. Modio Celeri
Tarracone
Ave

Do not injure your health, old soldier, while the weather is bad.
Nothing is so important that it cannot wait.
Vale Caesare m.p.

Epistula II
G. Modius Celer Hadriano Imperatori salutem dicit.
Concepti
Caesar, si vales bene est ego valeo.

I send you dreadful news. On visiting the home of T. Curt. Farus, I find
him recently deceased. His poor widow and children distraught. He,
who survived innumerable conflicts with *Legio VIIII*, was murdered
by thieves on the highway some two miles from Competum, his body
left in a ditch, his horse stolen. He rode alone with money bags, thus,
if he had not been my loyal friend of near fifty years, I would judge
him foolish. I have sought relief for his family from the council, or
else they must starve.

For lack of direction, the work on the shrine has been suspended: a
temporary roof of thatch covers it. The altar inscription is retained
in Londinium where I understand it has been set up temporarily on
the Governor's orders in the forum. It has created much interest
for it names the battle '*magna victoria Icenorum belli*' and gives its
position, '*m.p iii Competum; m.p. viii C. Ikelorum*'. A number of
visitors have come from Londinium to view the battle site and stay
in the settlement of Competum, of benefit to the place and its one
inn – from which place I write to you, Caesar.

I have also enquired of the *Victoria* statue in store in Duroliponte,
and there is bad news here too, for one of the wings has been cracked
badly through the carelessness of a slave and needs to be re-carved.
A sculptor will have to be found locally, and there is none available
at present.

Tomorrow, I ride to inspect the *tropaeum in loco tria flumina* where
I am told work has advanced, although delayed by the winter snows.
Vive valeque

Epistula III
G. Modius Celer Hadriano Imperatori salutem dicit.
C. Ikeniis
SVBEEV

Caesar, the roads here are not considered safe at present, and I could only make the journey to inspect the *tropaeum* in its isolated place by taking with me a bodyguard paid for by the *centurio regionarius*. The news of the construction is not good, I fear. The mound is but little advanced from the state when you saw it last. The ground has been long frozen, and the labour gangs were broken up during the winter and are now employed on repairing roads which have been damaged by frost and snow. There is none now to organise the work needed on the *tropaeum*. The steward, Frentius, has no instruction on the matter from his master, TC Verus. In my opinion, there is need of a direct command from the Governor's office and for the land to be taken into state ownership so the work can be centrally controlled, or it will fail. I wish I could write with better news, for I know you will have many other and greater concerns to deal with.
Vale

Epistula IIII
G. Modius Celer Hadriano Imperatori salutem dicit.
Fori Aelii
SVBEEV

Caesar, I write from my home, using the name of your planned town that is to rise nearby. Work has already begun there trenching for foundations. I have seen across the canal a great mast raised against the sky which I have been told is the working arm of a crane that will be used to build the tower you told me of. I know you will be receiving reports on this work, so you will not require any more from me except the expression of my pleasure that your plans are being fulfilled.

Regarding the works you have ordered on the battlefield, however, I have received no more information. I have not been able to visit again as I have been ill these past two months with a severe chill which went to my chest so that I was coughing up yellow phlegm and was advised to stay indoors with my hypocaust lit. I have not heard from you, or any official from the Governor's or Procurator's offices,

regarding the work. Now that I am feeling stronger, I shall be most pleased to receive further instruction as to your requirements so that I may endeavour to play my part in fulfilling them.
Vive valeque

Publius Aelius Hadrianus Augustus Imperator G. Modio Celeri
Cyrene
Ave

We thank you for your letters which are receiving our attention. We are preoccupied at present: war in these parts looks very likely. We will issue instructions on the matters you raise as soon as possible. In the meantime, *mi vetus amice*, look after your health. Report to us further only when you feel well enough.
Vale m.p.

I was left displeased and uncertain by Hadrian's last reply. The third person part of it was written as if by the Emperor's secretary, or perhaps by one of his scribes whose job it was to deal with the many routine enquiries that could not simply be ignored, but then the sudden change into the first person to call me *vetus amice* was as if Hadrian had cast a quick eye over the message and ordered that term added. The writing was not in his own hand, I felt sure, or even that of his secretary, but written up by scribes from dictation. Worse was that Hadrian had ignored completely what I had told him about poor Farus.

I had received another appeal from Virinia, the wife of Farus, for help, and was able to send her *xxxi denarii* I kept in a jar in the house, buried under the floor. This meant I had to send a sealed message through to my bankers in Duroliponte for a further supply of coinage to be allocated to me from the armed military barge that carries the soldiers' pay to the Northern Army. This is the way I generally obtain the money I need out of my own income – now principally my pension – to fulfil my obligations to my servants and slaves and meet the general running costs of my home.

I received a letter from Virinia, written in ink on a wooden leaf, offering me a thousand thanks and praising me to Minerva – I wondered if she had visited the shrine of Senuna – and saying she would repay me as soon as she could, something I had not wished and would not accept back. My friendship with Farus was forged in blood on many a battlefield, and is worth far more than anything money can buy.

I had wondered if I should take Virinia into my own home, but was pleased I had not made the offer when a second letter from her, following soon after the first, told me her position was now much better as she had been granted a widow's pension, which would be paid from the Governor's office in Londinium. She would also be allowed to live in the house that was to be built for Farus, only it would now be much smaller. She would not own it, but pay a small rent. I thought I detected the hand of the Emperor in this and felt immediately sorry I had doubted him – an Emperor who was probably at that moment making decisions on war and peace in a country as remote from Britannia as the frozen, white seas of the north are to the warm waters of *mare nostrum*.

It was in the early spring that I first began to hear rumours through Myru that there was some unrest amongst the *Iceni* people. The cause of this was not at first clear, but seemed to be occasioned by the works that I knew had begun on the far side of the canal to build Forum Aelium. Gavo had reported to me that some of the ditches excavated had been filled in again at night, and that stacks of building timber had been set alight. Some days ago, I had seen smoke rising in coils of twisting black, and had wondered at its origin.

At the dock a few mornings later, while taking a walk since the weather was fine, I came across three bedraggled men, freeborn land workers, I thought, but undoubtedly *Iceni* from the way their hair was cut to leave a sharp ridge on the crown. Sixty years ago, I knew one faction of the *Iceni* had cut their hair in that way to go into battle, which made it a disturbing sight today. The men had their wrists and ankles shackled in iron, and stood under guard waiting for an old tub of a barge to be towed out of the dock to take them down to Duroliponte. The guards I spoke to were ex-auxiliaries, probably *Germani*. They wore leather jerkins and breeches and carried long spears with daggers on their belts. When I got one to answer my questions, he simply shrugged his shoulders and answered with a heavy accent. "*Incendiarios*", drawing a grimed finger across his throat. I might have tried to find out more from my successor at the dock – the door to my old office was flung wide open to receive the morning sunlight and the sound of voices came from inside – but somehow I did not have the heart to do so. He and his staff might think I was trying to interfere. It is never pleasant for the new man to have his predecessor watching over his shoulder.

It was Myru who cornered me the next day when I was visiting the stable: she and Pyddr had been riding for me, exercising the ponies across the fresh spring grass of the meadow where Hadrian had had his camp set up last year. Already the impossibility of that event was retreating from me, muddling my thoughts, despite my daily efforts to make a written account of what had passed. At times, I wondered if I was inventing these happenings rather than recording the truth of them. My mind seemed to have grown increasingly murky of late.

Myru told me that her people were unhappy because the building of Forum Aelium meant that the site of an old enclosure of their forebears, most sacred to them, was to be disturbed. The enclosure was partly covered by trees, many of which, Myru said, had already been cut down by the construction gangs, which had also upset the people.

I knew that land considered sacred to the *Iceni* would hold a strange force for them if threatened. Emotions, long suppressed and denied, might rise to the surface, creating discontent, even violence. I determined I must ride across to where Forum Aelium was being built to see for myself what was happening.

I rode Ajax, perched on the pony's neck in the way I had now become used to, with Myru sat behind me. Diseta, learning of my intentions, had come out to the stables holding her cloak about her head in the chilly air, imploring me not to go. Why she was so concerned – frightened even – I had no idea. I told her roughly to go back into the house and to get on with her work, and she retired sobbing. I felt cruel. She had shared my bed last night and brought some comfort to my flesh. I slept badly now. My body often ached in the night, with sharp pains in my arms and legs as if my skeleton was about to pierce through the thin parchment of my flesh. It might not be long before it did, I thought grimly. My wishes, written down, were for my body not to be burnt, as was the usual Roman custom, but to be laid alongside that of my wife, who had been buried as a *Britanna*. And so we rode out that morning.

We had to cross the line of a new branch of the canal intended to run to the town. We passed over the muddy excavations by a plank bridge, seeing the slaves, including women, toiling away either side of us, wearing mere scraps of tunics, and the overseers halting the flailing of their whips to greet me with impertinent, over-loud salutes. I realised that to them I was now a figure of fun, I who had once led soldiers – men far better than they – into battle. I saluted them, though, in return, as Myru kicked at Ajax's sides and we trotted away.

It was this canal branch, in fact, that I saw was the cause of the local unrest. Its course was towards the ditches and banks of the abandoned *Iceni* enclosure, which occupied a peninsula at the edge of the marshes. The canal was to be dug across the peninsula to reach the site of the planned Forum Aelium, which lay on somewhat higher ground nearby. The canal would need to be completed before the actual building of the stone tower that would stand at the centre of Forum Aelium was begun. Many loads of timber and quarried stone for that purpose would need to be brought along it on barges.

We rode up to the enclosure. No one seemed to be about here. All the work that was being carried out was at a distance. A camp of wooden shacks and round huts for the workers had been built where the town would eventually rise. Smoke drifted in grey eddies against a clear, milky sky. The air bore the far off clink of pick and hammer, with the occasional muted shouts of men and braying of mules. I felt a sudden sense of great heaviness as if I was passing through some transparent, muffling wall of silence, penetrated here by the creak of Ajax's harness and the jolt of Myru's body behind me.

There had once been several ramparts surrounding this enclosure; even now, broken palisades of sagging timbers lined the tops of some of the banks, and beneath them ran ditches filled with pools of shining clear water. Ajax, head down, stopped to drink at one, and Myru allowed him to satisfy his thirst while I looked around. A causeway, once entered by a great gate of which the rounded posts were still in place, led into the interior: more ramparts crossed this inner space, and beyond them I could see the trees that Myru had spoken of, only a few small clumps of which were now left.

Seeing Ajax's head rise from the water, Myru urged him forward, and we proceeded at a trot across the enclosure and through another opening in the banks to the former area of trees. The felled trunks were piled up here, with cut branches stacked neatly beside. Great heaps of brushwood filled several carts, their draw shafts resting on the much-trampled earth.

Following the outer rampart, we came upon a group of women, wearing long, dark-coloured tunics, and with their heads covered, who were standing in a circle and chanting a mournful song, accompanied by a young man playing a pipe. Ajax started at their sight and pulled up, making a strange whinnying sound, his teeth bared. The piper stopped his playing and made a dash over the rampart, disappearing from view. I am sure the women too would have fled if Myru had not immediately called out to them in their own tongue. I saw their white, frightened faces turned up to her. I could not understand what was said. The women answered Myru with many cries, some tearing the shawls from their heads. One had the long, golden red hair of my Senuna.

Myru spoke into my ear, "They tell me of the cause of their sorrow, the reason for their lament. I did not know of this until now, although I had heard stories of it. It is very strange and troubling, yet it is wonderful too. *Domine*, we must go to the place they will show us."

I sat before her on Ajax, puzzled by what she meant. Then Myru turned Ajax, and we followed the women, who were crossing the clearing where the trees had stood, stepping between sawn-off stumps and trailing brambles, the hems of their garments splashed with mud.

It was here the canal was to cross and a dock would be dug out. Beyond the thin screen of the remaining trees, their branches yet bare of spring leaf, the marshes stretched away, the many channels of water catching the morning light, and the banks of brown-tipped reeds bent by the breeze, so that they looked like the long ranks of an army with heads bowed before an enemy's attack.

At a corner inside the outer rampart, which stood at this point to a height of some six feet, topped with the broken timbers of a palisade, the women stopped, and formed a circle to begin their chanting once more. Myru and I sat on Ajax's back, and watched as the women sang their lament, swaying their bodies and kneeling to lay their hands palm-down on the ground, then raising themselves again and flinging their arms upwards, crying out and clawing at the sky. They repeated this several times, then stopped and sank upon their knees and were still.

Within the bend of the rampart, the ground formed a shallow hollow. A thin sheen of water lay on the grass, which had been splashed up in silver drops as the women danced. Now they knelt in the water, their hands held out in front of them, their heads bowed.

"What are they doing?" I whispered back at Myru, trying to turn my head but only cricking my neck.

"They are praying to the gods. This is a sacred place of our people. A most sacred place. It must not be dug into."

"But it is going to be. Nothing can stop that!"

"*Domine*. Then there will be trouble. I have heard that some men are already arming themselves. Their blades are dulled from being hidden away so long, but they will sharpen them, and use them, as their forebears did."

I was both astonished and angered. "You talk of war!" I tried to bellow but it came out as something of a screech. I wanted to dismount, but I was trapped unless Myru did so first. "But why?! What has happened that it should bring the *Iceni* to another blood-letting?"

"They still remember the old war," Myru answered, her voice for once a little unsteady, yet insistent in my ear. "They remember their Queen who once led them against the Romans. They have never forgotten her. She lives for them still."

"Yes, yes," I heard myself mutter impatiently. "Old Boudica, Old Bodig. I know all about her. I thought I saw her face once...." The memories suddenly crowded back. I felt I was talking to Ajax's head rather than to Myru behind me – Myru with her dark-tanned skin and shining black hair. What was her origin, I wondered, that she should bring the genius of Epona to this part of the world?

"But why now? I exclaimed. "What are we Romans doing to anger your people?"

Myru dismounted, and helped me down, crushing my frail body against her tunic so that I felt the sharp mounds of her breasts against my thin chest. The *Iceni* women were rising and beginning to chant and dance again. Some had plucked the white heads of *conium* and were scattering them before them.

Myru faced me, holding me by both hands, looking into my eyes – I, who had been a soldier, felt now like a child before my slave. The chanting women, with their silly prancings, were beginning to annoy me. What was going on? My world was descending into disorder.

"The Queen is not dead. She is alive here."

"Alive here? That is nonsense Why do you dare to talk to me like this?"

"All those years ago – within your own life, *domine* – the Queen came here after her army was defeated. She lives now within the eternity promised by the *conium* that grows here. With the help of the *conium* she passed out of this life into another, yet she is present still."

"What do you mean?" I was astonished. I felt dribble on my chin. My bones felt very thin as if they could not stand the weight of the sun any longer.

"She was buried here in secret, *domine*. She lies beneath our feet. That is why this place must never be disturbed."

XXVI

Epistula V
G. Modius Celer Hadriano Imperatori salutem dicit.
Fori Aelii

The most extraordinary circumstances have arisen, Caesar. Upon attempting to find the source of some local unrest that had been interrupting the works at Forum Aelium – which I feel certain will have been reported to you already by the *praefectus gentis* – I have discovered that some numbers of the *Iceni* who dwell in this region, many of whom, in accordance with your instructions, are due to be moved from their homes to be resettled elsewhere, have been upset that one particular sacred place of theirs is to be destroyed by the building of the canal and port at Forum Aelium.

When I visited the site yesterday, it was to find a ceremony of the old religion in process within a banked enclosure that was once sacred to the *Iceni*, not a ceremony that could be said to be against Rome's rule as such, but one that commemorated ancestors long worshipped here. Foremost amongst these, Caesar – and I know you will find this extraordinary – is their Queen of the late wars that you were so anxious to learn about while in Britannia. I write of red Boudica, *regina sanguinis*, who killed so many of our people and left much of the settled province in ruin. The accounts say she took poison and was buried at a remote place that none can know of – that is, until now, Caesar, for Myru, my slave of horse – she is of the *Iceni* too – has told me that place is within this same sacred enclosure, which I have now seen with my own eyes. It lies at the very edge of the undrained marshes close by Forum Aelium.

Should the body of Boudica thus be dug up in the excavations for Forum Aelium, and treated as a common criminal, without ceremony, her remains burnt and her ashes scattered – as we Romans might feel they deserve – it will only increase the trouble in this land, and spread further unrest in a province to which you, in your great wisdom, Caesar, wish to bring your beneficence of reconciliation and peace.

I will write further should I learn more, yet I do not wish to seem to be interfering with those who now have command here in these matters. I propose, however, consulting the *praefectus* gentis, my near neighbour, Appius Claudius Numicius, with whom I believe I have an understanding relationship, and with whom, Caesar, your officials will probably be in contact, since he has responsibility here and much of the land in question was once, or is still, in his possession.
SVBEEV
Vale

T. Petronius Priscus ab epistulis imperatori Hadriano Augusto G. Modio Celeri
Ephesi
Ave

His Majesty commands that you do nothing in respect of the substance of your letter no.v, recently received, before receiving instructions through the office of Ap Cl Numicius Secundus, *praefectus gentis*. The Emperor is gracious to state that a further letter will be sent to you in due course, but affairs in Anatolia in which he is much engaged prevent him at present from writing.
Vale

I was much piqued by this letter. I had hoped Hadrian would reply on such an important subject himself. But the reply, which had taken over a month to reach me, had been written by a new secretary Hadrian must have appointed. I wondered what had happened to the last one, Valerius, whom I had seen with his tablets dangling about his waist. Perhaps he too had committed some indiscretion, in the way that Hadrian had told me of his predecessor, Suetonius Tranquillus. It is such conversations I will need to expunge from this account. Perhaps I have been foolish in writing them down.

Numicius, himself, paid me a visit shortly afterwards. It was the first time I had seen him since the ceremonies at the battlefield. His intention to call at my house on official business as *praefectus gentis* had been announced ahead of his arrival by his steward, who was riding a fat old pony that had been allowed to go to waste rather like its owner. Then Numicius, himself, appeared, borne through the warm, sunlit air in an open litter by no less than twelve sturdy bearers. I had him unloaded onto my garden seat by the pool, where we had sat with Hadrian that time ago. Numicius was wearing a double tunic bordered in green, with a shoulder mantle of a deeper green, both the stripes and their colours denoting his equestrian rank. In respect of that rank, if not of Numicius himself, I gave him an elaborate bow, my bones creaking with the effort. I snapped my fingers for the hovering Gavo to bring us bowls of water and wine, although the morning was yet young and my slaves were still sweeping the portico.

Numicius had surely put on more weight since I had last seen him. His mouth seemed to have retreated to a small 'O' within his puffy, red cheeks and jowl. He did not look healthy, although he was not even half my age. He picked at a cold chicken leg that Gavo had thought to bring him with the wine.

"Now, Celer," he said in his high voice, "how to deal with this remarkable matter without over-exciting the people? The canal has already reached the old *Iceni* camp and is now held up pending a decision on the best way to proceed. Our works office has recently heard from the Emperor on the matter."

I ignored the latter statement for the moment, still aggrieved Hadrian had not replied directly to me about the remarkable information I had sent him.

"Has there been any more trouble?" I asked, my mouth full of a toasted bun that Gavo had brought me, knowing this was a snack I liked in the mid-morning. On seeing it, Numicius had flicked his fingers for one too.

"A crane was overturned some nights back. The culprits were caught before they could set fire to it. They have already been executed. I signed the order. I had the power to do so without referral to Londinium."

He wrapped his chubby fingers around his bun. Butter oozed out around the gold and red signet ring he wore, the one which, stamped into wax, had sent several *Iceni*, slaves and freeborn, to their deaths. The horrors of sixty years past were returning in the bright spring sunlight of the present day.

"What does the Emperor say?" I asked reluctantly. I did not want Numicius to take control from me of matters I had first raised. Yet, I knew that was absurd. I had no part in the building works. I was just an observer, a relic of other times. He was the authority.

289

"The Emperor wishes the body – if body there is: there may be something there, but is it really of that long dead Queen? These people have many stories, mostly made up, and the truth is hard to gather...."

"The Emperor wishes the body, or any parts of the body, or any bit at all that's left, to be lifted with dignity, and preserved until it can be reburied somewhere else where the *Iceni* can see that being done with proper ceremony. Then the people can offer up their worship and their trinkets – or whatever else it is they feel they have to do for someone who led them to disaster – and, most hopefully, that will bring an end to this matter. Then we will be able to get on with our new town in which lies the future prosperity of these parts, and indeed of the whole province."

It was a long involved speech for the reclining Numicius, propped up amongst cushions on my stone bench, one full of assumptions and perhaps lacking a realistic conclusion, but I believed Numicius when he stated he had Hadrian's authority for what he said.

"So it must be done," I said as steadily as I could, although for some reason my nerves were jumping in my finger tips and my old heart was rattling its cage. "When and where will the body of the Queen, if what I have heard proves true, be reinterred, and by what custom?"

"In two days, " Numicius said decisively, "the grave – if grave it is – will be dug. There will be a cordon of guards around the site and the people kept away. We will tell them we are doing this with respect for their customs and traditions. Further decisions will be made, depending on what we find – if anything."

"My slave who trains my ponies is of the *Iceni* by blood. She is very certain that the Queen is there."

"Let us see," said Numicius, washing his hands in a bowl his steward proffered. "You will attend, Celer?"

"Nothing would keep me away," I said determinedly. And I knew it wouldn't, not aches and pains or the coughing up of blood, of which I had had signs of late, or anything else of which I knew, Minerva and Juno and Epona – all three of you – preserve me. "I shall bring my horse-slave with me. She rides with me now, or else I must be carried. She will be a witness for the *Iceni*. Whatever is found, she can tell her people of, so that they will know we Romans are not hiding anything."

Numicius looked thoughtful for a moment. "Yes, Celer. That is good. That is sensible. You are a lucky man. I have seen your slave ride." – I guessed what was coming, for the Emperor had thought me fortunate in Myru too – "Now, if you should ever wish to sell her...."

"I won't," I said firmly. "When I die, I shall set her free."

It was raining that morning, two days on from the scene I have just described. I had risen early; sleep had been difficult that night. I had called Diseta to me in the early hours, and she had shared my bed to rub warmth into me and whisper comfort into my ears. For some reason I do not understand – I try to keep my mind clear of such inturned melancholy – I had felt I was dying, yet when the dawn light, grey with rain, seeped between the shutters of the room, I felt strong enough to get out of bed without help, and to be shaved.

Before I had breakfasted – sparsely on fruit with a little seed-husked bread from the baker who runs a business at the dock – Myru had brought Ajax to the front of the house below the portico. I could see her draped in a grey cloak, greased with cooking fat against the rain, waiting patiently astride the pony, whose head was cast down on the gravel. I took pity on them, and wearing my old military cloak, and with a wedge of bread and meat still in my hand, I went outside. Myru helped me mount – hard to achieve with one hand already occupied, but I did not wish to give up the grisly meat that was difficult to chew with my bad teeth. Myru said but the one word "*Domine*" in greeting. I had already informed her of the purpose of today's expedition. When I had told her she was to represent the *Iceni* people at the disinterment, she had replied, "*Domine*, these matters are of concern to me."

"They must be done, Myru. There is no other way."

"I understand that, *domine*. But what shall I say to the people when you discover their Queen and take her away."

"If that happens, Myru, we shall find the words that are necessary at the time. I give you my vow that this matter will be handled well – to the honour of Rome and your people"

She gave me a long, dark look, but said no more. She urged the patient Ajax away from the house and through the courtyard gate, held open by Gavo. His face held its habitual worried look.

"Keep the servants to their work, Gavo I shall be returned by evening. *Vale.*"

"*Vale, domine.*"

There was a guard of auxiliary troopers spaced out all around the *Iceni* enclosure. They must have been sent here from a base to the north – perhaps the one at Lindum – because I knew of no depot of troops otherwise closer than Londinium. Beyond the ring of horsemen, knots of people sat in huddled groups upon the wet ground. There were not so many of them as I had feared: perhaps the light, but steady, rain had kept most away. Those who had made the journey from the settlements around, or from the further reaches of Icenia, had heard this rumour of the Queen's burial place – or perhaps such knowledge had long been retained in memory amongst their settlements – and they had come to see what we Romans would do now; in the same way as their forebears had once travelled to that great battlefield to the south.

We found Numicius's party sheltering beneath a dripping willow tree on the far side of the enclosure. There was Numicius himself, clothed now in the military-style leather cuirass of his office of *praefectus gentis* that I had seen him wear before, with slaves about him mopping the wet from his plump, flushed face and even from his calf-high boots, which were muddied again by every weighted step he took. And there too were controllers and supervisors of the building works, to whom I was introduced; thin-faced and gaunt, they looked, as if many years of exposure to the climate of Britannia had drained the sap of life from them.

The rain was easing. Only a few drops fell on us now through the drooping branches of the willow with its thin, spring veil of light-green leaves. Time for action, Numicius determined, his voice and look for once matching the authority of his office. As a group we walked to the spot by the rampart where the *Iceni* women had chanted and danced. A gang of slaves, huddled under pieces of sacking, had clearly long-awaited our arrival. I saw their dulled eyes move over our party – young men, I thought taken into slavery from some war or other, perhaps the one which lingered on in the North, their shape and physique hidden by the sacking. They took up spades, wooden with iron rims to their cutting edges, and, under the direction of an overseer in a leather corselet, bearing a whip, began attacking the turf.

It was soft digging. The grass and the black soil beneath came up in large clumps, which were stacked neatly, in legionary fashion, at one side against the rampart. Soon, a hole, some ten feet by ten in size, had been opened: it was already a foot or two deep.

Coming to us now, borne on the breeze that was blowing the rain away to the west, was the sound of lamentation, increasing in volume, then dying away – cries and chants from the *Iceni* gathered beyond the cordon of horsemen. I was also aware of a sudden confusion of men and horses in the distance against the far rampart: it seemed as if some hotheads had tried to get past the soldiers, and even now were being dragged away. We dug on.

The hole was now about three feet deep – a depth greater than half the height of a man – when all at once the spades, wielded by the slaves in relays of four at a time, began striking with loud thumps on some solid object. We watchers pressed forward. The overseer, his bare legs running with liquid mud, had ordered the slaves out of the hole and had jumped into it himself. With a short-handled spade, he was scraping aside the loose, wet soil, and was trying to scoop it up to chuck it out. Much of it splashed back on him and he cursed.

"It looks like a buried tree trunk," he called out eventually, and all at once my brain was racing. I had heard of the log coffins the *Britanni* used sometimes to bury their dead; these hollowed out tree trunks were usually reserved for the great ones of their society. The bodies of others – the ordinary people or the warriors who fell in battle – were either burnt, or committed to the lakes and seas, or sometimes even now – I had seen this practice years ago – exposed on platforms for the wild birds to pick away.

The slave gang was set to work enlarging the hole, until the long black shape we could see lying deep in water had been fully exposed. The section of tree trunk – part of a large oak tree, cut down and shaped – still with much of its bark attached, was the length of a man laid on his side with his arms stretched out, and some three feet in diameter. The top, I could see, had been flattened and smoothed, and through the water I could make out a horizontal line below running along the length of the log.

It was my time to shout out now, my words coming as something of a shrill croak, but they were enough to make the others start and gaze down more intently. "It is a burial – a log burial! You can see the lid!"

And then I tried to add, "The stories are right. The Queen is here", but I found my throat had closed in my excitement and the words would not come out.

Myru, who had stood all this time in the background, came forward now, laying her own woollen shawl over my shoulders and pressing my hand. "Take care, *domine*," she whispered, and my emotions were so affected by her care and by the sight of the black tree coffin before me that I felt the tears springing to my eyes. I hoped they were disguised by the wetness that was splashed all about us, and shared by everyone.

We sent for more slaves. They took a while to arrive, and we all stood around the hole while we waited, with only the occasional word to each other, scarcely believing the dark shape that lay below us still half-buried in water and mud. It would be necessary to raise the log to the surface to open the lid. A roar from the overseer brought a slave to us bearing wine from flagons at his belt and bread in a basket. I eat, but the bread stuck in my throat and the wine was coarse. Numicius, I could see, was eating voraciously, his face full of bread, and sausage too. I had to look away.

A gang of powerful-looking men from the labour camp, all in short black tunics with Numicius's personal monogram ACN woven at the shoulder, arrived at last. The sky was clearing. A bright shaft of watery sunlight shone on our scene as if the gods themselves wished a clearer view. What were we to find when the log was lifted out of the hole onto the grass?

It took many efforts to move it from the suction of the water, many brawny arms tugging, many bare feet stamping and sliding in the churned black mud. At first the log would not shift at all. Ropes and two oxen were brought up. All this activity, I thought, must be creating great speculation, fear even, amongst the distant, watching people: they must realise something of note had been found, and that the *Iceni* stories of the Queen might be made true. Even we Romans watching held feelings that were a mixture of awe and disbelief. I, for one, felt sure that something important would be found, but even I did not comprehend the reality of what was about to be revealed.

The oxen were able to drag one end of the log out of the ground using chains. The second labour gang, their tunics now smothered in mud, managed by brute force to lift that end higher and hold it up while the oxen were unhitched and the chains re-coupled to pull at the further end of the log. This was now raised too and held by the first gang, with bowed knees and floundering feet. Slowly, inch by inch, the log was lifted to the top of the hole, and then rolled sideways out onto the grass, there being no other way to do this. The lid, the edges of which could now be seen to run all around the smoothed upper surface of the log, did not break open, however. The contents of its hollowed out chamber, although perhaps shaken up, were still in place.

I remember thinking wildly that all this could be a subterfuge, a trick of the *Iceni* to lure we Romans away from the true burial site of their Queen; the find might prove to be just a hollowed out tree trunk, perhaps intended for a boat, abandoned here at the edge of the marshes. I knew these people had long been skilled in working wood – to build houses, to set up as columns in ceremonial rows, to construct carts and chariots and sea-going boats. Boudica might have been buried elsewhere, far into Icenia perhaps, safely interred in a chamber of white rock, at a remote place where no man ever came now; or perhaps her body had been burnt and her ashes long since scattered. Those at least were my tumbling thoughts in those last moments before the lid of the log coffin was prised off.

First, though, the trunk had to be rolled over so the long, flat lid was clear of the ground. A team of slaves, their skin and tunics covered in black slime like the mud- wrestlers I used to watch as a boy on the foreshore of Ostia's harbour, succeeded in doing this, their feet scrambling and slipping on the torn grass. Our group stepped back as the slaves struggled at this task, and then, when it was completed, we pressed forward eagerly again, arranging ourselves as best we could around the long, cylindrical length of shining, black wood. I could see Numicius jostling to gain an advantageous position. Perhaps in deference to my age, I found myself pushed forward with my slave against the trunk itself, so that I was able to run my hand over its wet wood, surprised to find how hard it still was. I picked at a piece of bark at the edge of the smoothed lid, but it would not yield to my fingers. Myru whispered in my ear, "Do you feel strong, *domine*?" I answered her that I did.

The overseer shouted an order to one of the least muddied of the slaves, and he ran off between the stumps of trees, returning after what seemed an eternity of time with a long iron bar bent into a hook at one end, such as I have seen being used to remove the metal tyres from worn-out carriage wheels. There had been a strange silence while we waited, as if no one wished to make a fool of himself by anticipating what might be discovered. The only sound was that of the breeze, stronger now, gusting amongst the few straggling trees and shaking the boards of the broken palisade above our heads; also, the occasional cough and muttered comment, and an oath or two from the overseer as he sought to wipe his legs and arms free of the clinging mud with tufts of grass.

The overseer seized the metal bar from the slave as if it was a weapon and he about to strike out at an opponent in the arena. With a sharp movement, he inserted the sharpened end of the hook into a gap at one end of the trunk-coffin's lid. With all his strength he pushed down on the bar. There was a creaking of the wood, and the lid was forced up a degree or two before the bar slipped out and the overseer fell to the ground, his arm gashed by the pointed hook. Crimson drops of blood mingled with the oozing, black mud. Some violent curses followed, and we all stepped back a little while he ordered a slave to bind a rag, produced from his tunic pocket, about his arm.

The overseer was clearly a stalwart man, and, after pushing me in the chest to make sure I was well back out of the way, he struck once more with the hook-ended bar, this time raising the lid a little towards its centre. His bandage had already slipped aside, and the red blood was running again in rivulets across his forearm. Like a man, wounded in battle, maddened by the sight of his own blood, he attacked the coffin lid once more, this time at the far end, and was able to force it up here to create a gap into which he could insert his fingers. Taking a grip, he heaved and heaved upwards, and we watched silently and in awe as the lid slowly rose, then was twisted sideways, and at last fell away free.

There was a gasp from the watchers that could be heard above the wind which at that moment chose to sweep our small clearing, stirring the hair and the clothing of the watchers. I found myself on my knees staring into the interior of the coffin – for coffin it was – my hands held forward, all of time seemingly framed by my fingertips, reaching out towards that past of which I had once been a part.

Queen Boudica lay there. I saw her clearly, her body covered by a dark cloak with a gold brooch at her shoulder, and a great twisted cord of gold about her neck. Her hair, flame gold too, framed her face, of which the skin seemed as white and plump as if in life, only her eyes were closed by shells brought from the sea.

As I watched, and this must have been in an instant, but seemed to me very much slower – as if an artist had painted the scene many times, with the slightest changing differences to each view, the scenes then made to move in synchrony so that one could slow them up at will – the white face turned darker, and grew black, and then the blackened skin fell away completely, revealing the bone and the teeth beneath.

Yes, I had seen the face of Boudica and recognised it. It was the same face – I understood now – as I had glimpsed at the enemy's camp as the riders surged past me. It was the same face too, I realised, in that same long drawn-out moment, looking from the breathing world of life into death's stilled darkness, as of the Sena of the temple – and the same as of my own Senuna, which had been mine to touch and caress.

The realisation was so enormous that I tried to reach into the coffin to take hold of the now ravaged, near vanished face, to hold it and kiss it, albeit that my lips would have met lips of bone – only others, including Myru, were holding me back, and a great blackness rushed upon me so that I felt I had died myself while looking upon death – but after a while I was able to open my eyes, and I saw light again.

It was Myru who was standing over me when I came to. I had been carried to one of the cabins of the workmen's camp and laid on a table top, with my own yellow cloak for a pillow. Two other cloaks were laid over my body to give me warmth. I struggled to raise myself, but Myru pressed down on me with her hands and told me to rest awhile yet. I did not have the strength to do more than obey my slave. The world swam away from me again, and when it returned the door to the cabin was open and a boy slave with a muddied tunic was ladling a thick stew from a metal bowl he carried into a wooden dish. Myru got me to sit up, my back resting against a wooden beam of the cabin wall, and made me eat. She spooned the meat and gravy at me as if I was a small child who was reluctant to eat. Obedient to her, I found my mouth opening and my throat swallowing. I felt warmth and strength returning.

Now I did get back onto my feet, pushing the bowl aside so that its remaining contents splashed onto the planked floor. Memory of what I had witnessed was sweeping through me. "I must go out and see her again," I said, trying to push Myru and the other slave aside. But my legs were still weak and Myru caught me as I fell.

"Sit, *domine*" she commanded, and she held me while the boy slid forward a stool onto which I collapsed while she supported my shoulders. This indignity could not be allowed to continue, I remember thinking, when the door to the cabin opened and Numicius with two of his slaves stood in the opening.

"Ah, better already, I see." His face was wreathed in a fat smile that, even in my weakness, I would have liked to wipe away.

"Where is she?" I said distinctly, and I saw the look of initial puzzlement replaced almost immediately by one of comprehension.

"You mean the corpse, I think. Do not worry, it has been taken somewhere that is safe. The mob out there, which has been in something of a turmoil, will not be able to get to it."

I could sense Myru's body stiffening behind me. Of course, she had stayed with me all this time. She did not know what was happening either. The corpse had been her people's Queen. Surely they, above all, had the right to view it.

"I am *praefectus gentis*. I have the Emperor's instructions," Numicius said in an oily voice. "Ah, yes, Celer: you see, it is not just you he sends his confidential messages to." Even in my enfeebled state, I found that maddening. I tried to stand, but Myru held me down.

"The Emperor has ordered," continued Numicius, "that in the event of any remains of the *Iceni* Queen, known to us as Boudica, being found they should be treated with dignity and a guard be placed over them until such time as they can be disposed of in an appropriate manner."

"Disposed of…?!" My voice broke, such was my anguish. "What do you mean 'disposed of'?"

"It is left to my judgement," said Numicius, his smile now vanished and sucking at his cheeks, so that he looked like a puffed-out fish blowing for air on the crystal surface of a pool.

My anger flashed like fire. Instinctively, I felt my right hand reaching at my hip for the sword that once had always lain there, but now, of course, had long since been put away: all my clawing fingers found was shrunken flesh and pointed bone. My anger at least brought back clarity and force to what I said. "The Emperor has asked for respect to be shown, so it is clear he would not want the body treated in any way other than by a dignified reburial. He should be informed straightaway of what has happened. I shall write myself. In the meantime, you should preserve the remains as well as you can and mount a guard over them. Use those auxiliaries who are here: get them off their horses and standing guard. And let some of the *Iceni* – their leaders at least – see their former queen. Unless you do, I would judge you will have a riot on your hands – and I don't think the Emperor will be pleased about that."

It was a good speech – I think – delivered to someone vastly my superior, with my head still swimming and my surging thoughts still attended by disbelief, but I did so with at least some of my former authority as an *optio*, and – dare I say – as a friend of Hadrian, one who had been his confidante even. I knew he would be both fascinated, yet horrified too, by what was going on here now.

I could see the annoyance in Numicius's eyes: he must have been far more upset by my upstaging him with the Emperor's affairs than I had realised. But he could not retain his anger. Anger demanded too much effort for Numicius. For all his arrogance and flaunting of his own position and status, it was clear he far preferred it when others were making the decisions and doing the work. He must have been as amazed as I by these developments, and did not know how to handle them in a situation where he would hold the immediate responsibility as *praefectus gentis* – particularly, in Hadrian's eyes, he being one of equestrian rank – however many other imperial officials were involved. My words must have shaken him through his buttresses of flesh. I saw the small, sharp eyes begin to soften, and he even held out an arm to me, which for a moment I feared Myru might push away. I could not see her, but I sensed her poised like a wild cat behind me ready to spring to my aid.

"What you say, Celer, does make sense," he said a little sulkily. What a business, this has been! What a total surprise! Who would have thought that we had that blood-soaked queen out of history in our midst all this time? I wouldn't wonder….." I didn't wait to hear what he wondered about.

"*Where has she been taken?*" I said with an intensity that I could see scared him. Perhaps he thought I was descending into madness. Of course, he knew nothing about the resemblance of the *Iceni* Queen to my Senuna, that I had seen before the air had caused the face to crumble away like the decaying bloom of a flower. Numicius must think it was just my bodily weakness before the blackened corpse that had caused my collapse, I who had seen such horrors in my years of fighting as he could scarcely imagine.

He responded, looking a little shame-faced, I thought, all his earlier arrogance before me now subsided. "She is to be taken to my villa. I have given the order. She will be on her way there now."

"To your villa! Where do you think to place her? In the middle of your atrium? That's about as suitable for a queen who hated Rome as sending our soldiers' dead bodies to lie in an *Iceni* round hut."

He stood his ground before my anger. "I have an ice pit in my grounds with a mound above it. It's well away from the house and will still be cold from the winter's frosts. I thought it would be suitable until arrangements are made. You see" – and he pinched his nose with his chubby fingers – "she may be a queen but she smells! The decay is fast, now that the body is out in the air, as if it seeks to catch up with natural time. The men who took it from the wood tell me it is already only black skin and bone – and a dreadful, stinking liquid; not something, I think, her people would want to look upon."

"You took it out the coffin?"

"Yes, there was no way we could lug that great bit of tree trunk about. It wouldn't fit a cart without standing it up, and that would have jumbled up the Queen in a way that would be hard to put together again."

"You do not show the respect, Numicius, the Emperor has asked for."

"On the contrary, Celer. I have done all I can. The remains were wrapped in the best red cloth, one with expensive gold thread, which happened to be in the camp: it had been ordered for the wife of the chief architect and was to be made into a stola for her birthday party. Now it's gone to dress a long dead, enemy queen. I shall have to pay for it out of my own pocket."

I had been wrong. I felt somewhat ashamed now, although I tried not to show it. It was clear, in fact, that Numicius had more than fulfilled Hadrian's instructions, even if, left to himself, he might have handled matters very differently. It did not pay to offend your Emperor, even about the body of someone whom Rome had once sought to hunt down and kill.

All becomes a little blurred now, for I think I became ill and dizzy again and was wrapped by Myru closer in the three cloaks so that I must have looked like one of those plaques you see carved with rustic gods wearing the *birus Britannicus*, with just my hooded face staring out through the many folds of cloth.

A closed litter with six of the black tunicked slaves as bearers was brought to the cabin door and I was helped inside, with Myru opposite me, and taken at a run to Numicius's villa. Someone must also have ridden my pony there because I learnt later Ajax was in the stables, whinnying with pleasure and tossing high Numicius's still fresh winter hay when he caught sight of Myru coming to take him home.

Numicius, and his wife Lucilla – I have neglected to mention her before: she was young and pretty and far beyond her husband in intelligence – looked after me well. I was given a heated room with a plain, red tiled floor. A window closed by shutters looked out onto a small courtyard with a fountain, surrounded by red and white painted columns. I slept well, with Myru beside me to perform Diseta's usual duties in dressing and feeding me, and taking my chamber pot away. She – my horse girl of Epona – showed no sign of resenting this bodily service. It puzzled me at times why she was so devoted to me.

I recovered fast. Early on my second morning, I walked with Numicius – he hobbling on a stick, for he had twisted an ankle – to the cone-shaped, brick ice house where Boudica lay. A guard, I was pleased to see, was at the door – two troopers of the auxiliary horse, with black plumes on their helmets and wearing corselets of chain mail. They saluted us, and let us inside through the low, arched entrance.

The smell hit me straightaway, and I placed a hand over my face and mouth while Numicius pulled a scented napkin from his tunic pocket. Boudica lay on the paved floor wrapped in the red cloth like a bundle on a carrier's cart. Light from the doorway lit the gold thread in the cloth making it sparkle. Outside, the sentries' boots stamped on the stone. It was cold here and I shivered. I bent forward and carefully unwrapped the cloth at its far end with one hand, my other still across my face. Where I had seen white flesh, there was now only grey-black skin covered by fragments of cloth, with the bones sticking through. The skull was turned to one side, the teeth set in a grin (of triumph or contempt, I did not know), but the mass of red hair was still there, glowing in the rays of the new sun penetrating the entrance. The shells over the eyes had fallen away and there were only deep, black pits there – as deep, I thought, as eternity. Boudica's spirit that had once led armies to victory was far from here now, chasing somewhere amongst the forests or skimming the seas or soaring into unknown distances amongst the stars.

I suddenly realised there was no gold neck ring in place, or brooch, or anything else that had once been in that log coffin other than these poor shrivelled remains. I turned to Numicius. "Where are the items she was buried with?"

He looked shifty. "I have placed them in my safe."

"I would like to see them. They must be reburied with the body."

"Of course. That is what I have intended."

I thought, you hoped I would not notice. There would be quite a market in Londinium – or in Rome itself – for objects such as those. There were many collectors of the treasures of the *barbari* who would be prepared to pay large sums, in particular if the person who had once owned them was notorious – and Boudica, recovered out of history, was certainly that.

We left the ice house. Some workers from Numicius's estate were gathered outside, being kept at a distance by the guards. One or two bore garlands of spring flowers. Another carried a lamb in his arms.

"They may place their offerings outside," said Numicius to the guards. "And make their obeisance there. They must *not* be let inside. Bar the door and keep it locked. If there is any trouble, let your commander report to me immediately."

I nodded my approval. I did not think there would be trouble now, but you never knew. Rumours must be flickering about like wild fire. It only took one agitator to spark the people's temper from reverence into violence.

In Numicius' own bedroom – where his wife was yet dressing, her body slave curling her hair with a hot iron – he showed me his safe set in the wall, which had an iron door hidden behind wooden panelling. He turned the lock with a great key, which he seemed to produce from the depths of the bed. He sleeps more securely with that, I thought, than he does with his wife, whose slim, supple body must surely be aching for a younger, fitter man.

Yet, I knew, it was unwise to judge the intimate affairs of others. That had been done about Senuna and me, and the sneerers and the gossipers had been quite wrong. Yet even I couldn't have imagined when I married her that my Senuna would prove to be the granddaughter of a Queen – for I felt sure now that the baby who had been brought to the temple from the fort at Competum had been born of one of the two lost daughters of Boudica. That old *Iceni* rascal, Catrig, had described the princesses at the final battle, but there was no record – *Iceni* or Roman – of their fate.

I had seen the face of Boudica in that of Senuna, and it could only have been carried there through one of Boudica's own daughters – captured, and perhaps raped, after the battle. Did she lie still in that small graveyard outside Competum – *'femina Britanna'*? The likenesses were too striking to be mere coincidence. And the royal line of Boudica was still carried on at the temple, now worshipped through both Senuna and Minerva – the last also a goddess of war in her gilded helmet. Was that the real secret of those furtive priests, one that was not written down amongst their records, but carried forward in memory? Did they, in truth, worship Boudica first and foremost – Boudica, whose name means victory, placed above all others, mortal or divine?

These facts and suppositions had all locked together in my mind in that one moment when I had seen the face of Boudica lying in the oak coffin, before it was lost again – this time forever.

From a box in the safe, Numicius produced the great torc that had been on the body, with its many twisted strands like golden rope about Boudica's neck, and the brooch at her shoulder, of polished bronze, that I saw now was enamelled with red and blue and green colours, all twisting and interweaving in the style the *Britanni* favoured. And also, a surprise – because I had not seen them before – a gold arm band incised with most delicate chevron patterns, and a large bronze spearhead in the shape of a leaf, still with a short length of its wooden shaft attached. Confronted with these wonders, my hands trembling as I touched them, all I could think to say was, "There was nothing else?"

"Only some pins in the hair and the buckles of her shoes. I ordered them left with the body. I don't believe anything was stolen. The clothes she was buried in – perhaps those she was wearing when she died – have decayed as fast as the flesh."

I believed Numicius. There was sincerity in his face. I knew him to be a bad liar, and there was no sign of him lying to me now. His wife had left the room with her slave. I had not even had the chance to kiss her hand, the usual morning greeting of a guest to his hostess. I think she had been put out by our sudden, unannounced appearance by her dressing mirror. I thought it was about time I made my farewells.

"Keep everything secure," I said sternly to Numicius, unconcerned now by our disparity in rank. "I shall view the body again before the re-burial. In the meantime we must await the Emperor's instructions. They will come to you first, no doubt."

"Of course, Celer." His greasy smile that I did not trust had returned. I knew that he would not wish to offend Hadrian rather more than he would not wish to upset me. So I had to trust him.

"We shall keep in close touch by messenger," I said, as Myru and I prepared to depart on a rested and saddled Ajax. Lucilla had reappeared to say her farewells, so I had the chance to thank her fully and to apologise for disturbing her at her toilet.

She replied in Numicius's hearing, "You have nothing to say sorry for. The fault – if any – is not yours." She left the rest of the sentence unsaid, but I thought Numicius might be in for a few sharp words after I had left.

"Look after your master," she said to Myru.

"*Ego vobis valedico et bonam fortunam.*"

"*Valete.*"

And we rode off home to be met by a distressed Diseta, who bundled me inside like an outraged mother. Myru turned away to the stables without a word. I knew now that without my loyal slaves, life for me must prove impossible.

While I have breath, though, I must see this story that I tell through to its natural end – in whatever form that will come to greet me.

XXVII

The next day, a mounted courier from the *cursus publicus* brought me the personal letter from Hadrian that I had long looked for. It was marked 'for your eyes only' and was written in a cursive script that I thought was the Emperor's own hand. It was tied with tape with a bronze seal locket attached. I opened the lid of the locket and inspected the seal, an imperial eagle stamped into red wax, and it looked intact, with the tapes uncut. Yet I could not be sure – and nor, I knew, could Hadrian be absolutely certain – that someone had not cast their wondering eyes over it. The Emperor writing a private letter to an unknown ex-soldier at the edge of the empire might have caused a few questions to be asked. Yet emperors can do as they wish, and have the power to enforce this, so anyone interfering, whatever their purpose, does so at the risk of their own life.

P. Aelius Hadrianus Augustus Imp. G. Modio Celeri solis tui oculi Claudiopoli
Salve Celer amice vetus

You may have heard by now from Cl. Numicius Secundus about the arrangements that must be made should your suspicions about the death site of the late Queen of the *Iceni* be proven true and that any remains of her body are discovered. We must do everything we can to see that the people of the region are not upset by such a discovery. The remains must be respected or else they may be the cause of further trouble, which we have so recently exerted ourselves to prevent breaking out once more in the province. This is especially true since reports have been made to me that there is unrest again in the North where the *pax Romana* is not yet imposed and where we have ordered a *vallum* and *x castra* built to make a *limes Britannica*.

I expect daily to receive an account from Numicius of any discoveries that may have been made at Forum Aelium, but, dear Celer, write yourself as soon as you can if there is an important story to tell. I am surrounded here by long-faced officials so that I feel at times like a mouse caught in a trap, although that may sound strange to you – an emperor confined in a prison when he should have limitless power. The prison, my friend – as I once related to you, and perhaps should not have done so – is within my mind, for there are none about me with whom I can share the deeper expressions of life. My inner spirit at times is quashed: at what place shall my poor, unnourished soul find sustenance?

All is not so dismal, however. The Empire is strong, and I am well too, at least in body. The Empress keeps her own court here and I only see her when it is necessary. My eyes have fallen on a person so wonderful, of so divine a form, I am quite unable to express my feelings to you. You have learnt of many of an emperor's anguishes, old comrade, but of this one matter I am not able, for propriety's sake, to say more. Yet, it shall perhaps bring me a new happiness when all about me still is war – and the talk of more war.

Write soon, from one soldier to another.

Cura et valeas

Bene vale Caesare

I replied immediately with a detailed account of the discovery, although I was careful to keep my account free of my own emotion. I remembered that Hadrian had told me once that I would look upon the face of Boudica again, and he had been right. Is there then some gift of prognostication held by those who will one day themselves be divine?

I had spoken to Hadrian about Senuna but I did not think it was the time now – or, most likely, ever – to discourse on those revelations most intimate to me. I described Boudica's face as I had first seen it with her full, white cheeks framed by her long tresses of red hair, and how the life-like appearance of her body had soon shrivelled away, and I told him of the gold objects that had lain with her and were now in Numicius's keeping.

I asked him about how the Queen should be re-buried. At what place should that be done and in what company? – in secret or in public? – what might offend we Romans least, considering there were some still alive whose parents had been killed in the terrible times this red queen had precipitated? – and what might please, and placate, the *Iceni* people most, without giving them the feeling that their Roman masters now tolerated, and even celebrated, violent rebellion?

I knew Hadrian would be taking advice from his chief officials in Britannia, including the Governor himself, as to what – if anything – was most fitting, and I knew he would want to link the Queen's reburial to the memorials to Roman arms that he had given instructions for. What was the state of those works, I wondered? Hadrian had asked me to report to him, but there was nothing new I could add, other than that they were much delayed. I must stir myself to find out, but that would mean another journey of inspection for which I did not feel I was strong enough at present. I put a note at the end of my letter that perhaps Hadrian would excuse me this task as I had been unwell, and delegate the responsibility to some other official who could send him immediate reports. I thought he would be displeased with me by that, but there was nothing I could do as I had little enthusiasm to attempt another uncomfortable long journey, with or without Myru.

All I wanted to do in truth was to potter about my house and remember Senuna's quiet shade, in the special places where her memory came back most keenly to me – in the garden where she liked to walk in the heated air of a summer's evening; in the kitchen, preparing a bowl of flower petals while a slave banged about with cooking pans, so she must raise a hand to her temple telling the slave to stop; in the moonlight that she loved so much which turned her hair to silver; in a chair which I had left in a corner of our bedroom, as she had liked it placed, with a needle in her hand at some task of embroidery while her eyes were fixed on the window grill by which a coloured bird had perched; in the meadow with my ponies running free and coming to her to place their muzzles in her hand, as if she was Epona herself, as in a way I knew her now to have been – of the royal line of Boudica. No wonder the slaves, brought from Icenia, had been so much in awe of her. Had they realised, through secret channels of which I had no knowledge, what I have only just come to learn?

When I finished my letter to the Emperor, and had it sealed up by Gavo and prepared for delivery tomorrow to the office of the *cursus publicus* in Duroliponte, I walked out into the chilled air of evening and crossed my meadows to the place where Senuna lay, and would lie forever with my body beside her, under the round, grassy mound I had had raised above her. Red bars of light crossed the western sky like the shores of distant lands glimpsed through fire, and the sky above was darkening into an intensity of purple through which the evening star bearing the chariot of Venus was already shining. "Farewell, my love," I whispered. "Daughter of Queens. Give me your peace, now and in all things, until the time comes – and I feel it will not be long – when we can be joined once more."

And I went back to the house and I wept. I think all the high emotion of the past few days had quite washed the martial virtues out of me. Later, I got out from the corner cupboard where I kept them, the battered, re-rolled pages of the *papyri* on which I am compiling this account of my life, and I wrote for many hours until Diseta came at last and extinguished my guttering flame and put me to bed.

XXVIII

The funeral of the *Iceni* Queen – that Queen whose kingdom was destroyed by we Romans and whose descendants rule no more – is to take place this day. It is a fine day of early summer, with a flower-scented breeze blowing through the sunlit gardens of the villa of Tiberius Claudius Verus, so that I sniff at their fragrance as Diseta helps me to dress. I have brought her, with Myru, to serve as my body slaves. We travelled in Numicius's grand carriage, all the slaves perched like coloured, chattering birds amongst the trunks and boxes on the roof, while Numicius with his wife, Lucilla, sat opposite me in the rattling, jolting privacy of the interior. Myru looked unhappy at being separated from her ponies and being placed with the other slaves – three of Numicius's household as well – so I allowed her inside the carriage beside me, despite Numicius's clear disapproval. He sniffed, yet said nothing. Lucilla held no such pretensions of rank, but chattered away with Myru, who answered her diffidently, her wide eyes cast down. And so we came to Verus's villa, which is a sprawling affair of two main porticoed wings set around an inner courtyard garden, with an outer courtyard beyond where the stables, granaries, barns, and other buildings of the farm are situated.

Verus is a grand and pompous man – a tall, dark man with black eyes – of noble *Catuvellauni* descent, but that descent now mixed with the blood of a good and prosperous Roman family from Gallia (they had been merchants supplying the Army), the marriage having added greatly to his already considerable fortune. When the Emperor, in his despatches to Britannia, had raised the question of a suitable site for Boudica's re-burial, it had been Numicius who had consulted Verus, who, although of mixed lineage, was elevated by his wealth to something suitably akin to equestrian rank.

Verus – as we have already seen – is a large landowner. Not only does he own the land outside Competum where the temple of Senuna Minerva stands, but also this extensive estate to the south of Civitas Ikelorum on which he has built his grand villa. On a part of the estate, Hadrian's planned *tropaeum* has begun to rise. Other land further towards Duroliponte, carved out of former *Iceni* territory, is his as well, it having come into the possession of his great-great grandfather at the end of the *Iceni* rebellion. There – as I have described – the scattered bones and relics of the dead of *Legio VIIII* were recovered in the presence of the Emperor. In the same area stands the circular, ramparted fort of the *Iceni* where we came across the old man, Catrig, who had accompanied us to the battlefield beyond the *Portas Album*.

All the soundings put out to the *Iceni* people through their new centre of administration at Venta Icenorum showed that a site for the reburial of the Queen on the borders of what was once *Iceni* territory, close to that long-abandoned fort, would be satisfactory to Romans and *Iceni* alike. The land for this was offered by Verus and approved by the *centurio regionarius*, and counter-approved by the Governor's office, providing that the expense of the whole affair was met by the *Iceni* themselves, and that no great crowds of onlookers should be allowed to attend – the actual ceremony to be conducted by Romans, and not *Iceni*.

Yesterday, the day of our arrival as guests of Verus, our host took out Numicius and me in a light carriage to see the planned burial site, which lies on the same ridge as the circular fort, but further to its west. From here against the northern horizon can be seen the smoke of the distant town of Duroliponte.

In the opposite direction, but more towards the setting sun, the land sweeps down into that broad plain upon which the great battle was fought. Hard against the line where earth meets sky can just be made out the low hills upon which the Roman Army had stood. It seemed suitable to me that the Queen should be buried at a place that was, on the one hand, at the gateway to her former kingdom, yet at the same time in sight of the battlefield where she had met with her last defeat. There is honour in viewing a field of war, reflecting on the courage of the men of both sides who fought there, that can help dispel the opposing hatreds of battle and become a place of quiet memory, rather than one of ever-renewing pain. That is what I hope will be achieved by reburying the Queen of the *Iceni* at this place – I who had fought in that war myself, and killed, and seen my comrades killed around me.

On the ridge top there are the mounds of forebears of the *Britanni* who have been buried here over the long years, some, I would think, in an age long before the *Iceni* themselves came to this land. It has been decided that Boudica will not be buried beneath such a mound, but in a square pit lined with timber that has already been prepared, where she will lie secure in the white rock forever. Only blowing grass and the small flowers that grow close to the earth will mark the place. It will not, therefore, become a marker to any thing or any person, past or present – yet man perhaps may stand on these hills in years to come – in a future that we cannot even guess at – and force consciousness back through time, to look out over the plain, seeing again how two great giants once battled here.

Epistula VI
G. Modius Celer Hadriano Imperatori salutem dicit.
Villa Vero

I write this evening, Caesar, to describe the reburial of the remains of Queen Bodig of the *Iceni* whom we call Boudica, which was held around the mid hour today. There were many present, *Romani* and *Britanni*, and many others of the *Iceni* who could not get near, but were held at a distance by a cordon of guards ordered by the Governor from the garrison in Londinium. There was no disorder, but the crowd who were kept apart wailed and chanted and threw wands of willow and baskets of flowers onto the earth. Later these were gathered and placed over the filled in grave.

The ceremony was officiated by Tib. Cl. Verus who holds honorary priesthood at the temple of Minerva near to Competum. The *Britanni* show an affinity now with great Minerva and link her with their local gods. The *centurion regionarius* was present, and Numicius Secundus, together with several other Roman officials, as well as representatives from the territories of the *Iceni* and *Trinovantes*.

Gifts placed with the body, which was wrapped in cloth, were rich. Jewels and silver, including two silver torcs, were laid in the grave, which was accompanied as well by feasting jars and bowls and *amphorae* of wine. The items recovered from the first burial were returned, and the great gold torc was set again at the body's head, with the gold brooch and arm band and the bronze spearhead to one side.

After the interment, following the custom of the *Britanni,* several bent and broken swords and spears were flung in the grave by mourners, with earthenware pots and flagons too that were smashed against the grave's wooden sides. The custom, Caesar, is to break the life of these things so that they can only be used by the dead.

310

The grave was filled in by slaves as we watched, and the soil smoothed over and covered with branches in leaf, then heavy balks of timber dragged on top as well so it will not be easily disturbed. There was no sign of any trouble from the watchers, and the crowd dispersed as soon as the ceremony was complete. I believe, though, as is the practice, there will be much feasting and drinking tonight amongst the small settlements of round huts that still scatter these lands.

You may remember, Caesar, the very old man of the *Iceni* who acted as our guide to the battlefields and to whom you once gave a bronze band from your own arm – his name is Catrig. He was present at the ceremony and was allowed to stand by the grave while it was still open. He performed some ceremony out of the old tradition of the *Iceni*, which I did not like and told him so. He looked at me, with one eye whole and bulging and the other half-closed, and told me I should watch the moon which is huge in the sky this night or it might fall on me. I do not know what he means by that, but I shall drink some wine later with Numicius and Verus when my writing is done, and hopefully I can forget.

My horse-slave, Myru, whom you have been good enough to speak well of in the past, was also at the graveside, she being of *Iceni* blood, I believe once well-born, although she came to me as a slave. She cried such tears as I have seldom seen before: they flowed like rain. She is normally the most self-contained of women. Perhaps the entire *Iceni* people cry tonight for their Queen who led them to disaster – yet, to be truthful, they were very brave.

I shall write again, Caesar, when I have news of the progress of the other works you have ordered.
Vale

I have returned to my room after a meal with Verus's other guests, of which I little partook, but the wine I drank still spins in my head. He had sought to make merry this night, which I did not wish, my thoughts being on that black-skinned corpse still crowned with her red-gold hair that we put under the ground today. The moon shines into my room, so there is scarcely need for the lamps that Diseta has lit for me. The moon disturbs me, although Senuna loved the moonlight and would walk outside in the garden bathing in its milky glow, with the stars like a million fires pricking the night. I recall that aged servant of the *Iceni*, Catrig – one, I believe, who still carries the secrets of the Druids – and what he spoke to me today: 'beware of the moon, for it may fall on you'.

The moon does seem overlarge this night as if it is heavy in the sky and finds it hard to rise. Perhaps its weight is too much for Luna to carry and she must drop her burden into the earth, just as mad Catrig spoke. I have never equated Senuna with Luna before, although their names make similar sounds on my lips. I remember somewhere learning too that Minerva herself is descended from an earlier goddess of the moon, so moonlight seems to have lit all my ways of late, yet I shall not be sorry when this light grows dark again.

I scramble for more of the *papyri* that Verus has been generous in giving me. Like those I make use of in my own house, they are the backs of earlier writings – of his steward, it seems, for they are lists of accounts: *'vi denarii* for fresh oysters', I have just read. It seems there is more wealth with Verus than in many an estate in Italia – and so the Roman world is made today.

I fought for Rome for other reasons than money, so have I been deluded? The battle cries of my soldiers are now as dust whispering in the grass, yet I think the fight was worth it, and we shall be remembered through the many generations to come. Were there ever soldiers like those of Rome before, and shall there ever be their like again? The wars may go on – have they ever ceased in the world? – but we were of the first and the very best companies of men. My purpose in writing this is to honour my comrades: it would not be seemly to praise myself. Yet, I hold my pride and shall take it to my grave, which will have no carved stone to commemorate it, as others have set up, but I shall lie most contently with my wise moon-goddess, Senuna, daughter of Queens, under the breathing earth.

I try to rest. I have blown out the last lamp. Diseta sleeps on a trestle bed beside me, at my call if I should need her. Myru will be somewhere in Verus's stables, asleep beside his horses, which she has ridden since we came here, astounding his stable lads. Sleep on, my Myru, brave and faithful girl, for I will need you yet.

Senuna, is it you who calls to me in the moonlight? I am coming, my dearest, I am coming.....

Statement of Myrag f.Seisyll, known as Myru, slave, as given to Gavienus Gavo, steward of the house of G. Modius Celer at Forum Aelium and written down by him.

'I was called by Diseta, slave to my master, in the early morning. My master lay dead in bed. He had died in his sleep. This was reported to Tib. Cl. Verus, *dominus* of the house where we dwelt. Arrangements were made to bring my master's body back to his house. The *dominus* loaned his horses and carriage and accompanied us, together with the *dominus* Ap. Cl. Numicius Secundus, to Duroliponte, where the body was placed on a barge and so brought by canal to the house.'

'The house has been in mourning ever since, the fires unlit, the shutters closed. On the seventh day, my master was buried in the place which he had instructed, beside his wife in the northern meadow, beneath a mound close to the lake. His *diploma* of military service was placed with him in the coffin together with the great staff that he was used to carry, also various *papyri* and writing tablets, as he had commanded. By the coffin were placed the head and hooves of his favourite pony named Ajax. The blood of Ajax was also offered as a sacrifice to Epona at the shrine where my master had often worshipped.'

'The household has wept ever since, and the house has been cold and in darkness. The slaves do not know their future, only that I and three others are to be freed.'

ABOUT THIS BOOK

I have long been both fascinated and intrigued by the story of the great rebellion of the Iceni queen, Boudica, which took place between 60/61 AD, seventeen years after the Romans' initial conquest of the province they knew as Britannia. It has been suggested that Boudica was not the queen's personal name but an honorific title meaning 'Victory'. However, other forms of the name Boudica are known from Roman-period tombstones, for example the British wife of a Roman centurion called Lollia Bodicca and the recently discovered grave in Cirencester of a Bodicacia. I think it more likely than otherwise, therefore, that the true name of the Queen of the Iceni, consort of King Prasutagus, was indeed Boudica, or some form close to this as latinised from the Iceni tongue – perhaps Bodig (which Celer preferred).

The events of the rebellion are known mainly from three ancient sources – two separate histories of the Roman historian, Tacitus, written about 115AD, and one of the Greek, Cassius Dio, set down around a hundred years later. Suetonius's account of Nero's reign in his 'Twelve Caesars' also includes a brief mention, although he does not name Boudica. After the fall of Rome in the West and the incalculable loss of so much of Greek and Roman civilisation, these written accounts survived perilously in Christian monasteries to be brought to light again in the late 14th century during the Italian Renaissance. Until scholars began to read the rediscovered texts, almost all knowledge of Boudica and the war she had fought against the Roman conquerors had been lost, other than for a scattering of distorted references by early, and later, medieval chroniclers, taken probably from Tacitus and Cassius Dio.[1]

---

1   The text of Petruccio Ubaldini in his *Le Vite delle donne illustri, del regno d'Inghilterra...* (1588), as translated in Frénée-Hutchins, 'Boudica's Odyssey in Early Modern England', is particularly interesting. Ubaldini, who at one time had been a mercenary soldier in

The plethora of sites associated with Boudica that are spread across much of Eastern England, as well as in other regions, must originate, therefore, at the earliest from the late medieval period. However, some credence can also be given to the idea of the possible survival of memory, out of such great and significant events, through oral transmission over the ages. It is possible, for instance, that, if we did find and prove the site of the great last battle, then we would see some clue in the landscape, or in local folklore, that has been hitherto overlooked. One major revelation often leads to others falling into place, which then seem obvious.

Archaeological evidence can be an invaluable aid in reconstructing the past. Layers of burning, dated to the mid-1st. century period, in all three towns that Boudica destroyed – St. Albans, Colchester, and London – indicate the truth of Tacitus's account. Other towns and settlements show comparable episodes of burning as well – such as Staines and Silchester, suggesting that an Iceni war band might well have operated south of the Thames striking into the territory of the client king Togidubnus, who ruled over large parts of the settled province to the south. Tacitus states that Togidubnus's loyalty continued up to 'recent times', and the reference to loyalty might be to the king's support for Rome during the rebellion. Other archaeological finds – of hidden coin hordes and plundered Roman goods – also indicate the disturbance and uncertainty prevailing at that time.

However, no definite archaeological evidence at all has emerged for any of the battlefields of the war, either the battle that concluded it (the site of which has been much sought), or the earlier, and in terms of Roman casualties, much more serious action, and defeat, of the VIIIIth Legion coming to the relief of Colchester. Indeed, no battlefield site of the Roman Army in Britain has ever been securely identified, either of the initial invasion campaign or the later actions against Wales and Scotland, including the defeat of Caratacus and the battle named by Tacitus as Mons Graupius, both of which have proved as elusive to place on the map as the

---

English employ, writes of the Romans before the final battle setting up camp close to their enemies so that they could not refuse to fight, and tells of the action taking place (in part, at least) beside marshes, both details not included in Tacitus and Cassius Dio. They do, however, happen to reflect my own theory that I had worked out long before reading Ubaldini! It is quite possible he had a primary source now lost to us. It is also just possible that a further ancient source may yet be rediscovered – amongst the Egyptian sands, or some European wetland, the largely unexcavated ruins of Herculaneum, or even some secluded Christian monastery or Arabic library. Tacitus, I feel, originally wrote a much fuller account. The one late Roman manuscript that has come down to us gives the appearance of having been shortened at some time before the copy was made.

final Boudican defeat. And nor – to expand this point – do we have any identifiable evidence for Julius Caesar's armies in Britain: few marching camps are known in the South-East of England and none can be ascribed to the late Republican-period Army. And yet, from Caesar's own accounts, 40,000 men, with their horses and equipment, were marching and fighting across the soil of southern Britain.

The exceptions to this lack of battlefield evidence are the various attacks that have been recognised against the fortified positions of the British tribes resisting invasion. Scatterings of Roman Army missiles and equipment, together with skeletal evidence of the defenders showing battle trauma, have been found at a number of hill top positions, in particular at Maiden Castle and Hod Hill in Dorset, but also at other places, including South Cadbury in Somerset (the Roman attack here interestingly being dated to the Neronian period). Recently as well, at Burnswark Hill in south-west Scotland, extraordinary deposits and spreads of lead sling-bullets – a missile employed by Roman auxiliary troops – have been located by metal detection, showing this hillfort to have been invested by fortified camps and attacked from two sides.

Celer has already informed us of the strategy of the Roman Army in the Boudican campaign. However, perhaps I will be forgiven for setting out the major points once more, this time from a modern perspective.

There have been many theories over the years as to the site of the final battle of the Boudican rebellion. Most pundits today prefer a site they call 'The Battle of Watling Street', indeed the term seems to have become so generally accepted that it is given in many on-line accounts of the rebellion as established fact. The theory is that Suetonius Paullinus, on hearing in Anglesey of the outbreak of the revolt, rode ahead with a force of cavalry to London, leaving the slower advance of the main body of his army – the foot soldiers of the XIIIIth Legion and part of the XXth, and some auxiliaries, – to follow behind, ready to receive further orders consequent upon whatever their commander would find in the rebel-occupied areas.

On realising he could not defend London 'for lack of troops', Paullinus then – the theory goes – abandoned St. Albans as well (and incidentally also the whole still-loyal south of the country) and retreated back on his advancing legions, who were following the main highway we now call Watling Street. Somewhere in the Midlands (a site near Mancetter, north-west of Nuneaton, is a favoured location – but other sites close to Watling Street are put forward), Paullinus was reunited with his main army and took up a defensive position, as described by Tacitus, against Boudica's advance. Here, he fought his battle and saved the province.

I find many things wrong with this scenario. Neither Tacitus or Cassius Dio, in fact, state that Paullinus separated his personal command from his legions, and galloped ahead with cavalry alone: they just say he pressed 'with great fortitude' through the midst of the enemy and reached London, which he then found indefensible. I believe Paullinus's approach, in fact, was much more cautious and militarily competent than a simple fast gallop with his cavalry force to reach a city which he could not defend, being apparently surprised by his lack of troops to do so. If he did indeed advance on London with cavalry alone, then he must have done so in the expectation of making a junction at the provincial capital with substantial numbers of legionary infantry – in fact, very likely, with the IInd Legion, which he had probably ordered to advance on London from the south-west. However, the IInd Legion had disobeyed orders and not marched, perhaps because it was divided, dealing with several disturbances in the areas it occupied (the Roman assault at South Cadbury and the burning at Silchester could be the result of two such incidents).

But now, without the IInd Legion, and because of the imminence of the Iceni attack, Paullinus had to make the decision to abandon London (and later St. Albans too) to their fate. The IInd Legion may not have come to the aid of London, as ordered, but at least it was available to cover the roads leading to the south and south-east in case a large Boudican force attempted to cross the Thames and penetrate those areas, the richest in the province with populations that had long accepted Rome (even perhaps before the Roman invasion). Perhaps there were indeed raids by various rebel war parties into the settled 'quisling' south, raiding and looting, which did damage but were fought off: in any such actions, the alliance of King Togidubnus would have been of great assistance to Paullinus.

The clue to where the final battle took place emerges by a consideration of what type of force, and its size, that the Iceni and their Trinovantes allies could have put into the field. The Boudican army that attacked and defeated the column of the VIIIIth Legion (this was probably a detachment of some 2000 men, which was the number of legionaries that Tacitus states had to be replaced at the end of the war) would have likely come from the warrior class of the rebels, with their retainers – well-led, probably, and ferocious in attack.

Petilius Cerialis, the VIIIIth's commander, seems to have had to give battle when in extended column of route. Probably, owing to the emergency, he had not been as cautious passing through enemy territory as was desirable. The Roman infantry, likely to have been attacked from all sides on the march, could not be defended by their cavalry, which rode off when the affair seemed hopeless, their commander amongst them: better perhaps not to sacrifice men to no purpose when there was still a chance for some of escape. The legionaries would probably have been cut off and surrounded in many places, then destroyed in detail. Any who surrendered would only have been killed later.

The numbers of the rebel force (their prime fighting men, no doubt, well-equipped) to achieve such a victory would have needed to be no more than those of the Romans. Two thousand men (perhaps some hundreds more) can do an awful lot of damage in a short time. You do not need large armies to capture and destroy cities where the defence is inadequate. Small forces are manoeuvrable and can surprise and cut off larger ones. Consider what in the present day a small number of ISIS fighters in Iraq achieved against much larger forces in a short time, occupying and holding great tracts of territory until a cohesive, well-equipped and well-trained army could be moved against them.

I believe that the idea of a vast army led by Boudica numbering tens of thousands, moving from city to city destroying each in turn is quite wrong. War bands of rebel fighters are much more likely to have been the forces involved, perhaps a few hundred here, a few hundred there, terrorising the countryside, entering the towns, looting, burning, raping – the scenario is sadly only too familiar to us today. As I have said, such highly mobile war bands of horse and foot, with chariots too, may have entered the south of the province as well, beyond the Thames, only the story of the damage they would have done has not (yet) been recognised in the archaeological record.[2]

Taking the above into consideration, the main points concerning the siting of the final battle are as follows (several of these Celer has already stated to you) –

Paullinus, for certain, needed to concentrate his forces as soon as possible into a strong field army, one sufficiently powerful to outfight the rebels on a ground of his choosing. Nothing could be left to chance. He had to find a

---

2   Professor Michael Fulford of the University of Reading, director of the recent excavations at Silchester, has written that destruction and burning, evidenced in the archaeology of that town broadly dated to the 60-80AD period, may well have been occasioned during the Boudican rebellion. There is also evidence of the Roman Army at the town.

prepared battlefield that he could entice the Iceni and Trinovantes to fight on. But where would that battlefield be?

In my view, leaving the south to be defended by the IInd Legion, and perhaps as well by forces of loyal Romano-British commanded by Togidubnus, Paullinus would have led his immediate force away from London (perhaps by a circling route to the west before again heading north-west on 'Watling Street') to meet the rest of his army, consisting principally of the XIIIIth Legion with cohorts of the XXth. This, I think, would have been at a place further to the south than the proposed Mancetter, perhaps at a point between High Cross and Towcester.

Tacitus states that Paullinus 'sought an end to delay'. This indicates to me that it was he who had to precipitate the final battle. Insurgents usually do not wish to engage in major battles unless they feel reasonably confident of the outcome. In a culminating battle you have to play your full hand. The revolt is over. You either win or you are destroyed. That was what was to happen now.

'The Battle of Watling Street' theorists have the Iceni and Trinovantes advancing out of their East Anglian fastnesses to give battle against a powerful and consolidated Roman force some 150 miles away. Why would they do that? How would they do that? Tacitus states that the rebels had brought their wives and children in wagons to watch the battle, and presumably other non-combatants as well – the elderly, for instance. Cassius Dio also mentions the wagons.

The whole host was said to be enormous, larger than any ever seen in Britain before. How many was that? 40,000? 50,000? More? Tacitus gives a figure of 80,000 rebel dead on the field, which, even allowing for considerable exaggeration, means the size of Boudica's army must have been enormous? How many of those fighters were well-armed? Arms and armour would have been recovered from Cerialis's destroyed column, but they would have only kitted out a few thousand. And how would you have moved an army like that, with wagons and oxen, food and other supplies, over 150 miles of tracks and roads? The column length alone would have occupied 30 miles of road. And would the Romans simply have sat and awaited their arrival without harrying such an enormous column? – a few overturned wagons with their supplies, set on fire. would have blocked a road for several hours. Iron Age peoples only made mass movements of that sort if a whole tribe had decided to upsticks and migrate – as happened, for example, in Gaul during Julius Caesar's campaigns. It is very unlikely the Iceni and Trinovantes were intending any such migration. Where would they be heading for?

The main point, anyhow, is that the Iceni and Trinovantes did not *have to* advance north towards the established Roman military area, nor, most certainly, did they wish to. Tacitus specifically states that the rebels avoided forts and other defended places, as all they sought was plunder, and they knew the consequences that would come. If they were going to advance anywhere with such an enormous army, surely it would have been better to move south where only one legion awaited them, and there were rich pickings.

I believe that by now there was little direction or cohesion in the rebel ranks. As so often happens in war, lucky initial victories had left a dearth of strategic generalship. The rebels knew the Romans would be seeking retribution. It would make little sense to make a difficult advance against them. If they had to fight a final battle, it would be far better to do so in, or near, their own tribal territory.

Having consolidated his field army, and added to it whatever extra auxiliary troops he could reach, Paullinus now knew he had to fight a carefully prepared battle where, by use of topography, field fortification, placement of artillery, and by superior discipline and tactics, he could hope to defeat – and defeat utterly – an enemy greatly out-numbering him. He would have left nothing to chance.

This last battle must not be looked at as one fought by two great armies manoeuvring in the field, challenging each other for the best strategic and tactical positions, but one where the Romans had carefully prepared the ground on which they were to offer battle, where secure lines of communication and supply were established, where signalling posts had been set up, camps prepared, field fortifications built, and the tactical positioning of the differing units of the defending army worked out to the finest detail. If the reader seeks a vivid representation of this type of battle, see the opening scenes of the film 'Gladiator'.

The consequences of defeat would have been apocalyptic for the Romans. They were likely to have been slaughtered to a man on the field or nearby in the enemy's sacred groves (as happened, for instance, to the three legions of Varus that could not escape from the Teutoburger Wald disaster in 9AD). The remainder of the Army in Britannia would then have been very vulnerable to attack and total destruction; perhaps its only hope would have been to seek a sea-borne withdrawal organised by the Roman fleet. Undoubtedly, the whole province would have collapsed into chaos, the client kingdoms in the south being overrun and much bloody vengeance exacted.

The Roman state too, in the person of the Emperor Nero, might well have lacked the will to re-invade. Indeed, Suetonius records that Nero and his advisers considered abandoning the province, which very probably refers to the events at this time. So a very great deal depended on Paullinus's battle plan when he drew up his forces in the place he had selected, probably in the early autumn of 60AD, with the aim of bringing the Iceni and Trinovantes armies into the field to put the matter to the test of battle once and for all.

It is important to remember that the Iceni, who had entered into a client kingship with the Romans from the earliest days of the conquest, had not been conquered in war. The first Iceni rebellion of 47AD had indeed been put down by the Roman Army in battle, but that seems to have been a fairly limited uprising affecting only one small part of the tribe: the fact that the client kingship was then allowed to be renewed shows so. Thus, when Tacitus writes of the Iceni of 47AD 'as not yet broken in battle', the comment is also valid for 60AD. That test of battle was now to come.

So what is the most likely area where the battle took place? Much of my reasoning has been set out in the narrative you will already have read, as seen through the eyes of the legionary veteran, Celer, and the Emperor Hadrian. As I have said, I believe Paullinus had to advance his army against the Iceni kingdom (which for convenience we can call Icenia, although there is no documentary or epigraphic evidence for such a name). The principal entry into Icenia (including certain of the territories of the Trinovantes) is by the ancient highway we now know as the Icknield Way (the very name probably retaining an echo of the Iceni). This Way follows the belt of chalk that runs from the chalk uplands lying in the south-west (the area of Salisbury Plain), forms the Chiltern Hills to the north-west of London, then extends into Cambridgeshire, and ultimately into Norfolk.

The chalk ridges and their lower slopes were always far easier to traverse than the river valleys beneath, and from remote time they had formed the great routeways of prehistoric peoples, of which the Icknield Way is but one example. Archaeology has shown in recent years that there was a far greater movement of peoples in prehistoric periods than had previously been thought. Clear, well-drained routes were needed for the movement of traders, sheep and cattle drovers, itinerant peddlers, farmers, wood-hauliers, quarriers, and the many others involved in activities vital for the sustainment of communities.

A prime need also was for the movement of armies, warfare being endemic in all periods of history and prehistory, despite the optimistic view of some commentators that there have been past utopian golden ages when strife was little known The belt of chalk that runs into Cambridgeshire out of Hertfordshire, upon which the Icknield Way is set, is thus highly significant in identifying the site of the Boudican battle.[3] East of the town of Royston, it narrows to a width of only some five miles, lying between marshland to the north (the first outlying reaches of the Fenland marshes found further to the north-east) and a line of low chalk hills to the south. Although these hills are also formed of chalk, their tops are capped with thick clay upon which – pollen evidence shows – thick woodland was growing in the Roman period, and indeed is still prevalent today. The contrast between the flat, open belt of grassland spread out below the hills, bordered on one side by marshland, and the dark line of trees occupying their summit ridges must have been very marked. The hillside slopes – like the comparable North and South Downs further south – have been moulded by millennia of erosion into smoothly-flowing spurs and re-entrants, a number of the latter forming dry, steep-sided valleys.

Such is the landscape at the very borders of Icenia, a landscape known from archaeological discovery to have been inhabited by the Iceni people. At a point further to the north-east, where this strip of chalkland widens again, stands another block of low chalk hills that can be seen as marking the very gateway into the former Iceni kingdom. They are known as the Gogmagog Hills – for reasons that must lie deeply buried in ancient folklore – and they are crowned by Wandlebury hillfort, a circular Iron Age fort with double encircling ditches and ramparts on a site which may have Bronze Age origins. The entire landscape of the Gogmagog Hills appears over the distant ages to have had a ritual purpose. Its summit peak, known as Little Trees Hill, was once encircled by a Neolithic causewayed enclosure, and in the Bronze Age ditches were cut into its lower slopes, with evidence for timber structures, forming what the excavators concluded may have been a 'sacred landscape'. Further archaeological sites in the area seem to have had a ritual rather than practical purpose as well, including aspects of Wandlebury hillfort itself, the siting of which, slightly below the ridgeline to the north, blurs any idea of a purely defensive function. On the top of Little Trees Hill is a massive round burial barrow, unexcavated, presumed to be

---

3   The Icknield Way should not be seen as one track (now conveniently signposted), but as a broad band of several tracks, perhaps dividing from the main route, curving away, and then joining again, spread widely across the chalk. A parallel is in 19th century South Africa where it was recorded by English settlers that main routes would often be as wide as six miles, spread in various branches across a plain, each branch having developed to seek a better track when others had become badly rutted or washed out by heavy rains.

of Bronze Age date. Forward of it, seen on aerial photographs, is a square feature cut into the chalk which is thought to be a burial chamber of the Iron Age or early Roman periods.

When I began to explore these landscapes in the early 2000s, I was impressed immediately by two factors – one, the area's suitability for a reasonable theory to be developed that the Boudican final battle had taken place somewhere within it, and the other, the fact that there was already much evidence, with further conjecture, of warfare happening there. A series of defensive dykes, as they are known (high ramparts and accompanying ditches), that still survive in the landscape, cut off the Icknield Way route as it crosses between marsh and forest. They are said to have been built by Saxons in the post-Roman period as a defence against possible re-invasion of their newly established Anglian kingdoms by surviving Romano-British peoples to the south. It has been conjectured, however, that the origin of one or two of these dykes may have been much earlier, and even date to the late Iron Age.

The real point to be made about these dykes is that they are testimony to the military importance of the Icknield Way route into East Anglia (or Icenia). In other words, they provide evidence of a militarised landscape, showing how the chalk route followed by the Icknield Way may always have been defended over the ages.[4] The greatest of these defensive barriers in terms of size is the Devil's Dyke, lying a little further to the north than the area just described: it is massive, with a deep ditch and high rampart that still dominate the landscape, so that one marvels at the collective labour necessary to build it. Another, known as the Bran Ditch (or Heydon Ditch), is in a much diminished state, having been ploughed away over the centuries, yet in parts its surviving bank may be clearly seen and walked. It runs between the village of Heydon (situated on top of the ridge to the south) and the marshes at Fowlmere to the north. We will look at these two places in more detail shortly.

Further evidence – or folklore memory – of warfare in these parts lies in the presence of the Bartlow Hills in a wooded valley six miles to the south-east of the Gogmagog Hills. These are four surviving burial mounds (out of seven or eight originally raised) dated to the early 2nd century – the largest such group in Western Europe. Local legend for long considered them to

---

4   In 1940, as an anti-invasion defence, the equivalent of another dyke was constructed by the crossing of the GHQ Stop Line (consisting of an anti-tank ditch and bank, fortified at points, with an outlying demolition belt): it crossed the chalklands just north of Wandlebury to run east of Cambridge.

be the burial places of warriors killed in battle. Because the nearby village of Ashdon has an unproven claim to be the site of the Battle of Assandun in 1016, those buried here were said to be some of the fallen of that battle. The story provides a further reference – if no more – of this landscape having once been one of warfare.

Another legend of the Gogmagog Hills – this one too fantastic to be taken literally, yet it might enshrine the idea of battles having at one time been fought upon these chalk heights – lies in the highly fanciful theory that the Trojan Wars of Homer's *Iliad* and *Odyssey* were not fought in modern Turkey, but within 'Lands of the Celts' far to the north – in fact, in no less a place than the Cambridgeshire Gogmagog Hills, where Troy has been squarely positioned. Other places described by Homer are also identified amongst the local topography. I mention this fantasy (because it is no more than that) simply to show how the landscape I now present as the one where Suetonius Paullinus's army fought the forces of Boudica has already been mulled over by others with military tactics and strategy in mind. It is strange how truth can sometimes emerge out of such collective, yet differing, analysis, the results for some being not those intended!

Tacitus describes the battlefield where Paullinus destroyed Boudica's army as having the principal landscape elements of a defile, or other narrow, enclosing feature (in which the Roman Army fought, thereby compressing the greater numbers of the rebel army onto a narrow front); a forest (behind the forward positions of the Roman Army), and a flat, open plain (upon which the great numbers of Boudica's armies were assembled, and which was free of places where an ambush of the Romans could be carried out). Two further elements might also reasonably be deduced – a good roadway, or at least track, by which both armies might have approached the battlefield, and some physical determining of the edge of the plain: there the Iceni would have drawn up their wagons from which their wives and children would have watched the progress of the battle, likely to have been a river or other water source (both armies would have required copious amounts of water, not least for the horses and draft-animals).

On my first exploring the landscape that lies south of Cambridge along the line of the low chalk hills running out of Hertfordshire into Cambridgeshire (which also acts in places as the boundary between Cambridgeshire and Essex), I became interested almost straightaway in the feature marked on the 1:25,000 Ordnance sheet as the Heydon Valley. This forms a long, narrow, dry valley running roughly south to north, its mouth debouching onto a level plain that stretches away north-east to the

Gogmagog Hills (and eventually Cambridge). Duxford Airfield occupies part of the plain closer to where the mouth of the Heydon Valley opens. More directly north, however, lies the marshy land around the village of Fowlmere, which was once far more extensive than the surviving lake and swampland now within the Fowlmere Nature Reserve.

The Heydon Valley forms a considerable re-entrant into the chalk hills, the chalk sub-soil here lying beneath a thick capping of clay, which once bore – and still does – thick belts of woodland. On the ridge itself lies the small village of Heydon. West of Heydon, the line of hills takes a south-westerly direction, reaching, in the rounded knoll known as Down Plantation (or on older maps, Chishill Down), a height of 140m (460ft). On the ridge top beyond this point lies the village of Great Chishill.

This is the battlefield that old Catrig of the Iceni shows to Celer and the Emperor. They viewed it first from a position just south of the village of Fowlmere, roughly on the line of the A505 road. It was in this area as well, but perhaps some few hundred yards further to the south, that the Emperor's grand ceremony of commemoration took place. The high point Celer and Hadrian rode to – from where I would speculate Paullinus at first directed the battle – is on Down Plantation. Between that point and the Bran Ditch (did this ditch, or linear rampart, perhaps originate as a Roman field fortification or was it already present on the battlefield as a late Iron Age defensive structure?), the hills form a broad hollow, which is where I think the main legionary force of Paullinus's army was drawn up, protected on its left by Down Plantation and the cavalry positioned there, and, on its right, by the steep height of Reeve Hill, just north of Heydon. Reeve Hill is the point from which the Bran Ditch begins its arrow-straight three mile journey to meet the marshes at Fowlmere, running across the narrowest point of the chalk belt between marsh and forested hill crossed by the Icknield Way – the centre of the proposed battlefield.

I have the Emperor's party riding to a ridge where they look over the steep-sided valley (the Heydon Valley) within which cohorts of the XIIIIth Legion fought off the main attack of Boudica's army, which was trying to outflank the Roman right. It was here that the action described so vividly by Tacitus was fought, with the Romans meeting the Iceni charge funnelled into the valley and destroying it – first, by thrown javelins (and possibly *carroballista* fire), and then, by a sudden advance in wedge formation. The point on the ridge above the valley – known as Anthony Hill – is where Paullinus commanded this decisive action of the battle, and it is where Hadrian wished his altar of victory to be built. In the 1840s, a Roman building was discovered here during digging for chalk (the chalk pit is still there). It was a solidly built, square structure of shaped chalk blocks and was interpreted at the time as a corn-drying kiln, but this is very unlikely in such a position. It is much more likely to have been a shrine or small temple.

The work to place the inscription naming the battlefield, together with a statue of the goddess of victory, within the building was never completed, and, as the years went by and the battlefield was forgotten once more, it may have served a purpose for the worship of other gods. Perhaps one day the inscription carved so carefully in London and put on display there may be found, although its presence in the Roman capital may cause some confusion today!

There is admittedly no direct archaeological evidence for my proposed site being the great battlefield of Boudica's defeat. I have seen metal detectorists on many occasions working their way across the hill slopes and on part of the plain beneath, and I wonder what it is they are finding. I questioned one who was working close to the modern track of the Icknield Way, and he showed me a Roman coin he had just found. I think the date of the coin was later than the first century, but that does not mean it had not been dropped by a Roman visitor, reading Celer's account and seeking the long-lost field.

There are no known Roman settlements on the plain below the hills, although slightly further afield by the village of Duxford and also at Black Peak near Fowlmere, where the Bran Ditch joins the marshland, both Iron Age and Roman settlement sites have been excavated. Near Chrishall Grange, on the eastern flanks of the suggested battlefield, there used to be a substantial *tumulus* said to be prolific of Roman coin finds, but now sadly ploughed away. Speculation might make it a place of commemoration as well, or even a burial mound.

At Great Chesterford by the River Cam, five miles to the east, is a known Roman fort dated to the Neronian period. An early Roman cavalry bridle pendant found there can be seen in Saffron Walden museum. A town developed later out of the fort and its attached vicus. One brick found in the 18th century, and since lost, is recorded as being inscribed with the word 'Ikelorum', making my interpretation of the site as Castrum Ikenorum, and then Civitas Ikelorum, plausible. This is perhaps the fort that Tacitus mentions as the one from which auxiliaries attached to Paullinus's army came: if not, it would certainly have been used in the follow up operations. Other possible Neronian period forts are known under Saffron Walden and also under Cambridge, out of which the town of Duroliponte later developed.

Further archaeological evidence of the presence of the Roman Army at an early period has been recovered within the area that I have determined as Tacitus's 'plain'. On Pepperton Hill, just south of Duxford Airfield, and thus very close to the proposed battlefield, one corner, and a length of ditch, of a first century Roman marching camp were discovered when a gas pipe line was being laid in 1994. At Sawston, some three miles to the north-east, two ditched enclosures thought to be of Roman military camps were found during a watching brief: this site is approximately half way between the battlefield and Wandlebury hillfort. At Wandlebury itself, and at the nearby Iron Age strongpoint of War Ditches, skeletal remains have been found showing battle trauma, although the dating evidence is inconclusive and some at Wandlebury may date to the Bronze Age.

At Thriplow, close to Fowlmere, a magnetometry survey produced the shape of a triple ditched enclosure, as yet unexcavated, with a 'playing card' corner that could be of a Roman military site. Other possible military enclosures are at Melborn, to the west, and at Flint Cross, close to the Bran Ditch, and also on Clay Hill, a prominent high point on the western flanks of the battlefield. A Roman military site was also identified at Shepreth three miles to the north-west, close to later Roman buildings. Amongst the rolling downland on the eastern side of the Heydon Valley, aerial photographs show a mass of soil marks, including enclosures, pits, and huts that may be of a considerable Iron Age, or later Roman, settlement. To the south-west of Great Chishill, the unmistakable 'playing card' shape of what looks like a small Roman military enclosure is revealed by crop marks, with further circular, dark marks showing possible structures within: this would be in an ideal position, with clear lines of vision, to have been a signal station. Another adjacent enclosure, of more irregular form, straddles a stream: water supply for Paullinus's army was, of course, as vital a matter as for the Boudican army.

From the above it is clear there is plenty of evidence of early Roman military activity around the proposed battlefield. That, without much more detailed and certain archaeological evidence, proves nothing, but it is at least indicative of the validity of my theory, that in this area the culminating battle of the Boudican revolt may have taken place – the largest battle in terms of numbers involved and casualties sustained that has very likely ever been fought in Britain.

Many novels have been written of Boudica and the Iceni, and of the events of the war. The very best of these, I believe, is *Imperial Governor* by George Shipway, first published in 1968, which has a convincing military background. Shipway gives the site of the battle at a point on the great road west out of London, half way between Staines and Silchester. It is still a plausible theory, did I not prefer mine! My conclusion that the site must have been close to Icenia itself, if not actually within its territory, is the decider, I am sure. Of course, with that determiner in mind, there are further possible sites, including other defiles into the chalk hills between Royston and Wandlebury. A long, narrow defile close to Royston is one candidate: it was used as a rifle range in the Victorian period, and probably later.

But other determiners – what the late Lt. Col. A. H. Burne called Inherent Military Probability – must also come into play. The entire Roman army could not have been concentrated in one defile, however important that feature was tactically in the fighting. There would have had to be ground where the Roman legionaries could deploy as well on a wider front, with cavalry operating in support of their flanks. Some aspects of the account of Cassius Dio may contain a more precise record of the battle than does Tacitus. Cassius Dio writes of a desperately fought, full day battle, with much hard, see-sawing fighting before the Romans won the day. Tacitus's account, on the other hand, indicates that it was the defence of the defile, and the subsequent Roman advance, that overcame the enemy relatively quickly. However, it takes an awful long time to kill tens of thousands of the enemy by sword and spear, although assisted as well by missile-firing artillery, arrows, and other projectiles. Death by crushing and suffocation probably accounted for a high percentage of the casualties. If the numbers on the field, and the numbers of dead, were anything like the ancient authors have told us, it must have been a long, desperate affair before the Romans finally gained the day.

The exhaustion of the victors – and the problems they still faced – would have been enormous. Prisoners would have had to be killed – as happened at Agincourt in 1415 – because their numbers would very likely have outnumbered the winning army. Without machine guns to assist the process, the killing of thousands of men, let alone the women and children and draft animals that Tacitus adds to the heaps of slaughtered, would have been a process virtually beyond our comprehension. The Romans then had to retire to whatever camps they had set up, feed themselves and sleep, while others guarded the thousands of prisoners and pursued the fugitives, who included Boudica herself. The next day there would have been arms to clean, armour to mend, bodies to strip, dead comrades to be gathered together for cremation, fires to be lit, water to be collected, tents to be set up for the surgeons, horses to be fed and watered, some to be put down. The list of tasks to be achieved by Paullinus's army was endless, creating a nightmare of duty for its commanders that would have been almost as great after the battle as before it.

Even when the enemy dead had been looted of valuables and their bodies cleared away, and the most obvious and desirable debris of the battle gathered up – the weapons and armour of the enemy, for instance, that would make trophies of war or could be melted down to make new weapons or projectiles (in a situation where supplies for the Roman soldiers were probably now very poor) – the battlefield would still have been littered with detritus. Hails of arrows would have been fired, storms of steel javelin heads thrown, thousands of lead bullets slung, hundreds of iron *carroballista* bolts fired, broken armour, cuirass hinges, horse pendants, the crests of helmets, finger rings, brooches, buckles, boot hobnails, dropped and trampled underfoot – the list of artefacts that might be found is long. Although over the many centuries, in particular on land that has subsequently been ploughed year by year, much of this might have been picked out of the soil, it is certain that much too must remain – somewhere.

A battlefield – in particular one where such a huge, destructive battle has been fought – surely cannot disappear entirely, so that no evidence at all remains. Metal detectorists' work on battlefields of the English Civil War, for instance, has recovered spreads of musket balls, which can show the position of opposing lines as they fired upon each other. Taking other examples, battlefield archaeology has enabled an entirely new theory on the closing stages of the Battle of Bosworth Field (1485) to be proven beyond reasonable doubt. And at Barnet, north of London, recent work has likely located that important battlefield of the Wars of the Roses (1471) at a different location from the one previously suspected.

And yet there can also be a remarkable lack of finds recovery on some battlefields, even those where the exact position of the fighting is well attested. The field of Hastings (1066), for instance, has such a dearth of evidence that the traditional site of the battle has been questioned. Can it be that the working of the soil over hundreds of years can remove virtually all trace of battle? That is surely unlikely. Arrowheads, for instance, may not just lie in the top soil waiting to be picked up, but may well have penetrated the sub-soil. Perhaps some artefacts lie deeper than the range of the average metal detector.

The first process to prove the battlefield I have put forward, however, should be to carry out archaeological examinations of some of the likely Roman military works in the surrounding area that are mentioned above. Any suspected earthworks on the field itself may include ditches and pits, which can be a good source of dateable finds. The Roman Army must have had a camp or camps adjacent to the battlefield, both before and after the battle. To find these sites might be a better way to prove the battle than simply seeking military artefacts within the soil.

Of course, to find a burial pit with bone evidence of battle injury which could be dated to the correct period should be sufficient to prove the field. However, the Roman Army would have cremated their dead, and almost certainly taken the ashes away to be buried at the depot forts of the various units, legionary and auxiliary. The Iceni and Trinovantes dead, where not collected (if so allowed) by kinsmen, would also probably have been burnt, or simply left on the field to be picked over by wild animals, until later 'tidied up' when the land reverted to agriculture: the discovery of some skeletal fragments is, therefore, possible. I speculate about some of the dead being thrown for convenience into the marshes, in which case fragments may survive to be discovered one day.

However, for all sorts of reasons of hygiene and religious taboo, mouldering flesh is normally cleared away and not allowed to rot in the open. It has always been a fact of wars and battles that the people who live on and work the land they are fought over have to set to their labour again once the armies have gone. They have to keep their land clean so it can grow food. Much of the clearing up, with little compensation from those who have caused the destruction, has to be carried out by them. It is possible, therefore, that some remains, gathered in the years after the battle, were buried in pits where they might yet be uncovered.

To return to my story: the bones collected by Catrig and shown to Celer, and those gathered by Hadrian's men on the battlefield, were due for reburial at the *tropaeum*. However, the idea of the *tropaeum* was probably never fulfilled, and was not followed up by Hadrian who was busy with a thousand and one other matters. The bones that had been gathered together were perhaps scattered again, or burnt, or simply placed in a pit. Tiberius Claudius Verus, who owned the land on which the *tropaeum* was being built, perhaps took the site over as his own family's burial ground. Certainly, the huge burial mounds at the village of Bartlow, on the Cambridgeshire / Essex border, held rich burials with Roman grave goods, although the style of burial is not Roman itself but of the custom of Romanised Iron Age peoples.

The four excavated mounds at Bartlow (excavated in the 19th century) are unusual in that they all seem to have been constructed at the same time, rather than reflecting the successive dynasty of a powerful family. A coin of Hadrian was found in one showing that a Hadrianic date for construction is likely.

In my story, therefore, Verus may have died suddenly with other members of his family, perhaps of plague, and they were all buried together next to a mound Hadrian had originally built for an entirely different purpose, now serving as Verus's own tomb. The central mound at Bartlow is unusually large as if it was intended for some special purpose. Whoever was eventually buried there was furnished with rich grave goods, including an iron folding chair – a symbol of administrative, and possibly military, authority.

The *tropaeum* at Adamclisi in Romania built in 109 AD (and reconstructed in the 1970s), adjacent to the site of a battle in the Dacian wars seven years earlier, although constructed on a much more lavish scale, with stone facings and sculptured friezes, than anything Hadrian would have intended in Britain, gives a good idea of what the Emperor may have had in mind if only Antinous and a few other matters had not taken his attention away.

The name of Tiberius Claudius Verus – the *praenomen* and *nomen* taken from those of the Emperor Claudius, showing how the family had thrown in its lot with Rome – is known from stamped bricks at the Roman villa of Piddington in Northamptonshire. Perhaps the site of this villa was one of Verus's later land grabs. One particular fragment of brick is impressed with 'VERUS' but with an 'SE' scratched by hand in the clay in front, making 'SEVERUS'. The Emperor Septimius Severus reigned from 193-211 and campaigned in Britain. A descendant of our Verus may have wished to ingratiate himself with the new imperial dynasty.

The Gogmagog Hills, which lie some four miles south-east of the centre of Cambridge, form an isolated area of chalk upland running broadly west to east. Wandlebury hillfort tops the north-western edge of the Hills, its ditch and rampart largely hidden by trees, and its enclosure occupied by the remains of a house and gardens built here in the 18th century. To the south-west, on Magog Down, stands the high point of Little Trees Hill (240ft) with a large burial mound on its summit. A little forward of this mound, on the grassy slope, is the site of Boudica's burial, the square-cut for the grave being visible on air photographs. The Roman road travelled by the Emperor Hadrian and his party runs to the north of Wandlebury. The track that follows the line of the road today can be visited from Wandlebury Country Park. It was on this road, a little further to the north-west near Wort's Causeway, that the column of the VIIIIth Legion was cut to pieces. Human remains have been unearthed nearby.

There are other striking features of the Gogmagog landscape. Copley Hill, beside the Roman Road, is a very large, unexcavated, probably Bronze Age barrow, while Wormwood Hill, closer to Wandlebury, is said to be a natural chalk knoll that might have been used for burial as well. In the 1950s, the archaeologist, Tom Lethbridge, was convinced, by soundings and excavations he undertook, of chalk figures cut into the flanks of the hills. These showed, amongst others, a warrior with raised sword, and a rather bulbous goddess with a chariot, which he determined as Epona (but perhaps was it a depiction of Boudica herself?). The outlines Lethbridge revealed by his probings have since been shown to be geological fissures, but did he, a parapsychologist as well as an archaeologist, nonetheless tap into some source of 'hidden memory' of the events that can now be reconstructed as happening close to these places. Lethbridge's earnest diggings can still be seen amongst the long grass of the Wandlebury Country Park.

Of the other places that come into the novel –

Celer's house: It stood at a short distance to the north of the great Iron Age enclosure of Stonea, which lies amongst the Fens south-east of the town of March. The house was by a dock on a branch of the Roman canal system now known as the Car Dyke. Still surviving amongst the grasses of this gravel island in the peat fens is the mound under which Celer and his wife, Senuna, are buried. A Roman settlement with a high central tower was built north of the Iron Age ramparts of Stonea fort. Excavated in the 1980s, the settlement was dated to the Hadrianic period, with speculation that the tower was the headquarters of an imperial estate spread over the Fens. Areas were drained for wheat production, which would have been taken in barges to the Army in the north. The canal system also connected with the River Cam to the south. Stonea was a strongpoint of the Iceni in western Icenia. Evidence of the Roman Army has been found there, and it is put forward as the site of the battle that crushed the first Iceni rebellion. Before the Romans developed the canal system to drain the land, it would have been difficult of access, just the place that a fleeing Boudica and her household may have eventually headed for in the course of their wanderings after the Iceni defeat. The interior of the inner enclosure is known from pollen evidence to have been wooded. The site of Boudica's first burial, where her log coffin was recovered, must be sought in the corner of the ramparts close to the present pond. It seems this part of the enclosure was never, in fact, disturbed by the digging of a branch of the canal, which aerial photographs show to have actually been built further to the north.

Numicius's villa: an unusually large and luxurious house for the early 2nd century period, it stood on the southern fringes of the present town of March. Although finds from the villa have occasionally been made, its foundations have yet to be located.

Verus's villa: this villa, known from 19th century and later excavations, is situated south of Linton on the banks of the River Granta. The Romano-British burials at Bartlow have long been thought to be associated with the house and its probable large and wealthy estate. The burial mounds can be visited by taking a footpath that runs from Bartlow church, or alternatively, by a footpath that is signposted on the left of the lane to Ashdon, a short distance beyond the old railway bridge. The camp of Hadrian's party visiting the *tropaeum* was around Great Copt Hill a mile or so to the south, where a heated Roman building is known.

Competum: this town is not recorded in the surviving records of place names in Britannia. Its site should be sought under modern Royston in Hertfordshire. *Burentum*, further west, is the name I have given to the substantial Roman settlement at Baldock.

Temple of Senuna Minerva: I have taken great liberties here with the discoveries made in recent years at Ashwell of a previously unknown goddess, Senuna. At the time of writing (May 2017), the full report on the excavations is much awaited. The figurine of the goddess, and other votive objects, are on display in the British Museum, with some finds as well in the museum at Ashwell. I have equated the Iron Age Senuna with the Roman Minerva and reconstructed her temple with accommodation and other buildings for both her worshippers and her priests (these remain to be found!). The idea of sacred prostitution came to me from recent speculation that a villa site in Buckinghamshire may have been a brothel owing to the very large number of burials of newly-born babies found there, many more than at the average Roman villa estate. Sacred prostitution, where a male devotee seeks a closer relationship with a goddess through sexual intercourse with a priestess, is well attested from the ancient world, although it does not seem to have been a practice officially approved by the Roman state. It is something, however, that one can easily imagine happening at one or other of the many shrines and places of sacred pilgrimage that are known to have been built across the Roman world, including, of course, in Britain, where there seems to have been an unusually large number of them. The merging of the attributes of Senuna with those of Minerva perhaps represents an even greater leap of the imagination, but the Roman practice of the conflation of their gods with local ones is well documented: the temple of Sulis Minerva at Bath is just one example.

The Icenia campaign: The place where the reinforcements from the XXIst Legion landed with auxiliaries must be imagined on the east coast of Norfolk, perhaps near Caister-on-Sea where a later stone fort was built, the remains of which can be seen today. The wooden fort of this campaign, I have named *Epocuria* – a name which appears in the writing tablets discovered during the recent excavations at the Bloomberg site in London. The coastline in the Roman period was greatly different from the present one. It would have been hard for an army to penetrate inland at first because of the many river courses draining into the bay where Great Yarmouth stands today. The raid towards the north coast of Norfolk was perhaps in the area of Wells, and the Iceni fort encountered, that at Warham, where the earthworks survive well. The sites of several 1st century Roman timber forts and marching camps are known in Norfolk. The VIIIIth may have been the first to build those at Scottow, Swanton Morley, Ashill, Saham Toney, and Threxton (the Castrum Harenae of the text). The chalk quarry where Boudica was nearly captured lay close to the village of Caistor St. Edmund, where the later town of *Venta Icenorum* was to be built. The Queen with her bodyguard would then have fled to the area of Stonea, where her desperate story was ended by hemlock.

Reconstructing the Roman past has proved a more difficult task than I imagined when first considering this project. So many things needed to be checked by research before they could be set down – the appearance of military standards, the differing ranks of Romans and non-Romans, slaves and free, the languages they spoke, coinage, wine goblets, window glass, horse harness, breeds of ponies, fighting tactics, writing tablets, seal boxes, Iceni hairstyles, Roman dress (male and female), temple furniture, styles of address, gods and goddesses, archaeological evidence, literary evidence – the list could go on for several pages.

Without the power of the Internet, this research would have taken immeasurably longer, but it still meant that on some days the writing would advance at no more than a few hundred words (or even less) in a day. I felt sometimes that, with Celer at my side, I was in a stone quarry picking out a giant slab with a toothpick. The more detailed and realistic you wish your reconstruction to be, the more labour there is in the writing.

Whatever is set down, however, there is likely to be someone out there with greater knowledge who will wish to correct it. That is inevitable, in particular with a subject so much researched, and re-enacted, as the Roman Army. I wait in some trepidation for the criticisms that will come. What I have striven for overall is the correct 'feeling' of the period. I have tried not to be anachronistic, in substance, thought, or language, but I have wanted my Roman characters to breathe the same air, enjoy the same sights (or similar ones), tremble at the same fears, see birds in flight and smoke rising, feel love and grief, as we do today. If I impart any pleasure, or any insights, in that regard, I shall be well satisfied.

For my interpretation of the battles of the Boudican rebellion, I have been greatly helped by the Emperor Hadrian's own testiness at not knowing where these great events took place. His problems were much the same as mine! If only Tacitus, or some other Roman historian, had taken the time to be more detailed in their descriptions. But that was not the Roman historians' way – although (as I have already written) I do believe Tacitus's original account may have been longer

History was meant by the Romans to be declaimed in public. You simply set the stage and then delivered the moralising monologues placed in the mouths of the historical characters. There was little place in the Roman canon for the type of detailed, penetrating research that historians carry out today, in which – coupled with other disciplines such as archaeology – different events, recent or long buried in the past, are analysed down to the last nut and bolt, and the participants' deeds, motives and consequences considered from every conceivable viewpoint.

How many more histories of the 'Titanic' disaster will come out? How many more accounts of D-Day? What fresh theories are there for the identity of Jack the Ripper? Yet all these subjects will have books written about them by authors not even born yet. The Boudican Rebellion, I feel sure, will be the same.

I think it is very possible that progress can be made in the landscape identification of events of the rebellion. It is more than likely, in fact, that the last battle site will be found eventually – perhaps in time for the 2000th anniversary! Of course, I have to declare with confidence that it will turn out to be exactly where I have said it is – but you never know! There is room for other ideas. But let no one any longer perpetrate the canard of the Battle of Watling Street.

Finally, I would like to set down a few notes about my reasons for interpreting other events of 60/61AD and 122AD (i.e. those not relating to the movements of armies) in the way I have done –

The raping of Boudica's daughters: Tacitus describes the rape of the two princesses as taking place at the same time as the flogging of Boudica, i.e. during the Procurator's first greedy grab at the kingdom of Icenia after the death of the king, Prasutagus. That, of course, is quite possible – the sort of thing that might be done by an out-of-control, armed force descending on an unsuspecting, unprepared, and perhaps weaponless household. I have chosen, however, to have the rapes happening as a consequence of defeat in the final battle. The princesses are stated to have been present there with Boudica, riding with her in a chariot. If captured on the field, a fate of rape or death, or both, was very likely. The princesses may, of course, have escaped with Boudica, perhaps to die with her later, or indeed been killed in the battle. Tacitus does not mention them again. If recognised as being of the royal household, they might very well have been taken into the care of a Roman officer, and one at least delivered eventually to a further place of safety – in the way I have interpreted the story. (I have not chosen to speculate on the fate of the other). It is the sort of thing that happened during British colonial wars, the stuff of Victorian novelists. The rumour of the princesses' rape after the battle by Tribune Floccus or Centurion Pilus might have been circulated later to be picked up by Tacitus when he wished more lurid details to add to his account of the reasons for the revolt.

The appearance of Boudica: From the descriptions of Tacitus and Cassius Dio, Boudica is normally presented as a tall, strong, angry figure, perhaps in her mid to late 30s, raw-boned, wielding a spear, and dressed in a tartan-type cloak of many colours. Her hair colour is usually translated as 'tawny', which may mean red, but could also mean blonde. I have chosen to give her hair a red-gold colour, and make her of a rather more delicate physique, a bit younger too – 33 or 34 perhaps rather than 38 or 39. Her daughters may only have been fourteen or fifteen in 60AD, and Boudica could have given birth to them in her late teens. She was certainly a determined woman and could well have been terrifying to behold when angry (as described by Cassius Dio and depicted on the jacket of this book). I believe she did not have active command of her armies, but would have left the main military decisions to her chieftains. It was in the Romans' interests to make her seem as strong a figure as possible to explain their early defeats. If she was then crushed effectively – and particularly in a way that showed her to have been a bad commander – the supremacy of male Roman society was securely reinstated.

Hadrian's friendship with Celer: I am told by those far more learned than I in these matters that such a friendship, involving the sharing of confidences by a man of the highest status with one very much lower, is unlikely. Indeed, it probably was. However, Hadrian always had the mystique of soldierly comradeship foremost in his mind, and he saw Celer and himself as noble fellow soldiers seeing off the corrupt civilian administrators with which he had largely surrounded himself. It is recorded by Cassius Dio that Hadrian often mistrusted those about him and preferred the company of the ordinary soldier. Of course, he could always have unburdened himself with the *praefectus* of the Praetorian Guard, but Hadrian – although certainly a tough soldier himself – was clearly a highly sensitive man, and he sought someone of fellow sympathy with whom he might be able to share his inner thoughts and worries. Celer, although outwardly the rough, tough ex *optio*, had a much softer, self-examining side as well – although he does admit to being amazed by Hadrian's revelations and indiscretions, some of it sexual. Hadrian's sexuality was clearly one of his problems, which he was only to come to terms with fully at a later date when he met Antinous, that person 'of divine form' he wrote about to Celer. Hadrian's Empress, Vibia Sabina, I turn (probably most unfairly) into a type of Messalina figure, yet there are records of her several indiscretions with men in Rome which led to their banishment from Hadrian's household. Rumours would certainly have been rife at the court, and beyond it. The view I present, therefore, must be considered to be taken from the scurrilous comments of the disaffected about Hadrian (and there would have been many such), something like the so-called trolls of today's internet, inventing other people's bad behaviour out of a sense of their own cleverness. The trolls of Hadrian's court, however, were taking a far greater risk than their anonymous contemporary equivalents. Sabina's estrangement from Hadrian (they had no children) was to be even more pronounced after he had brought Antinous into his household and into his bed. Even after his death, Antinous did not go away, having been turned by Hadrian into a god to be worshipped throughout the empire. Whether the neglected Sabina committed further indiscretions is not recorded. She died in 136AD, two years before Hadrian, and in turn was deified.

The reburial of Boudica: My idea that Boudica's body was first buried in secret and later reburied is based on the statement of Cassius Dio that 'the Britons mourned her deeply and gave her a costly burial.' With the body of Boudica, alive or dead, being undoubtedly the imperative target of Roman search parties for many months after the final battle, it is very unlikely that Paullinus, or another Roman administrator, would have allowed her any type of public burial, let alone one accompanied by ritual and the placing of rich grave goods. The last thing the Romans would have wanted was for her grave to become a place of commemoration at which the Iceni and their allies might work up a further thirst for vengeance. When the Americans killed Osama bin Laden, they made sure his body had been disposed of in the ocean less than 24 hours after he was dead. Similar hatred would have been directed by the Romans towards Boudica, who had been responsible for the deaths of tens of thousands of their countrymen. Hence, she must surely have been buried at first in secret. Tacitus does not mention a burial. So how did Cassius Dio's story of a weeping crowd and a rich interment arise? I feel my idea of her body being located and reburied, at a time when Hadrian was trying to consolidate the province and allow the Iceni back some of their former pride, has credence (after all a cowed people do not usually do the things, even in slavery, that produce wealth and prosperity, which is what most rulers boast of achieving).

Pronunciation: Celer himself provides notes on this subject: Boudica should best be pronounced by Romans as Bow (as in bow and arrow) -dika and, in the Iceni tongue, as Bodig, with a short 'o' and a guttural 'g'. Iceni is properly pronounced, as written on their coins, Eceni, the 'c' being pronounced as a 'k' and the first 'e' short, as in 'egg'. I have used Iceni throughout, however, as that is the form most recognisable to the general reader.

Visiting the 'Campo Albo' in the area of Heydon, Cambridgeshire.

The line of hills where the Roman Army stood can be viewed from the A505 west of Duxford Airfield, looking to the south. Several lanes lead from this road towards Heydon village, but it is best to take the one bordering Heydon Grange golf course. After half a mile, the road bends sharply to the left. Here (on the right) you can park your car where the Icknield Way crosses. A walk to the east along the Way will give you a view of the spur of Anthony Hill and the mouth of the Heydon Valley, where some of the fiercest fighting took place. Walking from your car to the west gives you a better view of the ridge and the positions of Reeve Hill and Down Plantation, the right and left of the Roman main position. You can ascend the ridge by the Bran Ditch. Near the top, where the path joins the lane, you have a superb view of the plain covered by the British host below you as far as the distant trees of the Fowlmere marshes. To your left is the curving ridge line towards Down Plantation where the legions stood before the battle and against which Iceni charges by horse and chariot, and on foot, were made. Another path that descends from Great Chishill towards New Buildings Farm provides you with an even better appreciation of this part of the battlefield.

Once you reach the lane above the Bran Ditch, turn left onto it and walk to the chalk pit on your left where the Roman building, thought to be a shrine, was discovered. Extensive views to right and left can be obtained at various points – on the left is the height of Reeve Hill with the expanse of the plain stretching beneath it, and on the right is the steep-sided cleft of the Heydon Valley where the particular action that Tacitus describes was fought. Beyond it can be seen the buildings of Duxford Airfield, whose visitors have no idea that they are walking across much earlier history! Heydon has an interesting church which was badly damaged in the last war by bombing. An inscription above the door states it was 'destroyed by Nazis'. Somewhere behind it, on the flat ridge top, was very likely a Roman camp, although no evidence from air photographs has yet been seen.

Taking the lane into Great Chishill (there are very fine views from the churchyard and an excellent pub: the Pheasant) and turning right at the crossroads, on the right towards the foot of the hill (before the windmill) is the site of a possible Roman signal station (seen in crop marks) with a further enclosure straggling the stream at the bottom. This stream once marked the boundary between the kingdoms of the East Saxons and Mercia, and now that of Cambridgeshire and Hertfordshire. It used to be one of the very few sources of flowing water on these chalk uplands, but today largely dried up.

If you drive to Fowlmere on the far side of the A505 and take the lane that leads north out of the village towards Shepreth, you will come to the track that leads to the RSPB nature reserve. Walking through the preserved marshland here, you can gain a very good idea of the conditions that would have prevailed far more widely at the time of the battle. At the southernmost point of the reserve, you can push through the trees at Black Peak, the place where the Bran Ditch met the marsh. There was once a late Iron Age and Roman settlement here, and a pagan Saxon burial site as well. Ahead of you would have been the positions of the Iceni wagon lines against which the Romans exacted their terrible revenge at the end of the battle. In my reconstruction, much of the debris of the camp was pushed into the marshland you have crossed, where it may yet be found.

RECOMMENDED READING

Aldhouse-Green, Miranda 2006. *Boudica Britannia*. Harlow: Pearson.

Breem, Wallace 1970. *Eagle in the Snow: A Novel*. London: Gollancz (not about the Boudican revolt, but inspirational for anyone reading or writing on the Roman Army).

Davies, John 2006. *The Land of Boudica: Prehistoric and Roman Norfolk*. Oxford: Heritage.

Davies, John & Robinson, Bruce 2009. *Boudica: Her Life, Times and Legacy*. Cromer: Poppyland.

Dudley, Donald. R. & Webster, Graham 1962. *The Rebellion of Boudicca*. London: Routledge.

Frénée-Hutchins, Samantha 2016. *Boudica's Odyssey in Early Modern England*. Abingdon: Routledge.

Hingley, Richard & Unwin, Christina 2005. *Boudica: Iron Age Warrior Queen*. London: Hambledon.

Jackson, Ralph & Burleigh, Gilbert [forthcoming]. *Dea Senuna: Treasure, Cult and Ritual at Ashwell, Hertfordshire*. London: British Museum Press.

Sealey, Paul. R. 1997. *The Boudican Revolt Against Rome*. Princes Risborough: Shire.

Shipway, George 1968. *Imperial Governor*. London: Peter Davies.

Spence, Lewis 1937. *Boadicea*. London: Robert Hale.

Webster, Graham 1978. *Boudica: The British Revolt Against Rome AD60*. London: B.T. Batsford.

GLOSSARY

I have used Roman place names (albeit in an anglicised form, i.e. Camulodunum rather than Camvlodvnum) in the main text (other than for the section 'About this Book'), but, for clarity, have replaced them with their modern equivalents in the sketch map. I have also preferred Latin words and terms when there is no exact English equivalent, or when I think they add a particular value to the Roman-period descriptions. Sometimes, however, I have made use of an English alternative, where the constant repetition of the accepted Latin word detracts from the narrative, e.g. 'sword' for 'gladius' (the main legionary sidearm) or 'first-centurion' for 'primus pilus'. Such decisions are admittedly idiosyncratic and unlikely to please everyone, in particular aficionados of the Roman Army, to whom the Latin terms are more familiar than any English equivalent; or indeed experts in the Latin language, who may complain about gender, case, and declension. I have tried to be as thorough and consistent as I can, but my apologies in advance for any major errors and omissions.

PLACE NAMES

ALBANIANA	Alphen-aan-den-Rijn, Netherlands
AQUAE SULIS	Bath
ARULA	River Aare
BRITANNIA	Britain
CAESAROMAGUS	Chelmsford
CALLEVA ATREBATUM	Silchester
CAMULODUNUM	Colchester
CIVITAS IKELORUM	Great Chesterford
CONFLUENTES	Koblenz, Germany
DACIA	Romania

DEVA	Chester
DUROBRIVAE	Water Newton
DUROLIPONTE	Cambridge
EBORACUM	York
GALLIA	Gaul (France)
GERMANIA	Germany
HISPANIA	Spain
ISCA DUMNONIORUM	Exeter
LINDUM	Lincoln
LONDINIUM	London
LUGDUNUM	Lyon, France
MARE NOSTRUM	The Mediterranean Sea
METARIS	The Wash
MONA	Anglesey
MONS GRAUPIUS	Site unknown, perhaps in Aberdeenshire
OSTIA	Ostia Antica, now suburb of Rome
PONTES	Staines
RHENUS	River Rhine
TAMESIS	River Thames
VENONIS	High Cross
VENTA BELGARUM	Winchester
VENTA ICENORUM	Caistor St. Edmund
VERULAMIUM	St. Albans
VINDONISSA	Windisch, Switzerland

OTHER NAMES

A Note on the Roman Army:

The Roman Army of this period consisted of its legions (made up of Roman citizens) and its non-citizen auxiliaries, many units of which were formed within conquered territories and officered by Romans. A legion was commanded by a *legatus* (legate), assisted by other senior officers including military tribunes. Each legion consisted of ten cohorts, which in turn were made up of eight centuries. The backbone of a legion was its centurions, one for each century, the more experienced of which might command the complete cohort. The centurion of the first century of the first cohort was the most senior (*primus pilus* – literally, first spear). The second-in-command to a centurion was an *optio* (Celer's rank) – perhaps equivalent to a lieutenant in today's British Army. The auxiliaries consisted of units of both infantry and cavalry. The latter were formed into squadrons *(alae or turmae)*, which were usually commanded by a Roman officer – a *decurio*

The term *Legatus* was used for the Governor of a province as well, for which he was also the Commander-in-Chief. I have preferred 'Legate' in reference to Suetonius Paullinus.

Other Army and administrative terms:

Procurator	the senior official, independent of the Legate in charge of a province's finances.
Praefectus Praetorio	the commander of the Praetorian Guard (referred to generally in the text as *praefectus*). *Praefectus* was also the term for several Army and other senior administrative ranks, such as Numicius's *praefectus gentis*.

Names of indigenous pre-Roman peoples of Britannia:

Atrebates	a people of the area of modern Hampshire, Berkshire, and West Sussex.
Brigantes	a powerful (still nominally independent: AD60) people occupying much of Northern England.
Britanni	a generic term for peoples within Britannia. *Britannus* is singular for a man and *Britanna* for a woman.
Caledonii	generic term at this time for peoples within Scotland.
Cantii	a people of the area of Kent
Catuvellauni	a formerly powerful, warring people of Bedfordshire, Hertfordshire and parts of Cambridgeshire.
Corieltauvi	a people of the area of the East Midlands.
Dobunni	occupying primarily Gloucestershire Oxfordshire and Wiltshire

Iceni	occupying much of Cambridgeshire, Norfolk and Suffolk.
Regnenses	a former client kingdom, occupying a region of southern England centred on Chichester (ruled by King Togidubnus whose residence may have been the 'palace' at Fishbourne).
Trinovantes	occupying largely Essex.

Peoples beyond Britannia:

Batavii	a Germanic people of the area of the Rhine delta.
Daci	people of modern Romania.
Galli	a generic term for peoples of Gaul (France).
Germani	a generic term for peoples of Germania. *Germanus* is the male singular.
Helvetii	a people of the area of Switzerland.
Ludaei	peoples of Judaea (Israel and Palestine).
Nervii	a people of the area of Belgium.
Tungri	a people from the Gallic borders with Germania.

General words and terms:

amphora/amphorae	large pottery vessels, usually of an elongated shape, used for carrying wine, olive oil, and other liquids.
armilla/armillae	Roman military decoration(s) worn on the arm.
barbarus/barbari	a generic term for savage or untutored peoples both within and beyond the Roman Empire.
basilica	large, aisled hall, often with an apsidal end.
birus Britannicus	hooded cloak, something like a modern duffle-coat.

bucinum/bucina	curved Roman military horn(s) similar to the *cornua* (q.v).
caerimonia commemorationis	ceremony of commemoration.
caldarium	very hot room in a Roman bath house.
carnyx	upright bronze trumpet used by the 'Celtic' peoples of Europe.
carroballista/carroballistae	mobile artillery of the Roman Army – a gun worked by torsion firing heavy iron bolts.
castellum	Roman Army fortified place, usually smaller than a *castrum* (q.v).
castrum/castra	Roman Army camp(s) or fort(s). The word can refer to a temporary marching camp or a permanent army base.
cella	inner chamber of a temple holding an image of the deity.
circus	outdoor arena, of greater length than width, usually used for chariot and horse racing.
cithara	stringed instrument similar to a lyre.
classis Britannica	Roman fleet operational in the waters around Britannia.
colonia/coloniae	Roman town established in conquered territory and settled by discharged legionaries – centres of Romanisation.
conium	hemlock.
cornu/cornua	curved musical horn(s) used in the Roman Army, primarily for signalling.
corona/corona muralis	Roman military decoration – the crown. The *muralis* was one of the highest awards for bravery, being literally the first over an enemy's wall.
cuneus/cunei	term, meaning wedge, for a small, irregular mounted unit: the same term was used for the legions' wedge-formation of sudden, shock attack (but for the latter I have prefered the English word 'wedge' in order to prevent confusion).

cursus publicus	state-run transportation and courier system throughout the Roman Empire (see also *mansio*).
cymbalum	percussion musical instrument, hand-held.
diploma	engraved bronze document recording a Roman soldier's honourable discharge, containing a record of his service.
dominus/domina	term for 'lord' or 'master', used generally by one of lesser status to his social superior: *domina* is the female equivalent and *domine* the vocative case, i.e. the form in which a *dominus* would have been addressed.
denarius/denarii	Roman monetary unit and silver coinage. One *denarius*, as a broad comparison, was worth about £50 in modern money.
emeritus	veteran soldier.
exercitus Britannicus	the army of Britannia.
frigidarium	cold plunge pool in a Roman bath house.
jugerum/jugera	unit of area equivalent to just over half an acre.
lares	protective deities of a household, worshipped at a shrine within the house, often a niche near the entry.
legio	a particular numbered legion.
limes	frontier defences.
lupa/lupae	prostitute(s) – literally she-wolf.
lupanar	brothel.
maiestas	a subservient form of address, meaning your 'greatness' or 'majesty' – (see Vindolanda tablet 344: 'tuam maiestatem imploro', just possibly a reference to the Emperor Hadrian).
mansio	posting station of the *cursus publicus* (q.v.), established at regular intervals on main roads, often consisting of a

347

	substantial courtyard with ranges of buildings for accommodation and stabling.
mausoleum	building housing one or more tombs.
papyrus/papyri	writing material, akin to thick paper, made from the papyrus plant, and pieces of such material.
phalera/phalerae	Roman military decoration(s) worn on the breastplate.
pharos	lighthouse.
rudiarius	usually an ex-gladiator now acting as an umpire at fights.
sestertius/sestertii	Roman monetary unit and bronze coinage. Four *sestertii* made up a *denarius* (q.v.): one *sestertius* was worth about £12 in modern money.
S.P.Q.R.	*senatus populusque Romanus* – the Senate and People of Rome.
stola/stolae	the traditional full-length garment of Roman women, corresponding to the formal toga worn by men.
temenos	sacred area around a temple or shrine.
tepidarium	room of medium warmth in a Roman bath house.
tesserae	small pieces of stone or tile used in flooring, pieces of differing colours being utilised to make a patterned mosaic.
testudo	a battle formation (the 'tortoise') used by small units of Roman soldiers against enemy missiles, making use of their shields to form a protective shell overhead and at the sides.
triclinium	dining room or other area, sometimes outdoors.
tropaeum/tropaea	monument(s) to commemorate a war and the Roman fallen, often topped with a representation of an armed but faceless soldier, akin to our 'unknown soldier'.

tuba/tubae   Roman military trumpet(s).
tympanum   a type of hand drum or tambourine.

SKETCH MAP SHOWING THE BATTLE SITES
OF THE WAR (ICENORUM BELLI)
SOUTH OF CAMBRIDGE

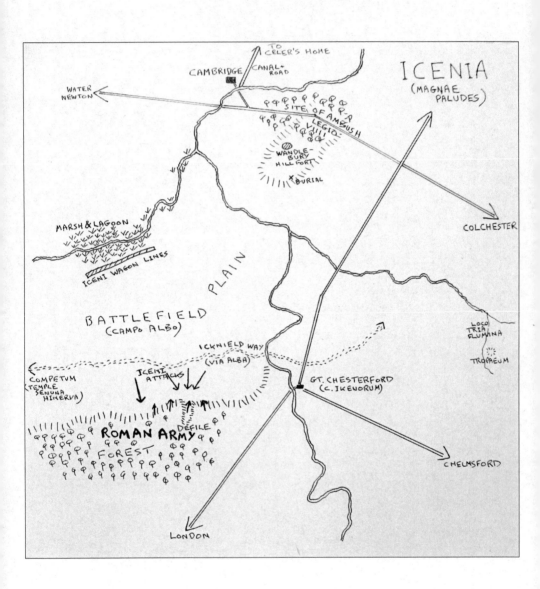

xK8yj T pgg hhb

VM 356 2066